David Roberts was educated at Eton and McGill University, Montreal. He was a publisher for thirty years including editorial director of Weidenfeld & Nicolson and a partner in O'Mara Books. He has published a series of ten detective novels set in the 1930s featuring Lord Edward Corinth and Verity Browne. He is married and lives in London and Wiltshire.

Praise for David Roberts

'Intricate and enthralling'
Michael Dobbs

'Lovers of golden-age crime fiction need mourn no longer. Roberts takes us back to the world of the aristocratic sleuth'
Natasha Cooper

'Roberts pays meticulous attention to period detail and the result is a really well-crafted and charming mystery story'
Daily Mail

Also by David Roberts

Lord Edward Corinth & Verity Browne Series

The MORE DECEIVED

A murder mystery featuring
Lord Edward Corinth & Verity Browne

DAVID ROBERTS

CONSTABLE • LONDON

CONSTABLE

First published in Great Britain in 2004 by Constable,
an imprint of Constable & Robinson Ltd

This paperback edition published in 2005 by Robinson,
an imprint of Constable & Robinson Ltd

Reissued in 2017 by Constable

1 3 5 7 9 10 8 6 4 2

A CIP catalogue record for this book
is available from the British Library.

ISBN 978-1-4721-2813-3

Printed and bound by CPI Group (UK) Ltd, Croydon, CR0 4YY

Papers used by Constable are from well-managed forests
and other responsible sources

MIX
Paper from
responsible sources
FSC® C104740

Constable
An imprint of
Little, Brown Book Group
Carmelite House
50 Victoria Embankment
London EC4Y 0DZ

An Hachette UK Company
www.hachette.co.uk

www.littlebrown.co.uk

For Sophie

I am grateful to the staff of the Brooklands Museum, Weybridge,
for their help and advice

Ophelia: I was the more deceived.

———————————

Hamlet: 'Tis the breathing time of day with me.
Let the foils be brought . . .

Shakespeare, *Hamlet*

April 1937

1

Lord Edward Corinth stood poised on the balls of his feet, prepared to meet the attack which he knew would be fierce and unforgiving. In the few seconds remaining to him, he assessed his stance and was satisfied. His knees were bent, his feet at right angles, the back foot turned slightly forward. His rear arm was raised to balance the épée he grasped in his right hand, arm outstretched breast-high. Beneath his mask, a trickle of sweat rolled off his forehead on to the bridge of his beaky nose causing him to move his head very slightly.

'Hold still! Keep your head perfectly still,' came the cry as he knew it would. 'No, don't look at your blade. Always eye to eye.'

Edward cursed silently. His knee, injured in a car accident two years earlier, was quite strong again despite his having fallen awkwardly on it while chasing a girl on the *Queen Mary* just a month ago but, if he did not move in the next few seconds, it might just betray him.

'*En garde*! Lunge! Keep your back foot flat. Good! Lunge – recover – lunge!'

Two hectic minutes later Edward felt his épée taken out of his hand as easily as candy from a child. As he heard, rather than saw it clatter across the floor, he stepped back and lifted his mask.

'For God's sake, what happened? I thought I was just about to *flèche*.'

His instructor laughed. 'It was bad of me, I know, but I couldn't resist it. You laid yourself right open. First I confused your sense of distance by having my arm more retracted than usual, then I went under your arm aiming at the wrist. Always remember, Lord Edward, the best time to attack is when your

3

opponent steps forward. You are tall – taller than me by nine inches – and I had to prevent you using that advantage. I had to keep you at relatively close quarters and attack your blade. You must try not to signal your intentions to your adversary, though. But you did well.'

'I'm so out of condition, Cavens. I hope you won't despair of me.'

Fred Cavens, Edward's instructor and swordmaster, was a graduate of the Belgian Military Institute. Whenever Douglas Fairbanks embarked on a film such as *The Black Pirate* or *The Iron Mask* in which he was called upon to bound across the set, sword in hand, duelling with some evil opponent, Cavens was there instructing him and occasionally stepping in for him when the fight became too acrobatic. He also arranged fights for Basil Rathbone and Errol Flynn, both of whom had become close friends.

Edward had once asked him why Belgians seemed to do all the fight arranging in Hollywood and he said, '*Les Français sont trop difficiles*. We Belgians are . . . more relaxed. You understand?'

Fenton, Lord Edward's valet, came forward with a towel and helped him remove his sweat-sodden clothes before proceeding to rub him down. They were in his rooms in Albany. Fenton privately considered the dining-room, even when stripped of its furniture and oriental rugs, an inappropriate place in which to take violent exercise and hinted as much now. Edward was adamant.

'You sound just like my dear departed Aunt Gladys. Of course this is the place to fence in. Do you not realize that these were Byron's chambers? This was his *salle d'armes*. He sparred just where we are standing with John "Gentleman" Jackson – "Bruiser" Jackson as he was known in the ring – boxing champion of England during the Regency. And with Henry Angelo he practised with foil and broadsword. It would be ridiculous for any of the other residents to object and they haven't, have they?'

'No, my lord, but . . .'

The telephone rang and Fenton excused himself and went out to the hall to answer it.

'Saved by the bell, eh? You know, Cavens, Fenton's the best valet in London but there are times when he makes me feel like a naughty little boy. I had a nanny just like him when I was a child. I had to get rid of her by putting tadpoles in her jam sandwiches.'

Cavens laughed. 'I shall go now. You remember that I leave for Germany on Friday?'

'Yes, I gather fencing is fashionable there at the moment. I know Mussolini has been encouraging it in Italy.'

'In Germany I number Herr Himmler among my students.'

Edward frowned. 'That man? I thought fencing was a sport for gentlemen.'

Cavens looked embarrassed and Edward felt he had been rude. 'Ah well!' he said with an effort at humour. 'Just because Fascists like to fence doesn't mean we have to give it up. My friend Verity Browne tells me that Karl Marx also liked to fence.'

Cavens smiled weakly. 'You know the old joke? The German said to the Frenchman, "After all, when the history of the Great War is written, it will be difficult to decide where the greater measure of blame lies." "Well, my friend," the Frenchman says, "the one thing history will not say is that Belgium invaded Germany."'

Edward smiled wryly. 'I say, Cavens, it's very good of you to spare the time to teach me. Are you sure I am not being a bore . . . wasting your time and whatnot?'

'No, indeed. You are a natural athlete, Lord Edward, and if it were not for your knee and your . . .'

'I know! My great age . . .' Edward was about to be thirty-eight.

'You are not too old. One of my pupils started at sixty. Fencing is like a physical game of chess. It helps to be quick and agile but if you are slower you can fence defensively. If you trained hard enough you could reach Olympic standard.'

'No, no, Cavens old man. It's true I did fence a bit at Eton but I hardly did anything when I was at Cambridge . . . had other fish to fry . . . so I'm terribly rusty now, as you can see.'

'While I am away, practise, practise, practise and then practise some more. When I am back we shall continue our search for *la botte secrète* – the perfect thrust, *n'est-ce pas*?'

At that moment Fenton re-entered the room. 'Sir Robert Vansittart is on the telephone, my lord. He wishes to speak to you.'

'His secretary, you mean?'

'No, my lord, Sir Robert himself.'

'Good heavens! What can I have done to deserve this?'

Vansittart was Permanent Under-Secretary for Foreign Affairs – the Foreign Office's effective chief. Not a politician but, nevertheless, highly political, he wielded immense power and could promote or vitiate the policy of his political masters. If he supported the Foreign Secretary – at this time Anthony Eden – he could be a most able servant but also a dangerous enemy. What this great man could have to say to him, Edward could not imagine. Wrapped in a towel, he hurried to the telephone half expecting to find one of his friends was playing a joke on him.

'Sir Robert, I apologize for keeping you waiting. I was just . . .'

'Ah! Lord Edward. I am delighted to have caught you. Something has come up which I thought might interest you. Can't say anything about it on the telephone but I wondered if you were free this afternoon? Forgive the short notice but . . .'

'Of course, Sir Robert. I have no engagement I cannot break. Shall I come to your office about three?'

'Could we say four? I have a luncheon which may drag on. The Italian ambassador . . . need I say more?'

Edward's elder brother, the Duke of Mersham, had once reprimanded him for dressing sloppily with the comment, 'If you cannot dress like a gentleman, you should at least dress like a Conservative.' Another piece of advice the Duke was fond of repeating was 'Gentlemen shop at gentlemen's shops' and Edward always had. His suits were made in Savile Row by Leslie and Roberts, his boots by Lobb and his hats by Lock in St James's Street. Thus it was that, when Edward set out for the Foreign Office, he was impeccably dressed in his most sober tie and black pinstripe suit. Fenton had urged him to wear spats but he had declined on the grounds that they were beginning to look old-fashioned. Fenton had pursed his lips and begun to protest but Edward had cut him short.

'I want to look reliable and . . . respectable and so forth but I don't want to look a complete fossil.'

The truth was that Edward wanted to be taken seriously. Over the past two years he had done several jobs – unofficial ones – for the Foreign Office or at the behest of Major Ferguson of Special

Branch but he had never met Vansittart. With war looming, he was anxious to establish his position with the powers-that-be on a more formal footing. It was not a question of money. He had plenty of that. It was more that he wanted to be useful . . . to have a purpose in life . . . to serve his country and be able to tell himself he wasn't just a useless *coureur de dames*. He was easily bored and the idea of office work of any kind filled him with horror. Politics was out of the question. All the hypocrisy, the lies you had to tell and the babies you had to kiss.

There was always the army but he was really too old to imagine he would be allowed to do any real fighting. No, what he was good at – if he was good at anything – was nosing out the truth and he had a feeling that this was where there was a role for him. Not spying exactly but . . . well, he supposed it was a type of police work. He had been told that Vansittart thought well of him – he had done some useful work preventing a scandal which might have touched the Royal Family – but to be commissioned by him personally . . . that was something else.

It was a glorious spring day and he decided to walk across St James's Park rather than take the Lagonda. He had, of course, no idea how he appeared to passers-by as he strode purposefully across the grass, recently mown for the first time that year. Tall, long-legged, with a look on his face which a foolish observer might have mistaken for vacuous, he exuded the confidence – some might say the arrogance – of the upper-class Englishman who had never had reason to doubt his place in the universe. In point of fact he did often doubt himself and, as he scattered the ducks drying their feathers beside the water, he was far from feeling satisfied with his position or rather his reason for existing. He had a good brain. He was, despite his age, still something of an athlete. He had a large circle of friends not just in his own social circle but in neighbourhoods and social classes in which aristocratic young men rarely ventured. He had no wife or child but an *amitié* – irregular and hard to define – with a young Communist journalist who exhibited an annoying preference for Europe's battlefields over the joys of Piccadilly.

He twitched his nose and sighed. A child in a perambulator looked at him pityingly and the child's nanny – a woman the size of a small sofa and of indeterminate age – pushed her charge out of danger with a snort of indignation. Five minutes later he found himself outside George Gilbert Scott's undeniably impressive building, the epitome of Empire. The Foreign Office, as Scott had planned it, was designed to impress and it certainly did make a statement. Scott seemed to be saying that even the grandest potentate, the richest maharaja, the most self-regarding president was, in the presence of the Queen Empress, of little account. That was the 1870s. Sixty-five years later Queen Victoria was dead and the British Empire had been undermined by a great war which had bled it of its best young men and reduced it to near bankruptcy but the illusion of power lingered on.

Edward wondered if this magnificent building would survive the next war. Stanley Baldwin had said the bomber would always get through, seeming to imply that there was no defence against the new air force of militant Germany. It was a grim thought. As he had a few minutes to spare, he walked round to stand in front of Lutyens' Cenotaph. With head bared and bowed, he stood for a minute or two remembering his older brother who, had he not been killed in France in 1914, would have been Duke of Mersham. He prayed fervently but without real conviction that Britain would not again be called upon to sacrifice its young men and thought particularly of his nephew Frank, now in America but soon to return home.

At last he entered the great quadrangle and made his presence known to a uniformed porter. After a muffled colloquy on an antiquated telephone, he was led by a frock-coated flunkey beneath the gilded dome, up the grand staircase and along a gallery. They arrived at an impressive door upon which the flunkey knocked. Edward entered a large room in which two female secretaries were clattering away on typewriters. A pleasant-faced young man rose from behind a desk and took Edward's coat and hat. He then knocked on an inner door and there was a brisk shout of 'Enter.'

The room was cavernous but Edward's eye was immediately drawn to Sir Robert's desk which was stacked with scarlet-and-gold despatch boxes as though he was the Foreign Secretary. A huge vase of flowers stood in the fireplace on either side of which were glass-fronted bookcases full of leather-bound tomes. For a moment he had the impression he was in one of those libraries in great country houses where the books are purely decorative and have never been removed from their shelves. There was a portrait over the fireplace of one of Sir Robert's distinguished pre-decessors and two or three other portraits of men in eighteenth- and nineteenth-century dress hung elsewhere around the room. The views from the windows were of St James's Park.

The man behind the huge desk rose and came round the side of it, his hand outstretched. 'Lord Edward, how very good of you to come and at such short notice, too.'

Sir Robert ushered him to a small sofa at one side of the room and sat himself down opposite. He was a handsome man, six foot one, strong-jawed with a twinkle in his eye. As Edward shook his hand his first impression was of a man alert and straightforward in a profession tending to the devious. As he knew, Sir Robert was not only a diplomat but a poet, playwright and novelist. His plays had been put on in the West End with some success and a play he had written in French performed to acclaim in Paris. He was a close friend of the Prime Minister, Stanley Baldwin, and had been his principal private secretary. He had become head of the Foreign Office in 1930 at the age of forty-nine and now, seven years later, was at his peak – assured, patrician, some would say arrogant. He had an abiding hatred of Germany – a country he knew well and whose language he spoke fluently – and a great love of France though he despaired of its politicians. As early as 1930 – before Hitler had become a menace to world peace – he had forecast that Germany would demand to become a great power with an army at least the size of Poland's and would seek union with Austria.

'My younger brother Nick was a friend of your brother's at Eton,' he was saying. 'I remember meeting him. It was a tragedy – one of so many – his dying like that in the first weeks of the war. It was a great pain to me that I was kept from the battlefield by diplomatic work. Those of us who survived the carnage must do whatever we can to prevent a second bout but it will be a miracle if we can bring it off.'

Edward said nothing but smiled and then, fearing he might seem inane, frowned and muttered, 'Indeed, indeed.'

Fortunately, the great man appeared not to expect an answer and went on talking. 'I have heard a great deal about you, Lord Edward, and I was particularly struck by the way you handled that unpleasant business of Mrs Simpson's stolen letters. Of course, I should call her the Duchess of Windsor now, though I must say it rather sticks in the craw. The point I'm driving at is that it appears you have a talent for discreet investigation and that's just what I need now . . . a discreet investigator. You come highly recommended by Major Ferguson of Special Branch.'

Edward had come across Ferguson when he had been trying to retrieve Mrs Simpson's letters and had then been commissioned by him to protect Lord Benyon on his recent trip to the United States.

'You want something investigated? A crime?'

'Not quite that. Have a cigarette? No? Well, you won't mind if I do.' Vansittart took a cigarette from a box on his desk and subsided once again into his chair. He was obviously finding it difficult to know where to start.

'No crime has been committed, or at least none that I am aware of, but there has been a . . . a lapse in security.'

'A foreign agent?' Edward hazarded.

'No, no, nothing like that,' Vansittart said hurriedly. 'Oh dear! I had better be explicit. I need hardly say that anything I tell you is confidential.'

'Of course.'

'Well then, have you met Mr Churchill?'

The question was so unexpected that Edward thought for a moment he had changed the subject but a glance at his face made it clear he had not. Through a cloud of smoke, Vansittart was peering at Edward and expecting a reply.

'No, I never have.'

'That's good!'

Edward looked puzzled. 'I'm afraid I'm not following you, Sir Robert.'

'No, of course you're not. I just wanted to be sure you were not a friend of Mr Churchill's because that would have made the investigation very difficult . . . if not impossible.'

'I have never met Mr Churchill,' Edward repeated.

'You are, however, aware of his political opinions?'

'On foreign affairs?'

'Yes.'

'I know from what he writes in the newspapers that he believes Germany is building up an army and air force which we would have difficulty in withstanding in the event of a war. And, I must say, I am sure he is right.'

'He is right in that, if in nothing much else,' Vansittart concurred. 'You do not have to be Talleyrand to see that Germany is a threat to the British Empire. As Mirabeau is reported to have said, "*La guerre est l'industrie nationale de la Prusse.*" The question is what to do about it. The government is rearming. We are doubling our expenditure on the Royal Navy and the Royal Air Force in the next two years.'

'I am no expert, Sir Robert, but surely one must respond, "too little, too late"?'

'What more can we do? We are already deeply in debt to the Americans. The government wishes to postpone war, if indeed it is inevitable, by negotiating with Germany – satisfying her legitimate demands and giving her no excuse for further aggression.'

'I understand. My friend, Lord Benyon, has explained to me how close we are to bankruptcy but, if we give ourselves more time to arm, surely that gives Germany time to do the same? A fellow passenger on my recent trip to the United States was a German Jewish aeronautical engineer. Fortunately for us the Nazis had been stupid enough to hound him out of his job.'

'Which was?'

'To work on the new jet engines which would make every fighter we have obsolete. However, if we allow Hitler the time, they will be built.'

'We too have jet engines in development,' Vansittart said, 'but, of course, there is something in what you say. In any case, as you know, it is not my task to make policy but to implement it.'

Edward was aware that this remark was disingenuous. Sir Robert was not a man to leave policy-making to the politicians.

'But no doubt you would like me to get to the point. It's a delicate matter. To put it bluntly, confidential information concerning our defences – particularly our air defences – is being passed to persons unauthorized to receive it.'

'You mean to a foreign power?'

'No! – at least not as far as we know. The information is being passed to Mr Churchill. The figures he quotes in his newspaper articles and in debates in the House of Commons are uncannily accurate.'

'So you think someone in the Foreign Office is giving him the ammunition to attack the government? '

'We're not absolutely certain it is coming from the Foreign Office or perhaps not *only* from the Foreign Office. You will be shown the complete list of those government officials who are authorized to receive secret information relating to our rearmament programme. These documents are circulated to twenty or twenty-five ministers and top officials and presumably they show them to their senior people though they are not supposed to.'

'I see. So, if I understand you, one or more of these people is passing secrets concerning our rearmament – facts and figures – to Mr Churchill so he can embarrass the government?'

'That's correct.'

'But what would be that person's motive? Money?'

'Probably not. We do not believe that Mr Churchill has ever given any reward for information. I think it is more likely to be from a misguided idea that alarming the British public in this way is patriotic. Of course, nothing Mr Churchill can say or do can alter the situation. As I said to you, we are increasing our armed forces very rapidly – as rapidly as our financial position allows.'

'And is Mr Churchill actuated by a patriotic desire to prepare Britain for the coming conflict or merely to promote himself?'

'Ah, well! There's the question. Personally, I think he is a genuine patriot but he does enjoy irritating his former colleagues. He had hoped to be taken back into government and he may be trying to make such a nuisance of himself that the PM prefers to have him on board rather than rocking the boat from outside. But that's by the by. Whatever his motives, the situation cannot be allowed to continue.'

'I have always admired his energy and determination but after Gallipoli . . .'

'Quite! Though, it has to be said, that fiasco was not entirely Mr Churchill's fault.'

'But he bears the responsibility,' Edward persisted.

'He does,' Sir Robert agreed, getting up from his chair. 'And he did the honourable thing and resigned. Joined his regiment and fought at the front. I admire him for that. As for Gallipoli, he was impatient . . . too impatient. The war in France was bogged down in trench warfare. He was prepared to risk anything to find a short cut to victory. He was a young man with the world's mightiest fleet at his disposal. He was a personal friend of Mr Asquith and could count on the unstinting support the British people always give their navy. He threw all these gifts away in sheer headstrong recklessness. He lost himself trying a short cut in unfamiliar territory and lost others with him. You know, Lord Edward, there is a broad gulf between the man of talent and the man of genius. One may perhaps feel that at the present time, when the empire is going through a most terrible economic crisis and faces the appalling prospect of another war, Mr Churchill's recklessness may once again imperil us. His facile phrases and unbalanced enthusiams are the last thing we need.'

Vansittart's bitterness surprised Edward. He must be seriously worried to give vent to his feelings so unrestrainedly. Vansittart, perhaps sensing he had spoken too freely, ceased his pacing and sat down again opposite Edward.

'Anyway, it is intolerable that top secret documents should be seen by unauthorized people, whatever their motive,' he ended lamely.

'I see. So you want me to go and see Mr Churchill and ask him who is giving him this information? I cannot believe I would be successful.'

'You are a neutral figure – if I may put it that way, Lord Edward. I agree Mr Churchill is unlikely to reveal his sources of information but you can at least warn him that we are aware of what is happening and when we do find our weak link . . . but there is another way of tackling the problem. When you receive the full list of those who have legitimate access to the figures Mr Churchill quotes so authoritatively, you can interview each of them. There may be fewer than a score – thirty at the most.'

'I will have to have some letter of authorization if I am to get anywhere.'

'That goes without saying,' Vansittart said with relief, making the assumption that Edward had agreed to undertake the investigation. 'You will be sworn in as an officer in Special Branch. You will have all the authority you need, I can promise you. However, the investigation must be most discreet. No word of our anxiety must reach the newspapers or we shall be pilloried. You understand?'

'I do, Sir Robert. And I report direct to you?'

'Myself or Major Ferguson. The fewer people who have to

know about this the better. And, by the way, commit nothing to paper. Any report you make should be verbal. We don't want any memorandum from you being reprinted in one of Lord Weaver's rags, do we?'

That seemed to Edward to be a warning. Vansittart must know of his friendship with the owner of the *New Gazette* and other newspapers with little love for the government.

'There is nothing else you can tell me? You have no suspicions yourself as to who may be talking to Mr Churchill? Presumably Major Ferguson must have made some preliminary investigation.'

'That is true,' Sir Robert said, rising to his feet to indicate the interview was at an end. 'He had a hint that one of my people, Charles Westmacott, a junior employee in Desmond Lyall's section, might have – how shall I put it? – a weakness for Mr Churchill. Major Ferguson made an appointment to see him.'

Edward was on his feet too. 'Which department is Mr Lyall's?'

Vansittart hesitated. Then he said, 'I suppose you will have to know. Lyall is Director of Industrial Intelligence. His job is to study arms deals amongst our European friends and possible enemies and gather and collate industrial intelligence from our people abroad. The department is most secret and must not be referred to outside this room.'

'And what was the result of Major Ferguson's meeting?'

'It never took place. Westmacott disappeared the evening before Ferguson was to interview him.'

'Disappeared? When was this?'

'Exactly a week ago.'

'And no one has any idea where he is?'

'No. Westmacott left the Foreign Office about his usual time – five thirty or six, we believe – and has not been seen since. Ferguson will brief you but he's in the dark along with the rest of us. Of course, this may have nothing to do with what we have been talking about but . . .'

'Would his knowledge have been useful to the . . . to other countries? Does he have access to secret documents?'

'Up to a point. Ferguson will give you all the gen.' Sir Robert seemed anxious now to get rid of his guest. 'He saw certain low-level secret documents . . . He was, as I say, relatively junior but Lyall trusted him. He might have seen more than he was supposed to. Ferguson will arrange for you to talk to Lyall. As you can imagine, Westmacott's wife is distraught but at least we have kept the news of his disappearance out of the press – for the moment anyway. Lord Weaver and the other proprietors have been most understanding.'

Always, Edward thought, there was this fear of the public knowing what was going on. Government kept control by not permitting the general public to know what was done in its name and what mistakes were made. However, perhaps in this instance there was some justification. As he said his farewell to Sir Robert, he realized he had never actually said he would take on the investigation. His agreement had been presumed. He sighed. No doubt in a few hours he would receive a telephone call from Major Ferguson and feel bound to respond positively. He could not deny that he was intrigued. Mr Churchill was a colourful character. He had seen him once in the House of Commons in full flood and been carried away by his oratory. His friend Marcus Fern admired him and Edward trusted his judgement. In fact, he had an idea that Fern was working for him in some capacity or other. But still, he thought, there was something of the charlatan about Churchill.

2

When Edward got back to Albany he found an irate Verity reading his correspondence and smoking furiously.

'Oh, there you are. I suppose you forgot you are taking me to the exhibition and then a slap-up dinner before I return to the front line?'

Edward tried to kiss her but she dodged him. 'Fiddlesticks! Don't think you can get round me with that sappy stuff. There's a hundred places I could be, instead of waiting on you. Where have you been, anyway? '

'Simmer down, old thing. I hadn't forgotten our dinner engagement but I was called to an important meeting at the FO, don't y'know.' He spoke loftily but Verity was unimpressed.

'Huh! I bet you were called in to polish a few boots!'

'On the contrary, my dear Watson, Sir Robert Vansittart himself wished to consult me on a matter of international importance.'

'Less of the Dr Watson. Well,' she added grudgingly, 'what was so important the FO wanted to talk to you about? Are you to be our next ambassador to Transylvania?'

'Can't tell you, I'm afraid. Sworn to silence. Sir Robert specifically warned me against talking to Communist journalists.'

'Blast you, Edward! Stop teasing. Tell me all about it,' she commanded him, stubbing out her cigarette in a potted palm.

'Sorry, I mean it – no can do. You'll have to get me drunk at Gennaro's tonight and see if you can loosen my tongue. By the way, where are you staying? You can't stay here, you know. The managers wouldn't like it.'

'I have no intention of staying here. If you want to know, I'm staying with Charlotte and Adrian.'

Adrian Hassel was a painter and his wife a successful novelist.

They were friends with whom Verity usually stayed when she was in London, no longer having a place of her own.

Edward saw that she was on edge. She lived on her nerves, eating little and smoking too much, courting danger, choosing to live the uncomfortable and occasionally dangerous life of the war correspondent. He knew from experience that a few days before she went back to Spain, where civil war now raged, she would become nervous and irritable, only regaining her equilibrium when she was actually in the front line. The anticipation was much worse than the reality, she said, but Edward doubted this. She had been out of Spain for a couple of months and the respite had done her good. She had put on a little weight and the dark circles under her eyes had disappeared. She had been with him on the *Queen Mary* a few weeks before and, although the trip to the United States had not been without incident, she had benefited from sea air and good food. Then she had spent two weeks meeting influential Americans: union leaders, left-wing politicians and Communist Party sympathizers.

There had been relatively few of these last, she had been disturbed to discover, and she had been dogged by FBI agents – at least she assumed they were FBI – who made it clear she was seen by the government as an undesirable. Edward and she had become lovers on the *Queen Mary*, or rather they had had one brief and interrupted night when, despite his having an injured leg which hurt whenever any pressure was put on it, they had managed to make love. It could hardly have been described as a night of passion but they had sealed some sort of emotional knot, though neither of them could have defined its nature. Verity was not the marrying kind. Most girls of her class were married by twenty-five with a baby or two and a husband at the office all day. She was racketing round the world doing a dirty job which, if it had to be done, most people would say should be left to men to do.

The English knew about war. They had not too long ago survived a particularly bloody one but they had relatively little interest in foreign wars. The civil war in Spain was of crucial importance to Communists and those on the left in politics but these were few in number if vociferous. Most readers of the *New Gazette* wanted to read about the Duke and Duchess of Windsor, who were shortly to be married in France, and the imminent coronation of King George VI. Verity was resigned to seeing her reports from the front relegated to a few columns squeezed on to the inside pages though she had written a series of articles about 'daily life' in the United States which had proved popular. As Edward sniffed, she might as well turn them into a book and call it *Inside America*. Two weeks was surely ample time to get the measure of that great country.

'I hadn't forgotten we were dining but I have to admit I had forgotten we were going somewhere first. Give me five minutes to shower and put on a clean shirt. You can entertain me while I change. Remind me where we are going first of all. It might affect my choice of necktie. And, please, don't tell me about all our Comrades in Spain without clean shirts or neckties. I really don't want to know.'

Just as he reached his dressing-room, he heard the sound of an épée falling on the floor.

'Hey! Desist! Leave my weapons alone, woman.'

'What on earth . . .? Don't say you are taking up fencing? At your age . . . ! What are you trying to prove?'

'I am not trying to prove anything. I was merely taking some exercise that would strengthen my leg and . . . Can you help me with this collar?'

'You men!' Bossily, sword still in hand, Verity bustled into the dressing-room.

'Here, I say, dash it!' Edward exclaimed as she tugged at the recalcitrant stud. 'What are you trying to do? Cut off my . . . ? Ouch! Don't do that!' He had his trousers round his ankles and was therefore at a disadvantage.

Verity laughed. 'Men look such asses without their trousers.'

'You're such an expert on male attire? Hey! Stop prodding me with that sword. I mean it. Unhand me, girl!' He drew her to him and relieved her of the sword. He kissed her on the lips and she made no protest except to say, her voice rather unsteady, 'What about Fenton?'

'I've just remembered, it's his evening off.' He hopped about, clinging to Verity with one hand while trying to remove the trousers round his ankles with the other.

With a gurgle of laughter, she pushed him on to the chaise longue. 'Why is it, whenever I kiss you, you fall over?' she said when she could breathe again. She was referring to how, on the

Queen Mary, Edward's damaged knee had made him unsteady on his pins. 'I begin to think it's a sophisticated seduction technique.'

Although she prided herself on being tough and certainly she instilled fear in both women and men over whom she did not consider it worth taking trouble, she was not half as hard-boiled as she pretended. She loved Edward but felt she would be at a disadvantage if she let him know how much. She was afraid she could never give him what he needed . . . what he deserved . . . and she had warned him that she could never be a wife to him. If he still loved her, as he said he did, that was fate and something she knew she could do nothing about.

'Huh!' he grunted. 'Why are women's undergarments more difficult to negotiate than a minefield?'

'Ouch! You're hurting. I suppose I had better do it myself.' She got up and slipped out of her dress and then removed her brassiere and knickers with a grace and lack of embarrassment which made it all seem so natural. 'I didn't mean for this to happen,' she said as she lay down beside him. 'The trouble is that, when I get cross, I get . . . Golly, this bed thing's narrow. There! You're sure it's Fenton's evening off?'

Edward said nothing. He thought there was something particularly erotic about making love on so respectable a piece of furniture as a chaise longue.

When they had finished and lit cigarettes, he said, 'We do love each other, then? I mean, I know I love you but . . . On the *Queen Mary* . . . it wasn't something you regretted?'

'Don't let's have this conversation,' Verity begged him. 'We go round and round in circles. Of course I love you. I'm not some tart who gets into bed with just anyone. Let's change the subject, shall we?'

'I suppose so. But I like going round and round in circles with you. I always think I might just understand it this time. However,' he went on hurriedly, seeing a look in her eyes which he knew meant her patience was being tried, 'you never told me where we are going, before dinner.'

'Oh my God! Stop whatever it is you are doing . . .' – he was in fact stroking her stomach – 'and get up. We're terribly late. We were late before this . . .' She gestured at the chaise longue.

'Well then, do we have to go at all?' Edward replied, lying back lazily, admiring her neat posterior as it disappeared into the bathroom. 'I bet it's one of your Communist gatherings where I catch people sizing me up with a view to hanging me from a lamp post.'

'No, it's not. Or rather André is a Communist but it's not a Party "do",' she called over the sound of running water.

'André?'

'André Kavan. He's a photographer and he's got this exhibition in Jermyn Street. That's what we have to go and see. It's opening today.'

'What sort of photographer?' Edward inquired suspiciously.

'A *great* photographer. He has his stuff in *Life*. You'll recognize it when you see it.'

'He's a war photographer? You met him in Spain?'

'Not just war but, yes, his photographs of the war in Spain are amazing. It makes me want to give up writing. You know what they say about a picture being worth a thousand words? Well, it's true.'

Edward, always jealous when he heard Verity enthusing about some man he did not know, wanted to ask if they were lovers and, as if reading his mind, she said, 'And before you ask, he has a girlfriend – Gerda Meyer. She's almost as good a photographer as he is. And she's beautiful which is rather unfair. I expect you'll fall for her the moment you see her. All the men do but be warned: she'd eat you for breakfast and have forgotten you by supper.'

'I don't need any such warning,' Edward said with hauteur. 'My heart is . . . well, you know where it is.'

'It wasn't your heart I was talking about,' Verity said drily.

'Really, V, wash your mouth out. When I think that, when I first knew you, you were pure as the driven snow. So how did you meet? On some ruined battlement?'

'We met in the Ritz in Paris, if you must know. André's a great friend of Belasco's. We were all having dinner together.'

Edward was wise enough to say nothing. Ben Belasco was an American novelist whom Verity had met when she first went to Spain and they had had a brief but intense affair. As far as Edward knew, that was all in the past. Certainly he was going to assume so.

'So is Mr Kavan – your photographer friend – French?' he asked instead.

'No, he's a Hungarian Jew. He was thrown out of Hungary by the Fascists. I suppose Paris is his home now but I think he has a Polish passport. He speaks about ten languages – all very badly. He's a gypsy.'

It was after seven when they reached the gallery but the party was still going strong. There were a lot of 'Comrades' present and Edward was rather proud to be escorting Verity. She was something of a star since her success with her Left Book Club bestseller and her reports from the front in the *New Gazette*. She had as many enemies as admirers, of course, who liked to gossip about her scandalous relationship with Lord Edward Corinth.

Verity was looking smart in a navy-blue coat with a wide belt covering the slightly creased little black dress which she liked so much. She loved hats and her navy lacquered straw hat with its white ribbon seemed to Edward just perfect. He could hardly believe that she was, in some indefinable way, 'his'. As she disappeared into the crowd to greet old friends, he was left on his own. He glanced at the photographs on the walls and then looked more closely. They were remarkable. Taken very close up, they were almost indecently intimate but, as he peered at them, the images became grainy and began to dissolve. They revealed faces wrenched out of their normal expressions by the horror of war. There were old women with babies in their laps and dishevelled younger women running across a square staring up at the sky from which it was obvious bombs were raining down. One particularly chilling image was of a Spanish soldier, head thrown back, one hand stretched out, his gun – some sort of rifle – falling to the ground. When Edward looked closer, he was shocked to see that this was a picture of a man caught at the moment of his death. There was no visible enemy, no blood, no gaping wound but there could be no other interpretation. A bullet had checked him as he ran and stopped him dead. Edward saw that the photograph was captioned 'Soldier falling'.

He was distracted by someone calling his name. He turned to see a flaxen-haired man of his own age. Edward's polite smile left his face as he recognized one of his least favourite people, one David Griffiths-Jones. He was Welsh but that in itself would not have prejudiced him in Edward's eyes. There was much more: he was a published poet much admired by left-wing critics; he was a senior figure in the Communist Party and was well known in

Spain as a ruthless organizer and committed Stalinist. Worst of all, he had been Verity's first lover and, though he had abandoned her when it had suited him, Edward still feared his malign influence over her.

'Corinth! Still slumming, I see. Do you think we workers at the coal face have a certain glamour or is it mere inverted snobbery? I certainly never expected to see you here. Do you know our André? But, of course, I am being stupid. Verity must have brought you. Where is she? Ah! I think I see her hat. So you two are still . . . friends?'

'Still friends, yes. How is it in Spain? I gather Madrid is shortly to fall to the rebels.'

'The reports of Madrid's imminent demise are, I am pleased to say, an exaggeration. Comrades from all over the world have rallied to her defence. The legitimate government will prevail despite the cretinous behaviour of the so-called democracies. Thank goodness for Comrade Stalin!'

David was being disingenuous as usual. There was no chance of Madrid withstanding General Franco's onslaught for very much longer. Moreover, the ramshackle alliance of anarchists and left-wing parties which had made up the Popular Front – the elected government of Spain before the civil war – could never be glued back together. Like Humpty Dumpty, that alliance was shattered beyond repair. If, by some miracle, Franco failed to win the war, a Communist regime would seize control of the country, taking its orders direct from Moscow. This was the reality and the reason neither France nor Britain would come out in support of either side.

'Have you met my friend Guy, by the way? He was up at Trinity with you, or was he a year or two after your time?'

'Guy!' Edward said, grasping the hand of a man with blue eyes and tight wavy hair. He had a boyish, healthy look and a charming smile that made Edward smile back but his fingernails, Edward noted, were dirty and badly bitten and, at a second glance, he wondered if his high colour was not fuelled by alcohol.

'Trinity and, before Cambridge, we were inky boys at Eton together, though we were not in the same house,' Guy cut in. 'But our paths haven't crossed since we came down from the University. I don't remember you being a Marxist, Corinth?'

'No, certainly not. As David says, I am here with a girl, Verity Browne. Do you know her?'

'We all know Verity,' Guy said smoothly. Seeing Edward's face fall, he added, 'But don't worry, Corinth. Don't you remember? Even at Cambridge my sexual preferences did not incline towards the female of the species.'

Edward was taken aback. He did remember now that Guy Baron was spoken of as 'one of those' but he never expected him to admit it so openly. He was spared from having to answer by Verity's reappearance. She had in tow a black-haired, black-eyed young man – in his late twenties or early thirties, Edward guessed – with an engaging grin and the dishevelled air of the artist. His shirt – vaguely military in style – was half in and half out of his black trousers and torn at the elbow. He was deeply tanned. Edward was immediately alarmed. True, Verity had talked about a girlfriend but this young man looked as though he might not attach much value to the idea of monogamy.

'This is André, only we call him "Bandi". Don't you think he's the most wonderful photographer? Oh, Bandi, this is Lord Edward Corinth.'

The two men shook hands. 'I haven't yet had a chance of looking at your photographs except the ones just behind me here. The crush, don't y'know, but I am very impressed. Where did you take this one of the falling soldier? It's an extraordinary image.'

'Outside Madrid,' André answered laconically.

'Amid so much horror,' Edward tried again, 'do you not want to do something – apart from taking photographs, I mean?'

'Do something?' the young man repeated in his complicated accent, a ripe mixture of several Continental languages. 'What do you suggest I do?'

'I am sorry, I didn't mean to be rude but, if you see a child in pain, don't you want to do more than take a photograph?' Edward knew he was being gauche but he could not stop himself. The photographer seemed too good to be true. He needed taking down a peg or two. 'Don't you want to intervene?'

André was silent for a moment. Then he said, 'I do intervene. These photographs,' he waved his hand at the wall, 'they "intervene". They say that here is pain and suffering. The innocent always suffer. Even you must have noticed,' he added with studied insolence. 'But why should I bother . . . bah!'

He turned away and was soon engrossed in conversation with Guy Baron. Verity looked at Edward in amazement. 'What did you do that for? I thought the one thing you were was polite but I see I was wrong.'

Before he could defend himself, she had flounced off. Edward's heart sank. What had possessed him? They were amazing photographs and all he had needed to do was say so. Instead he had accused the photographer of being a heartless voyeur. It was inexcusable and he ought to apologize. He sighed. It was going to be one of those evenings when he could do nothing right. He had visualized a romantic dinner at Gennaro's with the girl he loved and then perhaps, if he were lucky, back to bed. Now she would leave for Spain and there would be bad blood between them. He must do something to put matters right.

He looked around wildly for something he might do and found himself looking into the green eyes of a flame-haired girl who was offering him a cigarette and laughing. 'I guess you need this.' She'had a slight American accent and Edward was immediately charmed. 'Bandi can be a mite touchy about his art.'

'Bandi? Oh, you mean Kavan.'

'Yes, André. Some of us call him Bandi. Don't ask me why.'

Edward was always attracted to redheads and this one with her monkey face and freckles, her slightly twisted smile and the wicked gleam in her eye was – as black-haired Verity had forecast – hard to resist.

'Can photography be an art?' he asked in genuine surprise.

'Oh, don't let's get into that. It's true a few years ago Bandi was just another news photographer but things have changed since his stuff started appearing in *Life*. But you have to admit, they are good.'

'I haven't seen much of them yet but, as I tried to tell him, the ones I have seen are remarkable. I wonder, however, if my response is adequate? That's why I asked you if they were art. It might alter how I feel about them.'

'*How* do you feel about them?'

'I suppose I want better captions.'

'Meaning?'

'Meaning when I look at these pictures I feel sympathy and, in a general way, I would like to do something about the pain they expose – heal the wounded, stop the bombs and soothe the frightened child – but I know, after a good dinner tonight, I will hardly remember them. Only if Verity talks about her experiences in Spain and I argue with her will these photographs start to be important to me. Only with words to back them up will these images mean something. I'm sorry, I'm being pompous. Verity would have stopped me ages ago.'

'Someone said that a photograph is a secret about a secret. The more it tells you, the less you know.'

'Yes, that's good. I'm not sure what it means, but it feels right. You must be Gerda Meyer? Verity told me about you. To be accurate, she told me I wasn't to fall for you but you are going to have to help by not looking at me like that.'

Gerda turned away her head. 'Sorry! Was I staring? I suppose I was surprised. From what Verity told me, I was expecting to see a silly-ass, music-hall aristocrat with nothing in his face but a monocle.'

Edward found himself laughing again. 'Perhaps it was unwise of Verity to talk to each of us about the other. It leads to . . . expectations. Let's complete the introductions though. Perhaps you mistake me for someone else. I'm Edward Corinth.' They shook hands solemnly. 'You were in Spain with Verity? At the siege of Toledo?'

'With Bandi, really. We're lovers – at least some of the time.' She laughed. 'Have I shocked you?'

Edward shook his head. 'You are a photographer too, aren't you?'

'*I* think so but Bandi can be rather dismissive. You must know from Verity how difficult it is being a woman and a war reporter. Do you want to see some of my photographs? No one else does. They're over there in the corner.'

'Of course. I would like that very much.'

He followed Gerda across the room. A sequence of about thirty photographs of what was clearly a Spanish village devastated by war met his gaze.

'Not cheerful, I'm afraid, but it is necessary to tell the truth especially the truth no one wants to hear.'

Edward was transfixed. Beneath photographs of jubilant troops at Barcelona's train station captioned 'Off to fight the Insurgents at the Aragon Front' were pictures of what looked like a whole village in flight – men, women and children, most on donkeys but some in or on ramshackle vehicles, all with that bewildered look of refugees turned out of their homes by the brutal hand of war. The contrast seemed to say it all. How war shatters illusions, destroys lives and brings – not much-vaunted freedom – but despair.

'It was a place called Cerro Muriano. I took them a few months ago. It makes one sick to the stomach, doesn't it?'

'I'm sorry. I don't know what to say. They are magnificent. They wrench at your heart.'

'There are many worse scenes,' she said grimly. 'Dead bodies and so much grief but I didn't think them suitable for a fashionable London art gallery.'

'And for people like me to gawp at,' he said looking at her.

'That too,' she agreed.

Edward turned back to the black-and-white images on the wall and saw a group photograph of soldiers – some arm in arm – standing on or leaning against an armoured vehicle. 'Isn't that David?' he said suddenly.

'David Griffiths-Jones? Yes, of course, you know him, don't you? He's very good-looking, don't you think?'

Edward looked at her suspiciously. He thought he might be being teased. He was. He smiled. 'Yes, very.'

'But you don't like him?'

'No, I don't like him' he agreed. 'I expect he sees this whole exhibition in terms not of art but propaganda. You have to admit, powerful as they are, these photographs provide a one-sided view of the war. There's no room here for any atrocities carried out by Republican troops.'

'We can't be on both sides of the fence. My pictures aren't faked if that's what you're getting at.'

She sounded angry but Edward was imperturbable. He liked this girl but he did not like the feeling that he was being manipulated. Perhaps it was the presence of Griffiths-Jones, so pleased with himself, which made the hair on the back of his head stand up. 'I didn't say they were. I simply said that there are other atrocities which have not been photographed.'

'It's not my job to be "balanced" or "fair",' Gerda said, going red about the ears. 'I just take photographs of what I see.'

She spoke fiercely and Edward was quick to apologize.

'Forgive me. It's just what I said. Give me the context and I'll read these images and make sense of them. I admire your photographs and the courage it took to get them but in this place, surrounded by so many Comrades, I feel as if I am being told what to think and feel.'

He waited for her to stalk off or slap his face and watched as she thought about doing both of these things but then her irrepressible smile lit up her face.

'I can see why Verity finds you so irritating but it's probably why she respects you. You just refuse to toe the Party line, don't you?'

Edward did not answer but turned once more to the photographs.

'And that face. I know it . . . Who is that?'

'You've just been talking to him – Guy Baron.'

'Of course! How stupid of me. He was fighting in Spain?'

'No. He was just over for a few days "observing" but he rather fancied himself in fighting gear. I gave him a gun to hold and took his photograph. He was frightfully pleased.'

'So David's a friend of yours?' he said.

'Not really. He doesn't have "friends", you know – just comrades. Anyway, he's a bit ruthless for me. There was this pal of mine – an English writer. He wasn't very good at fighting. In fact they called him a coward. He wanted to leave the front line. David had a long talk with him and persuaded him to go back to the fighting. Secretly, he arranged for him to go to a place where he would be certain to be killed.'

Edward looked at the girl with horror and then said slowly, 'I can believe it.'

They gazed at each other in silence for a moment and there was an understanding.

Verity came through the mob. 'You don't mind, do you, Edward? I've asked David and Guy to eat with us tonight. Oh, I see you've made friends with Gerda. How do you like him? He's not bad for an aristo, is he?'

Edward hated Verity when she was like this, making smart remarks in bad taste, but realized she was still angry with him for being rude to André. He caught a glance from Gerda and stifled his angry retort. 'Not at all. Why don't you and André come too?' he asked her. 'Or are you being wined and dined by the gallery?'

'I'm sure we'd love to come. I'll just ask Bandi. Won't be a moment.'

She went off to find him. Verity said in a loud whisper as soon as her back was turned, 'I wish you hadn't asked her. André's all right but she's a nothing.'

'Verity! I'm ashamed of you. She's not a nothing. She's a highly talented photographer. Have you looked at these?'

'And you lust after her.'

'I say!'

'Well, that's why you invited her. Admit it. She's not . . . faithful to André . . . leads him a merry dance.' She was suddenly contrite. 'I shouldn't have said she was a nothing. She is a very good photographer and brave . . . much braver than me. She says she has to be *near* . . . always nearer to get the photograph that tells the truth. She's been almost killed dozens of times. But I still don't like her.'

'And I don't like David but I suppose I'll have to put up with it.'

'Oh, cheer up. You'll enjoy renewing old friendships and flirting with Gerda.'

'And I'll end up paying for all of them. It's a funny thing about Comrades, they regard it as undemocratic to pay their own bills.'

'Think of it as your contribution to the redistribution of wealth,' Verity said, squeezing his arm. 'Don't sulk. I think it a great compliment that David and Guy want to eat with you. After all, you are the enemy.'

Just as they were leaving the gallery, in bustled their old friend the Rev. Tommie Fox. Tommie had been at Eton and Trinity with Edward and then, to the amazement of his friends, had refused to join the family firm and earn a good living doing not very much. Instead, he had been ordained and was now a Church of England vicar. His father had still not forgiven him. Tommie had recently moved to a new parish in Hoxton and was always roping in his friends to help entertain 'my boys', as he called them. Edward admired him enormously. He was hardly ever daunted by the impossible odds against which he struggled. Poverty and its attendants, dirt and disease, were endemic in the slums and Tommie found himself ministering as much to the body as the soul.

Hoxton had its quota of respectable lower-middle class but poverty bred not only crime but political extremism. Like flies on a dung heap, Mosley's bully boys trawled the slums recruiting the unemployed and inciting hatred for the Jews and for enclaves of 'foreigners' – Italians and French principally but also dozens of smaller immigrant communities – refugees for the most part who, according to Mosley, had stolen their jobs. The black uniforms and boots were also a powerful inducement to join the British Union of Fascists. The semi-military 'get-up' gave the new recruits a spurious sense of importance and having someone who seemed to need them made the BUF very attractive. The Communists also recruited in the slums but their appeal tended to be to the better educated and there were not many of those in Tommie's parish. There were moments when he seriously thought a new war was exactly what his boys needed. Army life would harness so much wasted energy but, when it was borne in on him that he was recommending death and destruction to solve a social problem, he knew he was giving way to despair. There had to be another way.

'Thank goodness!' Tommie exclaimed. 'I thought I might have missed you.' He kissed Verity and shook Edward's hand so heartily it was almost painful. He was built like a rugby prop forward and had indeed gained a blue at the University but his first love was boxing, which was unusual for a vicar. You could tell from his squashed nose and cauliflower ears that he was a fighter but his expression was all sunshine and amiability. The boxing school he had begun in a disused warehouse was one of the most popular parts of the youth club he had set up.

'Verity invited me,' he explained to Edward, 'but I got caught up. There was a rumpus and by the time I had broken it up . . . well anyway. Has Verity told you about it?'

'Told me about what?'

'Sorry, Tommie, I quite forgot.'

'Typical! The thing is, we're having a football match the day after tomorrow – three o'clock – Old Etonians against my boys. One of my pals has pulled out at the last moment and so I need you. You'll say yes, won't you, old boy?' he finished breathlessly.

From time to time Edward had 'done his bit', as he thought of it. Eton had a 'mission' in the East End to which he had gone most holidays. Now he helped Tommie whenever he could. He liked teaching and found that most of the youths did not resent his presence once they saw he was not going to 'put on airs'.

'Oh, do I have to?' he wailed. 'I'm too old to play football. It's not my game and my knee's only just got right.'

29

'You must!' Tommie insisted. 'We can't let them down and you are my last hope. I'm scraping the barrel. Tell him, Verity.'

'Don't be a weed, Edward,' Verity backed him up. 'Guy's playing and lots of your old friends. It'll be like one of those school reunions or gaudies – isn't that what you call them? – you boys love so much. I was never at a school long enough to be invited to a reunion,' she added wistfully. 'I'll bring Bandi and Gerda. It will amuse them to see the primitive rituals of savages. Bandi will take photographs and Gerda . . . she can mop your brow when you fall in the mud.'

'Oh God! Must I? Why should your lads want to play games with Old Etonians? It's much more likely they want to kill us.'

'Nonsense!' Tommie said, putting an arm round Edward's shoulder and squeezing.

'There's a good little man,' Verity said patronizingly. 'You do what this nice vicar tells you.'

Some hours later they sat round a table at Gennaro's, the ruins of their meal in front of them, cigars and brandy to hand. Edward was feeling rather ill and resentful. The extravagant manner in which the restaurant was furnished was making his eyes ache. It had been redecorated since he had last eaten here and he did not like the result. The pink lamp-shades in the shape of exotic birds offended him and the maze of mirrors dazzled him. He knew he would be picking up the tab and it irked him. He hated them all – the red-faced, self-satisfied Guy Baron, the hard-eyed David Griffiths-Jones and the half-drunk André who he suspected was stroking Verity's leg under the tablecloth. Tommie had wisely refused to accompany them, saying he had a Mothers' Union meeting to attend. Only the presence of Gerda made the party tolerable. She sat beside him, a cigar in her mouth, her eyes narrowed against the smoke, patiently listening to him tell stories of Africa, occasionally squeezing his hand.

'You know,' Baron was saying, 'when David was in Moscow last month he had a pretty little *comsomolka* all to himself – slim, ardent, red bandana round her hair. . .' He hummed the 'Internationale'. '"Who was nothing shall be all . . .".'

'*Basta*!' David said, but not angrily. It was as if Baron was a naughty schoolboy – too charming to be thoroughly irritating.

'And you found the Soviet Union lived up to its promise? Is it truly a classless society?' Edward had no idea why he chose to bait Griffiths-Jones but it did not matter. David saw the question not as a challenge but an opportunity to lecture his flock on 'the promised land'.

'Soviet Communism is based on genuine social equality. To engage in socially useful work is a universal duty.' He looked at Edward with loathing. 'There is no exemption from this duty for possessors of wealth, owners of land or holders of high office. There is a single social grade, that of producer by hand or brain. This is what is meant by a classless society. But the principle of social equality goes much further. It extends to relations between the sexes – everyone lives in an atmosphere of group responsibility and freedom from servility. What is even more unique is the absence of prejudice as to colour or race . . .'

At this last assertion, Baron exploded with laughter. 'And what about buggers? Is there prejudice against them?' He was obviously determined to needle David. 'No prejudice! Even you cannot believe that, David. Take India, for instance. I am convinced of the incompetence and futility of the Party and the Comintern when I look at their policy. They want the British to leave India before its historic task is complete. The Labour Party agrees! Surrender and grovel. Only Mr Churchill and the right of the Conservative Party see what must be done in India.'

Baron relapsed into a drunken stupor but Edward smiled. Would Mr Churchill welcome such an ally, he wondered?

'What does Baron do?' he asked Gerda in a low voice.

'Do? He picks up boys and drinks. That's what he does.'

'He doesn't have a job?'

'He works for the BBC. He is in charge of a programme called "This Week in Parliament". He likes talking to politicians. Don't ask me why.'

When the party broke up, David Griffiths-Jones and Baron went off together. They were sharing a house in Chester Square. David said, insincerely, 'Good to see you again, Corinth. Shall I ever convert you to my way of thinking? No, I suppose not.'

Baron, very drunk, seemed about to kiss him and Edward backed away. Instead, he shook him by the hand. 'I like you, Corinth,' he said solemnly. 'We must see each other again. You're in the telephone book? There are things . . .' His voice tailed off and he looked about him vacantly. Griffiths-Jones pushed him into a taxi but, in a last burst of energy, he leant out of the window and said, 'Thank you for the . . . party. Very white of you, old man.' Giggling, he sank back into his seat as the taxi accelerated away.

Verity, who was also rather the worse for wear, refused to let Edward take her back to the King's Road. She kissed him wetly and said, 'When I get back from Spain . . . shall we . . . you know, live together? Oh God, why does my head ache so? Kiss me, Edward. Tell me I'm not drunk.'

Edward had never seen her drunk before and did not like it. His alert, bossy, irritating bird of a girl had softened at the edges. She had let her defences fall and it made her rather ridiculous but he excused her. She was shortly to return to war-ravaged Spain and she knew now what to expect. He guessed she must be frightened and he knew she had every right to be. She *had* to go. She could never live with herself if she funked going back. As for what she had said about their living together, he knew that to be a pipe-dream. Not only was it quite impossible socially but, more to the point, he knew she valued her independence too highly. He had resigned himself to the idea that he would never to be able to live with her but whether their love could survive on snatched moments of sex and the odd week or two in London he did not dare guess.

He kissed her forehead and put her gently into a taxi, murmuring words of reassurance. Gerda and André, who were going in the same direction, said they would see her home. Gerda threw her arms around his neck and kissed him on the lips. André did not seem to mind and Verity was already asleep. The taste of her intoxicated him and he walked back to Albany in a state of wild frustration, angry and ashamed of himself.

3

The following day, Edward was unsurprised to be rung up by Major Ferguson of Special Branch. He was equally unsurprised to find Ferguson knew with whom he had been consorting the night before.

'Interesting friends you have, Lord Edward. I always thought there must be something about you to get along with so many strange characters with political views so much at odds with your own. At least I assume they are at odds with yours.'

Edward sighed. 'I don't know why, Major, but I have rather a headache this morning so perhaps we could ease up on the witticisms. Do I take it you will be calling on me later in the day?'

'At three, if that would be convenient?'

'Quite convenient.'

Ferguson was a small man with a face easy to forget. He had a small scar on his forehead partly hidden by a lock of hair, heavy spectacles and a military moustache but these were his only notable features. As Edward had reason to know, he was a shrewd operator. He respected the Major's ruthlessness and his information network. His detailed knowledge of the party at Gennaro's was proof of that.

'How did you find out about last night? Was it one of the waiters? Say it wasn't Freddy?' Freddy was Gennaro's proprietor.

'Not Freddy,' Ferguson assured him.

'So, have you come to give me my orders?'

'How explicit was Sir Robert?' Ferguson countered.

'He said he wanted me to find out who was passing information to Mr Churchill about our rearmament, or rather our lack

33

of it. He said you would give me a list of those who had access to secret files on arms and the arms trade and might therefore be under suspicion. He also mentioned a man who had gone missing – Charles Westmacott. Is that his name?'

'Yes. The information is all here.' He handed Edward a brown envelope.

'What do you think might have happened? You have investigated?'

'We are completely in the dark. We thought at first he might have defected to the Germans but there's no evidence of that. We have contacts in their embassy but we have heard nothing. Anyway, he's too junior to be much of a catch. It's not clear what he might have to sell.'

'What does his wife think?'

'Naturally, she fears he may be dead. What other reason can there be for his not having been in touch with her?'

'Does she have any idea of the nature of his work and why he might have been in danger?'

'She's not telling if she does but my impression is that she is genuinely ignorant and innocent. I may be wrong, of course. I thought you might get more out of her than I did. You'll find a complete report on the investigation – such as it is – here.' He tapped the envelope. 'We alerted all ports as soon as we knew he was missing and informed the ICPO.'

'The what?'

'You've not heard of it? The International Criminal Police Organization was set up – what? in 1923, I think – to exchange information about criminals and missing persons. All the European police forces are members but it's based in Vienna. Since the Germans have all but taken control there, the ICPO is a bit of a dead duck.'

'Thanks very much! It all sounds impossible. Perhaps I should start at the other end and talk to Mr Churchill? He might have some idea why Westmacott has gone missing. Sir Robert seemed to think Westmacott might have had sympathies in that direction.'

For the first time Ferguson looked doubtful. 'It's very hard to know. I don't see any real harm but . . .'

'But?'

'I don't altogether trust you with him. He's very persuasive.

Sir Robert himself is not above feeding him information when he wants a particular point made in the House.'

'Good Lord! If *he* is leaking information what chance have we got to plug the holes in the bucket?'

'*Quis custodiet ipsos custodes*?'

'Who guards the guards? I thought you did.'

'*Touché*, but we have a job to do and we must try to do it. Though Sir Robert might ask Mr Churchill to raise a particular point in the House, that's quite different from systematically feeding him with secret information on the strength or weakness of our armed forces. If Mr Churchill is being fed information, perhaps our German and Russian friends are also getting their sticky paws on stuff they shouldn't. Some of your Communist friends might feel justified in passing secrets to Moscow.'

Edward nodded. He had to admit that was more than likely.

'There's another thing . . .' If Ferguson was capable of being embarrassed, he was now. 'Churchill's not sound.'

'Politically?'

'Politically, yes, but I was meaning financially. We know for a fact that he owes his stockbrokers, Vickers da Costa, £1800 and he has seriously contemplated putting his house on the market despite it being the great love of his life.'

'How do you know all this?'

'It's our job,' Ferguson said simply.

'I heard he earned a great deal from his books. *The World Crisis* sold millions, didn't it?'

'Yes, but rebuilding Chartwell cost him a fortune and he leads an expensive life. For the moment he has been saved by three millionaire businessmen of dubious reputation – a Moravian-born Jew, now South African, called Sir Henry Strakosch, Sir Abe Bailey and an Indian arms dealer called Sir Vida Chandra.'

'Good heavens!' Edward was taken aback. 'I have met two of them as it happens, when I was in South Africa. Bailey owns a lot of mines in the Transvaal, doesn't he? He may be a bit of a rogue but I liked him. Wait a minute! Didn't his son, John, marry Churchill's daughter? I'm not sure I wasn't asked to the wedding but I was abroad.'

'That's right. They're divorced now but Churchill and the father are still close friends.'

'And Strakosch . . . I met him too. He's chairman of Union Corporation. A big wheel! Didn't he represent South Africa at the Genoa conference?'

'That's the man. You do know all the right people, Corinth. That's one of the reasons you can be so useful to us.'

'Oh well,' Edward said, modestly, 'South Africa's a large country but a small place, if you take my meaning. I don't know the Indian – what was his name – Chandra? Tell me about him.'

'Don't know much about him. Secretive sort of chap. Hard to get a line on him but we think he's on the side of the angels. Of course, all millionaires are rogues. That goes without saying but he's no worse than most. He made his money in armaments during the war. Lloyd George sold him a knighthood. He lives in London now.'

'Hmm. Wait a minute! I think Chandra's a bit of a sportsman. Fred Cavens was talking about him. He's a fencer. Olympic standard, I believe.'

'He must be in his late fifties.'

'Yes, but Cavens keeps on telling me that age is not as important in fencing as you might think. If you do it regularly, it helps you keep fit.' Edward was silent for a moment and Ferguson did not interrupt his thought process. 'So these men are keeping Churchill afloat financially? Why?'

'I suppose they think they have something to gain.'

'Ferguson, you are such a cynic. Maybe they just think he is the man to save "the old country".'

'Maybe. I don't know their motives but it does mean Churchill is in their respective pockets. The press would have a field day if they could prove he was not as independent as he likes people to think.'

'So you would blackmail him?'

'Perish the thought.' Ferguson's thin lips twitched in what might have been a smile. 'I just wanted you to be fully briefed in case you do meet him. We're more concerned about information on how weak we are, militarily and in the air, getting to the Germans. If Churchill knows the facts, so might the Nazis. If Herr Hitler fully appreciated how little there is to stop us going under in the event of war, he would take even less notice of our protests than he does already. The Germans have an idea that there is a different way to wage war – *blitzkrieg* they call it, literally

36

"lightning war" – a massive attack, speedy, overwhelming . . .
tanks, aeroplanes. They are, we believe, planning to try it out in
Spain courtesy of Franco. If they unleash such a thing on us in the
first few days of a war . . .' He shrugged his shoulders expressively.

A chill went down Edward's spine. What if Verity was a victim
of this new kind of war? He shivered. He saw Ferguson looking
at him shrewdly and wondered if he guessed what he was
thinking. He said aggressively, 'You seem to have muddied the
waters, Ferguson. Now I don't know what I'm looking for. Why
don't I just stay in bed? I can't see I'm going to be any use to you.'

'Rubbish!' Ferguson responded cheerfully. 'You have a nose.'
Edward unconsciously massaged his proboscis. 'Go and see Mrs
Westmacott. Stir things up a bit. Maybe someone'll take a pot
shot at you. That would help us. Startle a few birds out of cover.'

'I'm expendable?'

Ferguson smiled. 'Not at all. There would be a frightful stink
if the Duke of Mersham's younger brother was bumped off.
There would be all sorts of things said in the gutter press about
police inefficiency. It wouldn't do my career any good, I assure
you.'

'I take the point,' Edward grinned wryly.

Ferguson noticed the épée lying on the window seat and
picked it up. 'I hope not – at least, not literally. I see this is
capped. Don't forget the weapons our enemies use have no safety
caps. Goodbye, Lord Edward. I shall be in touch. Oh, by the way,
if anyone questions your authority to investigate, I have included
in that envelope a letter and an identity card which you can
thrust under any noses you like.'

'So I am a policeman now?'

'I suppose you are, yes. Does that bother you?'

Ferguson departed without giving Edward a chance to reply.

Westmacott lived – or had lived until his disappearance – in a
modest two-storey suburban villa in west London. Wanting to get
the interview with Mrs Westmacott over, Edward telephoned her
as soon as Ferguson had left and asked if she would see him the
following morning. So it was, at ten o'clock the next day, that he
drove along Western Avenue as far as Park Royal and then
turned into an area of small houses and bungalows mostly built

37

in the past five years. He parked the Lagonda in Elm Avenue. It was a pleasant place – a quiet, leafy street, respectable certainly, but who knew what secrets were hidden behind the net curtains. Two or three other cars were parked by the kerb but children still played in the street without any fear of being run down. Little gardens between street and front door reminded Edward that not so many years ago this had been countryside.

Each villa had a name, not a street number, and Edward had to ask directions from a child playing hopscotch. The Larches proved to be one of the smartest in the avenue. It had a green front door with a pane of stained glass let into it, a well-tended garden, bright with spring flowers, and carefully cultivated window boxes. No larches to be seen, however. This was a house which was loved and, for the first time, Edward began to appreciate what Mr Westmacott's disappearance must mean to his family.

The door was opened by a serious-faced girl of about ten. Neither particularly pretty nor plain, she wore wire spectacles hooked lopsidedly over her ears and wire braces on her teeth. She was holding a *Rupert Bear Annual* and a Mari-Lu doll dressed in a leather helmet and goggles.

'Yes?' she said belligerently.

'I telephoned earlier. My name is Edward Corinth. I have an appointment with your mother.' He paused, hoping for an invitation to come in, but the child said nothing, preferring to stare at him. 'I like your dolly. Is she Amy Johnson?' he inquired weakly.

'No, she's not. She's a racing driver,' the child said crushingly.

'Ah, a racing driver,' Edward repeated, feeling he was failing to make a good impression. 'So, may I see your mother?'

The little girl bent her head to one side and looked at him critically. She did not seem to approve of what she saw.

'Mummy said nothing to me about seeing anyone. She is lying down with a headache. I say, are you from the newspapers?'

'Certainly not!' Edward was rather insulted to be taken for a reporter but then it occurred to him that perhaps the press had been adding to the family's troubles. 'I'm a sort of policeman,' he said, not a little embarrassed. 'Might I come in? I won't bite, don't y'know.'

A voice drifted down the stairs behind the girl. 'Who is it, Alice?'

'He says he's a policeman but he doesn't look like one to me,' Alice added sturdily. Edward wanted to ask against what image of a man of the law he was being judged. Was he supposed to be wearing a helmet and brandishing a truncheon?

'Didn't I tell you, dear, that I was expecting a visitor? Is it Lord Edward Corinth?'

'It is,' Edward confessed.

'I thought it must be. Alice, show Lord Edward into the sitting-room, will you, dear? I'll be down in a moment.'

Reluctantly, the child let him in and gestured for him to follow her. She took him into a room which seemed at first sight to be bursting with furniture. There was a small open grate, shiny brass fire irons resting on the fender in front of which were two armchairs, complete with lace-edged antimacassars, and an uncomfortable-looking sofa. Next to the fireplace there was a large wireless on a table protected by a chenille cloth and a Victrola gramophone beside it. China geese on the wall flew in a straight line towards a cuckoo clock. At the other end of the room stood a table and several upright chairs and the obligatory aspidistra in a glazed pot.

The girl looked at Edward as though she knew him to be what was now being referred to as a 'con artist' with a record as long as her arm. 'You don't look like a lord.'

'I am sorry to disappoint you, Alice,' he replied mildly. 'What should a lord look like?'

'He should have a . . . have a crown . . . no, I mean a coronet.'

'I left it at home,' he said gravely. 'You can't wear coronets on ordinary days.'

'I see . . . no. But why did you say you were a policeman?'

'I said I was a sort of policeman,' he prevaricated.

'Are you going to find my daddy?' she asked bluntly.

'I shall try to. I suppose he didn't say anything to you about having to go away?'

He wondered if it was ethical to question the child without her mother's permission but he soothed his conscience by telling himself that it was Alice who had mentioned her father's disappearance.

'No, not really. He did say I was to be a good girl and help Mary look after mother.'

'Who is Mary?'

39

'She's the maid but it's her day off. She looks after me when mother's sick.'

'Is she often sick?'

'She has headaches,' Alice replied, as if everyone knew this.

'When did your father tell you to look after your mother, or was that something he always said before he went to the office?'

'No, he never said it to me before.'

'Before?'

'Before that morning . . . on the day he didn't come home.'

Edward saw that he had gone as far as he could. The little girl was bravely trying not to cry. It would not do if, even before he met Mrs Westmacott, he reduced her daughter to tears.

They stayed silent for a full minute, eyeing each other, and then they heard the sound of Mrs Westmacott coming downstairs. She must, he thought, have been a beautiful young woman. Even now, under severe strain, she was striking. She was aged about forty, he guessed. She was tall and moved with a certain grace, as though she had been a good dancer, and maybe still was. She had glossy hair, almost blond, and her eyes were large but at this moment uncertain, scared.

'Alice, go and finish your reading, will you, dear?'

When the girl had departed, she said, 'She ought to be at school but since her father . . . perhaps it was wrong of me but I wanted her at home.'

'That's quite understandable,' Edward assured her. He wanted to put out a hand to calm her trembling but reminded himself that he was a policeman not a vicar.

'Please sit down, Lord Edward. It's very kind of you to come. I am afraid the police – I mean the local police – don't take Charles's disappearance seriously. I believe they think we must have quarrelled, but we didn't, you know.'

'I quite believe you, Mrs Westmacott. We think his disappearance may have something to do with his work. Did he ever talk to you about his work?'

'Never! I mean, I would say "Did you have a good day at the office?" or something and he would say "I'm a bit tired." Or he might say "There's a job I have to finish. I'll be late again tomorrow, I'm afraid."'

'Did he often work late?'

'Not until quite recently. He was usually home by six thirty or seven.'

'Then what would you do?' he pressed her gently.

'He would wash and then he would have a drink and read the evening paper and then we would have supper. Then we would listen to the wireless or he might have some reading to do. We were normally in bed by half-past ten.'

'The reading he had to do sometimes – was that work?'

'Yes, he would bring work home, but not often.'

'You never saw what the papers were he was reading?'

'No, they were nothing to do with me,' she said, sounding slightly shocked at the question.

'But you never saw any papers or files lying around and just glanced at them? It would be quite natural if you did.'

'No, he was very careful like that. He used to replace what he had read in his briefcase and lock it. It was so he did not forget anything when he went to the office in the morning.'

'I understand. So you never saw any of those papers?' he repeated.

'No. . . Well, as a matter of fact, last week . . . he seemed so tired and worried. He had to go upstairs to take an aspirin while he was reading . . . after supper, you know.'

'And while he was upstairs, did you happen to see . . . ?'

'I meant no harm,' she said, alarmed, 'but Charles seemed so unlike himself that I did get up and go round to his chair.'

'You were in here . . . in this room?'

'Yes. He sat where you are sitting.'

'And what did you see?'

'Oh, I don't know – nothing . . . nothing I understood, anyway.'

'But?'

'But I did see some of the papers were marked Secret and one was a file and it had Most Secret stamped on the outside in red.'

'So your husband was coming home late and tired and worried?'

'Yes, for about a month before . . . before he disappeared.'

'Did you ask him about it?'

'Yes, but he just said it was work and that things had piled up and it would be better soon and I wasn't to worry. We even talked about going to the seaside when the weather improved.'

'I see. Mrs Westmacott, how did your husband get to work and come home in the evening?'

'He went on the Underground – the Piccadilly Tube.'

'To Park Royal station?'

'Yes, it's only a fifteen-minute walk from here. He used to say that little walk saved his life.'

'What did he mean by that?'

'The walk . . . it did him good. He was always complaining about not having enough fresh air and exercise. So this little walk . . .' she hesitated and then repeated, 'saved his life.'

There was nothing else he could glean from Mrs Westmacott for the moment so Edward left, promising to be in touch before long. When he got back to his rooms, he once again read through the papers Major Ferguson had given him. Detectives had questioned staff on the Underground and regular passengers without finding anyone who could say for sure that Charles Westmacott had been on the train the evening he disappeared. The likelihood was, therefore, that he had never caught the train. He had left his office at about five thirty – he was not senior enough to have his own secretary but several colleagues had seen him leave the building. Then, who knows? Had he gone to meet someone? Had that person abducted or killed him? Or had he fled the country for fear of being exposed as some sort of spy? It was futile to guess. Edward threw Ferguson's papers on the floor in disgust and called to Fenton to bring him a gin and tonic before he walked to his club for a bite of lunch.

'Tell me,' he said to Fenton when he appeared with the restorative, 'if you wanted to disappear and you had reason to think the ports were being watched, what would you do? Go to some remote part of the British Isles and hunker down?'

'It depends, my lord. I might do that if I wished to absent myself for a short period of time but, if I wished to vanish for a prolonged period, I would lose myself in London or some other great city. In the country, a stranger stands out like a sore thumb and his presence would soon come to the attention of the authorities. In a London boarding house fewer people would ask questions. Everyone is a stranger and people guard their privacy.'

'Very true. But what if you had to leave the country quickly and without attracting attention?'

'Then I would take the Golden Arrow from Victoria station and reach France within the day.'

'Yes, you wouldn't go by aeroplane. Apart from the cost, you would be noticed. Damn! Needles in haystacks!'

'Indeed, my lord.'

At that moment, the telephone rang and Fenton went to answer it.

'It is Miss Browne, my lord.'

Fenton's disapproval of his master's choice of female companionship was evident in his tone of voice though it was never expressed in words. It was not his place to comment on his master's romantic attachments. Fenton was in many ways an unconventional valet. Edward would trust him with his life and, on at least one occasion, had done so. He could be daring and decisive and Edward had no secrets from him save those entrusted to him by Major Ferguson. It was true they never discussed Verity but that was because neither man would contemplate bandying about a woman's name. That was not done . . . 'bad form', as Edward would have put it. Fenton might be happy to break the rules when necessary but he liked the forms to be observed. He had old-fashioned views on what constituted respectability in a female. He admired Verity for her courage and enterprise but he was firmly of the view that it was not a lady's place to gallivant round the world reporting on wars. If his master loved her, as he reluctantly admitted to himself that he did, then she should tear up her passport, marry him and settle down to darn socks and have children. He suspected that Lord Edward and she were lovers though Edward, considerate of his feelings, had never thrust the evidence in front of him. He accepted that gentlemen had to be allowed their 'little adventures', as he put it to himself, but this was not a 'little adventure'. It was a strange courtship of which he thoroughly disapproved.

'Miss Browne's off to Spain in a day or two,' Edward said brightly. 'I was expecting her to ring.'

It was a subdued Verity on the end of the line. 'Did I behave atrociously the other night? I woke up with the most awful hangover so I think I must have.'

'We all got rather fried, I'm afraid.'

'You didn't like my friends,' she said accusingly.

'I liked Gerda,' he offered.

'Huh. You keep your hands off Gerda. She's dynamite. Way out of your league.'

43

Edward thought of several witty things he could say but wisely rejected all of them. 'Guy Baron's interesting.'

'Yes, I don't know what to make of Guy. He's not serious, or is he? It's so hard to know.'

Le style c'est l'homme?'

'There's more to him than he would have you believe.'

'Is he a member of the Party?'

'Gosh, yes. David wouldn't be so thick with him if he weren't.'

There was a silence and then Verity continued, 'Anyway, the reason I rang you is to remind you that you are due in Hoxton in an hour.'

'Agh!' Edward hit his forehead with the palm of his hand. 'I'd quite forgotten. Do I really have to?'

'I thought you might try that line. Of course you have to go. Anyway, it'll be a laugh.'

'For you, maybe,' Edward said bitterly.

'Buck up! You can't let Tommie down. Gerda and I will worship from the side lines or administer first aid.'

Edward groaned as he put down the receiver. 'Fenton, you'll never guess – I met Mr Fox at that party the night before last and he persuaded me to play football for the Old Etonians against Hoxton's bravest and brightest. It's the last thing in the world I want to do but Miss Browne says I can't let him down.'

'Very good, my lord,' Fenton said, pursing his lips. 'If I might say so, with your knee only just . . .'

'Don't say it! I agree, I agree! But, if Miss Browne says I must go, then I must.' Fenton could see no such necessity. 'Perhaps I've lost my footer boots,' Edward said, hopefully.

'No, my lord. I shall bring them to you immediately. Would you wish me to attend, my lord?'

'Very feudal of you but I think not. You can patch me up me when I return. If ever I do,' he added gloomily.

Less than an hour later he arrived at the church in a taxi – having decided not to risk the Lagonda in Hoxton – and was greeted by a wildly enthusiastic Tommie. 'I knew you would come,' he said, meaning he had expected him not to. 'You know most of the others, don't you?'

Edward felt better when he had shaken the hands of fellow victims of Tommie's moral blackmail, some of whom he had not seen since leaving school. Everyone seemed as disinclined for the fray as he was which cheered him. Another taxi drew up and Guy Baron got out. As Edward greeted him, he smelled the liquor on his breath. He seemed very excited. 'What fun,' he trilled. 'It's so difficult to meet working-class youths in the West End. It's going to be so delicious to be stamped on by the proletariat!'

Tommie looked doubtful. 'You will behave, Guy, won't you? You're supposed to be setting an example. Good clean fun and all that.'

'Bugger that!' Guy giggled.

They all walked round the corner to the 'pitch' which was little more than a piece of wasteland with goal posts at each end, bare of grass in the main but at least, Edward noticed, clear of broken bottles and tin cans.

'Aren't you playing, Tommie?' Edward asked, surprised not to see him in his sports gear.

'No, I'm holding myself neutral. It's better that way.'

'What a sell!' Edward grumbled. 'You could have played instead of dragging me out.'

'That doesn't sound like the Edward Corinth I used to know,' the vicar said piously. 'I hope all that good living hasn't rotted your soul.'

The two teams shook hands awkwardly and the Hoxtonites took off their cloth caps and rubbed their hands meditatively. The Old Etonians took off *their* caps – mostly gaily striped, recalling schoolboy triumphs – and jogged up and down stretching, with the exception of Guy who, capless, took a long swig from a small silver flask he had in his pocket and then collapsed on the ground. He was helped to his feet by Edward and Tommie who patted him doubtfully and asked if were all right.

'Fit as a fiddle!' Guy said, tripping over his bootlaces.

Without further ado the game began. There were a number of spectators – families and friends of the players, Edward supposed. He could not see Verity but he caught sight of Gerda's red hair and the thought that she was watching made him determined not to shirk. The referee was a thin, unprepossessing, bearded man who, Tommie said, was his curate. Edward took one look at him and decided he would not be able to control the game if it turned rough, as he suspected it might.

In fact, the first half passed without any major incident and Edward began to relax. His knee was bearing up well and he had even scored a goal. He looked out of the corner of his eye to see if he could spot Verity but there was still no sign of her. He began to think longingly of a bath and a well-earned whisky and soda.

He could not but notice that the Old Etonians were larger and healthier than their opponents. A poor diet and too much bad beer, combined with having nothing to do all day but wander around the streets, did not make for physical well-being. However, the captain, a man called Hawthorne, was a burly fellow who, Edward felt instinctively, had no particular love for Old Etonians. It was soon apparent that his restraint in the first half was merely a ruse to lull the opposition into a false sense of security. He seemed particularly incensed by Baron and Edward decided there was something about Guy's manner which could easily infuriate. He was not effete but he was 'camp' – a word he had heard his friend Adrian Hassel use. He flirted – that was the only word for it – with Hawthorne in particular, inciting him to retaliate. Guy often had to rest – cigarettes and alcohol had destroyed his wind. On one such occasion, Hawthorne was thundering down the pitch with the ball at his feet when Guy, sitting on the ground attempting to regain his breath, thrust out his leg and sent him sprawling. The curate chose to believe Hawthorne had tripped and refused to admit the foul, crying falsetto, 'Play on! Play on!'

Hawthorne got up, looked round like a half-dazed bull, saw his enemy still on the ground and kicked out at him. While the Old Etonians were dressed in football shirts and shorts and wore boots, the opposition possessed no such special clothing. They played in ordinary shirts and trousers and, instead of football boots, wore the working man's hobnail boots. To be kicked by a foot encased in one of these was no light matter and Edward winced as he saw Hawthorne's boot connect with Guy's nose. There was plenty of blood but Guy mumbled that his nose was not broken. After a short pause when the wounded man was hauled off the pitch, the game resumed – though now it resembled not so much a game as a full-scale war. Edward doubled up as he received an elbow in his stomach and then, allowing his bad temper to get the upper hand, tackled a young man with a small moustache and bad teeth with such ferocity that he fell to the ground squealing. Conscience-stricken, Edward stopped to help him up and received a fist to his eye that made him cry out in pain.

It was an altogether disgraceful performance, as Tommie said afterwards, but somehow the match ended in an almost palpable sense of camaraderie. It was as if the artifical politeness in which the game had begun had been replaced by mutual respect. Hardly a player had escaped injury of some sort but even Guy seemed not to bear a grudge and insisted on joining players and supporters at a local public house. The atmosphere was further brightened by the attitude of the spectators who appeared to have enjoyed seeing their loved ones assaulted. Any reserve there might have been between friends of the Old Etonians and supporters of the Hoxtonites had been broken down as, one after another, the players had been dragged off the pitch to have their wounds tended. A great deal of laughter was generated by the state of the players – ripped shirts, bloodied noses and mud over everything.

Unexpectedly – or perhaps not so unexpectedly – Guy Baron had struck up a particular friendship with the man Hawthorne who had put so much effort into reducing his face to pulp. Tommie looked suspicious when the two of them – after a mumbled conversation – waved goodbye and disappeared, no one seemed to know where.

'You were marvellous,' Gerda said kissing Edward. 'Your poor eye! Here, let me put some balm on it. I brought it knowing it would come in useful.'

'Ouch! That hurt. Where's Verity?' he asked. Surely it was reasonable to expect his girl to be there and cheer on his efforts, applaud his goals and wipe the mud off his wounds.

'At the last moment she could not come,' André said. 'Such a pity! She would like to have seen your eye.'

'She had a last-minute emergency,' Gerda confirmed. 'She sent her love.'

'Huh,' Edward said, enjoying having a grievance. 'I suppose she had to cover a dog show for the *New Gazette*. But what can one expect?'

'No, it was a real emergency,' Gerda said loyally, though sounding not displeased at his irritation.

'I took some wonderful photographs,' André said excitedly. 'You English are quite mad. In my country someone would have pulled out a gun and shot at his opponent. But see – you are all friends. It is magnificent! *C'est magnifique, mais ce n'est pas le sport.*'

Tommie came over clasping a pint of bitter and said apologetically to Edward, 'I am sorry, old boy. You have a ripe one there. Get Fenton to put a raw steak on it.'

Edward went with him to examine his eye in the broken mirror which adorned the urinal wall. 'Oh God!' he groaned. 'How can I interview important civil servants with a black eye? Blast it! Damn you, Tommie, and damn Verity for persuading me to come.'

'Why are you interviewing civil servants?' Tommie asked curiously.

'Oh, did I say that? Forget it, will you, Tommie?'

4

'So, how did it go?' It was Verity sounding cheerful.

'I only lost an eye, that's all.'

Edward had got back to his rooms to be ministered to by Fenton, who was suitably sympathetic. A bloody steak was applied to his eye and he lay back on the sofa and groaned. It was then that Verity had telephoned.

'I'm sure you are exaggerating. Put a steak on it.'

'One is clasped to my eye as we speak and dripping blood on to the floor.'

'Brave boy! Sorry I couldn't make it. Did you notice I wasn't there?'

'Of course I did, but it didn't matter.' He added nastily, 'Gerda looked after me.'

There was a silence but when Verity spoke she was, to his chagrin, sweet and reasonable.

'There's a story going the rounds – the *Daily Mail* is pushing it – that our people are shooting anyone in the International Brigade who won't take orders from Moscow. Ridiculous, of course, but Joe wants me to investigate.' Joe was Lord Weaver, the proprietor of the *New Gazette* and Verity's employer. 'I've got to go back to Spain earlier than I had planned.'

'When?' Edward demanded.

'In about half an hour.'

'I won't see you then?'

'Not unless you come with me,' she said, with an effort at humour.

'I can't see myself doing that. Well, I'll miss you. When will you be back?'

'Not for a bit. Apparently, there's a big effort coming to raise the siege of Madrid. Perhaps the tide is turning.'

Edward thought that unlikely. It had been obvious to him for months that without decisive intervention from France or Britain, the Republic was doomed. The Republicans – or rather the Communists – were getting aid from the Soviet Union but that was just enough to keep the war going, not to give them a chance of winning.

'Thanks for telephoning. I suppose it's no good asking you to be careful.'

'I'll be careful, silly. I'm not out to commit suicide. I was quite surprised, Joe said what you said – a dead correspondent was useless to his newspaper. He recommended whisky in the water to kill the bugs.'

'It wasn't bugs I was thinking about. It was bullets.'

'I don't intend getting shot. I'm an observer not a participant.'

'I hope you remember that.' He hesitated. 'I'll miss you.'

'You've got Gerda.'

'She's just to make you jealous,' he retorted.

'Well, I am, so that's all right, isn't it?'

'Anyway, she and André are going back to Spain next week.'

'I know. I must go now.'

'Take care then,' he said. 'Wear your solar topi if things hot up. That's a joke.' He risked, 'I love you,' knowing how much she hated sentimentality. To his surprise, she answered in a small, rather scared voice, 'I love you, too.' Edward could hear the tremor in her voice but, before he could say anything more, the line went dead.

The telephone rang again almost immediately. It was Marcus Fern with whom he had recently been closeted on the *Queen Mary*. Fern had accompanied Lord Benyon on what, Edward had since learned, had been a largely unsuccessful trip to America. Benyon had gone with the object of convincing President Roosevelt that it would make sense to bankroll Britain's rearmament. The President had been courteous but had ruled out any such thing and Benyon had returned with his tail between his legs. Edward had been acting as Benyon's 'protector' on the ship. Major Ferguson had feared there might be some Nazi-inspired attempt to prevent him carrying out his mission. There *was* such an attempt and Edward counted himself fortunate that it had not been successful. A policeman guarding Benyon had been killed and altogether the voyage had not been one he ever wished to repeat.

When the 'how-are-you's' and the 'isn't-it-good-to-be-back-on-dry-land?' polite generalities had been exchanged, there was a silence and Edward waited to discover why Fern had rung him. They had got on well enough on the *Queen Mary* but they were acquaintances rather than friends and he knew Fern was a busy man with interests in the City and elsewhere.

'I gather our friend was not pleased with his meeting . . .' Edward said at last. He mentioned no names because Ferguson had warned him not to speak freely on the telephone in case someone else was listening. Edward had pooh-poohed the idea that anyone would bother to interfere with his telephone but had, in practice, taken Ferguson's advice to heart.

'Our friend? Oh, you mean the President,' Fern said, making Edward feel silly for being so cautious. 'Yes, it was always going to be a long shot. The PM's only comment was "I knew you'd get nothing out of America, Benyon, except words . . . big words but only words." Rather good, don't you think?' Without waiting for Edward to respond, he went on, 'The reason I am telephoning is to ask – at rather short notice, I am afraid – whether you would be free tomorrow to meet a friend of mine. It's an awful cheek, I know, and you are probably otherwise engaged but I think you ought to meet him . . . sooner rather than later. Might save wires getting crossed.'

'No, I'm not particularly busy. In any case, I am intrigued. Who is this friend?'

'It may be too embarrassing for you and, if it is, you must say so but Mr Churchill would very much like to meet you.'

'Good heavens! Why should I be embarrassed to meet Mr Churchill?'

'Well, rumour has it that you are investigating certain of his sources of information. We had better say no more on the telephone.' Fern suddenly seemed to remember security.

'How does he know that?' Edward said, before he had time to think. He mentally kicked himself. He ought to have denied having undertaken any such inquiry.

'Oh, well, as I say, he has his sources.'

'Where does he want to meet me?'

'It's rather an imposition but he wondered if you would come down to Chartwell and have lunch with him. It's possible to talk quietly there but, if that's impossible, he will be in London next week.'

Edward hesitated. It seemed rather feeble to have such an empty diary that he could spend a day in Kent without inconvenience. However, his investigation, if it could even be called that, could go no further without talking to Churchill so it would be absurd to refuse the invitation because he did not wish to lose face.

'Yes, I can make it.'

'Good man! There's a train at eleven ten which will get you to Westerham . . .'

'I think the Lagonda would enjoy a spin so, if you don't mind, I'll drive.'

'Certainly! Do you know the way?'

'More or less . . .'

'Have you got a pencil?' Fern gave him details of how to find the house and then rang off.

Fenton appeared asking, 'Will you be eating in tonight, my lord?'

'Yes. Just a chop and a glass of claret. I think I'll turn in early. Tomorrow I'm going into Kent to meet Mr Churchill so I want to have all my wits about me.'

'Indeed, my lord. From what I read in the newspapers, Mr Churchill is a . . . remarkable gentleman.'

'But, apparently, not to be trusted, Fenton. Not to be trusted.'

He thoroughly enjoyed his drive, the first of many he was to make to Chartwell, though he could not know it. It was exciting to be going to visit a man who had been at the centre of events since Edward was a child. The Lagonda went like a bird and there was very little traffic once he was out of London and Croydon Aerodrome was behind him. In not much over an hour he was crunching over a gravel drive and drawing to a halt in front of an elegant eighteenth-century door. This had once belonged to another house and looked rather fraudulent in its new home, as if it had come down in the world and knew it.

Chartwell was different from what he had imagined. It sat in a green valley with glorious views over the Weald. The grounds had been improved with a lake and a sickle-shaped ridge of wood on the opposite side. Terraces, covered in sweet-smelling rhododendrons, made the best of the view towards the South

Downs. The house itself was Victorian red brick and he had expected it to be ugly but he should have remembered that Churchill was a painter.

Churchill had bought it in the 1920s and enlarged it but there was no feeling of being in a grand house. The hall and the passages running out of it were narrow and the ceilings low. The light came grudgingly through small, cottage-type windows. But it was alive – Churchill's presence had the same effect as that of a queen bee and people buzzed from room to room with the air of having important business to transact even if it were only replacing the garden flowers which Mrs Churchill liked to have in every room.

The butler ushered Edward into the drawing-room where he perched on an uncomfortable sofa and looked about him with great curiosity. Windows on three sides made the room light and airy and he rose to stare out over the garden and, beyond it, the heads of green trees marching inexorably towards the horizon, as Birnam Wood had marched to Dunsinane. The butler reappeared and he was taken up a narrow flight of stairs and along a corridor to the study. Before the butler knocked on the door, Edward could hear that slurred yet booming voice which could only be Churchill's – Edward had heard him speak in the House of Commons – dictating, Edward assumed, an orotund passage concerning the the battle of Blenheim. The butler did not hesitate, however, and Edward was ushered into Churchill's presence, mumbling apologies for interrupting. He was standing at a wooden lectern – of his own design, he was proudly to inform Edward later – a sheaf of papers in his hand, spectacles perched insecurely on the end of his nose, arrested in mid-sentence. He made no objection to being interrupted and nodded to a man taking dictation who left quietly, closing the door behind him.

Churchill's place of work was a room quite unlike any other in the house. The architect he had employed when he bought the house had removed the ceiling to reveal beams and rafters of the older house and, rather oddly Edward thought, introduced a Tudor doorway with a moulded architrave. The windows looked west across the front lawn to Crockham Hill and east across the garden to the lake.

'Lord Edward! How good of you to come. You find me correcting the proofs of my biography of my ancestor, the Duke

53

of Marlborough. I drive the printer mad by adding new paragraphs when I should leave well alone but I can't seem to get a feel for the shape of a book until I see it in proof. You seem to have damaged your eye. Have you been in a fight?'

Edward was unable to resist Churchill's wicked smile. Here was a man who would always enjoy a fight.

'I was playing football, sir, Old Etonians against a team from the East End. I'm afraid it degenerated into a brawl but the odd thing was that seemed to unlock a kind of comradeship and, by the time we got to the pub, we were all great friends.'

'I understand. I have always held that the nation is bound together by an invisible chain. Ordinary people take it for granted that the aristocracy will exploit them and rob them. But, on the whole, they don't think of them as the enemy in the same way the French peasant thought about the aristocracy before the Revolution. There's a bond that we must call patriotism which binds us class to class and which will, I pray, see us through the next conflict.'

'I must tell you, sir, that your account of the Great War did more to make me understand why we had to fight than anything else I have ever read.'

'It is kind of you to say so.' Churchill was suddenly solemn. 'Am I right in saying you lost an elder brother in the war?'

Edward was taken aback. Busy as he quite clearly was, Churchill had taken the trouble to brief himself about his family before their meeting.

'Yes, indeed, sir. My elder brother died in the first weeks of the war. I was too young at the time to feel the loss as much as I should have but my father was devastated. Franklyn was his heir.'

'A terrible tragedy suffered by so many families across the land. I would like to think we could avoid repeating it but, as the months and years go by, I am less and less sanguine. Friends of mine – good men like the Duke of Westminster, Lord Rothermere and my cousin Lord Londonderry – try to make me see Germany from, as Londonderry put it to me yesterday, a "different angle". They tell me Germany cannot risk war for at least four years. They discount the possibility of an invasion from the air. What do you think?'

'What do I think?' Edward could see no possible reason why Churchill should be interested in his views. 'Surely, sir, with all your friends in government there is nothing I could say which would be of any conceivable interest?'

'May I be allowed to be a judge of that, Lord Edward.'

'Well, sir, if you insist. I have no doubt that we shall be at war with Germany within four years and, more probably, within two. I hope you will tell me I am wrong.'

'You must be right,' Churchill replied fiercely. 'But are we prepared for war, do you think?'

'We are rearming but, I would guess, not fast enough.'

'You are right again. German aerial rearmament is the real danger. This cursed, hellish invention and development of war from the air has revolutionized our position. We are not the same kind of country we used to be when we were an island, only twenty-five years ago. In a week or ten days of unimpeded aerial bombardment much of London could be reduced to rubble and we can expect thirty or forty thousand people to be killed or maimed. In such a dreadful act of power and terror, in which bombs go through a series of floors igniting each one simultaneously, grave panic would infect the civilian popu-lation. I won't bore you with a mass of figures but I have infor-mation, which I have reason to believe is accurate, that the German first-line strength is between nine hundred and a thousand planes – that is military aircraft complete with machine-guns and bomb racks, plus civil aircraft capable of conversion to military use in a few hours. By the autumn of 1939 the German air force will have a total of three thousand aircraft. These are not secret figures, Lord Edward. They are known to the government.'

Churchill spoke with such sombre deliberation that it was impossible to doubt him.

'And the Royal Air Force?' Edward asked with a heavy heart.

Churchill ceased pacing the room and turned to him, his eyes brilliant with anger. 'The Royal Air Force is just one third the size.'

'But Lord Benyon says we do not have the money to rearm more rapidly.'

'If we have to borrow or raise through taxation fifty or a hun-dred million pounds, what can that matter when the alternative is to leave our country defenceless? The Rhine, not the white cliffs of Dover, is now our frontier.'

There was a pause. Churchill broke it by saying, 'I apologize, Lord Edward. I am on what my wife calls my hobby-horse. May I offer you a drink?'

He ambled slowly across the room looking every bit of his sixty-two years of age. Edward thought that here was a defeated man, bowed down by his fears for the future of his country. But, when he turned round, he saw the energy in those eyes and the expression on that face, reminiscent of a bad-tempered baby, and changed his mind. This was a man who burned with determination and was fuelled by an inextinguishable sense of purpose.

'Mr Churchill, you confirm my worst fears but why tell me all this? There is nothing I can do.'

'Have you not been charged with disrupting my line of supply? I mean my sources of information.'

Edward opened his mouth to speak.

'Do not deny it, Lord Edward. Let me tell you, these men who provide me with facts with which to chivy the government are patriots not traitors. I do not solicit information. I do not suborn hard-working civil servants to bring me the truth about our weaknesses. These men come to me of their own volition because they believe that I will listen when the government will not, preferring to bury its collective head in the proverbial sand. These patriots come to me from every department of state, from the armed forces, from industry and elsewhere. You cannot have any effect on this but it is very wrong of you to try.'

To be reprimanded in this way was a shock and Edward felt the blood leave his face. 'I . . . I have no wish to . . .' he stumbled.

Suddenly the formidable man who confronted him smiled and it was as if the storm clouds had parted and the sun had been revealed. 'I do not doubt it, young man. I ask you to go away and find out the real traitors in government – and they do exist. That is how you should serve your country and you can tell Sir Robert I said so.'

They lunched in the airy dining-room, part of the new wing, just the two of them at a round table which might have sat eight or ten. They drank champagne – a bottle and a half – but the meal was simple enough – vegetable soup followed by roast chicken. The conversation – or rather Churchill's conversation – was, however, rich. Almost as if he were talking to himself but not unaware of the effect he was having on his guest, he ranged over many topics from gardening to world politics. He was gloriously indiscreet and told stories about the Prime Minister and his colleagues which both horrified and amused. He told Edward that Baldwin was 'on his last legs' and that Mr Chamberlain would soon be at the head of a 'National Coalition Government' of which it was obvious he very much wanted to be a part.

They talked about the nature of patriotism and Churchill said that England's ruling class was sound morally and, like Edward's elder brother, prepared to die for their country but he complained that, though they could not be accused of treachery, they could be condemned for their stupidity. 'They read *Blackwood's Magazine* and thank God they're not "brainy",' he said derisively. He shocked Edward by saying the ruling class was not totally wrong to think that Fascism was on its side. 'Unless he is a Jew, the rich man has much less to fear from Fascism than Communism,' he opined.

'At least our rich are not bandits like the American millionaires,' Edward offered and Churchill chuckled.

'But will the next war be *lost* on the playing fields of Eton?' he asked gravely. 'If, by some miracle, we win the coming war it will be despite our ruling class not because of it. My complaint against Mr Baldwin is not that he is a bad man, because he is not a bad man. My complaint is that he has shown no leadership. He has chosen to represent the people and that is not sufficient.'

'You mean that, because most people prefer to know nothing about what is happening in foreign countries, he should have made them aware of the threat Germany presents, whether they like it or not?'

'Indeed. These good men are leading us to perdition because they have been terrified by the Nazis, like a rabbit caught in the headlights of a car. They won't accept that the Nazis have torn up the rule book. Vansittart knows this and he will tell you so. Those of us who fought in the war are not as frightened of having to fight again as those who did not. War is terrible but it is not the worst thing.'

After lunch they strolled down to the lake and Churchill took him to inspect a wall he was building in the kitchen garden and the

Wendy house he was making for his daughter. He seemed prouder of his brick-laying skills than his writing.

Abruptly, Edward asked Churchill if he knew Charles Westmacott.

'You mean is he one of my "sources"?'

'Yes, sir.'

Churchill looked at him shrewdly. 'You know I cannot comment on my sources, my boy.'

Edward took this as an admission that he did know Westmacott. 'You see, sir, he works in the Foreign Office on matters connected with armaments. Or rather I should say he worked. He disappeared a week ago.'

'I am sorry to hear that.' Churchill paused and then said, 'I don't think I can tell you anything which would help but, if I do remember anything or hear anything, you have my word that I will tell you and I would be grateful if you would let me know when he reappears.'

Edward knew this was as much as he would get out of the old man but at least Churchill had not shut the door on him. His invitation to pass on to him any news of Westmacott was a useful hint that he might stay in touch.

They walked slowly back to the house and Edward felt happier than he had for a long time. He had been profoundly impressed by Churchill. Here was a man whom he could follow whatever his faults and, thereafter, he refused to hear him criticized or derided. As he drove back through the leafy lanes of Kent, Churchill's parting words to him echoed in his head. 'The bright day is done and we are for the dark.'

He went over in his mind what Churchill had told him about Britain's unpreparedness to fight a war. Could Britain really be devastated from the air? Could London be turned into a blazing ruin within ten days? It was a nightmare but Edward was inclined to believe it was a nightmare that could become a reality. He remembered standing in Lord Weaver's office at the top of the *New Gazette* building in Fleet Street gazing at the city below. Weaver, too, had spoken of a burning city. What should he do? Churchill had warned him not to interfere and even Ferguson had sounded doubtful about his mission. It came to him that he had no wish to harass Foreign Office officials passing information to Churchill. It would be different if secrets concerning Britain's defences – or lack of them – were being sold to a foreign power but how could it harm the country to be roused from its apathy and face the terrible fate which was in store? It was not even as though the Foreign Office was Churchill's sole or even principal source. Civil servants, members of the armed forces, trade unionists all saw him as the only major political figure who could sound the wake-up call.

By the time Edward reached Piccadilly and drew up outside Albany, he had decided he would concentrate on trying to locate Charles Westmacott. It was something tangible he could 'get his teeth into'. Westmacott's disappearance was causing his wife and family anguish. He had the image of the little girl in his mind. She was doing her best not to show what she was feeling but for a father to disappear . . . that was not easy to bear. Better to know the worst than to be left in some terrible limbo. He would not immediately tell Major Ferguson of his decision because, if he said he was no longer looking for leaks in the Foreign Office plumbing, he might not be allowed to pursue his search for Westmacott. He needed to talk to this man Lyall, Westmacott's boss. He *must* know something.

5

The following morning at ten o'clock he was shown into a much less grand office than Vansittart's on the third floor of the Foreign Office building. This room had no expansive views of St James's Park and was by no means luxuriously furnished. There was a rank of filing cabinets in battleship grey, a depressed-looking aspidistra on the windowsill and two upright chairs of a Dickensian age and character forlornly standing in front of a battered-looking desk. The surface of the desk was hardly visible beneath files heaped high in metal trays, a cigarette box, two telephones and several photographs in frames. The etiolated, grey-faced man who now rose from behind the desk was long in the chin, with drooping eyelids which made it difficult to see the colour of his eyes. He had long tapering fingers, yellowed with nicotine, bare except for a signet ring. Edward noticed the ring bore the design of a fish or possibly a dolphin.

'Cigarette, Lord Edward?' Lyall said when they had shaken hands and sat down. 'They are Turkish – Murad.' Edward shook his head. 'Oh well, I'll have one. My wife used to say I smoked too much but . . . it was she who . . . who . . . but never mind.' He peered at him. 'Am I mistaken or have you a black eye?'

Edward explained the circumstances in which he had got his wound. Lyall barked a laugh and predictably suggested applying a raw steak to it. He had the distinct impression that Lyall was making a great effort to appear amiable. He supposed he must suspect that any man authorized by Sir Robert Vansittart to investigate his section was dangerous and had to be conciliated.

Edward asked bluntly why he thought Westmacott might have disappeared.

'I wish I could help but your superior, Major Ferguson, has already asked me the same question. I told him all I knew, which is to say nothing at all.'

'Yes, I have read Major Ferguson's report but he thought you might perhaps have remembered something, as one does sometimes after the initial shock has passed. You must constantly be turning over in your mind where he might be. You must be very concerned.'

Lyall looked doubtful. Either he was not concerned or he knew perfectly well where Westmacott was. Edward could not decide.

'No, I can't think of anything . . . I'm sorry . . .'

Edward tried again. 'What sort of man is Westmacott? He doesn't sound the sort of chap who would disappear without leaving word.'

'No, he was . . . is a sound man,' Lyall admitted. 'Very regular in his habits, very reliable.'

'You said "was". Do you have reason to believe he is dead?'

'Did I say "was"? A slip of the tongue. I suppose I do think something . . . fairly serious must have happened to him.'

'He was not suicidal?'

'I have no idea. I do not know him well. He is a private man, you understand, and I am not inclined to socialize with junior staff.'

'How junior is he? I am afraid I am rather in the dark about what this department is responsible for. Sir Robert said industrial intelligence but I am not sure I know what that means.'

Lyall hesitated, as if considering how much it was necessary to tell his inquisitor.

'This section was set up three years ago to analyse and, if possible, control arms dealing in this country and find out as much as possible about the armaments trade in Europe. We have no legal powers to prevent arms dealers based in this country supplying "unfriendly" governments. We sell arms ourselves, as you well know, but we will only use intermediaries who play ball with us. We keep tabs on the more reputable dealers and they keep tabs on their rivals but there's not much we can do except watch and make notes.'

'I see. So much of your work is hush-hush? How dangerous is it for Westmacott? Might he have been abducted?'

'It's a possibility – a most alarming one – but it seems far-fetched. He is privy to secrets, certainly, but I doubt he would have been worth . . . abducting, as you put it.'

Edward changed tack. 'How much industrial espionage is there? I mean do companies like Vickers, say, have security problems?'

'We try to warn British companies in the arms industry to keep their secrets secure. Espionage is rampant and I have no doubt the German government knows precisely what we are up to – which aircraft are being manufactured and at what rate and what engines are in development. As I say, we have a watching brief . . . that's all.'

'So you do not indulge in any spying yourself?' Edward inquired genially.

Lyall looked at him with distaste. 'Certainly not.'

'Could Mr Westmacott have got hold of something that worried him about either our rearmament or Germany's and tried to do something about it?'

'I don't know what you mean,' Lyall said stiffly. 'If Westmacott had a problem, he would have come to me with it.'

Edward wondered what else he could ask. He was getting nowhere.

'How big is this section, Mr Lyall? Had he any close friends in the department I ought to speak to?'

'There are two other men in this section with different responsibilities, Mr McCloud and Mr Younger. You could certainly talk to them. Major Ferguson has already done so but concluded there was nothing that either of them could tell him. Of course, you may have better luck.'

The disdain in his voice was palpable but Edward ignored it. 'And secretaries?'

'There are two. Miss Williams and Miss Hawkins. I trust you will not upset them.'

'Surely they must be upset already at Mr Westmacott's disappearance?'

'Indeed.' Lyall stubbed out a half-smoked cigarette as if he wished he was stubbing out Edward. 'If there is nothing else I can do for you . . . ? I have an inter-departmental meeting in ten minutes. Miss Hawkins will take you round the section.'

'Thank you. One final thing – did Westmacott take out of the office the night he disappeared any files or letters he ought not to have done?'

'He took two files, as I informed Major Ferguson, both on foreign arms dealers. You will have the details in his report.'

Edward felt rebuked. He nodded his head. 'Neither very important, I gather?'

'The press might have made a story out of them but, from the point of view of national security, the files contain nothing of great interest.'

'You are sure those were the only files he took with him?'

Lyall looked irritated. 'Miss Hawkins keeps a meticulous record of who has what file and nothing marked Secret may be taken out of the building without my express permission in writing.'

'What about these cabinets? If Miss Hawkins has all the files in the cabinets in her office, what is in these?'

'These contain certain top secret files. Only I have keys to them.'

'And you have checked them? There are no files missing?'

'No. How could there be?'

'You tell me. May I see the keys?'

Reluctantly, Lyall took his key ring out of his jacket pocket and pointed out to Edward the key to the filing cabinets.

'And what if you lose your key? How would you get into the cabinets?'

'I would not lose it but, if I did, there is a duplicate in Sir Robert's safe.'

'Tell me, are the files in your cabinets stamped on the outside in red Most Secret?'

'Yes, Most Secret or Top Secret. Why?'

'The files in Miss Hawkins's office are just marked Secret? She doesn't have any Top or Most Secret files?'

'That's correct, but why do you ask?'

'Because Mrs Westmacott remembers her husband reading a file marked Most Secret a few days before he disappeared. Can you explain it?'

'No, I can't. If it were one of my files I would know about it and, as I told you, they are never taken out of this room.'

'So he must have got the file somewhere else?'

'I really don't know, Lord Edward.'

'As a priority I must ask you to check again that you are not missing any files.'

'I will but I checked when Westmacott disappeared. I am sure there is nothing missing.'

Edward got up and, as he did so, noticed two photographs on the desk. One was of a young man in school uniform and the other of a fashionably dressed woman photographed by Lenaire who, Edward considered, made all his women look alike: beautiful but devoid of character. The young man looked vaguely familiar but Edward could not say why, unless it was because of his natural resemblance to his father.

'Forgive me if I am being impertinent but this must be your son? He looks so like you.'

Lyall's whole manner changed and his face, which up till that moment had been artificially amiable and then frankly hostile, was transformed. He looked at Edward with the eyes of any father: proud, anxious but loving.

'Do you think so, Lord Edward? I always think he looks more like his mother.'

Edward looked at the other photograph. 'She is very beautiful.'

'To my great loss, she died six months ago . . . cancer.'

'I am very sorry to hear it, Lyall. And your son?'

'James? He's in Spain. The wretched boy insisted on joining the International Brigade.' Lyall's voice trembled with pride and fear. 'If I were to lose him . . .' he said, almost in a whisper.

'I have a great friend in Spain: the journalist, Verity Browne. I don't know whether you have heard of her? If there is anything I can do . . .? Should I ask her to keep an eye out for him?'

'I would be most grateful, Lord Edward. I have heard nothing from him for over a month and, consequently, I imagine the most terrible things. But your friend must not let on that . . . that . . .' He hesitated. 'If James thought I was spying on him he would never forgive me.'

Edward walked through the department taking particular note of the filing system. For the next couple of hours – using Westmacott's office – he interviewed the members of Lyall's department without gaining much in the way of new information except the general feeling that Westmacott might have stumbled on something which upset him. He had not confided in his colleagues, or no one was prepared to admit that he had. Miss Hawkins, a severe-looking woman in her forties with grey hair held in a tight bun on her head, confirmed that Westmacott had taken only the two files Lyall had mentioned.

'Miss Hawkins,' Edward said, attempting to ingratiate himself with her, 'you are an intelligent woman and thorough, too. There must be something you noticed which would give us a clue as to why Mr Westmacott has disappeared?'

'I am afraid there is nothing else I can tell you,' she said stiffly, refusing to melt before Edward's charm.

'What do you think of him? Do you like him? Is he good at his job?'

This last question was a mistake. Miss Hawkins who, no doubt, could have done any job in the department, including Lyall's, better than the incumbent, was not about to criticize her colleagues.

'Mr Westmacott is a valued member of the department.' Edward could see her drawing herself up in the face of his impertinence.

In exasperation, he continued, 'Miss Hawkins, my questions are not an expression of idle curiosity, you know. Mr Westmacott may be ill or in danger. I am sure you want his safe return as much as Mr Lyall does.'

Miss Hawkins looked at him oddly but softened a little. 'I am concerned about Mr Westmacott – of course I am. It is just, as I keep on repeating, I have no idea of his whereabouts or why he has gone missing. Have you asked his wife?'

'Do you know the family?'

'I have met his wife at the Christmas party. She seemed a very nice woman.'

'And there is a little girl,' Edward said, piling on the emotion.

'Please, Lord Edward,' Miss Hawkins said, her frigid reserve visibly shaken, 'believe me when I say that if I could help you I would, but I cannot.'

Edward repressed a sigh. 'Did you feel something was worrying Mr Westmacott? Did he look tired or . . . different from usual?'

'Mr Westmacott kept himself to himself. I suppose I did think he looked a little worried but he was working hard. We all are and . . . and he was worried about the international situation.'

'He talked to you about it?'

'Once, when he came in for a file, he did, yes.'

'About these files – your system of recording files going in and out seems very good. Were the filing cabinets kept locked all the time?'

'Yes. There are three keys to the cabinets. I have one, of course – here on my chain.' She passed her key chain over to Edward.

'And Mr Lyall and Mr Westmacott hold the other two?'

'Yes. The files are secret and Mr Lyall is very conscious of the need for security.'

'There's a cabinet in Mr Lyall's office where the Most Secret files are kept. You don't have keys to that?'

'Only Mr Lyall has a key to that cabinet.'

'I do understand you must think I have a bee in my bonnet, Miss Hawkins, but will you look through your files once again? His wife remembers him reading a file marked Most Secret some days before he disappeared. I don't know how he got it, or why, and no doubt it was returned from whence it came but I am almost certain that Mr Westmacott left this building with some-thing he ought not to have had the day he disappeared.'

Miss Hawkins looked at him with fear in her eyes. 'I shall, of course, Lord Edward, if you so wish it but I hope you don't think I was . . .'

'No one is accusing you of anything but there is a puzzle to be solved and maybe you can help me solve it. Here is my card. Feel free to telephone me at any time of the day or night if you find anything that strikes you as not quite right. Now, may I speak to Mr McCloud?'

Miss Hawkins took the proffered pasteboard and seemed about to say something but in the end merely nodded before leaving the room.

'Statistics are my field, old boy, and analysing figures. You know the sort of thing? We get information and estimates in from all sorts of sources and I have to make sense of them. If one source indicates the Germans are building six fighter aircraft a month and another source seems to suggest the figure is nearer sixty, I have to put both through the wringer – that's what I call it – and see which retains its "shape". It's interesting work but, if anyone had told me when I was at the Slade that I would end up here, I would have laughed in their face.'

Angus McCloud was a bearded, ill-kempt young man – in his early thirties, Edward guessed – with a strong body odour. He smoked a pipe and there was a gap in his teeth where the pipe-stem lodged on an almost permanent basis. He obviously wanted to be taken for an artist rather than a civil servant and he did everything he could to impress upon Edward that he was different from other Foreign Office staff. He had to be a bachelor, Edward thought. No woman would have let him go to the office dressed in a check flannel shirt, dirty tie, corduroy trousers and brogues.

'Do you still paint?'

'At weekends – nothing serious.'

'But you still move in that world?'

'Not really. I bump into Rothy – Sir William Rothenstein – now and again and he asks me how the painting is going and I say not bad. Of course, I can't say what I'm really doing, not even to Rothy. I occasionally go to one of Lady Ottoline's "Thursday afternoons", and I see Tonks sometimes and Mark Gertler, of course.'

Edward thought he might ask his friend, the painter Adrian Hassel, what he knew about him. Adrian had been at the Slade and was about the same age as McCloud.

'What do you think has happened to Westmacott? Is he a friend of yours?'

'I get on with him well enough but he's a cold sort of blighter – keeps himself to himself. Harry and I . . .'

'Mr Younger?'

'Yes. We go out for a pint after work once in a while. He's a good kid, smart as paint, wasted here. He speaks quite good German, after a pint or two anyway.'

'But Westmacott did not join you?'

'No. Westmacott has to rush home to wifey.'

There was a rather unpleasant sneer in McCloud's voice and Edward wondered if the two men had quarrelled.

'He's got a girlfriend – Younger, I mean?'

'You'll have to ask him that. I think Jane – Miss Williams – is sweet on him but I've never heard he returned the favour.'

'And you?'

'Me? No such luck. I've had my chances but they take up too much time – women – not to mention money. There was a girl at the Slade I was keen on – a model actually – but . . . What's this to do with anything?'

'Sorry. I didn't mean to pry. I was just trying to get a feel for the department. You all get on together?'

'I suppose so,' McCloud said dubiously.

'Do you socialize out of the office?'

'Not at all.'

'You never see Mr Younger out of hours – apart from the odd pint in the pub?'

'No. We get on all right, as I said, but we have different interests. He wouldn't know his Picasso from his Matisse, if you take my meaning. He's sporty and I'm the opposite.'

'So you have no idea what might have happened to Westmacott?'

'None at all, old man. He's not the sort of cove that anything ever happens to, if you follow me. Dull as ditch water, I would have said.'

Edward immediately took to Harry Younger. He was a clean-shaven, clean-limbed, dark-haired young man who confessed to being twenty-three years of age. He was the most junior member of the department apart from Miss Williams. He said how much he hated being stuck in an office all day.

'But you are very young to have such an important job.'

'Is it important? It certainly ought to be but really, you know, it's all guesswork. Anyway, we know the score. Germany is building a huge air force and we have a very small one. You've got to admire what they have achieved. While we have to put up with idiots like Baldwin and Chamberlain, they have . . . I mean, I'm not saying I like what Hitler is doing but, well, he does lead.'

Edward looked at him quizzically. 'You admire Hitler?'

'No, of course not. What he's doing to the Jews . . . well, that's not right. I'm just saying . . . I'm just saying the Luftwaffe's going to be a worthy enemy. I know as much about the German air force as anyone, damn it. It's what I'm here to study and evalu-ate, so I know what I'm talking about. Look, I've been reading this book – as part of my job, you know. It's by a chap called Guido Mattioli – an Eyetie. It's called *Mussolini Aviator, and his Work for Aviation*. Rotten title but it's true Musso was always hot about war in the air. I wrote down a couple of sentences which

68

made sense to me.' He rifled through his pockets and produced a crumpled piece of paper from which he proceeded to read. '"No machine requires so much human concentration of soul and will power as a flying machine to make it work properly. The pilot understands the fullest meaning of the word 'control'. Thus it seems that there is an intimate spiritual link between Fascism and Flying. Every airman is a born Fascist."'

'You don't really believe that?' Edward asked, startled.

Younger looked at him and said hurriedly, 'No, of course not. Don't get the wrong idea. I'm a patriot. As soon as war breaks out, I'll join the RAF and get myself killed *doing something*, if you understand me. I sometimes feel I'll go mad here, helping compile reports on our weaknesses and the enemy's strengths and then watching as they are either ignored or made to prove the opposite of what they mean. Oh, sorry, I didn't intend to sound off like that. Hey, I say, didn't I watch you make a century at Lords during the Eton and Harrow match . . . when was it? 1922? I was just a kid but it stuck in my mind.'

Edward was embarrassed but agreed it might have been him. 'Were you at . . .?'

'No! I was at some tinpot place you would never have heard of but I play cricket whenever I can get away.'

'I must get you down to play for the Cherrypickers. It's a team made up of all us old men who can't quite believe we're not still young. We need some young blood.'

'I'd like that, sir,' he said, his face lighting up. The automatic 'sir' made Edward feel his age. To this young man he was ancient.

'What do you think of Westmacott and have you any idea where he might be?' Edward asked hurriedly.

'I have no idea where he is. Perhaps he's had a breakdown or something. He was looking a bit peaky. I know I often feel like running away and not telling a soul where I'm going.'

'You thought he looked ill?'

'Or worried. He works too hard or maybe he has other problems. I wouldn't know.'

'He isn't a friend? He doesn't talk to you?'

'No. Nor to anyone as far as I know. We get on all right but he's very reserved. He goes straight home after work and he doesn't . . . you know . . . fraternize. No reason why he should.'

'McCloud – you like him?'

'Angus? Yes, he's all right. We have a pint together now and again.'

'But you're not friends?'

'As I said, we get on but he's one of those arty types. Not me at all.'

'What's your idea of a perfect day?'

Younger's eyes brightened. 'Cricket in the summer but, just recently, I've been going down to Brooklands most Saturdays.'

'You race cars?'

'I drive a bit but it's the aeroclub there I'm interested in. I'm learning to fly so that, when the war breaks out, I can join the RAF – no questions asked. I think it's the nearest I get to being happy when I'm flying. The glorious thing about it is that one feels a perfectly free man and one's own master as soon as one is up in the air.'

'I know what you mean. I did a bit of flying in Africa.'

'Did you really, sir?' The boy looked at him with eager eyes.

'Isn't that expensive – learning to fly?'

'Yes, but the RAF helps a bit. They seem to have woken up to the idea that they are going to need chaps like me when the balloon goes up.'

The junior secretary, Miss Williams, was the antithesis of Miss Hawkins. She wore as much make-up as she dared and her little blue dress was not designed to hide her charms. She was twenty and it was borne in on Edward that there must be many girls like her for whom the war might prove a welcome adventure. He wondered how she had got the job in Lyall's department.

'You wanted to see me, my lord?'

Edward groaned inwardly. It was obvious she intended to flirt with him so he must be as dull as possible.

'Yes, thank you, Miss Williams. I'm just trying to discover if anyone in the department noticed anything which might explain Mr Westmacott's absence.'

Jane looked at her inquisitor regretfully. 'I can't think of anything, my lord.'

'You share an office with Miss Hawkins, don't you?'

'Yes. Or rather – perhaps you recall, my lord, – my office is separated from Miss Hawkins's by a screen.'

'Yes, I remember. Forgive me, Miss Williams, if I sound impertinent but it strikes me that you must find life in the department quite dull. Why did you apply for this particular post?'

'I'm good at my job,' she said defensively.

'I'm sure you are but don't you find it a bit boring here? There are no other young people – except Mr Younger, of course.'

'He's a dear,' the girl said, going pink, 'but I'm not his girlfriend or anything if that's what you're suggesting. He says he doesn't have time for girls – what with there being a war coming. Do you think there will be a war, my lord?'

'I hope not,' he prevaricated. 'So you don't find it dull here? What about Mr McCloud?'

'What about him?' she said, thrusting out her chin.

'He doesn't attract you? I promise anything you say to me won't be repeated.'

'No, he doesn't. To be honest, I tell them – both the boys – that I've got a boyfriend already . . . in the RAF.'

'But you don't?'

'No, but I might have one day.' She sounded so arch Edward wanted to spank her but then he thought, who was he to feel superior? A little fantasy makes the days go by that much quicker and it gave her status, too. No one wants *not* to be wanted.

'So you like the job?' he persisted.

'It's a job and it's quite well paid . . . and people are impressed when I say I work in the Foreign Office.'

'I'm sure they are and quite right too.'

She smiled and Edward thought that, behind the make-up, the bobbed hair and the chatter, lurked a rather sweet girl and he hoped she would find the man to make her happy.

'So you like the people here?'

'They're all right. The truth is Mr Lyall's a friend of my father's. I did a secretarial course and my father didn't want me to go into anything . . . anything common, so he wrote to Mr Lyall and it just happened they were looking for a secretary, so here I am,' she ended brightly.

'And do you live at home – with your parents?'

'Yes.'

71

'Where is that?'

'Camberwell, my lord.'

'Now, tell me about Mr Westmacott. As you know, we're very worried about him. Is there anything you can think of which might help us find him?'

'No,' she said doubtfully. 'I don't have much to do with him. Miss Hawkins does his typing and Mr Lyall's of course. I work for Mr Younger and Mr McCloud.'

'I understand but did you happen to notice if Mr Westmacott looked worried or upset in the days before he disappeared?'

'No, not really,' she said slowly. 'He looked the same as always but, as I say, I have very little to do with him. He hardly knows my name,' she added ruefully.

Edward tried another tack. 'Would you have noticed if any files had gone missing?'

'I wouldn't. Filing isn't my responsibility. Miss Hawkins keeps a record of any file taken out of the office. I don't have much to do with them myself unless . . . unless Mr Younger or Mr McCloud asks me to get one for them or sort some file out.'

'Yes, of course. So, no files are ever left lying about?' Miss Williams looked puzzled. 'I mean, could anyone go into Miss Hawkins's office – say when she was out of the room – and take a file from her desk without being seen by you or anyone else?'

She thought for a moment and then said slowly, 'It is possible. I can't see the whole of her office from where I sit. No one could take anything out of the filing cabinets – I would hear them being opened. They make quite a noise. But off Miss Hawkins's desk . . . perhaps. But why should anyone . . . ?'

'What happens to returned files? Are they put straight back in the cabinets?'

'Not if Miss Hawkins is busy. They sit in the in-tray until she has time to put them away.'

'You don't put them away for her?'

'No, I'm not allowed.'

'Well, you have been most helpful.'

Jane looked troubled. 'You don't think anything bad has happened to Mr Westmacott do you, sir?'

'I very much hope not, Miss Williams. I very much hope not.'

6

It was not until he reached Brooks's, his club in St James's Street, that Edward remembered why the photograph of Lyall's son had rung a bell with him. He had seen the young man arm-in-arm with Guy Baron in Gerda's photograph of Republican soldiers which included David Griffiths-Jones. He was almost certain of it. As is so often the case, a person in your mind suddenly materializes. Feeling he had earned a break, after a late lunch – potted shrimps, kidneys and bacon, washed down with a passable claret – he had called on Mr Berry to ask his advice on laying down a burgundy of which he had heard good things. Then, feeling much better, he had gone into Sonerscheins and, on a whim, bought an Etruscan two-handled vase the colour of the many suns which had baked it. It was hideously expensive but Edward had found himself unable to resist adding it to his small collection of ancient art. As he was leaving with his new treasure, he literally bumped into Gerda.

He apologized and raised his hat with one hand while clasping the vase tightly with the other. She was just about to move on, not appearing to have recognized him, when he said, 'Miss Meyer, it's me . . .'

Gerda raised her eyes and a pink flush came into her cheeks. 'Lord Edward, I'm so sorry. I was thinking of . . .'

'André?'

'No, not André. I was thinking of . . . something else. How is your eye? Did you put a steak on it?'

'I did, thank you, and the swelling has all but gone, don't you think?'

She looked at him critically. 'Yes, but it stills spoils the image.'

'The image?'

'You know, "the man-about-town". What's the word? The *flâneur.*'

'That's how you see me?' He was hurt.

'No, that's how you *try* to appear but it's not you at all.'

Edward was wise enough to take this as a compliment. She changed the subject. 'What have you been buying?'

'Oh, this? It's a vase – an amphora – very old and very beautiful. I say, why not come back to Albany with me and I'll show you. It's much more fun, when you've bought yourself a present, opening the parcel with someone else. Otherwise it's a bit like drinking on your own – a vice more than a pleasure.' Suddenly realizing he was being pretentious or at least over-elaborate, he changed tack. 'Anyway, you look as though you could do with a cup of tea.' He saw a look of doubt in her face and added quickly, 'But, of course, you must be very busy.'

'Where's Albany? Not New York, I presume.'

'No, it's where I have rooms, round the corner in Piccadilly, don't y'know.' He was stuttering now and aware he was sounding rather an ass. 'I expect you think I'm the most awful idiot boring you with all those stories of Africa at that awful dinner after the exhibition. I must have had too much wine. If it hadn't been for you, I wouldn't have stayed.'

'Was the exhibition awful as well?'

'It was rather – not the pictures but the people. The Comrades en masse always give me the heebie-jeebies, but I did like your photographs.'

'André's, you mean?'

'No, yours.'

Gerda, pleased, relented. 'I don't think you are nearly the ass you would like people to believe. You know, André was beastly to me when we got home after the party. He said I had made a spectacle of myself and . . .'

'And befriended a useless appendage of Verity's who could not appreciate his art.'

'Something like that,' she conceded, grinning. 'I've just finished at the gallery and, yes, I would like a cup of tea. Thank you.'

They made an odd couple as they walked into Piccadilly: Edward, tall, hawk-faced, clutching his parcel, covering the ground with long strides, Gerda half-running after him, her red hair escaping from under a small triangular-shaped hat.

'Could we walk a little slower?' she begged him. 'I'm pooped.'

'I'm so sorry!' he said, slowing down. 'Verity always complains about the speed I travel but she's smaller than you.'

'How did you meet Verity?'

'In a car crash. In fact, I sometimes think our relationship, if that is what it is, is a sequence of car crashes. Sorry! I'm talking nonsense again. I know what you're going to say – we make an odd couple. She's a red-hot Communist and I'm a . . . well, she calls me a superannuated member of a class consigned to the dustbin of history. Quite accurate, don't you think?'

Gerda laughed. 'But you are a . . . couple . . . like André and me?'

'How do you mean? Oh, I see. Well, that's a rather difficult question to answer. I love her and I think she . . . cares about me but she's a war correspondent – and a very good one, as you know – so she doesn't have time for marriage or any of that kind of thing – bourgeois and redundant she calls it. And then, of course, it's not very pleasant for her – being a Communist – to have to spend time explaining me away to the Comrades.'

Gerda laughed again. 'I don't know Verity as well as you do but she has a reputation for liking to have her cake while eating it. Isn't that the expression? But I'm sounding catty.'

'No, but that's what we all like, isn't it? But most of us can't quite manage it. You're American – aren't you?'

'I was born in Des Moines, Iowa, but I have lived all over since I ran away from home when I was fifteen – mostly in Paris and Berlin until it got unbearable, and now England.'

'And Spain?'

'Yes, Bandi – André, I mean – we go there to take photographs but you can't stay there all the time. It's . . .'

'It's bad, I know. Verity's told me some of it. She was at the siege of Toledo. Of course! You were there too. You told me.'

'Yes, Bandi and I. There were a lot of press there who had been invited to see the good guys capture the Alcázar but, as you know, it didn't work out that way. Didn't Verity tell us you and she had been in Spain at the outbreak of war?'

Edward was absurdly pleased to discover Verity sometimes talked about him to her friends. 'Yes, but after a few weeks I came home. I decided it wasn't my war after all.'

'What do you mean?'

'Well, it's very much Verity's war. It is not just any old war. It means something special to her. She can literally stand up and fight for what she believes in. Sorry, I'm not being very clear. Look, for you and Verity the rights and wrongs are quite obvious. You are fighting the "good fight" – good against evil – but I think it's more complicated than that. I had a brush with the SIM – the secret police – when I was in Spain and I realized Stalin and his minions are about as interested in seeing a free Republican Spain as . . . as Hitler is. Don't get me wrong, I share the Party's hatred for Franco and his Nazi friends but, if the Communists are the cure, I'm not sure I wouldn't prefer the disease. I don't expect you to agree with me – Verity doesn't – but I find the Communist tyranny almost as frightening as the Nazi tyranny.' Gerda looked shocked and he saw that he had gone too far. 'No, of course I don't mean that. We are all going to have to fight the Nazis before we start fighting among ourselves.'

'But to beat Hitler there is no room for amateurism. Only Stalin can do it. The Western democracies are finished and my country won't intervene in Europe again. Stalin is the only hope.'

They had arrived at Albany and, when they were in the apartment, they tacitly decided to change the subject.

'I just love these rooms,' Gerda enthused. 'Oh, now show me your vase.'

Gently, Edward unwrapped it and set it on a side table where it glowed. They stood back and admired it. 'It's beautiful!' she exclaimed.

'It is, isn't it? To possess something so old and so fragile gives me hope that perhaps what we value can survive despite everything.'

Fenton came in and served them tea and cucumber sandwiches. Gerda started giggling as soon as Fenton had closed the door behind him.

'Forgive me, but this is all so *Importance of Being Earnest*. I remember cucumber sandwiches and . . .'

'Yes, Jack lived in Albany. But I'm not Oscar Wilde.'

'No, I didn't think you were,' she said, putting her hand on his knee.

'Gerda,' he said, getting up hurriedly and spilling some tea, 'you . . . shouldn't do that.'

'Why? Because of Verity? I thought that was why you brought me back here.'

'Yes . . . no. I'd feel so . . . so beastly if we . . . I mean, I think you are . . . wonderful but afterwards . . .'

'It makes you guilty wanting to sleep with me when you love Verity?'

'You can say that, yes,' Edward said, shocked but grateful for her bluntness.

'I hate that word "guilt",' she said vehemently. 'It's such a cold, ugly word. Don't you think so?'

'I hadn't thought of it like that.'

'Why do you think Verity would mind if you and I had some pleasure together? It's not as if I want to steal you away or anything like that. It's only sex.'

'That's the way you see it? I'm afraid my conscience is rather fragile. Sort of delicate. Won't bear much betrayal.'

'That's middle-class privilege. I don't have time for conscience – not about sex, I don't. I must take my pleasure now, when I can.'

'If you don't mind, Gerda, much as I'm tempted, I think . . .'

'Well, if you change your mind,' she said, seeming unruffled by the rejection. 'Life's so short. I can't see either André or I making old bones. "The grave's a fine and private place but none I think do there embrace . . ."'

'I know it but somehow . . .'

'Say no more. Have I spoilt everything?'

'Not at all! Actually, there was something I wanted to ask you.'

'Fire ahead.'

'In one of your photographs, there was a picture of a young man standing between two friends, their arms entwined. One was Guy Baron. I don't know who the second man was but the third – the one in the middle – was a boy called James Lyall. Do you remember him? David Griffiths-Jones was also in the photograph.'

'I do remember him. Why do you ask?'

'I met his father yesterday. He's not heard from him for some time. I wonder if you know where he is?'

'I took that photograph when we were all resting behind the front line. I can't remember the name of the place but it was three months ago. I have no idea where he is now. Madrid, I expect. They are trying to raise the siege so everyone's concentrated there.'

'Do you know, the government has made it illegal to join the International Brigade?'

'That won't stop the boys. They'll be even more eager to go ... the great adventure. You should see them out there ... raring to go. A few know what they are in for but most think it's some sort of game.'

'And then they get shot ... not only by the other side, so I hear.'

'Whatever do you mean?'

'The Stalinists ... I met a school friend, Eric Blair, he'd been out there. He said the Comrades were taking the opportunity of rubbing out anyone who resisted their control. I gather Verity is going to prove it's nonsense.'

'I hope she does. I never saw anything like that,' Gerda said. She seemed put out, almost angry. 'I must go now. Thank you, Lord Edward, for the cup of tea and the cucumber sandwiches. It was just what I needed.' She grinned wickedly and Edward wished his principles had permitted him to accept her invitation to partake of something more. She must have seen the look in his eyes because she said, 'But you still look hungry. Next time you must have tea with *me*. But I forgot. That won't be for a few months. André and I are off to Spain on Friday and who knows when we'll get back.'

She kissed him, first on the cheek and then quickly on the mouth. 'Lucky Verity,' she said.

'Should I dust the vase on the side table, my lord, or would you prefer to do so yourself?'

Edward was dismembering a kipper the following morning when Fenton posed this question.

'Oh ... ah! I see what you mean. If it were to fall to the ground ...'

'Precisely, my lord. I understand the *objet d'art* to be worth a considerable sum of money.'

'Quite and it has managed to survive the Roman Empire and several major conflagrations, not least the Great War. It would be grossly irresponsible if it were to meet its end as a result of domestic carelessness. I intend to have a cabinet made in which to display it. It needs subtle lighting and should, perhaps, sit on a revolving stand. I am going to take expert advice but, until that time, I think we should leave it undusted.'

'My lord . . .'

'Yes, what is it?' Edward spoke irritably. He liked, if possible, to eat breakfast without conversation and, since he knew Fenton was aware he preferred silence until he had downed his last slice of toast and his final cup of coffee, he was surprised and not a little annoyed that the man was persisting.

'My lord, I thought I ought to mention that earlier this morning, while you were still sleeping, Sir Robert Vansittart telephoned.'

'Did he, by Jove? He's an early bird.'

'I informed him that you were not available to speak to him and he asked me to convey his respects and inquire if you had made any headway with your investigation. He said the Prime Minister had been "pressing him".'

'Yes, I can see that might be uncomfortable. Did you . . . ?'

'It would not have been my place to make any comment. I merely said I would pass on his message to you.'

Edward put down *The Times* and stared thoughtfully at the amphora. 'Perhaps you ought to have woken me. The trouble is, Fenton – I speak in complete confidence, naturally – I have been thinking.'

'Indeed, my lord?'

'Sir Robert has asked me to find out where Mr Churchill is getting his information concerning armaments – our armaments and German armaments. It seemed a relatively simple matter of talking to the twenty or thirty people with access to secret information and coming to a conclusion as to who was doing the dirty.'

'But since you returned from Chartwell . . . ?'

'That's the nub of it. Mr Churchill may be everything they say – unreliable, given to impetuous and sometimes disastrous schemes of which the Gallipoli landings are the prime example – but the fact remains he is a patriot. He told me he did not solicit information from anyone in an official position and I believe him. However, many officials who are worried that we are unprepared for war come to him with their concerns.'

'Why Mr Churchill, my lord?'

'Quite simply, he is seen as the only prominent politician willing to stand up to the government and speak out about our drift to disaster. Mr Churchill told me he receives information not only from officials in the Foreign Office but from senior people in other government departments and from the armed forces themselves. If a tyre develops a puncture, one can repair it with a sticking plaster. But, if it develops several holes, there is nothing to be done but throw it away. Besides, I find myself in the invidious position of sympathizing with those people who are sharing secrets with Mr Churchill. I fancy even Sir Robert believes we are not doing enough to prepare ourselves for the coming war.'

'You believe war to be inevitable, my lord?'

'I do, Fenton. Everything I have seen in the last two years makes me as certain of it as that the sun will rise in the morning. The only question is when. Will it come this year . . . next year or in three or four years?'

'Presumably, my lord, the longer it can be postponed the longer we have to prepare?'

'Yes, Fenton, but equally it gives the Germans longer to build up their air force and army. I am convinced that, unlike last time, the war in the air is going to be vital. If we lose control of the sky, the Royal Navy will not be able to defend our shores. You have seen what has been happening in Manchuria and what the Italians did in Abyssinia?'

'Yes, my lord, the bombing of women and children . . .'

'Bombs cannot be rained down upon us with any accuracy, thank goodness, but low level bombing by determined pilots could destroy battleships. It's a terrible thought but the Royal Navy might be disabled in just a few days if the skies above the English Channel belong to the enemy.'

Not feeling like finishing his kipper, Edward threw down his knife and fork. The telephone rang and Fenton went to answer it.

'It is Major Ferguson on the line for you, my lord,' he said when he returned.

Edward got up, feeling rather sick. He had a feeling that Ferguson would not be telephoning at half-past eight in the morning without it being bad news. He was right.

'Ferguson? What's the news?'

'Not good, I'm afraid. They have found Westmacott.'

'Dead?'

'A bobby found him at first light. He was hanging from a rope below Chelsea Bridge.'

'How do you mean – below the bridge?'

'He was hanging from one of the bridge's girders.'

'Good God! How frightful. That poor woman . . . and little Alice. It doesn't bear thinking about. Was it suicide?'

'It is conceivable but unlikely. His briefcase is missing – well he might have chucked that in the river before he did what he did but . . .'

'But what?'

'His hat was on his head and his umbrella was hanging from his coat pocket. Someone – the murderer, I suppose – was making a fool of him even as he died. His neck wasn't broken.'

'His neck wasn't broken? Oh, I see. How horrible! He was throttled?'

'Yes,' Ferguson said grimly. 'It must have taken him some time to die.'

Edward thought of the man twisting and turning in the wind, desperate for air, choking to death. Each moment must have seemed an age of torment. He shuddered and tried to put the image out of his mind.

'It's a terrible way to die, Ferguson. You're right. It can't be suicide.' Now the shock was passing he was beginning to think clearly. 'Assuming Westmacott was murdered, the odds are it was the work of political gangsters – Nazis would be my guess. It would be just their idea of a joke. A little dog belonging to Miss Browne was killed in a particularly nasty way and left in her bed – to scare her, you understand. This killing seems to have the same nasty taste to it. If Westmacott hadn't been who he was, one might have thought it was some sort of underworld gang killing, though, thank God, they are rare enough, at least in England. Or is London becoming Chicago?'

Ferguson agreed. 'But if it was a political killing, they would probably have employed gangsters to do their dirty work. The Germans – if say, the killers are Nazis – would not want there to be any visible connection with the German Embassy. The political situation is too tense at the moment. The police have put out the word. Most "decent" villains would have nothing to do with such a killing and will be as shocked as we are. We may get a tip-off.'

'Has his wife been told?'

'Not yet. In fact, I was going to ask you if you would tell her? You are the official she knows,' Ferguson heard Edward's groan,

81

'but, of course, you don't have to. Chief Inspector Pride will if you won't. It has to be done immediately though, before it gets in the papers.'

Edward groaned again. 'Pride? Is he in charge of the investigation?'

'Yes. Of course, you know him, don't you? Crossed swords with him, too, I recall. Well, he's a good man and you're going to have to get on with him.'

'Why?'

'You're going to be our representative on the investigation. The political element. It's not just a straightforward murder case.'

'You're taking it for granted that I'll agree? I'm not a proper policeman, you know,' Edward said sarcastically. 'I'm a rank amateur.' Ferguson made no comment. 'Have you told Pride you want me to work with him?'

'Yes. He seemed quite . . . quite taken aback.'

'I bet he was!' Edward said with feeling. Pride was not one of Edward's admirers and, though their paths had crossed on more than one occasion in the last year or two, there was no love lost between them. Edward's immediate impulse was to refuse to have anything to do with the investigation but then he thought of Alice's face. The Westmacott mother and daughter could not be left to the tender mercies of Chief Inspector Pride. It also gave him an excuse for bowing out of Sir Robert Vansittart's inquiry.

'I'll go to Scotland Yard straight away,' he said.

'Good man!'

'Will you be kind enough to tell Vansittart that I am otherwise engaged? I won't now be able to pursue my inquiry into how Mr Churchill gets his information.'

'Yes. Does this change of mind have anything to do with your trip to Chartwell?'

'Are you having me followed?'

'No, but people tell me things,' Ferguson said enigmatically. 'Anyway, I mustn't hold you up. You have a lot to do. You wanted a proper job, didn't you? Well, look on this as a test. Goodbye.'

7

It demanded courage to present himself at Scotland Yard and ask for Chief Inspector Pride but, as it turned out, the meeting was not as uncomfortable as Edward had feared. He was shown straight into Pride's large but unprepossessing office. Pride might enjoy his authority but he did not deign to display it an obvious way. His desk was bare but for two telephones and two wooden trays labelled respectively 'in' and 'out'. The other furnishings were similarly utilitarian – some chairs, a coat stand and, on the wall, a map of London divided into postal districts and another of England, alongside two framed certificates. On an otherwise empty mantelpiece a heavy clock with a loud minatory tick presided over a blocked-in fireplace. There were no pictures and the window, which was filthy, had no view.

Pride shook his hand and bade him sit down. The Chief Inspector favoured him with one of those smiles that curdled cream but his greeting was pleasant enough and, to Edward's relief, he made no comment on his inflamed eye. They chatted for a moment or two and Pride even brought himself to ask after the Duke, Edward's brother, whom he had met at Mersham Castle.

There was a hiatus which Edward broke.

'I don't wish to interfere in your case, Chief Inspector, but Major Ferguson believes this murder has a political dimension and he has asked me to . . . to help in this area.'

Edward had rehearsed this little speech and was pleased with it but he hoped Pride was not going to come back with questions concerning his official position which, despite his letter of authority, he still considered to be dubious. Edward would also have been stumped if Pride had inquired why Ferguson, or anyone else, thought he was qualified to advise on the politics of

83

the case, or was a Communist girlfriend qualification enough? Pride knew that Edward had no training in police work, that his relationship with Special Branch was tenuous but, for whatever reason, the Chief Inspector chose not to humiliate him with any awkward questions. Instead, he calmly went over the circumstances in which the body was discovered.

'It was at a quarter to five this morning that a police constable on his beat noticed something hanging from Chelsea Bridge. He thought at first it was a dummy – a Charlie Chaplin figure dressed in a pinstripe business suit and overcoat with a bowler hat on his head and his umbrella on his arm, or that was what it looked like. In fact, on closer inspection, it turned out the umbrella was hanging from his coat pocket. When he got nearer, he got rather a shock. He saw that it was a body – not a straw guy or something of that nature. It couldn't be got at from the bridge so the River Police were called.'

Edward felt sick to the stomach. He could so vividly imagine the scene. The pathetic scarecrow figure twisting from a rope over the muddy water.

'The constable saw no sign of any boat?' he asked. 'I gather from Ferguson it is more likely that Westmacott's body was attached to the bridge from below rather than from the bridge itself?'

'We think so. Even at five o'clock there were people on the bridge. Someone scrambling about would have been noticed. In any case, you would have to have had the climbing ability of an orang-utang to hang yourself from that girder. Not possible, I would say.'

'The constable saw nothing suspicious on the river?'

'No, but that's not surprising. Unless he had happened to witness the body being hoisted into place – which he didn't – I doubt he would have been able to see anything suspicious from the shore. A boat's just a boat, isn't it? Still, the River Police have already begun a search of boats in the area. My belief is that the constable spotted the body within a few minutes of it being strung up. If it had been there even half an hour, someone would have seen it and called the police.'

'Yes. It was getting light by five.'

'We can rule out robbery as a motive for the killing. The murderer or murderers made no effort to prevent us identifiying

Westmacott. In fact, they wanted to advertise who it was. His wallet, keys and other personal belongings were still in his pockets.'

Edward grunted in disgust. 'It's horrible enough that Westmacott was killed but to hang him like that . . . I wonder if it was meant to ape a judicial hanging. No sign of his briefcase?'

'Not a trace. That's the only thing missing. Can you tell me anything about what might have been in it? Ferguson was no help, blast him.'

'As far as we know, Westmacott was not politically active but we think he had access to secret papers – secrets that worried him. The files in his briefcase are thought to concern businessmen – arms dealers. It's possible he stumbled on something which made him dangerous to those gentlemen.'

'Or he was trying to sell secrets to a foreign power?' Pride suggested, stroking his chin.

'It's possible but, on the face of it, the secrets he had access to weren't valuable enough to interest a foreign power. What I would like to suggest, Chief Inspector, is that I attempt to interview the arms dealers whose names we know were in the missing files. I say "attempt" because most of these men are not based in London and move around the world the whole time. I can also make some inquiries among my friends in the Communist Party. It is possible they may have heard something.'

For a moment, Edward thought Pride was going to say something disparaging but, if he had been, he managed to suppress it.

'That would be helpful, Lord Edward. I confess I am rather out of my depth when it comes to politics. To my mind, they are all as bad as each other – Fascists and Communists. They're all troublemakers. Now, ordinary crime I can cope with but this . . . it makes me sick.'

'I don't disagree with you, Chief Inspector, but that is the world we live in, I'm afraid. I will get out of your way then. I am sure you have much to do.'

'I do indeed, Lord Edward. I am also investigating a series of jewel robberies in the Hatton Garden area so I have my hands full. London's almost overrun with petty criminals. We can only investigate the major crimes.'

'You're understaffed?'

'I should say so! The Met has only 1,400 detectives out of a force of 20,000. We are well under strength. The Home Secretary just won't find the money.'

'That bad, eh? I don't envy you, Chief Inspector. By the way, may I speak to the constable who discovered the body?'

'Constable Robbins? Yes, of course, but I don't think he'll have anything to add to what I have told you.'

'No, but . . .'

'He comes off duty at ten. Shall I ask him to come round to you at your rooms or would you prefer to see him here?'

'Could you ask him to come to Albany about two? No, better make it tomorrow. I may have to spend some time with the Westmacotts.'

'The Major said, since you have met Mrs Westmacott, you will tell her . . . about her husband.'

'If I must.'

'I'll send a police constable with you in case you need help. She is bound to be . . . very much upset. And there's a daughter too, isn't there?'

'Yes, a little girl aged about ten. Alice.'

'That's bad. They must be told at once before they hear it from a reporter. I've got a car outside. Tell Mrs Westmacott I will come and see her tomorrow.'

Edward nodded. 'By the way, have you informed Westmacott's boss, Desmond Lyall, about finding the body?'

'Yes. Ferguson informed Sir Robert Vansittart and he has told Lyall. I am interviewing him this afternoon with Sir Robert. What do you think of him? You know him, don't you?'

'Sir Robert?'

'No, my lord, Lyall,' Pride said, with just a touch of the asperity Edward associated with him.

'Sorry! Lyall. Yes, I have met him. I don't know what to make of him. I don't trust him and he's certainly not telling all he knows but I don't see him as a murderer. He's a bit of a cold fish. The only person he seems to care about is his son, currently with the International Brigade in Spain.'

Pride grimaced. He did not approve of young Englishmen who ran off to fight in a war which was nothing to do with them.

'His wife died of cancer six months ago. He's a lonely man,' Edward said as he rose to go. Pride rose too and put out his hand.

86

'It's good to have your help, sir. I know in the past you may have thought I was not . . . that I did not appreciate . . .'

'Say no more, Pride. I have always thought you to be a most capable and efficient officer. How would you like me to report to you?'

'Here is my direct number. I give it only to a few senior officers so I don't get swamped, as it were. '

'Thank you. By the way, talking of Communists – you remember the Cable Street riots?'

'I do indeed.' Pride spoke with feeling. Edward was referring to the worst street fighting London had endured for many a year. In October 1936 Mosley, the leader of the British Union of Fascists, had tried to march through the East End of London. The parties on the left – the Communists in particular – were determined to stop him. They had built barricades across Cable Street and, when the police tried to dismantle them, all hell broke loose.

'That chap, Jack Spot . . .'

'He led the rioters . . . almost killed one of my officers.'

'That's the one. Didn't I read in the newspapers that he had been sent down for GBH?'

'Yes, he went to the Scrubs for six months and richly deserved it. He's out now and I hear he's mixing with some right villains.'

'I thought as much. Would it be possible to pass the word for him to get in touch with me?'

'Why?'

'I thought I might employ him to find out who was behind this business. We need someone who knows who's doing what in London's gangland. Don't get me wrong, Chief Inspector, I am sure your men will dig up something but, as you say, you are short-handed and this might be a short cut.'

'I can't be seen to be employing villains,' Pride protested.

'No, of course not, but I can. My status is nebulous to say the least. You can't be responsible for anything I get up to.'

Pride actually smiled. 'Very good! I'll pass the word. Can I hint that money might change hands?'

'Indeed you can, Chief Inspector!'

The police car set off towards Park Royal at high speed with its bell ringing. Edward had to ask the driver to slow down and turn off the bell. Apart from the fact that he was not in the least eager to reach the Westmacotts' house, he did not want to scare Mrs Westmacott by arriving noisily and at speed. Bad news could never be too slow in coming.

The moment Mrs Westmacott opened the door and saw Edward with the uniformed constable, she let out a cry and clutched at her throat.

'He's dead, isn't he? My Charlie's dead.'

Alice came running to her mother and clutched her, looking at Edward with accusing eyes. 'Where's my daddy?' she demanded. 'You said you would find him.'

'I am so sorry, Mrs Westmacott. I'm afraid your husband *is* dead. I wish it were not so but . . . may I come in?'

He followed the weeping woman and the little girl into their living-room, leaving the constable outside.

When they were sitting, he told them about Westmacott's death and how his body had been found. It was one of the worst things he had ever had to do and he wished he could be a million miles away. Briefly, in the car, he had considered telling the mother but not the daughter. However, on reflection, he thought that Alice was in many ways more grown-up than her mother. In any case, he did not want Mrs Westmacott to have to tell the child. She would find it a terrible burden. He knew it would be some time before she could take in the details of exactly how her husband had been killed – at least he hoped so – and he did not want her telling Alice some garbled story or, worse, have Alice read about it in the next day's papers.

When he had finished Mrs Westmacott was distraught and Alice, too, was very shocked. He decided he could not leave without finding someone to look after them.

'You ought not to be here alone. Is there any friend or neighbour who could come round?' he asked gently. 'I can't tell you how sorry I am. I can only promise we will do our utmost to bring the people who did this to justice.'

He prayed he would not have to disappoint them again. At the back of his mind was the thought that, if Westmacott had been killed by some international gang, they might never be caught. The killers might already be out of the country or hiding in a foreign embassy.

'My sister, Georgina. I will telephone her,' Mrs Westmacott said, trying to control her sobs.

'If you have the number, I will talk to her if you would like me to,' Edward said.

The voice at the other end of the telephone was very different from her sister's. Georgina was clearly one of those horsey, loud women whom Edward generally avoided but who on this occasion filled him with relief. She listened while Edward told his story and then asked to speak to her sister. While they were talking, Edward sat down with Alice.

'I am afraid you are going to have to be very brave. I promise you that you won't be left on your own. There will be people from where your father worked who will come and see what they can do to help but I can't pretend it is not going to be awful for you.'

'Will you come and see us?' she asked pathetically.

'I will come at least once a week until we have caught the people who have done this wicked thing.'

'You promise?'

'I promise.'

'Will they come . . . the men who killed daddy . . . and kill us too?'

'No!' Edward said shocked. 'You mustn't think that. Your father was in danger because of the work he did. He was doing his duty but he must have known the risks. I think that was why he told you to look after your mother the day he disappeared. He knew secrets and other people – foreigners probably – wanted them, even if it meant killing your father. No one will want to hurt you or your mother. Promise me you won't frighten yourself by thinking any such thing?'

He put his arm round her shoulders and she cuddled up to him. It was probably not something a real policeman would have done and he was glad he was *not* a real policeman. 'Your daddy was a very brave man. He died for his country and you are to be very proud of him.'

Alice seemed a little comforted by his words and he prayed that he was right – that Westmacott *had* died for his country, and not for betraying it.

When Mrs Westmacott put down the telephone she had stopped weeping. Her sister, who lived in Weybridge, had promised to come at once.

Edward decided he would wait until she arrived so he went outside and told the constable to take the car back to Scotland Yard. He would find his own way back.

Mrs Westmacott made some tea and they sat talking about her husband. It appeared to ease her to talk and Edward sat back and listened. Alice curled herself up on the sofa and seemed to doze.

He asked her again about the files that her husband had brought home and she said, 'I have been racking my brains ever since you asked me if I remembered anything about them and, last night, it came to me. I *do* remember something I saw. It was a letter. I didn't read it but I remember the address because it sounded so nice – like a comfortable hotel – Bawdsey Manor, Felixstowe.'

The name meant nothing to Edward but he made a note of it.

When the sister arrived she turned out to be a plain but sensible woman with rather startling yellow hair, three or four years younger than Mrs Westmacott whom she addressed as Tilly which Edward assumed was short for Matilda. She was called Miss Hay – Georgina Hay – and she took charge immediately. To his relief, Edward was told he might go. Before he did so he warned the two women that they might have a bad time from press reporters and that, if they were a nuisance, they were to ring Chief Inspector Pride at Scotland Yard who would send a constable to keep them in order.

'I have a better idea,' Miss Hay said. 'Tilly, you and Alice can come and stay with me. I have plenty of room and you are best out of here for the moment.'

'Oh, I don't think . . .' began her sister.

'It's for the best, Tilly,' Miss Hay said firmly and Edward backed her up.

'I am worried about the reporters, Mrs Westmacott. I think, as your sister says, it would be best if you spent a few days with her.'

Edward gave Miss Hay his card and she wrote her address and telephone number on a piece of paper for him. 'I will give this to Chief Inspector Pride. I know he will want to talk to Mrs Westmacott, tomorrow probably. I will also tell Mr Lyall where you are.'

He was exhausted when he left The Larches but easier in his mind. He could not have slept if he had not himself given the mother and child the news they had been dreading. To have left it to the Chief Inspector would have been unthinkable. He was going to do his utmost to bring Westmacott's killers to justice.

Only then could he look Alice in the eye and say he had done what he had promised.

When he got back to his rooms, he telephoned the Chief Inspector to tell him he had broken the news to Mrs Westmacott and give him her sister's address.

'You know who she is, I imagine?' Pride said.

'Who?'

'The sister, Georgina Hay.'

'No, is she someone special?'

'She won the Double 12 Hour race at Brooklands in 1930.'

'I don't understand.'

'She is a racing driver. I saw her race once,' Pride confessed, giving Edward an unexpected and somewhat baffling glimpse of the private life he had never before acknowledged having. 'She was driving an Ulster Austin, I seem to remember.'

'Good Lord! Women do everything nowadays. But I thought you had to be rich to race motorcars?'

'Not necessarily. At any rate, I have never heard that Miss Hay was rich.'

'That explains why she lives in Weybridge – to be near the course.'

'Presumably,' Pride said, sounding as if he rather regretted having raised the matter.

When he had put the receiver down, Edward sank into an armchair and tried to think. Fenton brought him a whisky and soda and asked if he would be dining at home. He was not feeling like eating but Fenton persuaded him to have a bowl of soup and a cutlet and he did feel better for it.

Before he went to bed he put through a trunk call to Chartwell. He knew Churchill worked late. Churchill answered the telephone himself and brushed aside his apologies for disturbing him.

'I rarely go to bed before two,' he growled. 'It drives my wife mad.' He listened to what Edward had to say about Westmacott. 'This is the evil we face,' he said at last. 'Men are made monsters by ideology and good men pay with their blood. May I count on you to keep me informed of developments? I rely on you, my boy, to track down his murderers.'

As Edward climbed into bed he felt weary and depressed. Why did these people have confidence in his detective powers when he had so little himself?

The following morning PC Robbins presented himself at Albany. He was young, enthusiastic and in awe of Edward. He sat on the edge of the chair to which Edward had directed him, refused food or drink but accepted a cigarette.

'So you come on duty at three – in the middle of the night – and finish at ten?'

'Yes, my lord.'

'It's a long shift and some would say the worst. I suppose you are not married. I can't imagine a wife permitting her husband to leave home at what – two?'

Robbins laughed. 'No, I am not married. I like being up and about to see the dawn – though in winter it can be deathly cold. This time of year it's fair enough.'

'Is it a quiet time, I mean compared with the evenings?'

'Usually, my lord. But the safe-cracker and the cat burglar – they like the quiet, when respectable folk are in bed and asleep.'

'So it must have been a shock – well, of course, it would have been a shock – to see the body hanging from the bridge. Where was it? Near the embankment or in the middle of the bridge?'

'It was quite close to the embankment but it was a devil of a job to get it down and no mistake.'

'Could he have hanged himself, do you think?'

'Not from the bridge.'

'From the shore?'

The policeman thought about it. 'No, my lord. I don't see how he could. At low tide the lowest girder on the bridge – the one he was hanging from – was not so far above the ground . . . the mud I should say . . . but there was nothing he could have climbed on. It would have had to have been something quite large. A chair was no good. He couldn't have tied the rope to the girder from a chair, my lord, let along hanged himself. It would have sunk in the mud. And then at high tide – that was about two hours before I saw him – he would have had to have waded into the water. Suicide? It don't ring true, do it, my lord?'

Edward was forced to agree with him. 'So what would be your guess as to how the body got there?'

'My lord?'

'Well, do you think a car could have stopped on the bridge and . . .'

'No, my lord, it must have been done from below.'

'Not even one of your cat burglars could have climbed under the bridge to affix the rope?'

'I don't see how they could have managed it. If the poor gentleman was still alive . . .'

'He might have been drugged . . .'

'Even then, my lord, the body would have been too heavy to handle.'

'Someone on a boat?'

'I suppose so. One of them barges perhaps. They go slow but,' he scratched his head, 'even at high tide no barge could have got near enough to the shore, where the body was hanging. I think it's more likely it were done when the tide were lower with a ladder resting on a flat piece of wood – to make a platform laid on the mud, if you understand me – maybe quite soon before I saw it hanging there.'

'I suppose the person who put his hat on his head and hung his umbrella from his coat pocket would have removed whatever it was he used to get up to the girder?'

'It seems so, my lord. I would have noticed elseways. Shall I show you where the poor gentleman was hanging, my lord?'

'If you have the time, but I hate to keep you from your bed.'

'Nah, that'll be all right.'

They took the Lagonda down to Chelsea Bridge, the constable delighting to ride in such a car and asking technical questions about engine size and acceleration which Edward was only able to answer in the most general terms.

They parked on the north side of the bridge and viewed it from below. It was muddy and there was garbage floating in an oily pool bumping at the shoreline. Edward gazed at it for some time and then said, 'What's that shining over there in the mud?'

The constable peered into the debris at the water's edge and said, 'It might be a bracelet . . . no, wait a jiffy. It's one of them powder compacts the ladies use.'

'Do you think we can get it?'

Edward looked at the constable and the constable looked at Edward and sighed. 'I suppose so, my lord.'

'Good man!'

Muddied but triumphant Constable Robbins returned from the river clutching the compact. Edward looked at it closely. It was modern with what looked like a gold cover. Valuable probably, he thought and, when he opened it, he saw it had a design on the inside of the lid. He recognized it at once. It was a dolphin, similar to the design he had noticed on Lyall's ring. He knew he ought to turn it over to the Chief Inspector but decided that he wasn't going to – at least not yet. It was too much of a coincidence to find it here. It had to have some connection with Westmacott's death. But before he asked Lyall just what that connection was, he wanted time to brood about it.

He walked on to the bridge and leaned over the parapet as far as he could. 'I am inclined to agree with you, Robbins. It must all have happened from below the bridge.'

'Careful, my lord. We don't want another death.'

Edward dropped back to stand beside the constable. 'So how many people might have seen it before you did? It must have been very obvious from the shore.'

'There were very few people around and Londoners don't as a rule look about them as they walk but I take your point, sir. The body can only have been hanging there for a few minutes.'

'You're sure you didn't see a boat – one that might have been used by the killer to get away?'

'I don't rightly know, my lord. I weren't thinking of boats at the time. I was thinking of the body. I thought some poor soul had killed himself.'

'Well, you have been very helpful, constable. Now go and have a hot meal. It may be spring but the wind's cold.'

'Thank you very much, my lord,' Robbins said, touching his helmet respectfully and pocketing the pound note Edward had pressed into his hand. On his pay of sixty-two shillings a week and one shilling boot allowance, a pound was worth wading in the mud for. Bobbies on the beat had to augment their wages as and when they could but that did not mean Robbins was going to break the rules and have the Chief Inspector breathing down his neck. 'You will give the powder compact to the Chief Inspector, my lord?'

'Leave it with me,' Edward said smoothly. 'If you remember anything later, let me know. Here is my card.'

After the constable had departed, Edward remained leaning over the bridge watching the boats go by. He was glad of his coat and scarf because it was cold, even in the sunshine. It was a peaceful scene but Edward felt depressed. Chelsea was a favourite bridge of his and now it had been defiled. He would never be able to look at it again without thinking of Westmacott's body left dangling above the water. It was so deliberate, so callous. Whom was it so important to taunt with the manner of Westmacott's killing? Why was this gesture of contempt made? Why not just drop the body in the river as so many bodies had been dropped over the centuries? Indeed, until the Great Stink of 1858 had forced Parliament to do something about it, the Thames served both as sewer and morgue. He remembered how, in *Our Mutual Friend,* Rogue Riderhood had made his living fishing dead bodies out of the river, even murkier then than now.

He thought of Verity on her way back to Spain and felt even more depressed. Should he give up all this police work and go after her? He wanted her and these few days in London had been so unsatisfactory. Was he losing her or had he never possessed her? The idea of anyone possessing Verity was so ridiculous that he was cheered up again. There floated into his mind the image of Gerda Meyer and he toyed with the idea of telephoning her. She, too, was going back to Spain, with Kavan. Perhaps they had already gone. He really disliked the man. He wondered if it was simple jealousy but decided that, despite his being a superb photographer and no doubt a brave man, there was something showy about Kavan which grated – that ridiculous nickname for one thing – 'Bandi'! Still, you had to be brave to get near enough to danger to take those photographs but . . . He decided it would be demeaning to run after Gerda. In any case, he had rejected her and she must think him the most awful idiot. At least he could look Verity in the eye when he next saw her without feeling ashamed of himself.

It was all the more disturbing, therefore, when he arrived back at his rooms, to find Gerda waiting for him. She kissed him, asked after his eye and said he was looking tired. She had just been passing, she said unconvincingly, and thought she might come and say goodbye. Fenton informed him later that she had been waiting for forty minutes.

'I was just going to leave you a note but here you are.'

'I am so pleased you came. Have you had lunch? I'm starving.' Suddenly, it was true. His appetite, which had disappeared on Chelsea Bridge, had returned with a vengeance.

'No, and I'm starving too. I hoped you might ask me to lunch.'

'Where shall we go?'

'Somewhere grand, please. Don't forget, it's the condemned man's last meal. There's not much food in Spain now, or at least not where we're going.'

'Where's that?'

'Barcelona eventually, I think, but Madrid first.'

'Verity's going to be in Madrid, isn't she? She said the Republicans would be trying to lift the siege.'

'According to what I have heard, it doesn't look as though the siege *will* be lifted. They won't admit it but the attempt to throw back Franco's army has failed.'

'André's still here?'

'Yes. We go everywhere together.'

'He doesn't mind you having lunch with me?'

'He doesn't know I'm having lunch with you,' she said like a naughty schoolgirl.

They ended up at Claridge's. Charles Malandra, the maître d'hôtel, welcomed Edward warmly and reprimanded him for not having been more recently. They drank champagne – Krug '28 – with their smoked salmon and began another bottle with the *Barbue au Vin du Rhin*. Edward chose a '23 Romanée La Tâche to go with the *perdreau du Kent Souvaroff* – partridge served with foie gras and truffles. They ordered jam omelettes to follow washed down with coffee and brandy. He began to feel rather dizzy but Gerda seemed unaffected by the alcohol if rather over-affectionate. Edward suggested a prize for whichever of them spotted the most celebrities. Edward won by noticing Princess Marina in a corner with a good-looking young naval officer. Gerda demanded more brandy and suggested they share a cigar. By the time they had smoked the cigar and drunk their brandy, the restaurant, which had been full when they began their meal, was empty but Monsieur Malandra made no effort to evict them.

The brandy, on top of the champagne and the burgundy, had made them intimate and they bent their heads together as they exchanged secrets. Edward's tongue was loosened by alcohol and he began to spill out his frustrations, telling Gerda how much he dreaded losing Verity. 'Y'know, Gerda,' he said, feeling his tongue thick in his mouth, 'when I was first taken fishing in Scotland, a boy about my own age, from the village, taught me how to tickle trout. You lay your hand just below the surface of the water,' – he demonstated with the tablecloth standing in for the river – 'and wait for the trout to swim over your palm. My friend – Dougal was his name, I've just remembered – caught two fat trout that way. Try as I might, I never caught anything but once – just once and I'll never forget it – a small, thin fish rested on my hand for a second and I thought . . . I thought I *had* him but, with a little twist of his tail,' Edward waved the cigar in the air, 'he was gone. That's what I feel about Verity. Just when I think I have her, she wriggles out of my grasp. I say, am I becoming maudlin? Forgive me. I don't normally drink so much at lunch.'

Gerda put her hand over his, and took the cigar from him and put it in her mouth and sucked on it before answering, exhaling an aromatic cloud. Edward gazed at her almost in pain from desire and, when she had returned the Havana to him, tasted her on his lips.

'You'll never have Verity in the sense you mean,' she opined. 'If you want the quiet life, my advice to you is find someone else. But you don't want a quiet life, do you? Who needs to be *bored* to death when there are so many more interesting ways of dying? Verity cares for you more than she would ever admit. She's a man's woman. Most women don't like her – have you noticed? She's a threat to everything most of us value: home and beauty. You know what I mean? Don't struggle after what you cannot have, Edward – just be grateful for what she is prepared to give you. Is there any more brandy, do you think? Oops, sorry, did you spill that or did I?'

At last the conversation slowed to a halt and Edward stared into the girl's green eyes. She smiled enigmatically back at him and he knew he could take her to bed and she would come willingly.

'I've just remembered,' she said. 'You know you were asking about that young man in the photograph – James Lyall?'

'Yes.'

'Well, I saw him yesterday.'

'Where? Here in London?'

'Of course! Where else have I been? He was walking down Piccadilly.'

'Did you talk to him?'

'I'm afraid not. You see I was on the top of a bus – smoking.'

'You smoke too much,' he reprimanded her absently. 'So does Verity. I wonder,' he said, reverting to James Lyall, 'if he has been in touch with his father?'

'I doubt it. I don't think they get on.'

'But his father worships him.'

Gerda shrugged. 'I remember him telling me about some quarrel they had – about his mother, I think. Perhaps I got it wrong.'

Edward changed the subject. 'That photograph of soldiers resting . . . I get the feeling, Gerda, between the frightening bits you had boring bits, just hanging around. Am I right?' Gerda nodded. 'You see,' he went on, 'I met a chum the other day – an old school friend, Eric Blair – who had just come back from Spain. He said his part of the front was very quiet. Just like in the Great War, he sat in a trench and read books. But then he's a very modest man so he may have been playing it all down.'

'It depends where you are. André and I found enough danger to satisfy our cravings.' She smiled crookedly as though remembering what it was like to be in the middle of the fighting. 'I'm afraid I'm a junkie when it comes to danger. I get all jagged up and feel . . . I don't know what exactly . . . as if I'm untouchable.'

'And after?'

'When I come down I sit shivering, holding my knees and feel my brain turn to semolina.'

'And it's worth it . . . to feel so bad afterwards?'

'Of course it's worth it. It's what makes life worth living. To snatch a photograph in a moment of danger – to live on the edge. I remember once . . . I had only been in Spain a few weeks . . . we met – Bandi and I – a group of soldiers, only they wore no uniform and we never did discover which side they were on. I don't suppose they knew. Anyway, they waved their guns at us and shouted stuff we couldn't understand. Bandi gave them smokes but they weren't smiling. They began to paw me. They took my watch. I was sure as hell I was going to be raped. Then I had the bright idea of taking my Leica out of its bag. I showed it them and mimed that I wanted to take their photograph. They looked uncertain until I said *"journalista"*. They seemed to understand. I started clicking away and soon they were smiling and offering us some of their filthy brandy and we were all great friends. We parted with much goodwill – they even gave me back my watch – but when it was over my legs gave way under me and I burst into tears. Bandi wasn't very sympathetic. But the odd thing was it made me crazy to do it again. I mean, I ought to have wanted to go back home and keep safe but it was the opposite. I could not wait to be in danger again. The thrill of it . . .'

'But the boring bits – tell me about those. What did you do then?'

'André would never stop taking pictures. He would photograph villagers tending their goats, or troops resting or training. Sometimes, when the photographs were developed – it was so long after he had taken them and he had taken so many – he couldn't remember where or what was in them. You should see his Paris studio. It's chaos.'

'That must have been a problem when it came to captioning them?'

'He didn't bother or, if he was showing a photograph to someone and he couldn't remember where he had taken it, he would invent a place and a time. "What did it matter?" he would say. "The picture shows the real truth."'

'So you don't think photographs lie?'

She thought about this. 'The photograph doesn't but I suppose it can mean different things to different people.'

'And people can be misled by the caption.'

'What do you mean?' Gerda demanded, suddenly angry. 'Are you accusing André of something?'

'No, I'm not,' Edward said hurriedly. Suddenly they were intimate no longer and his head was clear. 'I was only thinking out loud. Look, come back to Albany with me and Fenton can make us some more coffee.'

But it was too late. The charm of feeling at one with each other and the haze of physical desire had dissipated with the smoke from the cigar smouldering in the ashtray. Gerda got up. 'No, I must go now. Thank you for my lunch.' She looked at her watch. 'I had no idea how late it was.'

She gave him her hand which he took. 'You don't know where Lyall might go if he didn't go home?' he asked, as the girl who minded the cloakroom helped her on with her coat.

'No. Ask David. He might know.'

'I thought he was in Spain.'

'He goes back with us tomorrow. He's still in Chester Square – or at least that's where he's sleeping tonight.'

They parted almost as strangers with no talk of when they would meet again.

When Edward got back to his rooms – a headache already on the horizon – he called on Fenton for an aspirin. On an impulse, he telephoned the Foreign Office and asked to be put through to Desmond Lyall.

'Lord Edward? What is it? I'm afraid I am just going into a meeting.'

'Sorry to bother you but I wondered if you had seen anything of your son?'

'Of James? No, why? Have you seen him?'

'No, but a friend told me he was in London.'

There was a pause before Lyall asked, 'Do you know where he's staying?'

'No, but I might be able to find out. In any case, I expect he will let you know where he is.'

'I expect so,' Lyall said uneasily. 'However, if you do find out where he is, will you call me?'

'Of course,' Edward said and hung up.

There had been a moment when he had contemplated spending the rest of the afternoon in bed with a beautiful, if untrustworthy, green-eyed, red-haired photographer but, since that temptation had been resisted or maybe had never been a reality, he decided he would look up David Griffiths-Jones. He glanced at the clock on the mantelpiece. It was five thirty. He wanted to find James Lyall. He had one of his ideas – nothing more than a notion – that the boy was in some sort of danger. It was probably his loathing for a man he considered a dangerous fanatic but the feeling in his gut was that, if Griffiths-Jones was giving him houseroom, the boy might need rescuing. As he went out of the door and thrust his hat on his head, the faintest shadow of Gerda's scent caught him by the throat and left him momentarily breathless.

8

Feeling rather weary, he took a cab to Chester Square. It was a pleasant place to be on a cool spring evening and he felt immediately refreshed. Iron railings reserved the garden itself for residents but the stately houses which surrounded it were grave and tranquil. Its church, St Michael's, might be a little gloomy but altogether the square had more charm than the smarter, more expensive squares nearby. Edward's friend, Lord Benyon, lived in Gerald Road, just across the street from St Michael's, and he thought that if Griffiths-Jones was not at home, he might call on him. Then he remembered Benyon was abroad at some conference on international finance – Frankfurt, he seemed to remember.

The houses in Chester Square were substantial and, though most were still occupied by families, a few were divided up into flats. As Edward checked in his notebook for the number of the house, a door opened a hundred yards from where he was standing and he saw Guy Baron on the steps of one of the biggest houses in the square. He looked first left and then right, as though he was an Edward G. Robinson gangster, and went back into the house leaving the front door open. Edward smiled to himself. Guy would never make a successful spy: he was just too theatrical.

Edward marched swiftly towards the open door and, as he approached the house, Bernard Hunt came out.

'Hello, Hunt! I had no idea you knew Guy – or is it David Griffiths-Jones you've been seeing?' Edward said in surprise.

Hunt looked flustered but managed a mumbled 'How do you do?'

Guy put his head round the door. 'Corinth? Is that you? Do I gather you two know each other?'

101

'Oh yes, we know each other,' Edward said. 'We were on the *Queen Mary* together. How did you manage with that Poussin, Hunt?'

Bernard Hunt was an art historian and dealer who had been trying to have a painting he believed to be by Nicolas Poussin authenticated by an expert in New York.

'The argument's still going on,' Hunt replied breezily. 'I'm sorry, Corinth, I can't stay and chat. I'm late for an appointment. We must have lunch sometime. Goodbye.'

He strode off hurriedly and Edward looked at Guy quizzically. It was all coming back to him. Hunt was homosexual and, if not a Communist, he was certainly a sympathizer. He suddenly felt rather sick. Guy was difficult not to like but he was hardly an admirable character. Hunt he had reason to suspect – Major Ferguson had called him a crook – and he loathed David Griffiths-Jones. If James Lyall had fallen in with these people, he certainly ought to be rescued.

Guy, quite sober for once, invited him in. Edward explained that he had called on the off-chance of seeing David. Guy said Griffiths-Jones was out and would not be back until late. Edward said in that case he would not stay. Guy insisted he had a drink before he went and Edward got the feeling he wanted company – any company. He asked if the house belonged to him.

'No. It belongs to a friend,' was all he would say.

The drawing-room into which he was shown was gloomy, under-furnished and dirty. A large American-made radiogram stood in one corner and, rather incongruously, a tank of tropical fish in another. The house had an air of being nobody's home but just a place where men – there was no sign of a woman's touch – were temporarily housed.

Several rather battered armchairs were scattered about the room but Guy made Edward sit on a sofa and, to his embarrassment, sat down beside him. Edward, still suffering from the wine he had disposed of so freely at lunch, did not want any more alcohol but decided that, since Guy would be drinking, he ought to drink with him. Guy was the sort of man for whom alcohol was an essential social lubricant and, if he wanted to pump him, he had to be companionable. He asked for a weak whisky and soda. Guy went over to an ancient-looking instrument resembling a pre-war telephone on the wall and started talking into it.

He returned to sit beside Edward on the sofa. It was rather awkward having a conversation with someone sitting beside one, involving as it did a constant twisting of the head as though watching tennis. Edward's discomfort was increased by the feeling that Guy might put his hand on his knee, and he wanted to get up and walk about. At that moment the door opened and a man appeared carrying a tray with a whisky decanter and glasses. Edward looked once and then again. It was Hawthorne, the youth who had so comprehensively beaten up Guy at the football match in Hoxton.

'You remember Jack?' Guy said. 'He's working for me for the time being.'

Edward smiled weakly and was surprised when, after pouring out the whisky, Hawthorne sat down and opened a bottle of beer.

'Do you like working for Guy?' Edward inquired, for something to say.

'He's a good bloke, ain't you, Guy? He's a toff but that's all right. I like him right enough.'

Guy looked pleased. 'Do you know, Corinth, Jack's a member of Mosley's mob – a fully paid-up member of the British Union of Fascists. I'm thinking of joining myself.'

Edward presumed he was joking but it was hard to tell.

They touched glasses and Guy said, 'Absent friends.' Edward repeated the toast, wondering exactly which absent friends they shared. Guy, as if in response, spoke of Verity which gave Edward the opportunity to ask if he knew where James Lyall was staying.

'He's upstairs. Why? Do you want to talk to him?'

Managing to hide his surprise – not that James was in the house but that Guy admitted it so easily – he said, 'I have a message for him from his father. He wants to see him . . .'

'How did you know James was here?'

'I didn't but Gerda Meyer said she had seen him from the top of a bus and suggested he might be staying with you and David.'

'Interfering little baggage,' Guy said playfully but there was an edge to his voice. 'He doesn't want to see his father. They don't get on.'

'That's odd because Desmond Lyall was saying to me only the other day how much he cared for him. In fact, I got the impression that, now he's a widower, James is the only person he *does* care for.'

Guy hesitated. 'The thing is, Corinth, James told his dad he was one of us and he didn't like it.'

'One of us? You mean a Communist or . . .'

'Yes, a Communist,' he giggled. 'As far as I know, James likes girls – if that's what you mean.'

'Of course! I didn't mean to suggest . . . '

'Talk to James if you like. Check I'm not holding him against his will – though what it is to do with you . . . You're not a police-man, are you?' Edward looked sheepish. 'You *are* a policeman. I say, do Old Etonians and Trinity men go into the police force nowadays? How priceless!'

Edward shifted in his seat, failing completely to disguise his discomfiture. For the first time, it dawned on him that he really *was* a policeman and how absurd it was. He wanted to get up and leave but instead said, 'Yes, I would like a word with him if that's possible.'

'Jack, be a love and tell James he's wanted, will you?'

Hawthorne got to his feet. He was very large and muscular and Edward thought Guy had got off relatively lightly in the football match. As Hawthorne passed him, Guy grasped his hand and laid his cheek lightly on the back of it. It was an intimate gesture and Edward found himself once again squirming with embarrassment. It was a public declaration of their relationship. Edward suddenly felt sorry for Guy. For all his bravado, it couldn't be much fun being homosexual in a society which branded you a criminal. And if he needed men like Hawthorne – from a different class and background and with different political views – he was courting danger. Hawthorne was probably a decent enough chap but how long would he tolerate Guy? He was asking to be abused and betrayed.

Lyall entered the room – a gawky boy in an Aertex shirt with a tie loosely knotted round his neck. His grey flannels looked the worse for wear and were held up, inadequately, by one of those belts prep-school boys wore, hooked in the middle by a metal snake.

'James, this is Lord Edward Corinth,' Guy said lightly. 'I strongly suspect him of being some kind of policeman so be careful what you say or he may lug you off to gaol. He knows your father.'

James looked alarmed and opened his mouth once or twice like a stranded fish but said nothing. Edward thought of his nephew

Frank who, like this boy, had run off to Spain to fight for the Republic. He had only been a schoolboy at the time and Edward had had to retrieve him from the front line before he got himself killed. Yet compared to James Lyall, Frank was a mature adult.

'James, how are you?' he said, shaking the boy's limp, sweaty hand. 'As Guy says, I know your father and he asked me to keep an eye out for you.' This was a slight exaggeration but justified Edward considered. 'He would very much like to see you. He's worried about you. He thinks you are in Spain so he'll be relieved to know you are in London.'

'I'm only here for a few days and then I go back to Spain.' He sounded hesitant but not aggressive.

'Well, give him a ring if you can. You'll want to put his mind at rest.'

'He doesn't care what I do,' the boy replied sulkily.

'I think you're wrong there. In fact, I would go so far as to say you're the only person he does care about. He loves you, that I do know.'

James looked at him with sudden interest and Edward, too, was surprised by his own fervour. He just could not bear to see this rather pathetic, lost-looking boy at odds with his father. He knew what he would feel if Frank would not talk to him – and he was only his uncle. To Edward's delight and amazement, Guy, instead of laughing, added his voice to Edward's.

'Corinth's right, old boy. Give your father a ring now and go and see him.'

James looked trapped but was clearly very much under Guy's influence because he said, 'I haven't got his telephone number.'

'I have,' Edward said, drawing his little notebook out of his breast pocket. 'Shall I dial it for you?' He knew he was being a bully but surely it was in a good cause.

'No, I'll do it,' the boy said and Edward passed him his notebook. There was a pause and then he was talking to his father's secretary and then to his father. Edward felt guilty at eavesdropping but Guy seemed to have no such inhibition.

'Dad, is that you? It's me, Jimmy.'

They could not hear the other side of the conversation but James listened for what seemed like a full two minutes before saying, 'I'm all right. I am staying with friends in Chester Square. . . . Soon. I am going back soon.'

There was another silence and then he said, 'You are sure you want to see me? . . . I just thought . . . All right, tomorrow about four. Bye . . . Yes, same to you.'

He put the receiver down. 'I'm going to his office tomorrow. Now, if you will excuse me, I've got things to do.'

Solemnly, he shook Edward's hand and left the room without another word. Edward said goodbye to Guy and departed, feeling as pleased with himself as a Boy Scout who has done his good deed for the day.

He went to his club for a bite to eat and afterwards telephoned Ferguson. The moment he mentioned James Lyall, Ferguson stopped him and asked him to get in a taxi and come to his office. Edward groaned but, wanting the exercise, said he would *walk* across to Duncannon Street. Ferguson's office was a modest three rooms over a pub. If one twisted half out of one of the windows one could glimpse Nelson's Column but Ferguson never did.

'You must get out of the habit of telephoning me and discussing your investigations for all the world to hear,' he reprimanded him.

'I haven't done any investigations,' Edward said testily. 'I merely wanted to say that I have put Desmond Lyall in touch with his son.'

'How did you find him?'

'I had a tip-off,' Edward said grandly.

'And he was where?'

'In a nest of vipers.'

'Which particular nest?' Ferguson inquired mildly.

'He's staying with Guy Baron and David Griffiths-Jones in a house in Chester Square.'

'Their own house?'

'No, they said it belonged to a friend.'

'You should have found out who the friend was . . . but no, perhaps it was better not to seem too curious. Give me the number and I will find out.'

'I think Baron guessed I was a policeman,' Edward said, a little embarrassed.

'How?'

'I don't know . . . because I turned up and started asking questions, I suppose.'

'You didn't admit anything?'

'Of course not!' Edward replied indignantly. 'Who do you think came out of the house as I arrived?'

'I have no idea. I'm not very good at guessing games.'

'Bernard Hunt.'

Ferguson was impressed. 'I should have known!' he said at last. 'Good work indeed.' Edward was pleased with the reaction. Ferguson said, almost to himself, 'David Griffiths-Jones, Guy Baron, Bernard Hunt: king, queen and knave! It needs looking into. Yes, you have done well, Corinth. Anything else?'

'Just one small thing. When I talked to Mrs Westmacott and broke the bad news, I asked her again about the files her husband had brought home to work on. The first time I spoke to her she said she did not know what they contained but that one was marked Most Secret. I concluded this meant it came from the cabinets Lyall keeps in his office to which only he has the key. Anyway, this time she said she remembered seeing a letter from this particular file. She did not read it but she recalled the address at the top of the letter because it made her think of a comfortable hotel in the country.'

'What was it?'

'Bawdsey Manor, Felixstowe. Does it mean anything to you?'

Edward saw Ferguson change colour. He took a drag on his cigarette and started coughing as the smoke went down the wrong way.

'Bawdsey Manor is a top secret scientific establishment. Westmacott had no access to files about the place. Indeed, Lyall's department has no authority to have a file about Bawdsey. Damn and blast! This makes it all more complicated. If the file didn't come from the department, where did it come from?'

'Does Lyall know about Bawdsey Manor?'

'Yes, he would know that such a place exists. He has that much security clearance but he would not – ought not – to know what is being done there,' Ferguson said slowly.

'Lyall would have to know about Bawdsey because the work being done there relates to our rearmament programme?' Edward hazarded.

'Yes, but he would also know it was absolutely top secret. I shall have to go over to the FO and talk to him. This could be serious. If the Germans get an inkling of what is being achieved there . . .'

'And, presumably, you cannot tell me?'

'No,' Ferguson said shortly. 'But you have done well . . . very well.'

The next morning Edward woke up feeling energetic. He was still enjoying a sense of well-being born of virtue rewarded. He had achieved quite a lot in a short time and he had been absurdly pleased with Major Ferguson's words of commendation. But now what to do? He was hungry and Fenton fed him bacon and eggs washed down with strong black coffee. He tried to read *The Times* but threw it down in disgust. There was an editorial praising Hitler as 'a man of vision' and the letters included a paean of praise for the new Germany from no less a personage than Lloyd George.

He paced around the room wondering what he could usefully do. His good humour was rapidly giving way to accidie. He knew he ought to go and see the Westmacotts but, then again, perhaps it was better to wait until there was something definite to tell them. All this stuff about Guy Baron and James Lyall had nothing to do with Westmacott's murder as far as he could see. He wanted exercise and it was annoying that Fred Cavens was not there to fence with him. He hoped he was having a bad time teaching Himmler *la botte secrète*.

He decided, on the spur of the moment, to go to Cleveland Row. The London Fencing Club, of which he had been a member for several years, was located opposite St James's Palace and was the place to watch the great fencers. Guards officers would come over the road to relax and the atmosphere was that of a gentlemen's club. It was considered bad form to be too aggressive and the ideal was to let your opponent feel he was your equal, whether he was or not.

Edward was warmly welcomed and, after changing, he had two or three bouts with friends before being introduced to the very man he most wanted to meet. He had noticed it was often like that. To gain an introduction to a powerful man by writing for an appointment was almost impossible – he would be too well protected by secretaries and underlings – but to be casually introduced by a fellow member of whichever club he belonged to was to meet a man at ease and, literally in this case, with his guard down. Edward might have felt a little guilty if this meeting had been planned – a gentleman did not deliberately seek out another member for ulterior purposes but this was a genuine coincidence.

Sir Vida had been fencing with a friend of Edward's and when, after the bout ended, Sir Vida invited him to try a bout with him, he could not refuse. Although he was quite fresh and his opponent – who was at least a decade older – was sweating profusely after his previous engagement, Edward still found himself dancing, dodging and parrying to escape ignominious defeat. Sir Vida clearly did not subscribe to the notion that you fenced with deference. He fenced to win. By a lucky chance Edward had the best of it. He slipped and, feeling his knee give a little, twisted his blade from underneath his opponent's arm and saw with amazement Sir Vida's sword clatter across the floor. He was nonplussed and Edward was embarrassed.

'How did you manage that?' Sir Vida said ruefully, pulling off his mask.

'It was just a fluke; something Fred Cavens was teaching me, but I had no idea I had mastered it. I think I was slightly off balance so you must put it down to luck. You are far my superior, sir.'

Sir Vida seemed mollified but still angry with himself as they walked to the changing-room to shower. Edward, seeing him without a shirt, was impressed by his physique. He was broad in the shoulders and narrow in the waist – muscular but not heavily built. As they showered, they talked sport and Sir Vida overcame Edward's modesty to the point where he was telling the story of his racquets triumphs at Eton and Cambridge – which he would never normally do. There was something about this man which made him want to keep his end up and not be dismissed as a nobody. His face was particularly expressive – large black eyes, a delicate bone structure and full, red lips. His looks combined with his wealth and his obvious energy and drive, must, Edward thought, be irresistible to the ladies. He briefly imagined Guy Baron's reaction to such a man and was devoutly grateful that he was not present.

At the bar, Sir Vida ordered orange juice – he declared he never drank alcohol – and Edward had a beer. They talked about Lord Desborough who, like Sir Vida, had been at Harrow. 'He was perhaps the best athlete of any age,' Sir Vida opined. 'He was a soccer star at school and set a school mile record that stood for over sixty years. He rowed in the famous 1877 boat race – the only one to end in a dead heat. He sculled from Oxford to Putney – 105 miles – in a day and fenced for England at the 1906 Olympics,' at – Edward was pleased to discover – the age of fifty.

The conversation turned to other famous fencers and Old Harrovians. Edward mentioned he occupied what had once been Lord Byron's rooms in Albany and Sir Vida expressed an interest in seeing them. Edward could hardly do less than invite him to walk back with him to Piccadilly.

Sir Vida's car was outside but he waved to the chauffeur to follow them. Fenton let them in and Edward explained that this was the old Melbourne House which had been divided into twelve apartments. Byron's bow-windowed drawing-room, now Edward's, had been carved out of the famous Melbourne library.

'And Byron fenced here?' Sir Vida said, looking round reverently.

'And boxed and seduced his women,' Edward confirmed. 'We live in a less heroic age, I fear.'

'That's a common fallacy, Lord Edward. From time immemorial each generation has thought the great men of its time inferior to those of previous generations. I don't think Byron thought highly of the great men of his time. What did he say? "The 'good old times' – all times when old are good – are gone."'

'Did he say that? It's a long time since I read his poetry. Wrongly, I am sure, I think of the man as more interesting than his work.'

'He was – what do they call it now? – a huge best-seller. *Childe Harold* made him famous "overnight", as they say.'

'Who then in this present age would you call great? Not Mr Baldwin, surely?'

'No, nor Mr Chamberlain. I believe there is one great man among us, though sadly underestimated – Winston Churchill.'

'Despite his recklessness – the Gallipoli disaster, for example?'

'Despite that.'

'But his views on India – do you subscribe to those? Do you think it can remain part of the British Empire for very much longer?'

'I do so. If the British wash their hands of the subcontinent, there will be years – decades perhaps – of religious war.'

'As it happens,' Edward said casually, 'I went to lunch with Mr Churchill at Chartwell just a few days ago. It was the first time I had met him and I confess to having come away believing as you do.'

His guest looked at him with interest. 'May I ask, Lord Edward, why you were there? I presume it was not just a social visit?'

Edward hesitated and then thought he would risk the truth. 'No. I was asking him how he came to have such accurate information about our rearmament programme and how he justified using such information to spread alarm about our weakness. I tell you this in confidence.'

Sir Vida thought for a moment. 'You are not a journalist so I can only suppose that you are a government official. You know, perhaps, that I am one of Mr Churchill's warmest admirers. I think what he is doing is patriotic and in no way harmful to the national interest.'

'That became my view after I had talked to him,' Edward said cheerfully.

'I'm glad to hear it. Does this mean our meeting this morning was planned?'

'Not at all. An accident, I promise you, but – to tell the truth – I did hope to meet you sooner rather than later.'

'Well, Lord Edward, I would recommend you put your questions to me now because this may be your last opportunity.'

'I hope not,' Edward said as smoothly as he could. 'I merely wanted to ask if you knew anything about the murder of a man called Charles Westmacott?'

'Westmacott? I have never heard the name.'

'He was a Foreign Office official. In fact, he worked in a department which took an interest in arms and arms dealers. He was found hanging from Chelsea Bridge.'

'Ah! That man! I read about the murder in the newspapers. No, I don't know anything about it. Why should I? Are you accusing me of killing a man I have never met?'

'I am not accusing you of anything. As a friend of Mr Churchill's, I thought you might know if he was one of his "sources".'

'Why ask me that? Presumably you asked Churchill himself.'

'I did. He was evasive.'

111

'I cannot help you, Lord Edward. Much as I admire Mr Churchill, I am not party to his political activities. I support his campaign to build up our military strength but I have no way of helping him with information.'

'Forgive me if I am being intrusive but surely you buy and sell armaments? Does that not put you in a good position to . . . ?'

'My business is my own affair,' Sir Vida said shortly. 'It has no bearing on my politics or Mr Churchill's – or anyone else's for that matter. Now, I think it is time I left. My chauffeur will think I have been kidnapped. It was good of you to let me see these rooms. I envy you them.'

'It was no trouble.' Edward silently cursed himself. He felt he had been clumsy and wasted an opportunity but tried not to show it. 'You live in London, Sir Vida?' he asked, helping him on with his coat.

'And Paris and New York. My business takes me round the world but, yes, I have a house in London – Chester Square – although I hardly ever use it. I prefer staying at Claridge's. I have a suite there.'

Edward assumed he meant a permanent suite and was impressed. 'You have been most patient. I apologize for button-holing you like this. I had an idea you might have been able to throw some light on what is a very unpleasant business but I see I was wrong.'

'I hope you aren't too disappointed.'

As he saw him out, Edward said, 'I am surprised a man in your position is not accompanied by bodyguards. You must have made enemies.'

Sir Vida's eyes flashed. 'This is London, Lord Edward, not Addis Ababa. Goodbye and good luck with your investigation though I am still not clear exactly what you are investigating and by what authority.'

Edward went back into his rooms and thought about what he had learnt. Had he said too much? Had he asked the right questions? Perhaps he would have done better not to have shown his hand but wormed his way into the man's confidence. But he knew he would not have been able to play the hypocrite so thoroughly. And, as Sir Vida had said, he was not in any one place for any length of time. If he had not asked his questions when he did, he might never have had another opportunity.

What had he learnt? Little enough: that Sir Vida owned a house in Chester Square. If it was the one in which Guy and David Griffiths-Jones were living, what did that prove? Nothing, but it was . . . interesting.

Weary after his jousting with Chandra, he decided to spend an hour or two at the hammam in Jermyn Street. He then spent a pleasant evening at Brooks's trying to forget he was a policeman. He returned to Albany about eleven and was relieved to find no urgent messages from Major Ferguson or anyone else. He went to bed and slept soundly, only to be woken by the sound of the telephone ringing. He heard Fenton go to answer it. He looked at the clock on the bedside table. It showed seven o'clock. A telephone call this early could only mean bad news. Without waiting for Fenton to summon him, he slid out of bed, slipped on his dressing-gown and slippers and went into the hall.

'Who is it, Fenton?'

'Major Ferguson, my lord.'

He grabbed the receiver and barked, 'What is it, Ferguson? Bad news?'

'I am afraid so, my lord. I thought you would want to know straight away. Desmond Lyall has been found dead in his office. It looks as though he was poisoned though as yet we don't know how.'

'Good heavens! Lyall dead? Poisoned? How? When?'

'Yesterday evening. Someone left some poisoned cigarettes in the box he kept on his desk.'

'Poisoned cigarettes?'

'Yes. Lyall was a chain smoker which ought to have made him more resistant to it but . . .'

A thought occurred to Edward. 'His son, James, was going to see him. Do you know if he managed to do so before . . . ?'

'Yes, he did. It was just a few hours later that his father died.'

'Where is James now? Do you know?'

'Pride's going to Chester Square in about an hour, as soon as he has finished at the Foreign Office. I thought you might like to be there.'

'Right. By the way, about the house – I have a hunch it belongs to Sir Vida Chandra.'

'Chandra! That needs thinking about. I'll get Pride on to it straight away.'

'James . . . I blame myself for suggesting he go and see his father. Do you think . . . ?'

'No one is saying James killed his father but he was, possibly, the last person to see him alive. The poisoned cigarettes could have been left at any time. It was a sort of Russian roulette. Lyall may have smoked several ordinary cigarettes before he pulled out a lethal one. As for sending James to see his father – you cannot blame yourself for that. Assuming he had nothing to do with his father's death, he may sleep easier for having had that last meeting. Perhaps they parted on good terms. We have to hope so.'

'No one witnessed the meeting, I suppose?'

'No. The secretary saw James into his father's office but was absent when he left. Sometime later she found him dead.'

'Miss Hawkins?'

'Yes. Look, I have to be somewhere in five minutes – the Foreign Secretary wants a briefing and then I have to see Vansittart. I'll catch up with you later.'

Edward put down the receiver and wiped his forehead with the back of his hand, an unconscious gesture which Verity, had she been there, would have recognized as indicating he was under stress.

The death of two fathers, he thought to himself. There might be many other things Lyall and Westmacott had in common but both had children who would suffer from their deaths.

'Fenton, bring round the Lagonda, will you. I am going out. Ferguson says Desmond Lyall has been murdered.'

'I am very sorry to hear that, my lord. I will bring the car round directly. Might I inquire if you think Mr James Lyall killed his father?'

'I do not, Fenton, but you can bet your bottom dollar that Chief Inspector Pride will think he did.'

Pride arrived at the house in Chester Square to find Edward gazing up at the shuttered windows. 'I have been knocking and ringing the bell but there is no answer,' he commented.

Pride nodded. 'The birds have flown? The boy must have known we would come looking for him here. However, I have applied for a search warrant. We may still find something.'

'It's all probably quite innocent, Chief Inspector. Guy Baron and David Griffiths-Jones were planning to go back to Spain and they have probably taken James with them. You know he joined the International Brigade?'

'So you told me. They're all Communists, I understand?' he said with barely concealed contempt.

'Yes, Chief Inspector, and I have a hunch the house is owned by Sir Vida Chandra, the arms dealer. I have asked Ferguson to check if I am right.'

'I've heard of him. An Indian gentleman, as I believe, with too much money to be honest.'

'Really, Pride, you do jump to conclusions.'

The Chief Inspector snorted derisively.

Back in his office the Chief Inspector finished telling Edward about Desmond Lyall's death. 'James spent an hour with his father and left about five. Miss Hawkins put her head round his door at six to say she was going home and found him lying across his desk.'

'He was still in his chair?'

'Yes. Miss Hawkins thought he had had a heart attack while he was working. She's a most sensible woman. Instead of panicking, she tried to revive him but, when it was clear he was dead, she called an ambulance and Mr McCloud – he was just leaving when he heard her cry out – telephoned the police. The call was put through to me.'

'What made him call the police? I mean, Miss Hawkins thought Lyall had died of a heart attack.'

'McCloud said he "did not look right".'

'What did that mean?'

'He could not quite say but it seems to have been the chrysanthemum.'

'The chrysanthemum?'

'It was dead and broken in half. McCloud found it underneath the cigarette box on the desk.'

'But this is April. There are no chrysanthemums in April.'

'That's right, my lord. As McCloud knew, they bloom from September to December. There's quite a folklore surrounding chrysanthemums, so I am informed. They can stand for life or rest but a dead, broken flower signifies death.'

'That's fantastic! Are you suggesting someone's sending us messages . . . ?'

Pride shrugged. 'Maybe, maybe not. The man is dead, that's for sure.'

'Can you tell me about how he died?'

'It looks like nicotine poisoning.'

'Good heavens! I'm afraid I have never heard of it. How is it administered?'

'It can be drunk or, as in this case, inhaled. Lyall smoked a Turkish brand – Murad – and one of the cigarettes seemed to have been laced with the poison. Probably more than one – they are all being tested. Anyway, the cigarette which killed him was still between his fingers so death must have been almost instantaneous. A lethal dose is about fifty milligrams and death is almost immediate.'

'But the cigarettes – the poisoned ones – could have been left in the box on his desk at any time. I remember him offering me one.'

'Did you smoke it?' Pride asked mildly.

'I did not.'

'If the murderer poisoned only one of the cigarettes then it could have taken days before he reached it but, if there were several, they must have been left in the box very soon before he died. He got through as many as forty a day, Miss Hawkins says. She often told him they were bad for him.'

'But not this bad! What are the symptoms? I mean, is nicotine poisoning a painful death?'

'The doctor says the diaphragm muscles are paralysed and death occurs from respiratory failure. In other words, you die of asphyxiation.'

'How horrible!' Edward said, automatically taking a deep breath. 'And it works fast?'

'As fast as cyanide.'

Edward rubbed his forehead. 'This must have been done by someone close to him. There must be a personal motive. He wasn't a sociable man so we ought to be able to narrow down the list of suspects. Could he have brought the poisoned cigarettes into the office himself?'

'Just possibly. He normally bought several boxes every week or two from the tobacconist over the road. We've talked to the man who served him – it's a most respectable shop, I should add – and he had not been in for ten days. They were expecting a visit from him.'

'You do believe the deaths of Westmacott and Lyall are connected, Chief Inspector?'

'I do but, as I am sure you would agree, my lord, the two murders are very different. Westmacott's was clearly the work of an organized group. It has all the signs of a gangland killing but so far none of my people – narks, snouts, that's what we call them – have got a sniff of who might be behind it. Which suggests to me that it's political.'

'Agreed. While Lyall's murder . . .'

'Is personal.'

'Although you could say that both men were asphyxiated. Have you had a chance to talk to his friends? I don't even know where he lived.'

'He had a service flat in a block near Portland Place. We have had a look round it but there's nothing there. Hardly any personal belongings – a portrait of his wife by Lavery – that's about it.'

'But was that where he had always lived?'

'No. His wife was a rich woman. They had a house in Cadogan Gardens and a country place near Oxford – Steeple Aston. After she died, he sold everything and went into a shell from all accounts. Never saw anyone or did anything. When his wife was alive they used to do the season. They were keen on racing and Sir Robert said he met him at Ascot one year. He even owned a racehorse, he was telling me. But Lyall was hard hit by his wife's death and when James joined the International Brigade . . . well, it was the last straw.'

'But Vansittart thought well of him?'

'Oh yes. He worked harder than ever after his wife died. Sir Robert said his work was exemplary, except perhaps he was too unsociable. His staff respected him but never "knew" him. He wasn't the sort of man to interest himself in their private lives.'

'Yes, that's the impression I got when I talked to him.' Edward took a minute to absorb what Pride had told him. 'So, we have two different murders to investigate?'

'But linked,' Pride repeated. 'Have you any ideas, my lord? You have not had anything from your political . . . friends?'

'Not yet,' Edward said stiffly.

'You talked to the boy, my lord. Did James hate his father enough to kill him?'

'I met him only briefly – we did not really talk – but I don't think so. They had quarrelled, certainly, but I got the feeling James loved his father, and Lyall certainly loved him.'

'What was the quarrel about? Do you know?'

'His going to Spain, I suppose, but it might have been something else. I don't know for sure. A photographer friend of mine, Gerda Meyer, who knew him in Spain said something about James blaming his father for his mother's death.'

'But that was cancer. How could he blame his father for that? He must have seen he was heartbroken.'

'We'll have to find James and ask him,' Edward said flatly.

They sat in silence for a few moments, then Edward said, 'May I talk to Miss Hawkins and the other people in Lyall's office?'

'I don't see why not. Our interviews will be over today. You must of course make it clear to them that they have no need to answer your questions. Your position is that of an observer and political adviser.'

'I quite understand, Chief Inspector, and I'll keep you posted.'

Returning to Albany in a taxi, Edward put his hand in his coat pocket and got a shock. He felt something round and smooth and immediately knew what it was – the powder compact Constable Robbins had fished out of the river near to where Westmacott had been found hanging. He had meant to question Desmond Lyall about it but had quite forgotten. He looked again at the dolphin on the inside of the lid which he was sure was the same as the design on Lyall's signet ring. Damn and blast! He had suppressed vital evidence. He felt slightly nauseous. He looked at it more carefully. It was a beautiful piece of work. He was no expert but he thought he had seen something similar in Cartier when he was buying a present for Verity. She hadn't been very appreciative, he remembered. He turned it over in his hand. It was probably part of a vanity case. He wondered if he ought to go straight back to Scotland Yard and hand it over to Pride but then thought that, before he did so, he would take it into Cartier and see if they could identify it. He knew they kept meticulous records.

Marcus Fern was waiting when he got back to Albany. 'Sorry to barge in on you. I hoped to catch you before you went out but your man said you left here before breakfast. I thought you never got out of bed before nine.'

'Ah well, something turned up,' Edward answered vaguely, refusing to satisfy Fern's curiosity. 'What can I do for you?'

When Edward had got to know Fern on the *Queen Mary*, where he was acting as Lord Benyon's secretary, he had thought him brilliant but rather cold. Benyon had been at pains to explain to Edward at the time that 'secretary' did not properly describe Fern's position or his work. He was Benyon's economic adviser and someone with whom he could discuss problems and ideas. He was about Edward's age and Benyon had forecast that he would one day be Governor of the Bank of England. However, Fern had unexpectedly taken up with Winston Churchill and his career had suffered as a result. He sat on the boards of several companies but his main concern – one might almost say the obsession – which he shared with Churchill was that Britain was quite unprepared for the war he believed would break out within the next five years. He made speeches on the subject and chaired a small group of like-minded financiers but alienated most of the people with whom he worked. They thought him a bore, a monomaniac, who ought to leave politics to the politicians. Edward admired his dedication – trusted him up to a point – and shared his views but they were not close friends.

'Well, the fact is, Corinth, Winston asked me to drop in with an invitation. He took to you and wants to see you again. In fact, he wonders if you would have dinner with us tonight?'

Edward had an idea he was being 'got at' but did not object. Churchill was trying to enlist him in whatever private war he was waging against those who opposed his crusade and Edward was not unwilling to be recruited.

'Tonight?'

'Well, I knew you would probably be busy but I thought I would ask.'

'No, I am free and, of course, flattered to be asked. Presumably not Chartwell?' he said with a grin.

'No, Morpeth Mansions, number 11. It'll just be a few of us who support the cause, you know. All men, I'm afraid.'

'I don't quite understand why he should be interested in me,' Edward said slowly. 'My influence does not even extend to my family. My brother Gerald thinks I am barking up quite the wrong tree. He is a great friend of Baldwin and very much admires Mr Chamberlain.'

'To tell the truth, I think he would like to consult you in an area where he believes you are an expert.'

'That being . . . ?'

'Protection, I suppose you would call it.'

'He wants me to be his bodyguard?' Edward asked with studied sarcasm.

'Nothing like that!' Fern said hastily. 'He has many enemies, as you know, but neither the time nor the inclination to worry about them.'

'I can't believe he has anything *to* worry about.' Edward was still cross. 'I can't see Mr Baldwin sending his "heavies" to beat him up just because they disagree politically.'

'No, of course not! But his views on both Ireland and India have brought him death threats. He takes very little notice but I, and one or two others, think he ought to have . . . advice.'

'Major Ferguson of Special Branch . . . he is the person to advise.'

'Special Branch is overwhelmed by its obligation to preserve the government from political adventurists from the far right and the far left of the spectrum. They can hardly be expected to worry about the safety of private individuals.' He paused but Edward still felt he was being approached with a view to becoming Churchill's private detective – a position he thought himself, rightly or wrongly, to be above.

'I am sure Mr Churchill can employ an ex-policeman to guard him.'

'Oh dear! I am afraid I haven't explained myself clearly. Mr Churchill has no need of a bodyguard. He wants – or we think he wants – someone not involved in politics to keep an eye on . . . threats to his safety. I am convinced – and I want to convince you – that Winston is our only hope. He is too important to us not to take precautions. You must understand.'

'You say he has received death threats?'

'Plenty. Although these are from lunatics and he burns them, I am convinced there is a danger. Have you heard of the Blue Shirts, for example?'

'Irish Fascists?'

'Yes, a group of idiots led by "General" O'Duffy, the President of Fine Gael and a former police chief. He's in Spain now with Franco but some of his people are still here and in Ireland.'

'What have they got against Churchill?'

'They don't like him for a whole raft of reasons – not least his opposition to Britain returning the ports to Eire.'

'What ports?'

'As part of the treaty with de Valera which established the Irish Free State, Britain held on to certain fortified ports which will be vital to us in the event of war with Germany – Berehaven, Cobh and Lough Swilly. The government wants to hand them over to de Valera but Churchill regards them as vital to our interests and says so at every opportunity.'

'I see.'

'And then there is India. He has done so much to oppose Indian self-government that there are plenty of fanatics who would be delighted to see him dead.'

'Well, I shall come tonight, as you wish it, Fern, but I don't promise anything. In the first place – I tell you this in confidence – I am involved in the investigation of the murder of Charles Westmacott, the Foreign Office man, and I strongly suspect he was passing secret information to Mr Churchill. And now his boss, Desmond Lyall, has been murdered.'

Fern whistled. 'Curiouser and curiouser.'

'It's all such a muddle! There has to be a link between the two murders but it's not obvious.'

'Political?'

'Maybe. Politics is so fractured. I agree with Mr Churchill that our leadership is criminally supine in the face of the threat from Germany but that's all I do agree with him about, as far as I can see.'

'That's enough to go on with. See you tonight then. No need to dress – just dinner-jackets. Winston has been known to wear his carpet slippers!'

9

Edward was beginning to be worried about Verity. The situation in Spain was going from bad to worse and it was obvious, even to the casual observer, that General Franco was going to win the civil war. Madrid was under siege and, when the city fell, inevitably the world would believe the battle for the Republic was lost. The Republicans might fight a guerrilla war for many months but the final outcome could not be in doubt. And when Franco did take Madrid the odds were that there would be a bloodbath. Hand-to-hand fighting, snipers, street-by-street battles – the city would not fall without a bitter struggle and any journalist still with the Republicans would be in extreme danger. Franco had no reason to love the left-wing press which had campaigned against him so vigorously for so long and, if he could revenge himself without attracting too much notice, he would.

Edward had been telephoning the *New Gazette* every other day to get the latest news and was just about to do so again when the telephone rang.

'Hello!' Edward spoke irritably, his mind on Verity and the peril she was in. The voice at the other end of the line was unmistakably cockney.

'Lord Edward?'

'Yes. Who is it?'

'It's me, Jack Spot. I heard you was wanting to speak to me.'

'Of course! Yes, I do.' For a moment Edward had quite forgotten asking Pride to pass Spot a message to get in touch. 'I need some information and I am ready to pay for it. Could you come round to my rooms in Piccadilly?'

'Naw! I don't think so. Not my territory, if you see what I mean. I wouldn't feel at my ease.'

'Where then?'

'Do you know the Cat and Fiddle in Seven Dials?'

'No, but I can find it.'

'It's in Earlham Street. Can you be there at six, before it gets busy? Ask for the snug. We can talk there private like.'

'Very good,' Edward said briskly. 'I'll be there.'

As soon as he had put down the telephone receiver he dialled the *New Gazette* and asked to speak to Mr Atkins on the Foreign Desk. Atkins collected and collated reports from the paper's foreign correspondents. He said he had heard nothing from Verity for several days and that Lord Weaver himself was worried enough to telephone the Foreign Office to ask what plans it had for rescuing journalists and other foreign nationals in the event of Madrid falling to Franco.

'And what did they say?' Edward asked.

'The FO said there was nothing they could do. Standing orders are for journalists to make for the nearest foreign embassy in a crisis.'

'When do you expect Miss Browne to be able to get through to you?'

'As you know, my lord, Madrid is under continual bombardment. Miss Browne warned in her last wire that all communications with the outside world might be cut off at any time.'

Edward's lips thinned and his brow creased. 'Is she in any danger, do you think?' It was an absurd question and one which he regretted the moment he asked it. He could sense the man at the other end of the line shrugging his shoulders.

'I can't see Miss Browne staying out of danger, can you, my lord?'

Edward could just imagine Verity leaving it too late to take shelter in an embassy. He was suddenly overcome with anxiety. He would give anything to be with her.

'If I wanted to go out to Spain . . . ?'

'I wouldn't advise it, my lord.'

'I'm not asking your advice,' he said, needing someone to shout at. 'I'm sorry, Atkins. I *am* asking your advice and I hope you will forgive me for not liking it.'

'Not at all, my lord. We are all worried. Many parts of Spain are quiet enough . . .'

'But not Madrid.'

'Not Madrid, no, my lord.'

While he had been talking to Atkins, Edward had come to a decision. He resolved to go to Spain – whatever the cost – and find Verity. James Lyall would be his excuse . . . his alibi for doing something no sane man would contemplate. He suppressed his guilt at using the boy in this way by telling himself it would be what James's father, if he were still alive, would want him to do. Only action, however futile it might turn out to be, could stem his anxiety which threatened to become panic. He knew he might not be able to reach Verity but to do nothing was intolerable. He would ask Vansittart to furnish him with a diplomatic passport. He picked up the telephone again but, instead of dialling, lowered the receiver and replaced it on its rest with a bang. He would go round to the Foreign Office and talk to the great man in person. Face to face, he ought to be able to persuade him to give him the help he needed.

He shouted to Fenton for his coat and hat and strode, grim-faced, into the bustle of Piccadilly. He did not need to be psychic to know Verity was in danger but the fear he felt now was something more than his usual nagging expectation of hearing bad news from Spain whenever she was reporting the war. Verity would pooh-pooh his fears and be thoroughly ungrateful if he did turn up beside her somewhere on the front line. And yet he could not rid himself of his premonition that she was threatened in some personal way and that only he could come to her aid.

It was good to be out in the fresh air and his head cleared a little. It suddenly occurred to him that such a busy and important man as Vansittart would probably not be able to see him on the spur of the moment and he wondered if he were about to make a colossal ass of himself. He was, however, fortunate in his timing and spent just fifteen minutes kicking his heels in an ante-room before being ushered into his office.

'You have some news about Westmacott's murder . . . or Lyall's?' Vansittart greeted him. 'It has been a nightmare. We are involved in the most difficult international negotiations and this has to happen. The press is pursuing me with questions I don't want to answer and, moreover, can't answer. Anthony had to field a question in the House today. He is hopping mad, I can tell you.'

Edward was suddenly overcome with shame. Here he was consumed with worry about Verity and ignoring the fact that Sir

Robert had, almost literally, the cares of the world on his shoulders. Added to which he had made him a promise and broken it. He had /agreed to find out who was leaking secret information to Mr Churchill and had deliberately done nothing about it. His excuse had been he wanted to concentrate on finding Charles Westmacott's killer but, although he had followed up a few clues, he had to admit to himself that he was still completely in the dark. In his mind's eye he saw Alice and remembered his promise to her. Before he went to Spain he had to go and see her. It was his duty. But would he have time? He would like to be on his way tomorrow.

He decided he must put the best possible face on what he had been doing and not sound ineffectual.

'I apologize, Sir Robert, for breaking in on you when you are so busy but I just wanted to report very briefly on what little we have discovered and to ask you to provide me with a diplomatic passport. I need to get to Spain to find James Lyall, Desmond Lyall's son, and possibly the last person to see his father alive.'

Vansittart frowned. 'Is that really necessary? You really think he killed his father?'

Edward hesitated. He did not think James had murdered his father but he had to make his trip to Spain sound worthwhile.

'I don't know but I do believe he is in danger and also that he has important information which will lead us to the killer. He may not know he has it but I believe the murderer suspects he has and will do his best to prevent him coming back to England.'

This was wild guesswork on Edward's part but, as he said it, he believed it and his earnestness seemed to convince Vansittart.

'I see. What else? Do you know anything about Westmacott's murder?'

'I am following up several leads along with Chief Inspector Pride. As soon as I leave here I am going to meet a well-known East End criminal who, I hope, will lead us to the men who carried out the murder.'

Vansittart still looked puzzled – as well he might, Edward thought. He was about to speak when his secretary knocked and entered to remind Sir Robert he was due at the French Embassy in fifteen minutes.

'Well, my boy, I hope you know what you are doing. It all sounds muddled to me but I have faith in you. Sanderson,' he addressed the young man who had interrupted them, 'Lord Edward requires a diplomatic passport and anything else you can think of to make it possible for him to cross the Spanish border. Will you see to it? Goodbye, Lord Edward. Report to me as soon as you get back from Spain, will you? I want to hear about your investigations in detail. And don't forget what Talleyrand said, "N'ayez pas de zèle" – don't be too impetuous.'

With a nod, Sir Robert left the room clutching his hat and overcoat. Two assistants who had been waiting, laden with briefcases, in the outer office fell in behind him like ducklings behind their mother. Edward sighed. He had bluffed his way and got what he wanted but he knew time was short. He had to find out what lay behind Westmacott's murder if he was to retain any credibility with Sir Robert. He did not fancy meeting him in a month's time and having to confess he still knew nothing.

After warning Edward that a diplomatic passport would only take him so far and that bullets were no respecter of passports, Sanderson said he would have the papers he needed sent over to Albany before ten but he would need a photograph. Edward cursed at not having thought of that and telephoned Fenton. That competent fellow relieved his master's mind by saying he had a spare which he would bring over immediately.

As he left the Foreign Office he looked at his watch and realized he just had time to go into Cartier and check on the powder compact before his appointment with Jack Spot. The manager, Mr Bainton, whom Edward knew well, confirmed that the compact was one of theirs.

'The dolphin design is a classic and we use it on many pieces of jewellery as well as items such as this.' He turned it over in his hands. 'We must have sold a few hundred compacts like this so we could not say who bought this particular one. But you say there was a ring with the same dolphin design? Let us consult our Mr Mason.'

When Edward mentioned Desmond Lyall's name, Mr Mason's face lit up. 'Oh, yes, my lord, I know Mr Lyall. He comes in once or twice a year to buy his wife a birthday and Christmas present – usually jewellery and always to this design. But wait a minute,' his face clouded, 'last time he was in – that was before Christmas – it was to tell us his wife had died. I thought he looked very sad, poor man.'

'And you have not seen him since?'

'No, my lord. Why, is there something wrong?'

'I'm afraid there is. He has been murdered. It will be in the papers, no doubt, but until then I would be grateful if you would keep it to yourself.'

The two men looked very shocked and shook their heads at the evil times they lived in. Edward contemplated buying something for Verity but on reflection desisted. She had very little time for jewellery though she loved buying clothes, hats in particular.

Edward took a cab to Earlham Street and had no difficulty in finding the Cat and Fiddle. Seven Dials was by no means the sink of iniquity it had been in Dickens's day but it was still an area where it made sense to keep your hand on your wallet particularly if, like Edward, your dress and demeanour signalled you were more at home in St James's Street and Piccadilly. He pushed open the dingy door and made his way to the bar. The place stank of stale cigarettes and warm beer but the brass rail below the counter was polished and the little tables were clean beneath the stains from countless dripping tankards.

He was directed towards a door in the corner, almost invisible behind a dark curtain. He found himself in a small room which was empty except for the large figure of Jack Spot seated in a broken-backed but comfortable-looking armchair.

'Mr Spot, how kind of you to meet me,' Edward said, putting out his hand. 'Can we get a decent pint here?'

As the man dragged himself to his feet, he saw that he had put on a lot of weight since his days on the barricades and had also gained a savage-looking scar which began high on his forehead, just below his thinning, wiry black hair, crossed his eye and travelled over his cheek into his nose which was consequently much misshapen. He wore a moustache and was smoking an enormous cigar.

'The man outside will bring us beer, my lord. But call me Spotty. Everyone does. How is Miss Browne, if I may ask?'

As a well-known Communist, Verity had met Jack Spot on many occasions and she had campaigned fiercely for his release from prison after the Cable Street riots. It had seemed most unjust to her that Jack should have gone to the Scrubs for fighting Fascists when that was what everyone *should* be doing.

'She's in Spain . . . in Madrid,' Edward said and, once again, cold fear gripped his innards and made him frown.

Spot saw his look and correctly interpreted it. He showed surprising tact, however, in not pursuing his question, simply adding, 'That young lady stands very high in my regard, my lord. She stood by me when most others abandoned me. Any friend of hers is a friend of mine. Tell me what I can do for you, sir.'

When the beer had been delivered and both men had taken appreciative gulps, Edward told him.

'Do you know anything about the murder of a man called Charles Westmacott, Spotty? He was found hanging below Chelsea Bridge four days ago.'

'That's not nice, that ain't. I read about it in the newspapers, of course, but I ain't heard any talk about it – not on my patch.'

Edward looked disappointed. 'You've not heard anything about who might have done it, Spotty?' he pressed him, leaning forward, his pint in his hand. 'We think it was probably a political murder. Mr Westmacott worked in the Foreign Office and he might have been killed for some secret papers he was carrying.'

'When you say "we", my lord, do I take it you mean you're a copper?'

'Yes, but . . . yes,' Edward said after the very slightest hesitation. 'Or rather I am temporarily attached to Chief Inspector Pride – you know him, don't you? – but I am *personally* interested in the case. There's a widow and a little girl. Death is bad enough but the way he died was horrible. Someone wanted to make mock of him.'

Spot took a sip of his beer and raised an eyebrow, which made his scar take the shape of a question mark. He looked thoughtful. 'Well, let's forget about that, shall we? I'm no friend of Mr Pride, nor him of me I should imagine. It was him who got me sent down. Let's just say you're a friend of Miss Browne and leave it at that.'

'Very good, Spotty. But you know nothing about the murder?'

'Naturally, I *know* about it but, there again, I *don't* know nothing about it. I ain't heard a dickey-bird and that's odd in itself,' he went on ruminatively. 'No one in my neck of the woods has been mouthing off about it. I mean, my lord, if it had been part of gang warfare, I would know who had done it. I think you must be right: foreigners must have done it.'

'But could foreigners – Germans for instance – Nazis – could they have organized this sort of thing in London?'

Spot shrugged his shoulders. 'Anything is possible if there's enough money. The thing that puzzles me is that the whole point of killing a man in such a showy way is to frighten off other people but if you don't leave a calling card and nobody knows who done it, then the whole thing becomes a bollux, if you'll pardon my French. Do you follow me, my lord?'

'I do indeed, Spotty.'

'Anyways, leave it with me and I'll ask around – tactful like. What shall I do if I hear anything?'

'Here's my card – telephone me.' Edward hesitated and then burst out, 'I am planning to go to Spain for a week or two. Things aren't too bright there and I want to reassure myself that Miss Browne is not in danger. Leave a message with my man, Fenton, if you need to while I'm away. I would be most grateful for your help in this, Spotty, and I'll see you're not out of pocket.'

'That's all right, guv. Anything I can do, I will – for Miss Browne. Fine young lady that, my lord. I trust you will find her well but, if I'm any judge, look for her on the barricades – same as me in my younger days.' He looked a little wistful.

'Good, very good! Thank you. I rely on you. What are you doing now?' Edward added, to be polite.

'I work the racecourses with Darky Mulley's mob.' He touched his misshapen nose with his finger. 'Green Carnation in the four o'clock at Newbury, my lord. Ten pound on the nose and you'll do yourself a bit of good. Take it from Spotty.'

Still possessed by a fever of anxiety, Edward returned to his rooms to dress for dinner and warn Fenton to expect delivery of his passport while he was out.

'I have it already, my lord,' Fenton said. 'Mr Sanderson signed the papers when I went over to the Foreign Office with your photograph.'

'Excellent! You see, I'm determined to leave for Spain tomorrow.'

'Indeed, my lord.'

He fondled the passport and the letter of authority Fenton gave him as though together they comprised a magic key to Spain and so to Verity. 'Can you book whatever you think will get me to Madrid in double-quick time, Fenton?'

'Very good, my lord.'

Edward hesitated by the telephone and decided it would only complicate matters if he were to say he would go to Weybridge the next day to see Mrs Westmacott. In any case, he had so little to report that it was hardly worth it. He would salve his conscience by telephoning. Georgina Hay answered the phone immediately, as though she had been expecting it to ring. He explained that he had to be out of the country for a few days but, as soon as he was back, he would come and see them to report on progress.

'So you're no further on?' she said in her disapproving-headmistress voice.

'Nothing definite yet, I'm afraid, but we're following up several leads.'

He thought he had heard Pride use this phrase and it sounded as though something was being done. He felt guilty but then he seemed always to be feeling guilty, though his sins were mostly sins of omission.

He rang the Chief Inspector and told him that he had met Jack Spot and hoped something might come of it. 'I'm going to Spain tomorrow to find James Lyall,' he added.

'You don't have to do that,' Pride said, sounding surprised.

'It's all right, Chief Inspector. I won't be charging up my trip to you.'

'I didn't mean that, my lord. I meant . . .'

'I know what you meant. The truth is I am worried about the situation in Madrid and I want to see that both James and Miss Browne are safe. If at the same time I can discover what James knows about his father's death, that will be even better. It worries me that he may not even know his father is dead.'

'He may have seen an English newspaper.'

'I don't think that is likely. Remember, Madrid is under siege. Anyway, I expect to be back in a week or ten days. From everything I hear, Madrid is not a place to be if you want rest and relaxation.'

'As you say, my lord.'

Pride still sounded puzzled by Edward's sudden decision. He no doubt thought of it as a whim which only a rich man could afford to indulge and Edward could see it must seem like that. How could he explain to Pride, when he could hardly explain it to himself, his strong premonition that Verity was in danger? Of course she was in danger. Anyone in Madrid must be and she had been in danger before – notably during the ill-fated siege of Toledo but then he had been completely unaware of her predicament and had not been troubled by any premonitions.

Churchill's apartment in Morpeth Mansions turned out to be a relatively modest duplex at the top of a purpose-built block of flats behind Westminster Cathedral. It was convenient for the House of Commons but much less grand than the house in Eaton Square which the Churchills had rented before.

In the taxi, Edward wished he had telephoned to say he could not come to dinner after all. His mind was entirely on his trip to Spain and he doubted he would be able to concentrate on what Churchill had to say about the state of the world. However, in the event, it did not prove to be an altogether wasted evening. As Marcus Fern had said, it was an all-male gathering. Apart from himself and Fern, Churchill had invited Sir Vida Chandra, a scientist called Robert Watson-Watt and his adviser on scientific affairs, Professor Lindemann. The latter proved to be a most eccentric character – tall, balding and opinionated, he was a vegetarian, non-smoking teetotaller. He did not seem to mind that Churchill drank champagne throughout dinner after which he smoked a Havana cigar with a large brandy and soda.

Edward had decided to keep his head down and say nothing, which he managed quite successfully until he was eating his Dover sole. Churchill was sounding off about Republican atrocities in Spain. His sympathies seemed to lie more with General Franco than with the Republic which he saw as a tool of the Soviet Union. Edward, who had been in Spain when Franco had plunged the country into civil war, agreed that the Communists, under orders from Moscow, were almost certainly taking over the direction of the war in the name of the legitimate

131

Republican government but that Italy and Germany's involvement on Franco's side was much more worrying.

'You see Germany using Spain as a rehearsal for the wider European war to come, do you?' Churchill asked.

'I do, sir. We did not stand up to Mussolini in Abyssinia or to Japan in Manchuria. Now we leave Hitler a free hand in the Iberian peninsula. Hitler must think we are sending him the clearest message – that we have neither the will nor the means to resist him.'

'And you are going to Spain tomorrow?'

'Yes. I hardly know why, to be honest with you. I feel some crisis is coming to a head there and wish to see how my friend, the journalist Verity Browne, is managing to report the war. I also wish to locate James Lyall. He is the son of Desmond Lyall, the Foreign Office man who was murdered.'

'Lyall, yes indeed. That's a bad business. It must be connected, don't you think, with the death of that poor fellow Westmacott? I can confirm to you, now that it can do him no harm, what I think you already know. From time to time he supplied me with invaluable information about the lamentable state of our defences. He was a patriot and I trust his efforts on my behalf did not contribute to his murder. I don't know about Lyall. He was Westmacott's head of department, wasn't he? Van told me there was a nasty smell in the department and you were going to find out its source.' There was a pause but Edward chose to say nothing. 'You must find out who did it, Corinth – both murders. It is essential that the lives of the people who help me are not put in danger. Do you think Westmacott was the victim of a Nazi killer?'

'I cannot yet say who killed either man but I intend to find out.'

Everyone round the table looked at him but he refused to expatiate.

The only other time that Edward was drawn out of his silence was when, after coffee was served and they had moved into the drawing-room, Lindemann and Watson-Watt got to talking about Bawdsey Manor of which, apparently, Watson-Watt was Superintendent.

'Before Bawdsey was taken over by the government,' Churchill said meditatively, 'it was owned by a charming fellow, Cuthbert

132

Quilter – a brother or cousin of the composer. It was a delightful place. But that's all in the past, I fear. It's a place of war now. Bring us up to date with what you're up to, Bob.'

Either they had no concept of security or a touching faith in the probity of their fellow guests for they held nothing back. Edward glanced at Churchill but he appeared unconcerned, sucking at his cigar and gulping his brandy. He was remembering happier days. Edward decided he might as well take advantage of the situation and learn something about Bawdsey. Major Ferguson would never tell him anything. Lindemann was being very critical of the Tizard Committee, the government's official advisory body on scientific matters. He had had an idea for aerial mines supported on parachutes and was angry that the government refused to set aside funds to develop and test the idea. It sounded a mad scheme to Edward but he told himself he was no expert.

'That's all very well, Bob,' Lindemann said, when Watson-Watt echoed Edward's doubts, 'but you've come up with a host of ideas – some of which have proved unworkable while others have been invaluable. You can't tell till you have done some basic research. I mean, who would have guessed that your "death ray" was not some wild fancy dreamed up by H.G. Wells?'

Edward caught a look on Sir Vida's face which, though he immediately controlled himself, was recognizable as avid interest and intense excitement. He thought that, despite his junior position among these distinguished men, he must alert them to the danger of talking freely about secret scientific work.

'Forgive me for saying so, Professor Lindemann, but ought you to discuss such experiments here? Might not one of us inadvertently drop some hint of what Mr Watson-Watt is working on when we are at some other dining table and thereby enlighten someone who ought not to be enlightened?'

'You are right to remind us of our responsibilities,' Churchill interjected, 'but I can personally vouch for everyone round this table. We can speak freely here. Please go on, Bob.'

Edward felt he had made his protest and could now listen to what Watson-Watt had to say with a clear conscience.

'It's nothing new. As long ago as 1922 Marconi proposed to detect ships by means of reflected radio waves. In 1931 the Signals Experimental Establishment at Woolwich invented a pulsed radio system on a wavelength of about 50 centimetres for detecting ships and the *Normandie* has a similar system for detecting icebergs.'

'But your experiments have gone much further than that?' Sir Vida urged.

'Indeed. Early in 1935 I used radio waves from one of the transmitters at Daventry in the 49 metre band to target a Heyford bomber flying at 10,000 feet. It was successful and I was then able to develop what we now call radiolocation. At Croydon Aerodrome I was able to detect an Imperial Airways aircraft using infra-red rays. However, the Tizard Committee would not believe there was anything in the idea and, despite Lindemann's encouragement, I wasn't at that time able to prove that infra-red could be viable.'

Watson-Watt broke off almost in mid-sentence as though suddenly recalling where he was – at a dinner table in a politician's flat, not in his laboratory.

'However, Lord Edward is right. It would be wrong of me to go into any great detail at this time. My experiments are proving most interesting and I hope to have something ready for the Tizard Committee by the end of the year. I can say no more.'

'But why not?' Lindemann demanded. 'There are no spies here.'

'I wasn't suggesting there were but we all need to be careful. There was a so-called journalist named Dr Hans Thost, the correspondent of the *Völkische Beobachter*, in the lab a few months ago. I found him examining my experiments. Damn cheek! Don't know how he got in.'

'What happened?' Edward asked.

'I spun him a cock-and-bull story about what I was working on and, when he was gone, reported him to the authorities. I am glad to say he was deported by the Home Office a few days later. I have no doubt there are many other spies masquerading as journalists and whatnot who have not yet been deported, so we owe it to ourselves to be careful about what we say.'

Edward was frustrated not to hear more from the scientist about his work but relieved that Watson-Watt had pulled himself up. He knew he might well be wronging Sir Vida but felt in his bones that the man was untrustworthy and even wondered if Churchill himself might not prove too talkative in his cups. He was certain Churchill would never knowingly betray any of the secrets with which he had been entrusted by men like Watson-Watt or Westmacott but both Major Ferguson and Vansittart had called him unpredictable and impetuous.

Edward made his excuses soon after and left the others to talk into the night. He had an early start the next morning – or rather, he saw, looking at his watch, *this* morning – and he was far from certain it would prove an easy journey.

When he got home Fenton was still up.

'A good dinner-party, my lord?' he inquired, as he relieved his master of his coat.

'Instructive, Fenton, certainly instructive. Each time I meet Mr Churchill, I find him more fascinating. I am inclined to think, despite his age and his record, that he may still have work to do.'

'That is most interesting, my lord.'

'Have you booked my flight?'

'Yes, my lord. You leave Croydon for Le Bourget at ten. Then you are booked on the Blue Train through to Marseilles. There you will have a plane waiting to take you over the border but I understand there is no guarantee of how near to Madrid you can get.'

'Very good. As efficient as ever, Fenton.'

'Will you want me to drive you to Croydon, my lord?'

'If you don't mind. I have no idea how or when I will return. I would like to be back in London in ten days but I will wire you when I know exactly what my plans are.'

10

In the morning Edward was still in an odd mood but his feverish anxiety had given way to a brand of fatalism which left him listless and unable to concentrate. It was a good thing Fenton was driving or he might never have reached Croydon Aerodrome. A few moments before they left the telephone had rung and Edward had almost not answered it, fearing it might be an order from Vansittart or Ferguson to delay his trip. It was fortunate that he had, however. It was Atkins from the *New Gazette*'s foreign desk.

'I am so relieved to have reached you before you left for Spain, Lord Edward. I feared I might be too late.'

'Well, you are not too late,' Edward said ungratefully, 'but I'll miss the plane if I don't go this minute so, if you have anything to tell me, get on with it.'

'Sorry, my lord,' Atkins said in confusion. 'I only wished to report that we had a wire from Miss Browne late last night. It appears she is now in Bilbao following up on some story. It was a very brief message. She said she was staying at a hotel called Torrontegui.' He spelt it out for him. 'No further details, I'm afraid, but no doubt you will find it if you decide to go there. But I should warn you, my lord, that our information is that Bilbao is under constant bombardment and that the port is mined so no ships can enter or leave. In other words, the city is besieged.'

'Thank you for your concern but I can look after myself.' He recognized he was being ungracious – after all, if Atkins had not bothered to telephone, he might have embarked on a long and dangerous wild-goose chase. 'I'm most grateful,' he managed, before putting down the receiver and joining Fenton in the Lagonda.

Each passenger was called by name and walked out of the terminal and across the grass to the waiting aircraft. The other fifteen passengers included a famous actress and a millionaire motorcar manufacturer. Wrapped in his own dark imaginings, Edward saw neither. There were no tarmac runways at the aerodrome and, as the plane bounced over the uneven turf, he wondered momentarily if he would reach France, let alone Spain. At least Bilbao was much nearer the French border than Madrid but how he was to get into the city, if it really was besieged, he had no idea. He closed his eyes. The main thing was that he was off. He was obeying this extraordinary compulsion to get to Verity and defend her against some unnamed, unknowable threat. It was mad. He knew it was something he could never explain, not even to Verity, but he also knew he would find no peace until he held her in his arms and – like doubting Thomas – felt for himself that she was safe. She lived in danger. Given her job, that was inevitable and he had long ago reconciled himself to it. So why could he not rid himself of the fear that she was in some *special* danger? It was an almost anamnestic experience – as though he had lived it all before. He grinned to himself, his eyes still closed, and the motorcar millionaire wondered idly of what girl this hawkish-looking Englishman was dreaming.

At Le Bourget he scrambled into a taxi and was taken to the British Embassy in the rue du Faubourg-Saint-Honoré. The ambassador was away but a competent attaché went over his papers and added two more letters designed to ease his passage over the French border into Spain. The young man from the embassy insisted on his eating and, since there was nothing to do until the Blue Train – the famous overnight train to the Spanish border – departed in four hours, they had a long, late luncheon at the Colisée on the Champs Elysées.

The Gare d'Orsay was all confusion and Edward was most grateful to have the attaché at his side to summon a blue-smocked porter and see him to the sleeping-car. To cries of '*En voiture s'il vous plaît*', they shook hands warmly and Edward sank back in his seat, thankful at last to be on his own. He glanced at his newspaper, *Paris Soir*, but tossed it aside almost at once and stared out of the window at the last-minute hubbub of parents parting from children, husbands from wives, and lovers weeping in each other's arms. Finally, just when it seemed to him that his journey would never begin, with a whistle and a hiss of steam the great train pulled out of the station.

A moment later an attentive steward knocked on the door of the compartment to ask whether he would be dining in the dining-car or preferred to eat something where he was. The steward fussed around him showing him how to work the lights and checking he had everything he needed. In another mood – with Verity beside him, perhaps – the palaver would have amused him. He enjoyed being pampered, but now he became irritated and the steward hastily retreated. Fenton had put a book in his bag – *Our Mutual Friend* – but after a few pages he gave up Dickens in favour of watching the little stations flash by with their advertisements for Michelin, Dubonnet, Gitanes and Gauloises. The inspector, smart in his blue uniform and peaked cap, demanded '*Votre billet s'il vous plaît*' and was impressed by the English milord with his perfect French, smoking Turkish cigarettes and seemingly deep in thought.

Edward remained in a dream until they reached the Spanish border. At dinner, he failed to notice that the self-proclaimed Russian princess, dispossessed by the Bolsheviks, so she said, was propositioning him. Dismayed that her allure had failed to fascinate this aristocratic Englishman, she comforted herself with the thought that he was probably *un voluptueux* and, like most of his class, a follower of *le vice anglais*. Even when, in desperation, she spilt wine on him, he had merely favoured her with a slight bow and returned to his compartment. He slept well enough but awoke before the steward called him and was ready to disembark as soon as the train whistled itself to a halt at Hendaye.

It was then that his problems began. The border was closed and, despite waving his passport in front of several senior officials, he was told there was no possibility of his crossing. He was recommended to pass the time on the beautiful beaches and wait, but for what no one could tell him. The delay maddened him and made him ready for any effort, however desperate.

He went into town, found a disreputable-looking garage, and bribed the owner to show him another way to cross into Spain. Some miles inland, there was, apparently, a frontier post called Dancharia. Little more than a village, the local farmers were permitted to use it to take their produce into Spain. He bought a motorcycle from the garage owner and, with the aid of an inadequate map, found his way to Dancharia. He had a beer in a small café close to the border crossing and watched the world go by. It was a peaceful sight – local peasant farmers dressed, he imagined, much as their grandfathers and great-grandfathers before them, in smocks with pattens on their feet, drove their animals through the centre of town towards the frontier. Everyone knew everyone and the farmers were waved through with the minimum of documentation. There was a no-man's land of a few yards and then the Spanish frontier. Again, there seemed to be very little delay in passing the barrier – a brief look at papers and then the single beam which barred the road was raised by a bored offical.

Edward contemplated just walking over the frontier. After all, he had his passport and his documentation was in order. However, his instinct told him that, whereas a local farmer bringing much-needed food would not be turned away, an Englishman with no obvious reason for being in Spain might well be hauled in for questioning or even arrested as a spy. He could not risk it. With his heart in his mouth, he walked back to his motorbike, rode it to within a hundred yards of the frontier, waited until the barriers were up on both sides of the frontier to let through a farm wagon, revved up the engine and sped through, ignoring the shouts of protest from the guards.

As he accelerated hard up empty roads into the Pyrenees, he threw back his head and let out a scream of pleasure at being relieved from intolerable frustration. Several miles further on he halted, suddenly aware of the danger he was in. He had a sketchy map of the area and enough petrol to take him between fifty and a hundred miles, depending on the speed he chose to go. He was far from certain which of the warring parties controlled the area but he reckoned that, if he were stopped by either side, he might be sent back over the frontier or, more likely, shot as a spy regardless of the papers he carried. His only hope was to reach Bilbao by nightfall and claim the protection of the British Consul who could regularize his position in the country.

He suddenly felt inordinately hungry and thirsty. He cursed himself for being in so much of a dream that he had not thought to bring with him some of the food which had been thrust on him on the train and so contemptuously spurned. And those elegant blue bottles of water in his compartment – how idiotic not to have put two or three in his bag. He laid his bike on the grass and walked up to the top of a knoll and looked about him. He saw first a creek and, beyond that, a rough stone hovel which he presumed must be some sort of peasant farm. Crouching low over the broken ground to avoid being seen, he reached the creek and slaked his thirst. It was then that he heard the dogs. He stood up and looked down toward the hovel. What he saw had him staring about him wild-eyed.There were at least six of the brutes, as big as Alsatians but of indeterminate breed. Their tongues lolled out of their mouths and, as they loped towards him, Edward realized there was only one thing to do and that was run.

Their presence should not have been a surprise to him. The Spanish peasant had to defend his little flock of sheep from predators more dangerous than the wolves which still occasionally left their lairs in the mountains to raid the sheepfolds. His real enemy was any stranger, whatever his politics. Politics meant nothing to him. A stranger would be looking for food, most likely with a weapon in his hand. These half-starved dogs were his defence. Edward considered, just for a second, stopping to explain who he was and that he had gold to pay for what he wanted. Then it came to him that his Spanish was not good enough and, anyway, the peasant might very well speak only Basque of which he knew not a word. He might be badly bitten before he could convince the dogs' owner that he was not a marauder. An undignified run to the motorcycle was the only alternative. He reached it at the same time as the dogs. Kicking them away, he struggled to start the engine, cursing as a piece of Savile Row tweed was ripped by the yellow teeth of the largest of the animals. He gave a cry of relief as the engine started and he sped off, pursued by wild barking. It was borne in on him that Spain was no longer a country which welcomed tourists.

Ravenously hungry, weary beyond anything he had ever imagined, dishevelled and covered in oil – and worse – but happier than he had been in months, Edward rode into Bilbao at seven that evening and asked the way to the Torrontegui Hotel. The city was quiet but everywhere he looked there were ruined buildings and bomb craters. Bilbao, capital of the Basque region, was, as Atkins had warned him, under siege. The Basque nationalists had supported the Republic from the beginning of the war because it had promised them an independent Basque country. In their hearts they now knew the Republicans would be defeated but they fought on with dogged determination, understanding full well that under General Franco they would be mercilessly repressed. General Mola, whom Franco had charged with subduing the Basque region, had reduced the area round Bilbao to a desert and the city itself to something resembling a last redoubt. Without being aware of it, Edward had had amazing luck. He had found a way into the city when anyone in Bilbao would have told him there was none. He had taken minor roads, often little more than mountain paths, avoiding road blocks and patrols, which had brought him safely through the encircling army.

Bilbao was hungry but no longer starving. Mola's fleet in the Bay of Biscay had threatened to sink any ship bringing supplies but, just a few days before Edward's arrival, English ships had broken through with food and humanitarian aid – an 'interference' in Spain's civil war which Franco's sympathizers in Britain had been quick to condemn. However, the Basques had no air force to speak of so there was nothing to prevent the daily bombing of the city. Once again Verity was in the front line. When Bilbao fell, journalists supporting the Basque cause could expect no favours.

When Edward stumbled into the lobby, he was immediately surrounded by about a dozen journalists who had made the hotel their headquarters. With a great effort he asked for Verity. She was upstairs and someone was sent to fetch her. While he waited, patient in his exhaustion, he drank the Spanish brandy and soda he was offered and the ache in his limbs began to ease.

'Edward, is that really you?' The voice was unmistakably hers. He turned to see Verity standing at the top of the stairs, one hand on the banister.

He looked up at her with a pleasure indistinguishable from pain and stumbled over to the foot of the stairs. 'Yes, it's me. I'm afraid I . . .'

He got no further. Light as a bird, she hopped into his arms, indifferent to the watching journalists. He held her close enough to hurt her but she did not complain and, when they kissed, did not seem to notice that he smelt of sweat and dirt. When at last he let her go, she asked gently, 'Why are you here, Edward? I mean, it's wonderful that you are but is there something wrong at home or . . . ?'

'It's such a relief to see you, V. I know you must think I'm mad and perhaps I am mad but for the last few days I haven't been able to think straight. I've had this awful feeling that you were in danger and, now I'm here, I see that you are. I've got to get you out of here.'

'I can't possibly leave now,' Verity said, scandalized, 'and, anyway, I couldn't. I can't think how you got in. When I came back here I had to pull every string I could think of to cross the border and I'm an accredited journalist. The only way out now is by sea and that's dangerous. They say the harbour's mined. In any case, if you think I would desert my friends now . . . Someone has to be here to report what is happening.'

'But does it have to be you?'

'Silly! Of course it does. I don't mean that – if I wasn't here – someone else might not get the story but, you see, I *am* here. It's as simple as that.'

Edward was too hungry and tired to protest further. 'Is there anywhere we could get something to eat? I can't talk until I have eaten.'

'My poor lamb! Despite everything, there are still some restaurants open. We'll go to the Excelsior. I'm due to meet Bandi and Gerda there in any case.'

She shooed away the others who wanted Edward's 'story' and took him up to her room to wash. And there on the narrow bed, despite his hunger and fatigue, he made love to the girl he now knew he needed whatever the cost.

Bilbao was not Madrid with its sophisticated café life. It was a manufacturing city and its concerns were serious: money, not pleasure, but the siege had left it weakened and gloomy. However, as is always the way, the poor might be on half rations but the rich – and this included the foreign journalists – could still eat well. Edward assuaged his hunger with a highly seasoned pork stew washed down with a rough local wine which made his head swim.

He told Verity of his mad journey, his eagerness to see her and be assured she was well and of the excuse he had come up with – finding James Lyall.

'He's not here. I don't know where he is. He's probably in Madrid.'

'Why did you leave Madrid? I'm glad you did, of course. I

might never have got there and, anyway, I suppose one has more chance of being killed there than here.'

Verity raised her eyebrows. 'You think so? You wait until tomorrow. The morning bombing raids are . . . well, you'll see.'

'Mola has a strong air force then?'

'It's not under Mola's command,' she said bitterly.

'I don't understand.'

'They're German planes – the Condor Legion to be precise.'

'German planes flown by German pilots?'

'Yes. No one will ever admit it, of course. One theory is that Hitler told Franco he would like to try out some of his weaponry before the real war starts.'

Edward was very tired and his brain was fuddled by wine but he tried to think. 'How do you know they're German?'

'We can see the markings on the planes as they fly over. There's almost no anti-aircraft fire from the city so they can fly as low as they like.'

'But you don't know they are flown by Luftwaffe pilots.'

Verity leaned towards him confidentially. 'You asked why we came here. We were sent. David Griffiths-Jones got information from a spy in Franco's headquarters that they are going to try something special here – to show how near they are to winning. We don't quite know what but David wanted witnesses.'

Edward wiped the sweat from his forehead. 'I'm too tired to follow all this. What sort of thing have you been sent to witness?'

'A major attack on Bilbao, I guess.'

'Oh God! I wish I could take you back to England. You oughtn't to be here. It's too dangerous.'

'Dope! That's why I wanted to come. No one cares about the war any more in England. I need a scoop to wake people up to what's going on here. Sitting in the Hotel Florida in Madrid, talking and drinking with Belasco and Sefton Delmer – you know him? He's my rival at the *Daily Express* – that wasn't good enough. I mean, there were some good moments. I remember once, when Sefton forgot the blackout and hadn't drawn his curtains, the police fired through the window as a warning. You should have seen Sefton's face when the mirror behind him broke and he realized he had missed death by a hair's breadth.'

Edward wanted above anything to sleep but had not the energy to get up and walk out of the restaurant. At ten o'clock –

143

the time most Spanish considered eating dinner – the restaurant began to fill up. Gerda and André arrived having obviously quarrelled. Gerda expressed her amazement at finding Edward there. Kavan did not trouble to hide his indifference and made nasty little jokes about Edward's appearance, which was certainly bizarre. He had cleaned up in Verity's room but the clothes he was wearing were still the torn, dirty trousers and shirt in which he had ridden into Bilbao. Matters were made worse by Gerda's delight in hearing from Verity – Edward was almost asleep – how he had broken through the frontier on his motorbike. She stroked his forehead and murmured endearments to rile Kavan the more.

At last they staggered back to the hotel – all of them the worse for wear. It was natural that, with death an ever-present reality, those who watched and waited should drink too much but Edward, through his fatigue, was aware that Verity was very nearly drunk. He thought that on another occasion he would reprimand her. He hung on to Gerda with one hand and Verity held his other arm. Kavan followed, muttering to himself. Edward was provided with a room at the Torrontegui – apart from journalists, and there were not many of these, the hotel was empty – but he found himself in Verity's bed and the last thing he remembered thinking before sleep finally overcame him was that she smelt of sweat and wine and it was the scent of paradise.

Edward woke the following morning to the 'crump' of bombs falling quite close by. It was not a sound he had ever heard before but it was unmistakable. He tumbled out of bed just as Verity came into the room fully dressed, excited and bright-eyed, as though she had been given a present.

'The manager says we ought to go down to the basement but I'm going on the roof. Are you coming?'

Edward still ached in every limb and his head hurt but he could not say anything other than that he would join her as soon as he had washed and dressed.

'No time for that! It'll be over in a few minutes and you will have missed all the fun – not fun, I don't mean that, but . . . oh, get a move on, do.'

144

From the roof, Edward could see huge plumes of smoke rise above the city and people running around the streets in panic looking for shelter. He noticed inconsequentially that it was going to be a lovely day. There was no wind and the sun was rising in a cloudless sky. The crushing superiority of the enemy's air power was manifest. An occasional pop-pop from an anti-aircraft gun somewhere behind them was all the defence the city could muster and it was treated with justified contempt by the pilots racing through the sky above their heads. One plane flew low over the hotel roof and Edward and Verity instinctively ducked.

'That wasn't a German plane. That was Italian,' Edward shouted.

'It's the so-called Italian Legionary Air Force. Mussolini's trying to prove he's just as great a murderer as Hitler,' Verity shouted back. The sound of the screaming engine and the feeling that a bomb was just about to blow them heavenwards was terrifying but Edward was damned if he were going to show his fear with Verity hopping about, notebook in hand, as unconcerned as if she were reporting on a deb dance in Eaton Square. 'They are based in Burgos and give the Condor Legion support, not that they need it. They fly Savoia Marchetti 79s and 81s. I'm getting quite good at aircraft recognition,' she informed him as the noise of explosions all around them increased.

Edward looked up to see another aircraft hurtling towards them. He could actually see the face of the pilot in the cockpit and noticed, quite dispassionately, that he was smiling. He threw himself down on the roof, grabbing Verity in a rugby tackle as he did so. Machine-gun bullets whistled over their heads and, as Edward pointed out later, he had not even had his breakfast.

The Basque militiamen, known as *gudaris*, could do nothing but fire their ancient rifles at the swooping planes and shake their fists. It was pitiable and Edward wondered why General Mola did not enter the city immediately and end this charade.

As suddenly as the raid had begun, it ended. The bombers departed to refuel and replace their bombs. The silence was almost deafening, broken only by the cries of the wounded in the street below and the crash of collapsing buildings. Clouds of black smoke, stinking of dust, death and the depredations of the enemy in the air, rose lazily all about them. Edward dressed hurriedly, grabbed a cup of watery coffee and went into the streets to find Verity. She had not waited for him nor even washed the black marks off her face or put a plaster on her knee, scraped when Edward brought her down on the roof. She had not gone far, however. The road outside the hotel was partly blocked with rubble from a fallen building and he thought it was a miracle the hotel itself was still standing. She laughed when she saw him. He had left his bag somewhere – probably at Hendaye – and all he had to wear was the pair of filthy trousers he had almost destroyed the previous day. He had at least been able to borrow a shirt from the hotel manager to replace the dirty rag which had once been one of Jermyn Street's finest.

'They're all I have,' he said apologetically.

'What price Savile Row?' she quipped. 'I wish your tailor could see you now! Don't worry, Bandi's about your size and I'm sure he'll lend you something until you can loot a clothes store.'

Edward was not sure Kavan would be so accommodating but said nothing. He looked at Verity and was amused to see that she was wearing some of the fruits of her shopping spree in London. She had never been poor – her father gave her a generous allowance – but had spent little on clothes until she had made some money from her book on Spain. She had then become a client of the famous designer Schiaparelli. She was now wearing one of her creations – trousers and a wool-jersey top fastened with a zip which Schiaparelli had designed especially for her. It was, Verity told him, warm but light and she said she even slept in it when she had rough lodgings. From her neck flowed a chiffon scarf she had bought in Harvey Nichols and perched on her head a black beret with a golden arrow pin on the front – Schiaparelli's again, he thought. She looked wonderful and he was delighted that, even on the front line, she liked to look chic.

They soon came across Gerda and Kavan who were photographing in the ruins.

'What's happened here?' he asked Gerda. The bodies of three women and two children were lying beside the road.

'They were machine-gunned by one of those cursed Italians as they ran for cover,' she said curtly.

The air was full of dust and Edward found himself coughing and choking. They came to a makeshift field hospital and saw twenty or more men and women lying on stretchers waiting to be taken to the city's main hospital. An exhausted nurse watched apathetically as Gerda and Kavan took photographs.

'There's very little point taking them to hospital,' Verity said shortly. 'They have no drugs and not much else. I was there yesterday and saw them treating wounds with peroxide. I'll never smell ether again without thinking of that place.'

As the day wore on Edward became more and more uneasy. Why had he come here? Was he just a voyeur – an unwilling witness to other people's misery? He wasn't a journalist. Verity did not need him and all his premonitions of danger seemed ridiculous. He decided that, to justify his journey to Spain, he *must* find James Lyall. If that meant he had to go to Madrid, that is what he would endeavour to do, however difficult.

In a more than usually sombre mood Verity, Gerda, Kavan and several other journalists sat that afternoon in the hotel discussing the situation. It was self-evident that Bilbao would soon fall to Mola. Thanks to the daring of the English ships, the city was no longer in danger of starving. Food was not plentiful but there was enough. On the other hand, with no navy or air force of its own and with only a few antiquated weapons which were no match for the well-equipped army poised for the assault, it did not take a military strategist to see the game was up.

'I doubt the Basques can hold out for a month,' opined the man from *The Times*, George Steer.

'Should we get out now while we can?' the man from *Ce Soir* asked nervously. 'I don't fancy Mola's men will take many prisoners or bother to examine our letters of accreditation. I've been talking to Captain Roberts. He says the *Seven Seas Spray* will take us off but the English ships will not stay for ever.'

The *Seven Seas Spray* was a small merchantman, the first ship boldly to ignore the warning that the entrance to the harbour was mined, which had brought aid – though not arms – to the besieged city. Captain Roberts encountered no opposition and no mines, docking to cries of *Vivan los marineros ingleses!* and *Viva la libertad!* Roberts's daring was all the more remarkable given that he had his wife and daughter on board.

'It is too early to despair.' The voice was very familiar to both Verity and Edward but the last one they had expected to hear. It was that of David Griffiths-Jones who appeared like a genie from a bottle and with none of the signs Edward had displayed like medals of having made a difficult and dangerous journey. His arrival energized the company and even Edward was encouraged. They were not after all a forgotten outpost. David kissed Verity and Gerda and shook hands with Edward. 'What are you doing here, old boy?' he asked. 'If it is to report the death of the Republic, your trip is premature.'

'I am happy to hear it! But how come you are in Bilbao?'

'I have been sent to assess the situation and report back,' David said easily. 'Only a flying visit but necessary to judge by what I heard as I came in.' He settled himself down among the journalists to raise their morale. Making light of the threat from Mola, he promised that fighters from the Soviet Union would soon be chasing the Heinkels and Dorniers from the sky above them.

'And Mola,' he continued, 'is facing serious mutinies in his ranks. There are many Basques among his troops and they will not long tolerate this war against their own people.'

Edward was impressed. He did not like David, partly because of his skill as a propagandist which he was at this moment exhibiting, but he could not deny his courage and devotion to the cause. He just wished the cause had been more worthwhile. David's unquestioning faith in Soviet Communism, regardless of the price other people had to pay, was obnoxious but it was also admirable in its way. For him, Comrade Stalin was the answer to everything – a Messiah figure whose judgements, inexplicable, contradictory or perverse as they might seem to an outsider, were to him divine revelations to be obeyed without question. Edward sat back and admired the way he raised the spirits of those clustered round him like children seeking reassurance. He was an accomplished speaker and, without raising his voice or using oratorical flourishes, he changed the mood of the journalists in just a few minutes from defeatism to optimism.

Of one thing Edward was certain: if the Basques threw off the Nationalists and the Republic was victorious, Comrade Stalin would never permit a free, independent Basque state. It was this cynical use of men and women with ideals they associated with the Republican cause which Edward found so abhorrent. Griffiths-Jones was just another liar and con man in a world which bred them like flies. Whatever he said, Mola would take Bilbao. The Soviet pilots would never arrive to chase the Dorniers from the skies and many hundreds of Basques would die for a cause which was already lost. The pre-war Spanish Republic was gone for ever. Though Verity would never admit it, the choice now lay between two tyrannies, each as bad as the other.

By dinner that evening everyone, except Edward, felt happier and there was no more talk of getting aboard an English ship and leaving Bilbao to its fate. David explained that the following day he was going on a lightning tour of the city's defences and anyone who wished to accompany him would be welcome. Afterwards he took Verity aside and spoke to her earnestly – giving her instructions, Edward imagined uncharitably but, as it turned out, accurately.

When she returned, her eyes were burning bright and she took Edward's hand in hers.

'David has given me the chance of an exclusive story – a real scoop – what I've dreamed of. Some of us are going to Guernica. It's only about an hour's drive from here. David says he has had news from his spy in Mola's camp that the Condor Legion are going to attack the town and we should be able to get incontrovertible proof that, despite their denials, the Nazis are directly involved in the war. Gerda and Bandi are coming too, to take photographs, and then we will rush back here. David is going to lay on a plane or a fast boat to take our reports and photographs back to London.'

Immediately, the anxiety which had driven Edward to come to Spain and which had left him as soon as he reached Bilbao, seized him once again in an iron corset and left him breathless. He struggled to find words.

'Good God! Why would they attack Guernica? I thought it was a tourist town.'

'Yes, it's the historic capital of the Basque country. David says they're going to destroy it because it's a symbol of Basque independence.'

'But that's . . . that's vandalism. Has he sent the town a warning so they can evacuate civilians?'

'I expect so,' Verity said breezily, 'but don't you see what a terrific propaganda coup it will be for us if the Germans are seen to be attacking a defenceless town with no military value?'

'Oh, Verity! It's "us"' is it, now? You seem to have given up any idea of objective reporting. A propaganda coup! You're talking about human beings who may . . . who *will* be killed unless they are warned.'

'How dare you say that to me, Edward. I have never pretended my sympathies are anywhere other than with the Republicans. I am a Communist and proud to be fighting Fascism. Is it my fault that people would prefer to read in newspapers about Mrs Simpson and all that shit instead of "sentimental stuff about refugees" – as the editor called it when I was last in the office? I'm sure he suppresses my stuff and, if it wasn't for Joe Weaver, nothing of mine would be published. I *am* objective in what I report – I tell the truth. I have no need to exaggerate or embellish but Fleet Street is so reactionary that not much gets through. Steer says it is the same at *The Times* because Dawson is terrified of hurting Hitler's feelings. Bandi says *Life* is just as bad. Thank God for the *Daily Worker*. You know what slogan Weaver has fixed to the *Gazette*'s masthead: "There will be no war". It's a promise he'll live to regret. So don't preach to me about prejudice.'

Edward was shocked at her language and the force with which she spoke of her beliefs. For a second he hated her and everything she stood for and was only prevented from saying so by Griffiths-Jones appearing.

'Edward wants to know if Guernica has been warned about the attack?' Verity still sounded angry and refused to look at Edward.

'Of course!' Griffiths-Jones said calmly, putting a hand on Verity's shoulder, as if to calm her, and giving Edward a look of cool distaste. 'The mayor knows and he will take the necessary precautions. By the way, Corinth, Verity says you are looking for the English boy – what's his name? – James Lyall. I thought you might be interested to know that he is with the militia in Guernica.'

'In Guernica? Why there? I thought he was in Madrid.'

'I'm afraid he was a bit rattled. Madrid's not a very healthy place to be at the moment so we thought we might send him somewhere less dangerous. A rest from the heat of battle, you understand.'

'But you've just said the town is going to be bombed!'

'That's new information. We didn't know anything about that when we sent him. Guernica's of no value strategically.'

'But now he's in the firing line,' Edward said bitterly.

'He'll have had warning,' David said comfortably. 'He'll have plenty of time to take cover. I think then,' he added meditatively, 'we'll ship him back to England. He's not of much use to us now, I'm afraid. His nerve's shattered.'

Edward had an almost overwhelming desire to punch him in the face. It was all very well for David to talk so easily of bombing raids and warnings but he had no reason to trust him and he feared they were being led into an ambush.

Later, when they were all calmer, he tried to talk to Verity about his fears but she refused to listen, only saying that if he did not want to come he was welcome to stay behind.

'This is a great chance for me, Edward, you must see that. I need this story and nothing you can say will stop me getting it.'

He knew he was defeated and spent half an hour writing a letter to Major Ferguson and another to Lord Weaver at the *New Gazette* describing the situation in Bilbao and David Griffiths-Jones's invitation to Verity to see Guernica attacked. He felt better when he had signed and sealed his letters and given them to the hotel porter to be delivered to the British Consulate. If they were going to die – and it seemed a distinct possibility – he wanted two people he trusted to know who was responsible. An hour later, Griffiths-Jones was reading the letters in his bedroom, smiling grimly as he did so. When he had finished, he tore them into small pieces and burnt them in the grate.

They reached Guernica about three the following day. The town lay about five miles from the sea, near the Mundaca Estuary on the Bay of Biscay. Twenty miles of rough country separated it and Bilbao and the four of them – Gerda, Kavan, Edward and Verity – arrived thoroughly shaken up, their throats dry from the dust of the road. Their driver, a Basque chosen by Griffiths-Jones, Edward thought, because he spoke not a word of English and not much Spanish, smiled broadly as he indicated that they had reached their destination.

Largely constructed of wood, the houses looked much as they had a hundred years before. It was market day, as it was every Monday, and the place was bustling with people and animals. They got out of the car, stretched cramped limbs and took deep breaths of warm, fresh air. They started to stroll around, enjoying the sun and the *normality* of the scene. At a bar, Kavan ordered beer and for a moment they felt like tourists. The only sign there was a war on was that there were fewer men in the market than there once might have been and small groups of militiamen stood on street corners smoking and talking.

Gerda and Kavan started taking photographs and Verity wandered off to see if she could find someone who understood her Spanish. Edward was not happy. It was unnerving to see children tormenting a lame dog, a woman seated on a wooden box in the shade of a tree selling eggs, an old man guiding a flock of sheep into the marketplace, seemingly unaware that war raged not twenty miles away. It was quite evident that this was not a town which was anticipating attack and he prayed that Griffiths-Jones's information was incorrect. How could this peaceful little town be a military target? Nevertheless, Edward knew from bitter experience that Griffiths-Jones was a storm petrel, a bird of ill-omen. Wherever he went, his companions were always the same: death and destruction.

Edward went loping off in search of someone in authority. He found the town hall without difficulty but it was empty. An old woman was cleaning the mayor's office but she spoke only Basque and Edward was unable to make himself understood when he asked where everybody was. Was it possible that the mayor *had* received notice of an attack and had chosen to leave without warning his fellow citizens of the danger? It was unthinkable. He was probably on official business somewhere in the marketplace.

He walked back to the car, angry and frustrated. He wished now that he had insisted on a driver who could interpret for them but somehow there had not been time to insist on anything. Had he tried to do so, he might well have been left behind. As David had pointed out, he wasn't a journalist, just a sightseer. Like any other tourist, he received good-natured smiles and stares from the locals but could find no one who could understand his primitive Spanish. At last he thought to ask some militia for *el muchaco inglés*, the English boy. He found one youth more intelligent than his fellows who seemed to understand. Edward produced a small coin and in sign language asked to be taken to him. They set off together and reached the gardens of the Casa de Juntas, the building in which the Basque archives were housed and where the ancient parliament used to sit. The gardens contained two oak trees sacred to Basque liberty, one no more than a blackened stump said to be three hundred – some said six hundred – years old. Beside it stood the second tree, impressive in bulk and very much alive, belying its great age.

Edward was beginning to feel that he was in one of those nightmares where, bursting with news of vital importance, he could not even open his mouth – a dream from which he could not rouse himself. It was with considerable relief that he saw, sitting on a bench in the gardens, the unmistakable figure of James Lyall. He was half asleep, loosely cradling an ancient-looking rifle to his chest. It suddenly occurred to Edward that he had no idea what he was going to say to the boy. It was out of the question to blurt out that his father was dead. First, he had to explain what he was doing in Guernica and make him aware of the danger they were in.

'James, it's me, Edward Corinth. Do you remember me?' he stammered.

The boy looked at him in amazement, hardly believing his eyes which he rubbed like a child waking from a deep sleep. 'Lord Edward? What are you doing here? Is there something wrong?'

This gave Edward his cue. 'There is something wrong, yes. I am here with Verity Browne and she has had information . . . secret information . . . that Guernica is going to be bombed. It may be the mayor has already had the news but I thought . . . we thought we ought to be sure . . .' It seemed impossible to explain the situation. 'I mean, the people ought not to be having their market. They should be taking shelter.'

'I'm so sorry, Lord Edward, but I have no idea what you are talking about. Why should anyone bomb Guernica? There are no troops here unless you count the barracks outside town. There's the Astra gun factory but that's miles away. That's why Mr Griffiths-Jones – David – sent me here, because it's safe. I think there has been some mistake.'

'There's no mistake.' He took James by the arm. 'I'm deadly serious. The mayor – where is the mayor? You must take me to him.'

'I don't know where he is. I don't think he is in town. Look, why don't we go and talk to my captain about it?'

'But I can't speak Basque.'

'He speaks Spanish. He's from Madrid and my Spanish is very good now.'

'Where is he based?'

'We're billeted in the Augustine convent on the Bermeo road. It's about twenty minutes away.'

'Oh God, I don't know if there's time,' Edward said, rubbing his forehead with his sweating hands.

By now James had been infected by Edward's anxiety and his languor vanished. 'Well then, we must go to the marketplace and order people to take cover. Mind you,' he added ruefully, 'we're going to look pretty silly if nothing happens.'

'I'll risk that,' Edward replied grimly. 'Do you know enough Basque to make yourself understood?'

'I think so . . . I hope so.'

When they got to the marketplace, James started shouting and ordering people around but no one took much notice. They looked at the English boy and smiled as if to say: we know the English are mad and this proves it. Edward also started shouting and this seemed to add to the confusion. He got entangled in a flock of sheep which caused considerable amusement.

Verity arrived with Gerda and André who seemed to be photographing everything they saw.

'What on earth are you up to?' Verity inquired. 'You're making a spectacle of yourself.'

'But don't you see? We have to warn them.'

'Warn them?'

'Of what's coming.'

'But we don't know what's coming.'

'But I thought David said . . .'

'It was vague. Maybe he was wrong. There are so many rumours and counter-rumours. We can't do anything about it without making fools of ourselves.'

'There are worse things!' Edward said angrily. 'Verity, we have to do something! I have this feeling in my bones. There's going to be a disaster here and we have to warn people.' He waved his hand at the crowds pushing past them.

Her attention was caught by a shadow which, for a second, darkened the sun. She looked up into the cloudless sky, shading her eyes with the palm of her hand. 'What's that? Is it a bird or is it . . . ?'

Other people looked up as they heard the droning sound of an aeroplane above the lowing of cattle and the bleating of sheep. A single aeroplane grew in size and seemed to fill the sky. It was flying low over the town so that it was almost possible to see the pilot's face, masked by a leather helmet and goggles. The busy marketplace went quiet. Everyone stared into the blue sky, curious, nudging neigbours, gesticulating, uncertain of what they were seeing. There was still no alarm. They had not seen many aeroplanes and they supposed this was one of their Russian allies. Some children even raised a ragged cheer. Then, as it grew nearer, it was possible to see the wing markings. It was not a Russian plane but a Heinkel 111.

The church bell rang out in clamorous warning and its urgent jangling seemed to wake the town to its danger. People began to run in all directions. Mothers grabbed their children and dogs started barking as the sheep took fright and milled about. There were shallow dugouts at one end of the marketplace and some cowered there while others ran to take refuge in the cellars of their houses. Then the aeroplane was gone and those who had taken shelter got to their feet feeling rather foolish. But then, as they once more looked up into the sky, straining their eyes against the sun, they saw the Heinkel turn to make another run over the town. Reassured that he had met no flak or anti-aircraft fire, the pilot decided he had nothing to fear.

Like some terrible excreting bird, Edward saw six bombs fall lazily away from the open bomb hatch. They fell on the railway station and the square in front of it, sending huge fountains of earth into the sky. Flames from incendiaries dropped with the bombs set the station alight and the houses around it.

'The swine,' James cried and began to rush towards the station with other militiamen.

Edward turned from staring at the Heinkel to see Verity and Gerda also running towards the station. André had vanished.

'Wait, Verity,' he shouted. 'I'm not sure . . . there may be more planes.' But he, too, was drawn towards the carnage. As he turned the corner, he saw a dreadful sight: burnt and mangled bodies, some still with suitcases in their hands. A child lay with his mother, hand in hand, killed by the blast as they had run in fruitless search of shelter. He stood staring, unable to take it all in. It was these first images of death and destruction which were to stay in his memory more vividly than many of the more terrible sights he was to behold in the hours that followed.

From out of the sky there came the noise of another engine and a second aircraft appeared. Its target appeared to be the centre of the town and its bombs set alight every house in the area. Wildly, the militia began to run back to the marketplace where they were faced with the sight of sheep roasted by flames, stinking of death. The market stalls were also ablaze. In less than a minute, this second Heinkel had transformed the most peaceful of scenes into an inferno.

In the tumult, Edward found himself separated from Verity and the others. The cellars of their houses, to which many people had run for shelter, offered only an illusion of safety. As the burning houses collapsed, the timbers trapped those who had taken shelter beneath them. Screams from a house close to where he was standing drew Edward's attention away from the horror in front of him. Here was something he could do and his mind, dazed by the sudden assault, was calm again. He joined several militiamen as they attempted to remove a burning beam which had completely blocked the door behind which a woman and several children were trapped. They had nothing but their bare hands to work with and Edward felt his palms blister as he tugged at the beam to no avail. Then, a man arrived with a rope which was looped round the burning beam. Straining every muscle and choking on the dust, their faces covered in sweat because the heat was increasing with every moment which passed, they heaved. At first nothing happened but, after one final effort, the beam moved a few feet to one side leaving a gap wide enough for a child to squeeze through. A little girl came tumbling out, screaming with fear and pain, her hair alight. Someone caught her and stifled the flames in a blanket. Edward watched in horror as, behind her, the whole building lurched and fell in upon itself. He had to leap back as the flames billowed towards him. The face of the woman still inside was momentarily visible in the hellish light of the flames and then disappeared.

He turned towards another house whose roof was burning. A woman standing at a first-floor window shouted at Edward. She had a bundle in her arms and he realized it must be her baby. He held out his hands and the woman threw it at him. He caught it and a strong wave of love for this unknown child washed away his fear. Feeling the warm bundle safe in his arms, he remembered a famous catch he had made long ago at the annual Eton and Harrow match at Lords. It had won Eton the match. He had once thought that nothing in his life could ever be sweeter than that moment. A shout reminded him that there was still the mother to be rescued. He placed the baby gently on the ground and stood to catch the woman. She was quite light and he had no difficulty breaking her fall. As he held her in his arms, she put her hands around his head and kissed him. Then she scooped up her baby and left him.

He turned to see where else he could help and then remembered Verity. Once again, the cold fear which had brought him to Spain gripped his heart. He began running – not knowing where he ran – shouting her name. He stopped himself angrily. Running about like a demented chicken was not going to help. There was no point shouting her name. The noise of burning buildings, the drone of aircraft and the crump of bombs made it impossible to hear anyone call unless they were right next to you. He must think. Where had he last seen her? He decided she would be where the fire was fiercest so he went back to the marketplace and stood – uncaring of the target he made – looking around him. Just when he was giving way to despair, he saw first Gerda and then Verity. He could not see André. The two women were standing beside a dugout and, when Edward came up beside them, he saw that they were staring at a pile of bodies lying higgledy-piggledy in the shallow pit. Several women who had taken shelter there had been strafed by machine-gun fire and their clothes were torn and bloodied. Gerda was taking photographs. Verity was rigid, unconscious of the tears which flowed down her sooty cheeks. Seeing Edward, she turned to him, her eyes blazing with anger.

'The bastards! This isn't war. It's murder. How could they do this? I won't rest until I have told this story to the world. These are criminals – not Spanish, thank God! – at least not that! They were all German. I saw the swastikas on their wings. Whatever they say – and I know they will lie and lie and lie – the men who did this to defenceless women and children were German. The Luftwaffe,' she said with scorn, 'trying out their weapons on innocent women and children.'

157

Amid the turmoil, Edward saw the figure of James Lyall limp towards them.

'I think they're gone,' he gasped, coughing in the smoke that swirled about them.

He spoke too soon. They could not see it but they could hear it – another plane – a fighter. It roared over their heads, its machine-guns blazing. They all ducked, pointless though this was, and Edward saw a scatter of lights as the bullets raced like a burning fuse towards a group of militiamen huddled behind a stone drinking trough. One of the men did not move quickly enough and was thrown backward by the bullets which tore apart his head and chest. With a cry, Verity began to run across the square followed by Gerda, trying to ready her camera as she ran. Then Edward heard the drone of yet another plane. 'Come back!' he screamed but no one could have heard him. Once again he watched the tracery of light – so beautiful and yet so deadly – rake the square and race the two women to the stone trough. There could only be one winner and Edward watched in horror as both Gerda and Verity dropped to the ground like puppets whose strings had been cut. They tumbled among the mangled sheep and lay still. By the time Edward and James reached them, it was too late to do anything but gather them up into their arms and carry them out of the maelstrom into the shelter of a ruined house. As Edward clasped Verity to him, he knew this was what he had feared so much. It had come to pass as he knew it must and it was cold comfort – but comfort nevertheless – that he was with her. Panting, they laid the two women beside each other. Edward's heart leapt. Verity was unconscious but breathing. She was bleeding from the shoulder and there was a bad gash on her forehead but she was alive. He looked across at Lyall who was cradling Gerda. He raised his eyes to Edward's. 'She's dead. Look, her stomach . . .'

Edward turned away his head, the bile rising in his throat. To see that beautiful girl, her monkey face and green eyes alight with mischief, reduced to a bleeding piece of meat was almost unbearable. A moment ago she had been running and now she was dead. It did not seem possible that life could be snuffed out so quickly. She still had in her hand the camera she had been carrying as she raced across the marketplace. He took it from her knowing that the one thing she would have wanted above all was that her work should be saved. More powerful than a bookful of words, despite his churlish remarks in the gallery when he had first seen her images of war, her photographs would speak of what she had seen. They would survive her and be her witness and her memorial. He would see to that. She had said that to get the picture which made people stop and take notice, she had to get close and 'close' meant danger. She had died as perhaps she might have wished, getting close. He murmured the words from *Antony and Cleopatra* which Winston Churchill had used at Chartwell: 'Finish, good lady. The bright day is done, and we are for the dark.'

He got to his feet and found that André Kavan was there. He gave Edward a look which seemed to be full of hatred, as though he held him in some way responsible for her death. He put out his hand for Gerda's Leica and Edward gave it to him. It was his by right. He stepped aside and went back to Verity. James was using his bandana as a rough bandage. Verity moaned and tried to move but Edward hushed her.

'You've been wounded. You are bleeding and you must lie still until I find a doctor.'

She seemed to understand because she lay back again, her eyes still closed. Where amongst all this carnage, Edward wondered, would he find a doctor? James, as though reading his thoughts, said, 'Stay here. I'll be back in a minute or two. I know where the doctor is. I will fetch him.' Then he smiled a sweet smile, 'Don't worry. Verity will be all right.'

But Gerda. She was dead and Edward found he mourned her as he would have mourned a lover.

Ten minutes later, three more planes – Junkers this time – rained down bombs and incendiaries. And so, for three more hours, it continued. Even after dusk the wooden houses, burning like beacons, lighted the pilots to the pyre that was Guernica. The hospital was hit, killing twenty-five children and two nuns. When dawn came the town was a scene of utter desolation. Nothing remained unscathed except, miraculously, the Casa de Juntas with its ancient oak trees, and the church of Santa María, though its beautiful chapter house had been consumed by the fire. A long and weary trail of refugees pushing wheelbarrows or handcarts, some with a donkey or pony to aid them, wound down the road towards Bilbao. It was a sight with which the world was to become only too familiar in the years ahead but as yet was not hardened to such a spectacle.

As one German officer put it, the bombing of Guernica was 'a complete success for the Luftwaffe'.

11

Verity was sitting up in bed reading the newspaper. It was not so easy, given that her back and shoulder were swathed in bandages, but she managed it.

Over a week had passed since Edward and James Lyall had commandeered a car belonging to the mayor of Guernica to transport Verity, still in considerable pain and floating in and out of consciousness, down the column of refugees to Bilbao. André and Edward had found a simple wooden coffin in the crypt of the church of Santa Maria and had laid Gerda's body in it, nailed down the lid and strapped it to the roof of the car. Edward insisted James accompany them, using the excuse that, without him in his militia uniform, they would never make it to the city. Edward knew that, if the boy stayed at his post, he would be captured and almost certainly killed. When General Mola's troops entered Guernica just three days after its destruction from the air, they found it deserted.

Bilbao was in chaos, its hospitals full, its streets cratered and many of its buildings destroyed. It had been continually bombed for ten days and, with no big guns or aircraft to protect it, the city seemed likely to fall to the enemy within days. In fact, it was so fiercely defended it held out for two more months. Edward discovered that Captain Roberts was preparing to take his little ship, the *Seven Seas Spray*, back to England and would be happy to take them with him, along with other refugees. André did not accompany them. He insisted on taking Gerda's body over the frontier into France, which he did with great difficulty. He said that France, not England, was their home and that he would have her buried in Paris, a city she had always loved.

David Griffiths-Jones was said to be back in Madrid. He was certainly not in evidence in Bilbao. Edward absolutely insisted that James return with them to England. James said his duty was still with the Republicans in Spain but Edward informed him – and Verity backed him up – that Griffiths-Jones had specifically told them he was no longer required and was to be shipped home. After much anguishing, he bowed to Edward's demand. When he was determined to have his way, Edward was not easily denied. Until they were at sea he said nothing to James about his father's death. He feared that if James knew he was alone in the world, he might give way to despair and prefer to meet his fate in Spain.

Roberts's nineteen-year-old daughter, improbably named Fifi, and the wife of the chief engineer proved able nurses and, by the time they reached England, Verity was able to walk, though she was still very weak. At least one bullet was lodged in her shoulder and there was a deep scar on her forehead but the trauma which had almost killed her was passing. However Gerda's death and the horror of what they had seen in Guernica had left all three of them depressed and deeply shocked.

The story which Verity filed the moment she reached England, even before the doctor had dug the bullet out of her shoulder, made the front page of the *New Gazette* and was copied across the world. The Nationalists quickly retaliated with stories discrediting her as a Communist who saw only what she wanted to see and it was these lies that she was now protesting against vociferously. On the bed lay all the daily papers and she was beating the *Daily Mail* with the back of her hand as if she could correct it by force.

'Listen to this! "The Reds took advantage of the bombing to set fire to the town." "There is no German or foreign air force in National Spain," said General Franco's spokesman. "There is a Spanish air force, which constantly fights against Red planes – Russian and French – piloted by foreigners. We did not burn Guernica. Franco's Spain does not set fires." Damn them to hell! We *saw* the Heinkels with our own eyes!'

Her friends, Charlotte and Adrian Hassel, with whom she was recuperating, sat at the end of her bed trying to calm her. Edward, his hands still painful from helping rescue the child trapped in the burning building, lay slumped in an armchair. Morosely, he leafed through the *The Times*.

'It's only to be expected, V,' he said. 'They couldn't let your story go unchallenged.'

'But it's not just my story. Respected journalists like George Steer, who inspected the ruins of Guernica and interviewed witnesses, say what I say: that the town was destroyed by the Luftwaffe.'

'Of course! And most people will know it's the truth but there will always be people who don't want to believe it.'

'But they're saying that the militia destroyed the town; that there is no Luftwaffe presence in Spain; that in any case the weather was too bad for any aircraft to fly, when we know it was a hot cloudless day.'

'They would say that, V,' Edward said calmly. 'You have to accept that this is a great propaganda coup for the Republicans. It's exactly what David was hoping for . . . why he sent you. He can now brand the Fascists as murderers and criminals. There's no way Franco and his henchmen are going to take that lying down. They'll mobilize all their allies to try and discredit you. It's going to be hard for you but you have to look on it as a back-handed compliment.'

'Huh!' she said dismissively but she looked a bit happier.

Edward, on the other hand, looked wretched. He wanted to point out something Verity would find unpalatable. Tactfully, knowing that he wanted to talk to Verity alone, Charlotte and Adrian made their excuses.

'You two will be all right? We shouldn't really leave you unchaperoned, Verity, but . . .'

'Go, for goodness sake, Adrian. If I could throw anything at you, I would.'

When the door had closed behind them and they were alone, Edward said, 'V, I don't know whether you have thought about what took you to Guernica.'

'What do you mean – what took me to Guernica? As you say, David gave us exclusive information. I owe him a lot. He gave me the scoop of a lifetime.'

'Yes but . . . You're not going to like this, V . . .'

'Well, spit it out.'

'Doesn't it occur to you to wonder if David ever did warn

anyone in Guernica? I could find no evidence that he had. We went to Guernica because he sent us, but have you thought *why* he sent us?'

'To give us a scoop and enable us to prove to the world that Franco's a murderer.'

'Precisely! He didn't give us the information that Guernica might be bombed just to help your career. He wanted a first-hand account of the destruction so he could blaze it forth to the world. There would be no point in having something like that to report if no one knew about it. And he didn't care if you died getting it.'

'Well, what's wrong with that?' Verity said belligerently. 'I would never have forgiven him if he had gone to some male journalist because he thought women ought to be kept out of danger.'

'This was more than danger – this was almost certain death. He knew you and Gerda would risk anything to get your story. He could count on you not to be skulking in some cellar.'

'You are trying to tell me that he sent Gerda to her death deliberately? That's obscene. And it doesn't make sense. You've just said he needed eyewitnesses to the bombing.'

'He would expect one of us to survive, I suppose.'

Verity still looked scornful. 'You hate David. You always have done. You're letting your dislike of him get in the way of common sense. Why would he want to kill me? Answer me that!'

She stuck out her chin and gave Edward a look of loathing but he was not dismayed. This was his opportunity – however unkind – of making her see for herself the nature of the cause she espoused.

'See here,' he said, 'David knew you had been sent by the *Gazette* to find out if it was true the Communist Party was ... what's the expression they use? – "purging" the International Brigade of Trotskyists and Anarchists and so on. I don't suppose he liked that.'

'And I didn't find any evidence – not really. There are stories about Anarchists and Trotskyists being thrown out of the International Brigade but that's not surprising. We have to be united.'

Verity had gone very pale and Edward wondered if he had been wrong to alert her to his suspicions while she was still in a state of shock.

'When you're better, V, I want you to talk to James Lyall. He joined the International Brigade and, without really under-standing the difference, joined POUM. David "rescued" him.'

POUM was the United Marxist Workers' Party. Although Marxist, it was anti-Stalinist and its leader had been a close ally of Trotsky.

'I know David can be ruthless . . .' she said slowly, 'but I can't believe he would send someone to their death. It's a beastly, ugly war but it's not fair to blame it all on David.'

Edward suddenly remembered Gerda telling him in the gallery that David had done just that – sent someone to their death. A writer friend of hers had wanted to get away from the fighting, she said, and David had sent him to a part of the line where he knew he would be killed. He decided not to say any-thing to Verity. For one thing, he did not want to go on about Gerda. Verity had got it into her head that he had slept with her and André Kavan had convinced her of it. He had implied that Gerda had said as much and, though Verity said she believed him when Edward had denied the charge, it was obvious she wasn't really convinced of his innocence. It was rather galling, he thought, given the temptation he had resisted, but perhaps he deserved it. Was the thought as bad as the deed?

'Well, anyway, I must go,' he said, looking at his watch. 'I'm picking James up from his aunt's house in Clapham. We are going to see Pride at Scotland Yard.'

'Oh God!' Verity exclaimed. 'Don't tell me Pride is back in our lives?'

'I fear so though, to tell you the truth, he has been quite reasonable so far.'

'So, why is Pride allowing you to sit in on his investigation into James's father's death?'

'I'll explain it all when I get back.'

'No, tell me now. We're a team, aren't we?'

Edward was touched. Verity might be a tough war correspon-dent who had just survived a bullet in the back but she was also a vulnerable, lonely woman. The life she led did not make it easy to develop friendships and the friends she did make tended to be either déraciné gypsies like Gerda and André Kavan or Party members. Edward sometimes thought he and the Hassels were the only friends she had from the 'normal' world she had turned her back on when she decided to become a journalist. If it helped her get over the trauma of Guernica, he would involve her in the investigation, even if it meant bending a few rules.

'I hope you are right about Pride,' she was saying. 'I won't believe it until I see it. By the sound of it, he's barking up the wrong tree as per usual. James is now one of my heroes and I can't believe anything bad about him. He found a doctor in Guernica and saved my life and you say he found the car that got us out. What can we do to help? Does he need a lawyer? I could telephone my father.'

Verity's father was the well-known barrister, D.F. Browne. He spent his life supporting left-wing causes which left him little time to be a good father. It was typical that he was now in New York and had spoken to Verity only once, very briefly, on a crackly line shortly after she had arrived back in London. When she would get to see him was anyone's guess.

'Tell me what this is all about, will you, Edward? I get the feeling I have missed something.'

'I don't think Pride's going to accuse James of anything – at least I hope not – but he does need to question the boy. He may have been the last person to see his father alive. Actually, Pride's been quite good and allowed him time to recover from his ordeal before asking him to come into the Yard.'

'So James's father was poisoned – is that it? And wasn't someone else killed? You told me about it on the boat but . . . I wasn't really concentrating.'

'You really want to hear this, V?'

'It'll take my mind off other things.'

'In a nutshell then – and this is not for repetition – there is a department in the Foreign Office whose job it is to monitor arms sales, here and abroad, with a view to making accurate estimates of the military strength of our potential enemies. One of the junior members of the department, Charles Westmacott, took secret files out of the office – presumably to give someone – and ended up hanging from Chelsea Bridge.'

'And that was definitely murder not suicide?'

'He wasn't the suicidal type. He was a family man. He was left hanging from the bridge, his hat on his head and his umbrella made to look as though it was on his arm. Only his briefcase was missing. Anyway, who would commit suicide by hanging themselves from a bridge? Why not just jump off a tall building? That's what stockbrokers did in '29 after the Crash.'

'Right, so it's murder,' Verity said decisively. 'What next?'

'Subsequently, Westmacott's boss – Desmond Lyall – was found dead by his secretary. He had died from nicotine poisoning. He was a chain smoker and someone had left him with cigarettes laced with enough of the stuff to finish him off.'

'How easy is it to get nicotine . . . as a poison, I mean?'

'Not difficult at all. You simply soak cigarette butts in water and evaporate the extract. You get a yellow liquid which becomes a brown sticky mess. If you want to poison someone, you can either put it in the victim's drink or, as in this case, inject it into cigarettes.'

'And they wouldn't notice?'

'Not if you were a chain smoker like Lyall. He put one cigarette after another in his mouth – probably without being conscious of what he was doing.'

'And it's a killer?'

'As quick as cyanide. It stimulates and then depresses your nervous system. The muscles in your diaphragm are paralysed and you die of respiratory failure.'

'What's the lethal dose?'

'About fifty milligrams.'

'You've boned up on this?'

'Yes. And Pride showed me the preliminary medical report.'

Verity meditated. 'So James was the last person to see his father alive?'

'Probably, but that's not so important as anyone could have left the poisoned cigarettes in the box on Lyall's desk. We can only guess how long it would have taken him to reach them. If they had been put at the bottom of the box – it held about a hundred – it might have been a couple of days even at the rate he smoked. There were just two cigarettes left in the box when he was found dead, only one of which was posioned.'

'Maybe someone removed the other unsmoked cigarettes when they knew he was dead?'

'It's possible, V.'

'So tell me about James. He and his father had quarrelled?'

'They had been on bad terms but, unluckily as it turned out, I had persuaded him to go and see his father because I knew that

Desmond really loved him. He had admitted as much when I interviewed him. James, at my urging, went to see his father. They met and possibly quarrelled. James left for Spain unaware that his father had died.'

'When did he find out?'

'That was one of my main reasons for going to Spain. I mean, apart from being worried sick about you. As it turned out, I didn't have an opportunity to tell him until we were on the boat coming home.'

'What was his reaction? I wasn't taking much interest in anything at the time.'

'He was very upset – genuinely, as far as I could tell. I tried to get him to talk but he clammed up. I thought it best to leave it. We were all pretty exhausted.'

'And you have got involved because of Vansittart? I remember you told me he had asked you to investigate something for him.'

'It wasn't Westmacott's murder he wanted me to investigate, only his disappearance. I'll tell you the whole thing but don't forget I was sworn to secrecy. It was thought he was one of the people leaking information to Mr Churchill so he could bring pressure on the government to rearm more quickly. Vansittart thought his disappearance was tied up with that in some way. When it turned into a murder case, I was asked to look after the political side – represent the FO, don't y'know.'

Edward wasn't being quite frank. He did not think Verity would approve of him being a policeman. He had never told her that he had worked for Major Ferguson of Special Branch in the past and had comforted himself with the idea that it wasn't a formal relationship. Now it was formal but somehow it seemed too late to tell her. She hated Special Branch, considering them to be anti-Communist and pro-Fascist. He would have to tell her sometime, of course, but just for now it was his guilty secret. It wasn't his secret to share anyway – at least not without Ferguson's permission.

'I have met Mrs Westmacott and her daughter, Alice, who's a clever little ten-year-old. I promised I would find out the truth for them. You can imagine how distressed they are. Mrs Westmacott has a sister. She's a well-known racing driver, of all things. Pride knew about her – Mrs Hay. Have you heard of her, V?'

She said she hadn't .

'Could the nicotine poisoning have been a mistake? Perhaps Lyall just smoked himself to death?' she asked, reaching for her cigarettes.

'It's not possible, although I haven't seen the autopsy report yet. I'll know more later but, as I told you, one of the two cigarettes remaining in the box on his desk had been tampered with.'

'You'll never convince me James murdered his father,' Verity said decisively.

'No. I don't think so either. There is one other complication though. When I found him in London – that was when I told him he should go and see his father – he was staying in Chester Square with David and Guy Baron. What's more, I have reason to believe the house is owned by a rather – what shall I say? – dubious millionaire called Sir Vida Chandra who just happens to be one of Churchill's main financial backers.'

Verity looked as if she were going to jump to David's defence but, in the end, said nothing. Instead, she pondered what he had told her and Edward was pleased that at least she had stopped worrying about what the Fascists were saying about Guernica.

'You said you met Churchill?' she said at last. 'What did you think of him? I don't trust him. He's an aristocratic windbag and he makes you look like a friend of the people.'

'Yes, I thought that too but I've changed my mind. Having met him, I thoroughly approve of him. In fact, I think he's the only politician to understand what we are really up against.'

'I don't like him,' Verity reiterated. 'He's the enemy of socialism, of everything in which I believe. You know what he did in the the General Strike? He was ready to order in the army, even put tanks on the streets.'

'He supported the miners in their claim for better wages,' Edward said without much conviction.

'He did his best to prevent women getting the vote. Sylvia Pankhurst was his sworn enemy.'

'V! That was before the war.'

'I don't care. Do leopards change their spots? If he is so clear-sighted why didn't he support us going in to help the Spanish Republic? David says he's a reactionary of the worst kind.'

'I think Churchill felt – forgive me, Verity – that entering the Civil War would be a distraction. It would drain us of what little we had in the way of armaments and leave us seriously weakened when war with Germany starts.'

'And he doesn't like Communists.'

'No, he doesn't but he hates Fascism more, if that makes it better.'

'No, it does not. My view is, as you very well know, that if the democracies had stood up to Franco it would have sent the right message to Hitler. Oh well, it's too late now. They have shown the dictators they can walk all over us.'

'Getting back to Westmacott,' Edward said, not wanting to get into a political row, 'the question is, was he killed because he was giving secret information to Churchill?'

'Churchill admitted he had been in touch with Westmacott?'

'He did, yes.'

'You're not implying that Mr Churchill could have had anything to do with Westmacott's death?'

'No, of course not – not directly – but Westmacott may have been killed going to meet one of Churchill's people – Marcus Fern, perhaps. And Churchill does have round him some characters like Chandra who may support him for the best of motives but who are ruthless when they think they have to be. Chandra is by no means whiter than white.'

'Well, if he's an Indian he wouldn't be, would he?'

'Don't play the giddy goat, Verity. This is serious.'

'I know it is. I'm sorry,' she said humbly.

Edward was secretly surprised and delighted she could make even a bad joke.

'What's much more likely,' he said, 'is that someone did not want Westmacott to give certain information to Churchill and killed him.'

'Yes, of course. Let me think about this while you take James to see Pride. I need something to get my teeth into. Lying here thinking of the lies being told about me in the press is going to drive me crazy.'

Edward opened the bedroom door and called to Adrian. 'I'm going now. I'll be back this evening, if that's all right.'

'Of course,' Adrian said, appearing with a drying-up cloth in his hand. 'Charlotte and I can't keep her in bed if she gets too bored but the doc was adamant. Verity, you must rest.'

'How can I ever thank you for taking me in?' Verity said with transparent sincerity. 'You are my only true friends.'

'What about Edward here?'

She looked almost puzzled and then said, 'Edward's more than a friend, Adrian. You know that, don't you?'

'I do,' he said seriously, 'and I'm glad for the both of you.'

Edward felt his eyes prickle and, not wishing to make a fool of himself, said, 'By the way, Adrian, there's something I've been meaning to ask you. Do you know a chap called Angus McCloud? He was at the Slade – perhaps when you were there? Now he works in Desmond Lyall's department at the Foreign Office. He was a bit too keen to tell me he was an artist and not a civil servant when I met him. A phoney, I thought, but I may be wronging the man.'

'Angus! Oh, I remember Angus all right. I wondered what had happened to him. Fancy him ending up in the FO. He *was* a bit of a phoney, I always thought. Old Tonks couldn't stand him. He had a beard.'

'He's lost that but he's still rather shaggy. And he's got a pipe.'

'Yes, I remember his pipe. It was a horrid, smelly thing. In fact, he was a smelly man. Not much interested in personal hygene.'

'Typical bachelor,' Verity said. Edward gave her a look. 'Not you, idiot!' she corrected herself.

'Would you mind asking around a bit, Adrian. See if there's anything fishy there. For instance, I don't even know if he's married.'

'Will do. You think he's Lyall's murderer?'

'No! It's just one lead to follow up. I didn't tell you, V, I've got your pal Jack Spot doing some sleuthing for me in the underworld. Damn useful that he seems to fancy you. Mind you, I fancy you myself.'

Verity tried to throw a pillow at him but gasped as a stabbing pain hit her. Edward saw her wince and go pale. 'Hey, steady on, old thing. Lie back and . . . you know, think of England. I'll come by this evening and report.'

'You don't seem worried that James could be in any real danger?' Adrian asked, to give Verity time to recover. 'You were telling me the police want to interview him.'

'I don't think even Pride is going to make a case against the boy but I need to find out what evidence he does have. It seems an age since I talked to him. Maybe he has the case solved by

171

now. As for James, he's a good lad and he just needs someone to put him on the right path.'

'That'll be you, I suppose,' Verity said sarcastically. 'You'll knock all that silly Communism stuff out of his head, no doubt.'

'I would like to try.'

Edward left before Verity could throw something harder than a pillow at him.

'Can we just run through it again?'

Chief Inspector Pride was being reasonable and finding it all rather an effort. 'At Lord Edward's suggestion and in his presence, you telephoned your father and arranged to go round to his office?'

'Yes, I walked. It wasn't so far and I needed to think a bit. The truth is I wasn't too keen to have this meeting but Lord Edward had persuaded me my father really did want to see me. And I was thinking I might get killed in Spain – I'd had a few narrow squeaks already. It seemed a bit hard on the old man if I was killed without – you know – making my peace with him.' James sounded embarrassed. In a typically English way, he did not want to be accused of sentimentality.

'But in fact it was he who was killed,' Pride said flatly.

'Yes, it was,' the boy said soberly. 'That makes me glad I went and saw him. I would have felt so guilty if I hadn't made the effort . . .'

'He disapproved of you joining the International Brigade and going to Spain – that was what you had quarrelled about?'

'Yes that and . . .' He hesitated.

'And what?'

'I regret it now but I said some things about mother – about how he treated her.'

'They didn't get on?'

'It wasn't that. I am sure he loved her but he was always working. He often didn't get home until nine or ten.'

'He had an important job. Presumably she knew that.'

'She knew but that wasn't it. He was . . . oh, I don't want to talk about this.'

'Of course not,' Edward said. 'It's private and painful but the Chief Inspector is trying to find out who killed your father so he has to ask these questions. You want to help him, don't you?'

'I do but . . .'

'Your mother became ill?' Pride probed as gently as he could. 'Was your father upset?'

'He didn't know. He didn't realize. Neither of us did.'

'So when your mother had to go into hospital, it was a great shock?'

'Yes and I'm afraid I blamed my father. I said he ought to have known. I said I hated him. I didn't really mean it. I was just angry and scared.'

'And so – when she died – you said you were going to fight in Spain to . . .?'

'To spite him, yes. Though I did believe in what the Republic stood for. I was a Communist at school.'

'That was brave,' Edward encouraged him. 'You were at Wellington, weren't you? That's an army school. I don't suppose there were many who felt like you?'

'Not many,' James said reflectively, 'but that made the few of us who were Communists even keener.'

'And are you still a Communist?' Pride inquired.

James hesitated. 'I don't know what I believe, to tell you the truth. I've seen such . . . such things. What happened at Guernica . . . that was worse than anything I had imagined.'

'Lord Edward has been telling me how brave you were . . . how you saved Miss Browne's life.'

'I didn't do anything special,' he said, looking at his shoes, but Edward could see he was pleased that they thought he had done well.

'You've done your stuff, anyway,' Edward said. 'You're not going back there.'

'No, I don't think I will,' he said slowly. 'It wasn't just Guernica. It was what Mr Griffiths-Jones said.'

'What did he say exactly?' Edward's tone was acid and Pride looked at him with interest.

'Oh, don't get me wrong. They were very good to me. When Guy heard I didn't want to go home when I came back to London, he suggested staying with him and Mr Griffiths-Jones in Chester Square. I was very grateful. I had nowhere else to go. I . . . I didn't want to bother my aunt. She's my father's sister and she would have said I had to go home . . . to my father.' James sounded suddenly very young and alone.

'Guy – he didn't . . . didn't try anything on? I mean,' Edward found himself blushing, 'he didn't try to . . . to be too friendly,' he ended lamely.

'I see what you're getting at,' James said, smiling. 'He didn't touch me, I promise. I wouldn't have let him. I don't like that sort of thing but he didn't anyway. He was very kind. And David was there – Mr Griffiths-Jones.'

'What do you think of him?'

'He's a great man but sometimes . . . sometimes he frightens me. I don't know why. I think he would do anything for – you know – the cause. Anything.'

'He frightens me too, sometimes,' Edward said drily.

'I told you,' he said, turning to Edward, 'that he made me transfer out of POUM to a different unit.'

Pride looked at Edward for clarification.

'POUM was not strictly part of the International Brigade, Chief Inspector. It was Anarchist and Trostkyist while the International Brigade is Communist-controlled. As soon as they were powerful enough, the Communists liquidated POUM and other non-Communist fighting units.'

'Liquidated?' Pride asked, puzzled.

'Told them they had to join the Communist Party.'

'And if they wouldn't?'

'They got killed, one way or another,' James said.

Pride looked shocked. It was just as he supposed. Communists and Fascists – there was nothing to choose between them.

'Let's get back to the day your father died,' he said. 'What time did you get to the Foreign Office?'

'I got there about three thirty.'

'But you didn't get to see him until four thirty. What did you do for an hour?'

'I walked about a bit. I remember I stood on the bridge in the park and watched the ducks. I wanted to think things out, don't you see. It was warm. I sat on a bench.'

'You brought your father a present?'

James blushed guiltily. 'I didn't *buy* him anything. I just noticed that Guy smoked the same cigarettes as my father – you know, those expensive ones.'

'Murad – Turkish, aren't they?' Edward put in.

'That's right, and when I told him, Guy said why didn't I take him some.'

'You took a packet or was it a tin?' Edward asked urgently.

'They were in a box.'

'Loose? They weren't in the manufacturer's box?'

'No. Guy took them out of their box in the drawing-room and put them in another one – a cigar box, I think it was – that was sitting on the table.'

It was not until he was back in Albany – after delivering James to his aunt – that Edward remembered he had still not told the Chief Inspector about the powder compact the constable had found in the Thames near to where Westmacott had been found hanged. He wondered if he had *really* forgotten or if he had *deliberately* forgotten. He had been reading Freud again and found his theories on the unconscious most illuminating. He was about to dial Scotland Yard and confess everything when the telephone rang. He picked up the receiver to hear Jack Spot's rather hoarse voice at the other end.

'I'd heard you were back, my lord, and that Miss Browne had been wounded.'

'Yes, Spotty. Her friend, Gerda Meyer the photographer, was killed. Verity was lucky,' he said grimly.

'Could I see her, do you think? I mean, not if she's too ill,' he added hurriedly. 'But everyone is saying she did wonders and that her reports in the *New Gazette* and the *Worker* did more for the cause than anything.'

Edward thought for a moment and was about to speak when Spotty added, 'And I've got some information about . . . you know.' He was being discreet.

It occurred to Edward that it might cheer Verity up to have an admirer at her bedside and that it would take her mind off her woes if she got drawn into the investigation about Westmacott's death. So he said, 'Yes, indeed. We mustn't tire her but I know she would like to see you again and hear what you have discovered.'

Edward gave him the address of the Hassels' house in the King's Road and asked him to be there at six unless he rang to say she was not well enough. When he telephoned Verity, she was eager to hear what Spotty had to say. 'Why not ask James to come and we could all have a cosy supper here? Charlotte won't mind, will you, Charlie?'

175

There was a muttered colloquoy off stage and then she said, 'Charlie says she's out at a conference this evening but that would be all right. She'll leave us a shepherd's pie.'

Edward rang James and he accepted with alacrity, sounding eager to remove himself – if only for a few hours – from his aunt's house. Edward talked to her and fortunately it turned out she 'liked a lord' and was quite charmed to hear that he had taken an interest in her nephew.

'I tell him, Lord Edward,' she simpered, 'he ought to give up this Communism. Such a lot of nonsense. I've told him, I'll have no Communist in my house.'

Edward felt deeply sorry for James. He hoped, however, he would be sensible enough not to tell his aunt that he was also going to see the arch-Communist, Verity Browne, along with the socially acceptable Lord Edward Corinth.

'Well,' Spotty said with satisfaction, 'I can tell you who didn't kill Mr Westmacott.'

Through the blue haze of cigarette smoke – Edward, Verity and Adrian Hassel were all smoking and Spotty was puffing away at one of his foul-smelling cigars – expectant looks could just be made out. They were sitting around Verity's bed. She had wanted to get up but the doctor had refused to allow it 'for at least another week'. It had been quite touching to see the way Jack Spot had greeted Verity. He was genuinely in awe of her and it came to Edward that she was now a famous figure and, for the Left, a hero. Spot shook her hand and bowed. 'I'm greatly honoured, Miss Browne.' He touched the scar on his face. 'Now you, too, wear one of these but, whereas mine makes me want not to look in the mirror of a morning, yours is a medal to wear with pride – makes you look . . . dashing.'

Verity blushed but said with dignity, 'Thank you, Spotty. It's really Lord Edward and Mr Lyall who are the heroes. Without them, I would be dead. Simple as that.'

She had not looked at Edward and kept her eyes firmly on the ugly face of the gangster in front of her but Edward felt his heart go out to her. It was not her way to be gushing but she was acknowledging that she was glad he had followed his instincts and gone to Spain to be with her in her hour of extreme peril.

Suddenly he felt claustrophobic. It was a big room but the four of them – James, Adrian, Spotty and himself – were squashed together and he was feeling stifled.

'Open a window, will you, James?' Edward said, coughing. 'My brain can't breathe. Who's at this conference of Charlotte's, then, Adrian?'

'Bloomsbury lesbians,' Adrian said dismissively.

'What's a lesbian?' James asked.

Verity told him and he looked stunned.

'I knew about Guy, of course,' he said, trying to sound grown up,' but that's . . . toe-jam. Women don't do that sort of thing, do they?'

'Women do whatever men do,' she said in her lecturing voice.

'Everything?' James looked horrified. He saw Edward smiling and blushed. He got up quickly and struggled with the window. Soon a breath of cold evening air dissipated the smoke. Stubbing his cigar out in an onyx ashtray, Spotty went on. 'It weren't either the Communists or Mosley's mob.'

'I never thought it could have been Mosley's lot,' Edward said. 'Vicious though they are, they don't have the balls for that sort of enterprise.'

'And I never thought the Party would sanction murder,' Verity remarked, with what Edward decided was unjustified confidence.

'So, Spotty, who was it? You look like the cat who's got the cream'.

'The evidence points to it being one Major Stille, from the German Embassy.'

'No surprise there, then,' Edward retorted.

Spot looked put out that his news had gone for nought.

'Sorry, Spotty,' Verity said, 'but you see we have had dealings with Major Stille before. Don't you remember? At the battle of Cable Street, I discovered Stille in civilian dress on *our* side of the barricades, making trouble.'

'Yes, I do remember now, Miss Browne.'

'What's your evidence that Stille's behind this?' Edward demanded.

'It's all a great secret. No one will talk. Usually, when someone's taken out a contract I'm the first to know about it. But not this one. Top secret and that costs, I can tell you.'

'What's that – a contract?' James inquired.

'You see, sonny, when you wants someone done away with there are always a few hard men that'll do it for you . . . for a price, mark you. But not as much as you might suppose.'

'So how did you find out who had done it?'

'I set the dogs on it and they ferreted it out. Can't say any more than that, my lord. More than my life's worth.'

'No evidence to stand up in court then?'

Spotty looked indignant. 'Who said anything about court, my lord? You wanted to find out who killed Mr Westmacott and I've told you. Tell you any more and I'm dead meat.'

'I understand, Spotty,' Verity said, 'and we're very grateful, aren't we, Edward?'

'Yes, of course, extremely grateful. If there's anything . . .' He touched his jacket where his wallet lodged.

'Certainly not, my lord! I'm no informer. I am happy . . . always happy to aid Miss Browne in her investigations but I don't need no money.'

'I'm very sorry, Spotty. I had no wish to insult you. So there's no way we can express our gratitude?'

'It's enough being here with Miss Browne, my lord, in her bedroom. They'll be green with envy when they hears it.'

Verity coloured but smiled. 'You'd better call it my sickroom, if you please, Spotty.'

'Do you think this has anything to do with my father's murder?' James said in a small voice.

'Oh, James. You must think we are being very heartless. We ought not to be facetious talking about murder . . .' Verity checked herself.

'I don't mind. I want to help if I can. You see,' he went on bravely, looking at Edward, 'if you solve Mr Westmacott's murder, I think you will find out who killed my father.'

'You know, James, I think you are right,' Edward said, patting him on the shoulder. 'Tomorrow, I am going to have another talk to the people who worked with your father and Mr Westmacott. Pride says they have nothing more to tell – that they know nothing – but I don't believe it. I think he hasn't asked the right questions.'

'I hope you do find out something,' James said, looking very pale, 'because I think Chief Inspector Pride believes I killed my father. It looks bad, doesn't it? I gave him cigarettes just before he died of nicotine poisoning. I had quarrelled with him. I was the last person to see him alive. But for all that,' he looked around him as if wanting to impress a jury, 'I didn't kill him. I loved him and I would give anything to have him back.'

Vansittart had appointed an earnest young man called Alfred Caddick to run the department and take over Lyall's work. However, Caddick had not yet taken up his position and Edward commandeered his office to interview the staff.

Harry Younger was complaining about the extra work. 'It's all very well, you know, but it's not fair, sir. We were working flat out as it was and our work is important.'

Edward liked the young man rather less than he had the first time they had met. He was still the clean-limbed, ex-public schoolboy but there was something in his tone of voice which grated on Edward's ear. Still, he reminded himself, Younger was a cricketer so he couldn't be all bad.

'You live at home?'

'I do. My mother's a widow and I'm . . . you know, her favourite. Anyway, it's easier and cheaper to live at home.' He giggled nervously. 'I don't have to worry about my washing and she's the best cook in the world.'

'But it must be difficult to see girls – socially, I mean?'

'It's a bit of a bind, I grant you. To tell the truth, I don't see many girls. I go down to the pub most nights.'

'So, no girls?' Edward felt he was prying and tried to sound as if he were one of his pub friends.

Younger sounded annoyed. 'I didn't say that. I get my oats, though I don't see what it's got to do with you.'

'You're quite right,' Edward responded hurriedly. 'I apologize.'

'That's all right,' Younger said huffily.

'I suppose I was just trying to get a feel for the department's social life. You don't seem to see much of each other outside the office.'

'McCloud's all right but I don't go much for art. As I told you last time, we sometimes have a pint together after work though. He's stuck on Miss Williams but she won't have any of it. She's got a steady. In the RAF, she told me once.'

'She seems a nice girl.'

'She's a doll. Quite a looker but she don't look in my direction, worse luck. Talks a bit too much though for my taste. Women should be seen and not heard, eh?'

He gave Edward a rather sly look which he could not quite interpret.

'Miss Hawkins rules you all with a rod of iron?' Edward smiled to show whose side he was on. Younger responded with a dry laugh.

'We call her the Hawk. You can see why – we can't get away with anything. Mind you, she had a soft spot for Lyall. I don't think he noticed but talk about slavish devotion.'

'So how could Westmacott have had papers in his briefcase that Miss Hawkins knew nothing about?'

'Did he? I thought he only had . . . Well, if he did, he must have got them somewhere else. What papers were they, anyway?'

'It's easy to get hold of secret papers, is it?'

'I didn't mean that. I just meant if Westmacott had taken a secret file on Bawdsey Manor, he must have got it from somewhere else. Savvy?'

'Bawdsey Manor?' Edward asked sharply. 'Why do you say that? What do you know about the place?'

'Nothing,' Younger said quickly. 'Lyall told me about it. I saw a file on his desk and asked him.'

'Well, he ought not to have told you. It's top secret.'

'Of course,' Younger looked chastened, 'I wouldn't say anything to anyone outside this office.'

'Nor inside either, I hope,' Edward said grimly.

'No, certainly.'

'How's the flying going?' he said as he showed Younger out.

The boy looked at him, startled and, Edward thought, almost frightened. He pulled himself together.

'The flying? Yes, I told you about that, didn't I? Haven't done any recently as a matter of fact. Overworked – don't have the time.'

McCloud was louder than ever and his body odour more noticeable, even above his foul-smelling pipe. Edward wondered if it was because he was nervous. He was altogether too obvious and Edward was reminded of what Adrian had said about him the previous night while they were eating shepherd's pie.

'He's clever – no doubt about that. He was a wiz at crosswords. I'm not surprised, now I think about it, that he ended up at the Foreign Office making sense of statistics.'

'But . . . ?'

'But he was a rotten painter. I know I'm no great shakes but at least I'm me, if you understand what I'm driving at. McCloud could imitate well enough . . . turn out a passable Monet or Whistler. I remember him doing a copy of a Sargent – an aristocrat – riding boots, breeches, coloured waistcoat, riding crop. It was brilliant.'

'I know the picture you mean,' Edward said. It was a painting of his father and hung at Mersham Castle but he was not going to mention it. McCloud must have seen it when it was shown at an exhibition of Sargent's work at the Tate some years back.

'In a funny sort of way, he was likeable – a pet monkey or perhaps more like an ape. He got a lot of women because he could make them laugh but they didn't stay. Women are better at spotting fakes than we are and he was a genuine fake.'

'Mr McCloud,' Edward began, 'sorry to bother you and all that. I gather from Younger that you're pretty busy.'

'That's right. Van hasn't really got down to reorganizing the department. Between ourselves, I don't think this man Caddick's going to be up to the job.'

'You know him?'

'No, but people talk,' he said, tapping the side of his nose with his finger.

Edward was certain Sir Robert would object to the familiarity of 'Van' but, if McCloud wanted to show off, he would let him.

'So might they put you in charge of the department?' he asked, feigning wide-eyed innocence.

'Not quite the right type,' McCloud said, taking the pipe out of his mouth. 'Van wants pinstripe suits not artistic types like me. Too creative, I suppose.'

'Shame. You don't mind me asking a question or two? I know the police have been through it all with a fine-tooth comb but there are just a few things . . .'

'Carry on, old boy. Anything I can do to help.'

'You found Lyall dead?'

181

'No, Miss Hawkins did. I was just leaving the office – had my hat and coat on – when I heard her call out.'

'You telephoned the police – why?'

'I don't know. It didn't look right somehow. Lyall had clearly died in pain but that wasn't it. It was just something about the body . . .'

'There was no smell or skin discoloration?'

'Not that I noticed. He always looked yellow . . . too many smokes.'

'And the chrysanthemum . . .?'

'Yes, I moved the cigarette box and there it was. I thought it was odd.'

'You didn't put it there yourself?'

'Of course not! What are you suggesting . . .?'

Edward ignored the outrage in McCloud's voice. 'Could anyone in the department have slipped the poisoned cigarettes into Lyall's box?'

'I suppose so. Or a visitor – though he didn't have many of those. Yes, we were always popping our heads round the door to ask him something or make our reports.'

He seemed either unworried or unaware that Edward was implying Lyall must have been murdered by a member of his department.

'And you had weekly meetings, I gather?'

'Yes, on Mondays, but that's by the by, isn't it? It wasn't just a question of access to Lyall's office. You would had to have been there alone for at least a minute to give you time to take the cigarettes out of your pocket and slip them into the box on his desk.'

'True. So that lets you out?'

'Hard to say. I don't remember being left alone in his office. I mean, it would be quite difficult to engineer. It might happen that Lyall would slip out to fetch something from Miss Hawkins's room but you wouldn't have known when that would happen. After all, he would normally use the buzzer to summon Miss Hawkins if he wanted anything.'

'What about Younger? Was he ever alone in Lyall's office?'

'I wouldn't know. You'd have to ask him that but, I say, who is likely to tell you the truth? You're hardly going to admit you had the opportunity of murdering him, are you? And what about visitors? As I say, he didn't have many, ours being a secret operation and all that, but he had some.'

'There's no record of his having had visitors in the two days before he was killed.'

'Apart from his son, of course.'

'Apart from James, yes. Did you meet him?'

'Never met the boy, I'm afraid. Can't help you there but people say they weren't on good terms.' He coughed. 'Not that I'm saying he murdered his father but, look here, Corinth, what motive could either of us – Younger or me – have had for killing Lyall? I don't suppose either of us liked him much but that didn't mean we were going to kill him.'

'Quite true! And I wasn't suggesting any such thing. It might have been, as you say, some visitor from outside the department we don't know about.' Edward put on a 'chummy' voice. 'McCloud, you're a bright fellow. I'm sure you've been turning all this over in your mind. Does nothing suggest itself?'

'About who murdered Lyall? I don't know that it does. I suppose the only person who had every excuse for being alone in his office was his secretary but the idea of Miss Hawkins murdering Lyall is absurd. Marrying him, possibly – I always thought she had a *tendresse* for him – but not murder.'

Jane Williams was delighted to be questioned by Edward again. He had a nasty feeling anything he said to her would be repeated throughout the office and beyond but he could hardly blame her. She must find it exciting to be involved in a murder investigation and be questioned by Lord Edward Corinth.

'Miss Williams, or may I call you Jane . . . ?'

'Call me Jane, my lord, if you wish. I am sure Mervyn would understand.'

'Mervyn?'

'Since we last met, my lord, I have become engaged . . . to Mervyn Last. He's in the RAF,' she said proudly.

Edward kicked himself. Jane had indicated to him last time they met that she might become engaged to an RAF pilot and he had dismissed it as fantasy. In fact – he would have to look up his notes – hadn't she admitted it was a fantasy?

'Is Mervyn a pilot?' he asked.

'No,' she admitted. 'He's an engineer. He works on the engines, you know.'

Her eyes pleaded with him for reassurance and he gave it to her gladly. 'Well, that's very good news. Where would the RAF be without engineers – a vital job. You must be very proud.'

'I am, my lord.'

'So this happened before Mr Lyall was found murdered?'

'Such a shock it was. As it happened, we got engaged the day Miss Hawkins . . . you know . . . found the body. Miss Hawkins was kind enough to give me an afternoon off as Mervyn only had a day free before he went back to the base.'

'Where is that?'

'He says it's a secret, my lord. He's not allowed to tell me.' She opened her eyes wide to signify that she understood how important it was to keep a secret.

'Have you seen him in his uniform?'

'Not yet, my lord.' She seemed to find some comfort in intoning 'my lord' whenever possible. 'He says it's a surprise for the wedding. I thought that was ever so romantic.'

'Has he been to the office?'

'Oh no, my lord.' The girl sounded shocked. 'Miss Hawkins doesn't allow us to bring . . . friends to the office.'

Edward had a sudden sinking feeling in his stomach. Could it be that Jane was being taken for a ride? Was Mervyn not quite what he pretended to be? Not to have told his fiancée where he was based . . . that did not smell right. He would ask Ferguson to check up on him.

'So what did you do on your afternoon off?'

'We went to Kew. I had never been. Miss Hawkins recommended it. She said Kew was very respectable and it was.'

Edward thought he detected a note of disappointment in her voice but he was mistaken. She was merely battling with herself about how much to tell him about the day's events. She surrendered to her desire to share her pleasure. 'I shouldn't really tell you, my lord but at Kew he gave me this ring.'

Edward peered at a piece of what he was almost certain was coloured glass. 'Very nice, Jane.'

But she had not finished. She blushed and the words came tumbling out.

'It was in the tropical pavilion. He was perspiring so I said, "Is it too hot for you, Mervyn?" and he said no, he was just nervous because he had something special to say. Then, right there, in front of . . . oh, I don't know how many people, he got down on one knee and put the ring on my finger. I went all weak at the knees and people started to clap. The ring . . . But there I go chattering on, my lord. You ought to have stopped me. My dad says I'm worse than the wireless, the way I talk.'

'The ring is perfectly splendid,' Edward said at his most avuncular. 'What did you do for the rest of the afternoon?'

'We went to a Palais de Dance he knew at Hammersmith and then Mervyn had to go back to base.'

'He took you home first?'

'Oh yes. He's very much the gentleman. It was very late, almost eleven. He had to rush to catch the last train.'

'Well, that's very good news. Do your parents know about your engagement?' He felt a cad asking. Jane looked uneasy.

'Not yet. They're rather old-fashioned. I couldn't say I was engaged to a man they had never met.'

'Of course,' he said hurriedly. 'I quite understand.' Jane smiled at him uncertainly and he saw how very young she was. 'Have you told them about Mr Lyall being killed? '

'I did and my mother was horrified. She said I ought to resign at once and that it wasn't suitable for her daughter to work in a place where people got murdered all the time and might I not be next, and I said, "Oh, mum!" because who would ever want to kill me?'

'And your father?'

'He was quite excited – upset, of course. He knew Mr Lyall – I told you, didn't I? When I was looking for a job – after I had left school and taken my Pitman course – my dad wrote to Mr Lyall and he very kindly gave me an interview.'

'How had your father met Mr Lyall?'

'At one time my father was a messenger at the Foreign Office. That was years ago. He's been retired for ten years at least.'

'So your father wasn't worried you might be working in the same office as a murderer?'

'Ooh! If you put it like that . . . But I can't believe anyone here would . . .'

'No,' Edward said, wishing he had not alarmed her. 'I'm sure you have nothing to worry about, Jane. So, your father was excited when you told him Mr Lyall had been murdered? That seems odd.'

'You don't know my dad. He reads a lot of detective stories and thrillers – Rex Stout's his favourite. He gave me one to read and I said, "Dad, this is rubbish. I can't think why you bother with such stuff." He asked me if Mr Lyall had any enemies. I said, "Not unless you mean Mr Westmacott."'

'Mr Westmacott and Mr Lyall were enemies?' Edward interrupted the flow.

'Not enemies, exactly,' she said hastily. 'I just remember hearing them one evening going hammer and tongs. I was passing the door to Mr Lyall's office and I couldn't avoid hearing. Mr Westmacott was shouting – so unlike him. He was a perfect gentleman. I had never heard him raise his voice before.'

'Did you happen to hear what they were quarrelling about?'

'Not really,' she admitted. 'Mr Lyall was asking him to lower his voice and Mr Westmacott said, "Why should I? What you are telling me to do is wrong ... quite wrong and I won't stand for it." Then Miss Hawkins came and I went back to my desk.'

'When was this, Jane?'

'About a month ago. No, six weeks. I remember because it was the only time I ever heard raised voices in the office.'

'You have been most helpful. Now, I want you to promise me that you won't talk about what we have discussed even to your father and mother.' Though I know that's asking too much, he added silently.

'Oh, I won't, I promise you. When Mr Lyall interviewed me for my job he said he wanted to impress on me that the work I was doing was top secret and that I was to discuss it with no one, and of course I don't,' she added virtuously.

'Oh, that reminds me, Jane. You remember when we first talked, before we knew Mr Westmacott had been killed?'

'Yes, my lord.'

Edward tried to sound casual. 'You said returned files would sometimes lie in Miss Hawkins's in-tray until she had time to put them away. Do you remember ever seeing the Bawdsey Manor file in her tray?'

'Bawdsey Manor? Now why does that ring a bell? It can't have been because I saw the file in Miss Hawkins's in-tray because the files – at least on the outside – don't have a name on them. They're just marked Secret in red.'

'But you saw it at some point?' Edward said, trying not to sound over-eager.

'Yes, I know! In Mr Westmacott's office! I saw it lying open on his desk, the day before he disappeared. I saw a letter or a report marked Bawdsey Manor.'

'Are you quite sure?'

'Yes, because when he disappeared and Miss Hawkins was checking to see if there were any files missing, I said, "Have you got the Bawdsey Manor file?" And she bit my head off. She said there was no such file. I said I had seen it on Mr Westmacott's desk but she told me I was a silly girl and I wasn't to tell fibs.'

'So you didn't tell Chief Inspector Pride?'

'No, why should I? He never asked. I didn't think it was important and Miss Hawkins said I had made a mistake. Anyway, what is Bawdsey Manor? Is it important?'

Edward thought Lyall must have been mad to employ such an empty-headed gossip but perhaps he reckoned she would do her work and not understand the significance of the documents she was typing. But supposing she had been got at by someone and made an innocent dupe?

'It might be important,' he said thoughtfully and then, pulling himself together, added, 'Now this really is secret, Jane. You have to promise me on your word of honour that you won't mention what you have told me – especially the name Bawdsey Manor – to anyone, and I mean anyone. Do you understand? Not to your parents, not to Mervyn, not to anyone.'

Miss Hawkins, when Edward asked her about Jane's story of overhearing a quarrel between Lyall and Westmacott, was predictably dismissive.

'I believe Mr Lyall had questioned the basis on which he – Mr Westmacott – had worked out certain figures. You see, the arms merchants we considered friendly were asked to make their own reports on what deals had been struck and so on. Mr Lyall was beginning to feel that this was not adequate. For instance, Sir Vida Chandra had provided us with a list of arms deals he had been involved in during 1935. Mr Lyall was convinced the department was being hoodwinked and that many deals were not being reported and the records of those that were, were incomplete.'

'Incomplete?'

'Sir Vida would inform us he had sold so many anti-tank weapons to a French arms dealer and we would be reasonably certain that the dealer was just the middle man and that the weapons were really destined for Germany. Mr Lyall thought Sir Robert Vansittart might have to ask Parliament for new powers to make arms dealers co-operate with us. I am sure Sir Robert himself can inform you more fully.'

'Thank you, Miss Hawkins, that is most useful.' Edward was unpersuaded by her fluent account of the disagreement between the two men. He did not doubt that Vansittart would confirm these issues were under discussion but if Jane was right – and she did not appear to be the type of girl to invent an overheard conversation – Miss Hawkins's account could not explain why Westmacott would have used the words, 'Why should I? What you are telling me to do is wrong.'

To pursue her on this point would, he was sure, be counter-productive. Much better for her to think her answer had satisfied him. She would, he hoped, be more relaxed when she answered some other questions he wanted to put to her.

'You remember the ring Mr Lyall wore?'

'The signet ring with the dolphin design?'

'Yes. Was it a family crest or anything like that?'

'Oh no, I don't think so. I believe it was a present from his wife. He always wore it.'

'The odd thing is that this was discovered close to where Mr Westmacott was found hanging.'

He passed her the powder compact. 'Open it.'

Miss Hawkins did so, her fingers fumbling at the catch. When she saw the dolphin design inside, she went quite white and dropped the compact. Edward picked it up.

'What is this?' she asked, her voice strangulated by emotion. 'Are you trying to trap me in some way, Lord Edward?'

'Not at all but you must admit it seems odd to find Mr Lyall's wife's compact near Westmacott's body. It would seem to implicate him, would it not?'

'Chief Inspector Pride never mentioned this when he interviewed me.'

'He did not know I had found it,' he answered truthfully. 'Have you seen this before?'

'I may have,' she said at last. 'I remember at the Christmas party – the year before last – she and I were both powdering our noses in the cloakroom. I may have seen it then.'

'You have a good memory, Miss Hawkins.' She was lying, he was sure of it. 'But you could not say how the compact got where it did?'

'No, I cannot but Desmond Lyall was not a . . . not a murderer, if that's what you are trying to tell me.'

'I'm not trying to tell you anything,' he replied mildly.

'Have you got any more questions for me? I have a great deal of work to do and we are very short-staffed.'

'I quite understand, Miss Hawkins, and I won't keep you for very much longer. Miss Williams said you very kindly gave her time off the afternoon Mr Lyall was killed.'

'I happened to know from what she told me that her young man was going back to his base – apparently he's in the RAF.'

'Apparently in the RAF? You don't believe her?'

'You must have noticed that she never stops talking about her private affairs, Lord Edward. I got the feeling he might be leading her on or he might be . . .'

'Not what he pretended?'

'Yes. I suggested they went to Kew. It's a favourite place of mine and I thought she might get to know a bit more about him.'

'He gave her an engagement ring.'

'Yes,' she said shortly.

'I can't help finding it odd that a girl like Jane should be employed in a department like this. As you say, she is a gossip. Surely it would not do if she were to talk about the work that goes on here?'

'She is a gossip but, to be frank, I don't think she understands what we do here. She's not stupid but she is little more than a typist. She is not involved in anything else. In any case, Mr Lyall knew her father and wanted to help the girl.'

'Do you think she said anything to her young man about the work the department does? She might have been tempted to show off?'

'No, I don't. She knows what we do here is secret but I agree she has a wagging tongue. I'll talk to Mr Caddick about it when he takes over properly next week.'

'Still, I suppose you could say that the department does not in fact deal with secrets which, if they got out, would damage the country's defence. Am I right?'

Miss Hawkins visibly relaxed. 'No, indeed. There are things in the files . . . information about rearmament and about arms deals which might embarrass Sir Robert and the government if it got into the press but nothing vital.'

'So neither Mr Lyall nor you had access to very secret documents?'

'I don't, certainly, but Mr Lyall has . . . had files in the cabinet in his room which are Most Secret. I suppose he would also have seen certain documents from other departments which would be top secret – at heads of department meetings, for instance.'

'I remember you said you did not have keys to the cabinet in Mr Lyall's office?'

'No.'

'What happened to Mr Lyall's keys when you found him dead?'

Miss Hawkins went pale and Edward wondered if he was being too brutal.

'The police took them,' she said shortly.

'How do you explain that Jane says she saw a file about Bawdsey Manor on Mr Westmacott's desk the day before he disappeared?'

Miss Hawkins blanched. 'Bawdsey . . . ? She must have been mistaken. We don't have any such file.'

Edward looked at her and she met his eye. He decided it was better to leave things as they were.

'Thank you, Miss Hawkins. You have been most helpful and I apologize if I may have seemed to be asking you too many questions but I know you are as anxious as the rest of us to get to the bottom of these two deaths. And you effectively run the department, do you not?'

'Certainly not, Lord Edward. Mr Lyall ran the department and, from Monday, Mr Caddick does. I am merely an administrative secretary.'

He thought he might manage to leave the Foreign Office without seeing Vansittart but, as luck would have it, he bumped into him on the stairs.

'Were you looking for me?' Sir Robert said, putting his arm round Edward's shoulders.

'I was going to . . .'

'Well, come up to my office. I've got ten minutes before my next appointment. Much rather talk to you than go through my red boxes.'

Unwillingly, Edward found himself following the great man into his room. Vansittart's secretary tried to buttonhole him as he strode through the outer office but he waved her away, saying, 'I must have ten minutes with Lord Edward. The world crisis can go hang itself. I want to hear about that ghastly business in Guernica. You seem to have a knack of being in the wrong place at the wrong time.'

He was obviously pleased with himself and Edward dared to say, 'You sound cheerful, sir. Can I take it your negotiations are going well?'

Vansittart looked at him shrewdly. 'Is it as obvious as all that? Yes, I am beginning to think it may, after all, be possible to avoid war if we stand up to Hitler. In a month, if I'm any judge, we'll have a new PM. SB is set to resign and Chamberlain is a good man. Not as good as his brother, perhaps, God rest him, but a good man. I remember Austen saying to me once – this was years ago, before Hitler came on the scene – "Concession provokes not gratitude but some new demand which, but for the concession, they would not have ventured to put forward." He was the best Prime Minister we never had but his brother is good: modern, hardworking – SB is so lazy! – firm but reasonable. I'm optimistic.'

He suddenly recalled that Edward was not in fact on his staff and added hastily, 'I need hardly say, that's not for repetition. If Dawson thinks I'm optimistic, he'll just about elect Herr Hitler Prime Minister. I sometimes think the leaders in *The Times* are written by Ribbentrop, not Dawson. But enough of that. Tell me about Spain. I haven't got the time now to hear the full story. You're to come to dinner and tell me in detail but it was a terrible warning of what the bomber can do and will do to civilian targets.'

'There is no doubt that Guernica was destroyed by the Luftwaffe. I saw the swastikas on the wings of the Heinkels as they flew over. It was cold-blooded murder, Sir Robert. Not

191

content with razing the town to the ground they dropped incendiaries to burn what remained and machine-gunned women and children as they fled the fires.'

'And this is what war is going to be like! We've made every sort of protest but there is nothing we can do. Franco has won the civil war. It may take a year for this to be clear to everyone but I'm sure it's true. If we use our air force to combat the Luftwaffe in Spain, where will it be when we need it to defend our own country? Though perhaps we never will. I pray not, anyway. We're just not ready for war.'

Edward was not totally convinced but this wasn't the time to argue with the Permanent Under-Secretary for Foreign Affairs. He got up, hoping to make his escape without having to report on his progress – or lack of it – investigating Westmacott's death and working out how Lyall's murder tied up with it. He was mistaken.

'Westmacott?' Vansittart inquired, raising his eyebrows. 'I've put Caddick in to sort out that department. He's a good man but I'd feel better if I knew the cancer had been cut out of it by you.'

'I'm optimistic, to use your word, Sir Robert. Give me another week.' He wasn't quite sure why he was suddenly confident that he could 'crack the case' but he was. He had that odd feeling he had had once or twice before. Aristotle called it *anagnorisis* – the moment of discovery that forms the thin blue line between knowledge and ignorance.

'Good man!' Vansittart said, eyeing him with surprise and some respect.

Edward shivered when he went out into the street. Whether because of the promise he had so rashly made or because of the chill wind, he did not know. Then, looking up at the Cenotaph, he remembered Vansittart's easy optimism. It was that which had made him shiver, he decided.

12

Weybridge was Edward's destination but he slowed when he saw the signpost indicating that he was only three miles away. The Lagonda was so easy to drive fast that he sometimes found himself somewhere he did not want to be before he was aware of it – and he certainly did not want to be visiting Mrs Westmacott. Nothing he could do or say would bring back her husband or wipe away the memory of how he died, grotesque and undignified. It was this, almost more than the murder itself, which made him so angry. She did not deserve to have her memory of her husband sullied in this way. He would have liked to wave a magic wand and bring relief to the widow and her child but he had no magic wand.

He had discussed his theories with Pride and been listened to in silence until he proffered the powder compact at which point the Chief Inspector had exploded with anger. Edward heard him out, admitting his guilt and the justice of the Chief Inspector's tongue lashing. At last Pride ran out of expletives and he was asked to report on his investigations. He had questioned the tobacconist nearest to the Foreign Office, in Cannon Row. Lyall had been a regular customer, buying once a week several boxes of his favourite cigarettes. McCloud and Younger also patronized the shop.

Edward asked Pride to run further checks on the background of each member of the department and on Jane Williams's boyfriend, Mervyn Last. They discussed all the evidence and Edward put forward his theory, which the Chief Inspector was good enough to admit was plausible. Edward explained that he was going to Weybridge to interview Mrs Westmacott and her sister and, grudgingly, the Chief Inspector gave him what might pass for his blessing.

Before going to Weybridge, he also called in on the Hassels to find Verity very much better though easily tired and not very mobile. She was eager to be briefed on the investigation and Edward went over with her all he had learnt. Predictably, she was unconvinced by his theory as to who had committed murder and he knew her well enough to take her criticisms seriously. She had a sharp mind and, not being as close to the evidence as he was, she was able to be more objective.

'It would never stand up in a court of law, you know, Edward. Anyway, I think there is something fundamentally wrong with your theory which I admit I cannot quite put my finger on.'

'I was reading *Our Mutual Friend* on the Blue Train on my way to Spain and I was struck by something Mr Inspector said, that it was always more likely that a man had done a bad thing than he hadn't.'

'Oh, that's nonsense. Dickens was always talking nonsense.'

'I wish you could come with me to Weybridge,' he said, holding her hand.

'I wish I could, too. Next week perhaps. The doc says I'm making progress.'

'You are,' he said fervently. 'But you must take care. I can't forget how near I was to losing you.'

Verity looked suddenly stricken. 'Gerda had no guardian angel to save her. I've had a lot of time to think, you know, and I am beginning to believe we are fated to . . . to look after one another. Whatever it was that drew you to Spain . . . your premonition that I was in special danger . . . that's something between us, isn't it? A tie . . . a rope. Do I make sense? Or am I just being sentimental?'

'It's not sentimental to say what we think. We don't do it often, do we, V?'

'I do,' she said tartly. 'I may be wrong but I say what I think.'

'You're the most honest person I have ever met.'

'But wrong?'

'Not often but . . .'

'But sometimes . . . ?'

194

'It's just that you see black and white where I see grey.'

'Huh! Well, we won't get into that. You're wrong about this murder, I think. Or, if not wrong, then not wholly right.'

'Well, I had better get it right, hadn't I?'

'You go off then. James is coming in to see me in a few minutes. He wants to discuss Spain. Unlike you, he has a – possibly exaggerated – respect for my views. He seems to be suffering from some sort of crisis of confidence and thinks I can help straighten him out.'

As he drove slowly into Weybridge, Edward thought about the two murders – so obviously linked but so different from each other – and sighed. He thought back to the other investigations he had conducted with Verity and missed her badly. He had an idea she and Alice would get on well together. The little girl seemed to have something of Verity's intelligence, laced with common sense, and she was certainly determined, not to say obstinate.

Alice opened the door to Edward. 'Have you found out what happened to my father?' she demanded, without giving him a chance to catch his breath. 'Mummy is so unhappy. I think it would do her good to know but . . .'

'I am not quite sure, Alice,' he said, looking her straight in the eye, 'but I believe I do know who was wicked enough to kill your father. It may be a week or two before I can prove anything. I'm afraid you will have to patient with me a little longer.'

'I understand,' she said very seriously. 'But when you do know for sure . . .?'

'Then I'll tell you and your mother but you will have to go on being brave. I may be able to tell you why your father was killed and who the wicked person was who did it but that won't necessarily make everything better. It may not even be possible to punish the person who did it.'

'I know that. I'm not a child,' she said scornfully. 'It won't ever be better but it will help mummy and me if we can understand why.'

'Of course. I know you're not a baby and I won't treat you like one. I just wanted to warn you. When are you going home? I think it would be safe for you to go back now. The newspaper men have gone away, the Chief Inspector says.'

'We're going home after Aunt Georgina's race. I want to go back to school.'

'Your aunt's race?'

'Oh yes, didn't you know? It's a special one and she's going to win it. She's driving a Napier Railton. It's absolutely wizard. She let me sit in the driving seat.'

Miss Hay came in at that moment and looked pleased to see him. 'Lord Edward, how kind of you to come and see us. I read in the papers all about your terrible time in Spain. How is Miss Browne? I do admire her. We women who take on men on their own turf must stick together. Perhaps you could bring her to the race meeting on Saturday?'

'It's very kind of you but she is still recovering from her injuries. The doctor says she must not do very much for another week or so.'

'Oh, but that's such a shame. She must be dying of boredom. I know I would be. I have quite a pull at Brooklands, though I say it who shouldn't. I'm sure we could fix her up somewhere to watch the race in comfort – VIP treatment, you know?'

'It is very good of you,' Edward said dubiously. 'She *is* bored and I'll certainly discuss it with her but . . .'

'Good! That's settled. Now, Lord Edward, I expect you have come to see Tilly. I'll call her. Can I make you a cup of tea?'

Mrs Westmacott seemed calmer than when he had last seen her but she was still nervous – her handkerchief, with which she repeatedly dabbed her mouth, was wrapped tightly round her fingers.

'I am so sorry to have missed the funeral,' Edward began. 'It must have been a terrible ordeal for you.'

'Everyone was very kind,' she said vaguely. 'The church was full, you know,' she said, almost aggressively.

'I am sure it was. I know all the people who worked with your husband thought very highly of him.' It wasn't quite a lie and it pleased the widow.

'Yes, they were all there. Mildred, of course, and that Mr McCloud. He's a painter, he told me. Sir Robert was abroad but he sent a representative – Mr Caddick. They've given him Mr Lyall's job. Did you know? He said Charlie would be sorely missed. He said his work was . . . what was the word he used? Ah! I remember, "impeccable". He said his work was impeccable.'

Edward feared she would begin to cry so he said hurriedly, 'Who is Mildred?'

'Miss Hawkins, Georgina's friend.'

'I didn't know Miss Hawkins knew your sister.'

'Oh, yes, they are great chums. They've been together for years.'

'Together? They don't live together, do they?'

'No, but they ... they go about together. They are old friends. They met at ... where was it? Georgina was taking a Pitman's course just after the war – you know, shorthand and typing. She thought it would be useful so she could earn some money as a secretary. She always wanted to be a racing driver but she was never silly enough to think of it as a job. It wasn't until Sir Vida agreed to support her that she was able to live out her dream. We said she was mad to do it but she was obstinate. Even when she was a child, she always did exactly what she wanted whatever anyone said.'

Edward had still not fully recovered from learning that Georgina and Miss Hawkins were old friends. Now there was this new information to take in: Georgina Hay was being sponsored by Sir Vida Chandra. He cursed himself. For all his clever questioning – and Pride's, too – this had never come out; not that there seemed to be any secret about it. He had just failed to ask two obvious questions. Still, it was odd that neither woman had volunteered the information. But how did it affect anything? He tried to add this new information to the pattern in his mind and suddenly he saw how it must fit in.

'I had no idea Sir Vida was financing your sister's racing career.'

'Yes, didn't she tell you? Do you know Sir Vida? He is the most wonderful man. He has been kindness itself to all of us.'

'How did you meet him?'

'With Georgina. He likes car racing and all those other things rich men enjoy like horse racing and even ... what do they call it? – power boats, I believe.'

Edward decided not to pursue the connection until he had had time to mull over its significance. Instead, he returned to Miss Hay's friendship with Miss Hawkins.

'You said Miss Hawkins was also doing a Pitman course when she met your sister. How long ago was this?'

'I don't know. You'll have to ask Georgina. Shortly after the war, as I said. Fifteen years ago? More, probably. Charlie and I weren't married then. Georgina's four years younger than me.'

She saw the expression on his face and said accusingly, 'You thought it was more?'

He couldn't deny it. Mrs Westmacott had aged even since he had seen her last. Her husband had been her rock and anchor. Now she was adrift in hostile waters and he feared she would find it very difficult to weather her loss.

'You have suffered, Mrs Westmacott. It is natural that it has taken its toll on you. I know it's easy for me to say but time may heal, or at least deaden, the pain. You have got Alice to think of.'

'You don't have to tell me that,' she said sharply and, once again, he wished Verity had been with him. She would have found the right words to say. 'And it will help if you and the Chief Inspector can tell me why Charlie had to die. The muddle . . . it all seems so meaningless. If I could think he died for . . .' he thought she was going to say 'for his country' but in fact she said, 'for some reason, then it would be easier to bear.'

'I promise you I will find the reason your husband died but I wish I could promise it will make it easier for you.'

She looked at him and did not like what she saw in his face. Stubbornly, she said, 'I won't believe Charlie did anything to be ashamed of. I knew him better than anyone and he was honest to a fault.'

Georgina returned with tea and they talked over the progress of the investigation. Edward asked whether the Foreign Office was looking after them properly.

'I've got nothing to complain about,' Mrs Westmacott said, sounding as though she was complaining. 'They paid Charlie's salary up until the day he died and then I get the widow's pension. It's not much but I suppose I should be grateful. The man who came to see me said I might lose the pension if it is proved that Charlie was . . . I don't know, betraying secrets or something. He didn't betray any secrets so they can't prove anything, can they, Lord Edward?'

'I shall talk to Sir Robert myself, Mrs Westmacott. I can assure you,' he said grimly, 'there would be the most awful stink if they tried to do you out of your pension. I'm sure it won't happen.'

He had a vision of Verity writing indignant articles in the *New Gazette*. It seemed amazing to him that the Foreign Office had not been more understanding of the poor woman's position but that was typical, he supposed, of any institution of its size run by men for men. He checked himself. He must remember to tell Verity that she really *had* influenced the way he saw things.

With tea over, Edward made ready to depart but Georgina suggested he might like to run down with her in the Lagonda to look at the course and view the car she was going to race. He was going to refuse but then thought it might be interesting and perhaps Georgina wanted to say something to him without her sister hearing. Alice wanted to come but rather meanly, Edward thought, her mother insisted she stay behind and do her school work.

'When you go back next week, I don't want the school to say that you are so far behind you'll never catch up.'

Alice went into a sulk but Mrs Westmacott was adamant. He wondered if perhaps he had been wrong about her. Beneath her air of fragility and vagueness, she might, after all, be tougher than he had imagined. With her husband gone, she seemed to realize she was going to have to fight her own battles.

As they swung out into the road, Edward said, 'Alice told me that it's a special race. Did I read something in *The Times* about a new circuit?'

'Owning a Lagonda Rapier, you have no excuse not to know about it,' Georgina Hay rebuked him. 'Is it really possible you haven't been to Brooklands before?'

'I'm afraid it is. It must be terribly expensive – racing cars. Did your sister say you were helped financially by Sir Vida Chandra?'

'Yes, do you know him?'

'I've met him. Without wishing to be rude, why did he choose you to sponsor?'

'He loves racing. He's involved in a lot of sports, you know. He owns racehorses and he fences up to Olympic standard.'

'Yes, that was where I met him – at the London Fencing Club.'

'Oh, you fence, too?' She looked at him with interest.

'Not seriously,' he said quickly. 'But you haven't told me where *you* met him?'

'We met at Mr Churchill's house in Kent many years ago. I was Mr Churchill's secretary for a few months.'

'How interesting!'

'Yes, it was. I had done my Pitman course and I applied for several positions. This one came up and seemed the most . . . unusual. I'm afraid I've always dreaded being bored.'

'I know what you mean!' Edward interjected with feeling.

'It must have been fifteen years ago – something like that. Time passes so quickly.'

'But you didn't stay long? Why was that?'

'You seem very interested in my career, Lord Edward?'

'Not really. It's just that I have recently met Mr Churchill. He's quite an impressive figure, isn't he?'

'Yes, I am a great admirer. It would be difficult to work for him and not be an admirer.'

'So?'

'Well, I was young and I wanted a social life. You couldn't have that if you were working for Mr Churchill. He demanded the whole of you. After a few months – regretfully – I decided to get a less demanding job. Simple as that.'

'Hey! I don't want to be rude but what is that stink?'

As they approached the track, a strong fruity smell of rotting vegetables and worse became impossible to ignore.

'Oh, that's the sewage farm. It doesn't always smell as bad as this.'

'Sewage farm?'

'Yes, it's right next to the Aero Clubhouse. Planes sometimes end up in it which causes merriment, as you can imagine.'

'Of course! I had forgotten. Brooklands is also used by flying enthusiasts, isn't it?'

Georgina looked at him with scorn but, fortunately, he did not see her expression as he manoeuvred the Lagonda through the iron gates.

'It's much more than an aero-club. Brooklands is a centre for the development of the new generation of aero-engines. Look, there's the Vickers Armstrong factory.'

Edward whistled. 'I didn't know. It's an impressive outfit,' he added thoughtfully.

As they pulled up outside the clubhouse, he said, 'But you still haven't told me what's happening on Saturday.'

'It's the opening of the Campbell Circuit.'

'The what?'

Georgina, who was about to get out of the car, sank back in her seat and sighed. 'I suppose I had better give you a lecture. Brooklands has been worried for some years that its existing track isn't suitable for road racing.'

'Sorry, I don't understand. What is this track if it isn't a road?'

'It's too small. It's all right for mountain racing. The steeply banked part of the circuit was unique once but times have changed. Cars are bigger and more powerful than they were twenty years ago. The track at Donington and the new Crystal Palace road course is making Brooklands look old hat. To race at full speed along a straight road is impossible in England, so we often go over to Germany to race on the autobahns. Three months ago I raced a Bimotore Alfa Romeo from Munich and clocked up 137 mph.'

Edward was impressed. 'And this is official? I mean, the Germans close off the autobahn?' This time he did catch her look and apologized. 'Of course they do. I'm being stupid.'

'You can't race modern cars on ordinary roads and our track here needed improving so that's what we've done.' She waved at a slim, petite brunette in an open-necked shirt and carrying a leather flying helmet. 'That's Kay Petre. You must have heard of her? Canadian – she's married to Henry Petre, the flying ace.'

Mrs Petre waved back and walked over to the Lagonda. 'Hi, Georgie. Introduce me to your friend. I didn't think you had any use for . . .'

Georgina hurriedly interrupted. 'Lord Edward Corinth . . . Kay Petre.'

Edward got out of the car, raised his hat and shook her hand. It was a small hand and he wondered how this tiny woman controlled a racing car.

As if she had read his thoughts – no doubt everyone she met thought the same thing – Kay said, 'As long as I can reach the pedals, I can beat anything on wheels.'

'Oh, I'm sorry. Was I so obvious?'

She laughed and Edward found himself smiling. Before either of them could say anything more, Georgina said, 'See you later, Kay. I'm taking Lord Edward over to look at the Campbell Circuit.'

Suddenly serious, Kay said, 'It's a marvel but I'm worried about Saturday. The dirt on the concrete . . . we'll kick up a storm out there and, if we're not in front, we'll see nothing.' She shrugged and added, 'So I'm going to be leader of the pack if it kills me.'

'Kay's the fastest woman on wheels despite having to use a special collapsible seat because she's so small,' Georgina said as they walked towards the new track. 'Two years ago she lapped the old course at 127 mph in a V12 Delage. The car was so big that they had to adapt it for her by extending the pedals and raising the seat so she could see the track. Then she raced Gwenda Hawkes and clocked up over 135 mph.'

When they arrived at the track, Georgina said, pointing, 'The trouble is, as you can see, by the time they had avoided the sewage farm and the aerodrome there wasn't a lot of space for new track.'

'And this was designed by Sir Malcolm Campbell?'

'Yes. It's thirty-two feet wide, increasing to forty feet on the corners, and two and a quarter miles to the lap. The idea is to provide a really fast circuit by super-elevated bends and long straights.'

'I don't know anything about it but it looks fantastic . . . amazing.'

'So you'll come on Saturday? It's only five shillings to park beside the course.'

'Certainly I'll come.'

'And do bring Miss Browne. Come back to the clubhouse and I'll show you the room reserved for ladies where she can rest if it all gets too much for her. There'll be a parade . . . everyone with a car – not just us in our racing cars. Everyone will admire this.' She stroked the Lagonda. 'It's a great car. I'm quite jealous.'

'And then?'

'Then we race.'

In the clubhouse they drank champagne and it was obvious to Edward that Georgina – or Georgie as they all called her – was a popular figure. There was much joshing and back-slapping and Edward was looked at with curiosity. His Lagonda was admired and knowledgeably assessed. He met Kay Petre again and she introduced him to a charming young woman called Barbara – he did not catch her last name, Cartland, he thought – who seemed to be one of the Mountbatten set. Then there was Elsie 'Bill' Wisdom who, Edward was surprised to discover, was married.

He was introduced to the Clerk of the Course, Percy Bradley, who took him away from the ladies to talk to him in his office in the Paddock buildings.

'This new track looks magnificent,' Edward said tactfully. 'Is it safe, do you think?'

'Quite safe. It's been engineered to the highest standards. Sir Malcolm oversaw the whole thing. Why do you ask?'

'I don't know anything about it, of course, but there seemed to be a lot of stuff on the track – builders' rubbish – and there doesn't seem to be much in the way of barriers to prevent an errant machine ploughing into the crowd.'

'It'll all be cleaned up by Saturday, I assure you, and the barriers reinforced. We have a very good safety record, you know, but cars break down, and crash even – the famous Brooklands "bumps" see to that.' Georgina had told him about these. They were almost too sizeable to be termed 'bumps' and even the heaviest car could find itself airborne coming across one of them at speed.

Although Bradley would never admit it, the concrete with which the track had been built was not suitable for the use it was put to. It was too 'shiny' for one thing and in the rain it could be lethal. Even in the best of weather, steering required huge effort and the ladies had to struggle to drag their cars round corners. In general, tyres were narrow for the size and weight of car and engine and were made of poor compound rubber which never warmed up. Although engines had been developed to an extraordinary degree, there had not been the same progress in developing gears and brakes. Brakes were still fitted only to the back wheels so stopping was an uncertain art and might take some time.

Fortunately, Edward was ignorant of the hidden dangers of racing cars at high speed and Bradley was not going to enlighten him.

'I am glad to say fatalities are very rare,' he said comfortably. 'In fact, since I have been Clerk of the Course, there have been no deaths . . . injuries, of course, but no deaths. I don't wish to sound complacent, Lord Edward, but our drivers know what they are doing.'

'But they are always pushing themselves to go just that little bit faster. What am I talking about?' he said, feeling he was being rude. 'I suppose, if there wasn't some danger, then there would be no excitement.'

'That's correct, Lord Edward,' Bradley said smiling.

Georgina was to drive the Napier Railton in the parade but not in the race, contrary to what Alice had told him. In what would be the first of three races, she was scheduled to drive a supercharged single-seater Austin. They strolled down to the garages together where they found her mechanic, 'Barney' Mackintosh, working on the Railton, pipe clenched between his teeth. Round his neck a red silk scarf fluttered in the breeze.

Edward was introduced. 'This man is a marvel,' Georgina said. 'He has a gift for it. He can tune an engine to perfection. I've never gone faster than in one of Barney's babies – that's what I call the cars he has nursed.'

'It's quite beautiful,' Edward said, and it was. Huge wheels, dark unburnished metal, an aerodynamically designed body – the Railton was power personified.

'How fast can you go in this?' he asked.

'Over 160 mph, eh, Barney?' Georgina chipped in.

'Good Lord! Not really?'

'Certainly. I think she might do much more if pushed.'

'Aye, she's sweet as a nut,' the mechanic agreed, wiping his hands on an oily cloth. 'She'll do as much as you ask of her.'

'What about the Austin?' Edward asked.

'She'll do 100 mph on the straight – no trouble. But you be careful, Miss Hay. If it doesn't rain, there'll be dust. If it does rain, you'll be slipping and sliding around like it's an ice rink.'

'It won't rain before Saturday, Barney, and the dust will soon blow away. Have you seen the windsock? The wind's already beginning to sweep the track.'

'What's that?' Edward asked, pointing to something on Barney's work bench which looked like a dead flower.

'I don't know for sure, my lord, but I think it's a chrysan-themum. Someone left it on the seat of the Austin but – if it were one of Miss Hay's admirers – I'm afraid they made a mistake. It was quite dead by the time I found it.'

13

Verity cheered up the moment Edward told her about the invitation to Brooklands.

'I'm going quietly mad sitting here while you have all the fun. Of course I'm coming with you on Saturday.'

'But, V, the doctor said you were to rest and not get excited. We don't want you getting puerperal fever or whatever it was he said you might get if you gallivant around. Have you been taking your Yeastvite tablets?'

'Idiot! I haven't had a baby, thank God. The only fever I'll get will be anxiety fever. Charlotte and Adrian can come and nurse me while you're detecting. Please . . . daddy, say I can come.'

'Huh! I have no wish to be your daddy . . . not even your sugar daddy. To be honest, I wish you would come. Twenty-four hours ago I thought this was all pretty straightforward – the two murders – but now I'm not so sure. It's the chrysanthemum which puzzles me.'

'Well, look. Why don't we go through it all again, right from the beginning. We've done it before and it seems to work.'

Edward looked into the bright, intelligent eyes, very black in her pale face. He suddenly had a desire to crush her in his arms and pour out his love for her but he knew she hated what she called 'slush'. So nearly losing her at Guernica had made him realize fully how much he did love her. He might want to go to bed with other girls – Gerda with her red hair and her monkey face – but he loved only Verity and the bond between them had been strengthened by everything they had gone through. There was something . . . not softer exactly, but more reflective – sadder – about her since she had come back from Spain. She had had several long talks with James Lyall and he got the feeling that she no longer saw 'the cause' – the Communist 'crusade', if that wasn't a contradiction – in quite such clear-cut terms as she had only a few months earlier when it was a simple fight between good and evil. He would not broach the subject. She would tell him about it when she wanted to and he was happy to wait.

'The beginning then,' he said, taking his feet off the bed. It was eleven in the morning and Verity was sitting in an armchair beside the bed which Edward – having thrown off his shoes and taken off his jacket – had appropriated. He was drinking black coffee 'to stimulate the brain cells', as he put it. Charlotte had tactfully left them alone after plumping up the cushions behind Verity's head and making her put her feet on a low stool.

He took up a sheet of paper and a pencil. 'This is how I see it. Charles Westmacott was feeding information to Churchill which he thought would help Churchill challenge the government's complacency. In his department he saw alarming figures which made it clear that Germany was arming much faster than anyone seemed to appreciate.'

'But he did not meet Churchill himself?' Verity prompted him.

'No, his contact was Sir Vida Chandra, Churchill's friend and financial backer.'

'And how did he know Chandra? Westmacott did not move in those sort of circles.'

'Through his sister-in-law, Georgina Hay. She had met Chandra when she worked for Churchill as his secretary some years ago.'

'I see. So now Chandra sponsors her. Were they lovers, do you think?'

'I have no idea, V, and I'm not going to ask. Chandra is involved in a lot of sports. Let's leave it at that.'

'Hmm! All right, but if it becomes important to our investigation, you will have to ask her . . . or him.'

'Most of the lady drivers have financial backers except one or two who are rich in their own right.'

'Or married to rich husbands,' Verity said with sarcasm.

'V! Wash your mouth out. It doesn't always come down to sex.'

'Huh! It does with the men I know,' she said. 'Money and sex.' Seeing his face fall, she added, 'Not that I mind that, poppet. There are some men . . . no, *one* man I like having money and . . .'

'Be that as it may,' Edward went on hurriedly. 'The fact is, I think Georgina is a lesbian.'

'Now who should wash their mouth out?'

'No, I do, V. I'm serious. All the chat in the clubhouse suggested it was an accepted fact. You know, "I didn't expect to see you here with a man" sort of stuff. What's more, I think her lover was, or maybe is, Miss Hawkins, Desmond Lyall's secretary. They live close to each other and Mrs Westmacott – quite innocently – gave me the impression they were more than just "chums".'

'I see where you're going! Miss Hawkins killed . . . No, I don't! Continue to expound, master. I am metaphorically – and in fact – at your feet.'

'Jane Williams, the junior secretary to Miss Hawkins, heard Westmacott having a row with Lyall just before he was murdered.'

'When was this exactly?'

'About six weeks ago. She heard Westmacott saying, "Why should I? What you are telling me to do is wrong." Then Miss Hawkins turned up and stopped her hearing anything more, unfortunately. And Mrs Westmacott said he was worried by papers he brought home, one of which she happened to catch sight of. It pertained . . .'

'"Pertained"? What sort of word is that?'

'She saw the address on a letter. It was the address of a secret defence establishment which Lyall might have known about, but not Westmacott.'

Edward felt guilty. He knew he could not be quite frank with Verity. She was a Communist and she was a journalist and he could not trust her with any details about the nature of the work done at Bawdsey. It saddened him but there it was.

'So what was Westmacott doing with these papers?'

'I think he had found them on Lyall's desk and had jumped to the conclusion – probably correct – that he was passing them on to . . . well, I don't know . . . a foreign power, let's say.'

'So what had Lyall told Westmacott to do which he didn't want to?'

'That's the question! We can only guess. Miss Hawkins gave me some anodyne hogwash which I did not believe for a moment. She said they were arguing about the accuracy of

Westmacott's reports but I would say Lyall was asking Westmacott not to report him to Vansittart or the police.'

'Perhaps, but Miss Hawkins may have been telling the truth and you may be jumping to conclusions. Your theory doesn't hold water. If the file in question was Westmacott's only evidence against Lyall it doesn't amount to much. Lyall had a right to read this file, according to you. Westmacott certainly didn't. Surely, it was Lyall who could have . . . *should* have reported him for leaking secret stuff to Churchill?'

'He may not have known Westmacott was leaking information.'

Verity thought for a moment. Then she asked, 'Would Churchill have wanted to read the file – the top secret one?'

'No. I happen to know that the information in the file wasn't the sort of stuff Churchill was after. It wasn't facts and figures about the strength of the RAF or the Luftwaffe, which is what Mr Churchill needs. Furthermore, I happen to know that he already knew what this file contained.'

'How?'

'From other sources.'

'And you can't tell me what the file was about?'

'Sorry, V, but no.' Surprisingly, she did not challenge this. 'Perhaps there was some other evidence Westmacott had that we don't know about,' he suggested.

'So Lyall murdered Westmacott to save his own skin after Westmacott threatened to expose him?'

'I think so, V, but I admit I'm only speculating.'

'But the hanging . . . Could Lyall have done that himself?'

'I don't think so. We have to trust Spotty on that. It was our enemy, Major Stille. One, or maybe two, of his men hanged him at Lyall's request.'

'You mean Lyall alerted Stille, to whom he was passing secrets, that his position was threatened and so Stille killed Westmacott?'

'Yes.'

Verity shivered.

'Are you cold?' Edward inquired solicitously.

'No, I was just remembering what Stille did to my little dog. Poor Max! No one is safe until the Nazis are . . .' She stopped and then asked, 'But I don't understand why Stille should make such a song and dance of it. I don't mean that,' she said hastily – a

208

vision of Westmacott's body twisting in the wind underneath Chelsea Bridge coming into her mind – 'I mean, why make his murder so showy?'

'Well, I can only think the Nazis were making it clear to others how they would deal with their enemies. Frighten people – after all, that's why they killed Max.'

'Well, they didn't frighten me – the bastards.' She stopped again, as if trying to eradicate the memory of her dog lying on her bed with its throat cut. 'And the powder compact you found?' she said, trying to put the picture out of her mind.

'It belonged to Lyall's wife. I think he must have been torn by curiosity or even – let's give him the benefit of the doubt – remorse. He went to see where Westmacott was murdered and left the powder compact there by mistake. It must have fallen out of his pocket.'

'Two questions: why did he carry around his wife's powder compact and why are you sure it was only after the event that he went to Chelsea Bridge?'

'To answer your second question first: Chief Inspector Pride's men are thorough. If the compact had been there when they took down the body, they would have found it. As to why he had the thing on him in the first place, I think it was part of a very special present – a wedding or anniversary present – he had given his wife. After she died, he wanted something to remind him of her – to have by him all the time. I can understand that.'

He looked at Verity and wondered, if she had been killed at Guernica instead of or with Gerda, what he would have had to remind him of her. He realized he had nothing – no ring, nothing.

She may have read his thoughts because she hurried on. 'So Georgina found out somehow, perhaps through Miss Hawkins, that Lyall was the murderer and she persuaded Miss Hawkins to poison his cigarettes and revenge her brother-in-law's death?'

'That's what it looks like.'

'Do you think Lyall knew about Miss Hawkins being a chum of Westmacott's sister-in-law?'

'I have no idea but it doesn't affect things one way or the other. Pride has checked up on how Miss Hawkins and Westmacott were employed. They were both working in the Foreign Office when Lyall's department was set up and there is no evidence in the files that, when they were transferred to this new department,

209

the fact that they knew each other ever came up. I think it suited both of them to keep it quiet. They are – or in Westmacott's case were – reserved, private people who would hate gossip of any kind. Neither of them socialized outside office hours, but, of course, Lyall *may* have known. Did I tell you, Jane Williams was appointed because her father was a friend of Lyall's?'

'No, you didn't. It's all too . . . matey. I bet you would find that most people in the Foreign Office – and I may add in all government departments – are where they are because they "knew" someone. Pulling strings! There ought to be proper examinations and interviews open to anyone.'

'Oh, come on, V! You can't mean that. People need to trust each other. You have to recruit people you know . . . who play by the same rules . . . who won't betray . . .'

'Tosh! According to you both Lyall and Westmacott *did* betray the secrets they had been entrusted with.'

'*Touché,*' Edward said. 'But still, you know what I mean. There are always rotten apples but, on the whole, people . . . you know, from our class . . . well, they don't betray.'

Verity looked at him strangely. 'Do you really believe that? You call me naïve but that's . . . For a start, I thought you believed all we Communists were . . . Oh, forget it. Let's get back to the murders. One thing you'll never make me believe is that Miss Hawkins murdered Lyall, the boss she obviously adored, because she knew he was responsible for the death of her friend's brother-in-law. She might have been torn by conflicting loyalties but she would have needed a much stronger motive for killing.'

'No one is suggesting that.'

'So, you have got it all wrapped up, nice and tidy?'

'I thought I had but now I'm not so sure. It's the chrysan-themums that worry me. What do they signify and why was one found in Georgina's car?' Edward told her what Barney, Georgina's mechanic, had said.

'If Georgina had killed Lyall to avenge her brother-in-law, might she not have left it there to mislead you?'

'It's possible, V, but what was the chance of me ever seeing it unless she thrust it under my nose? I got the feeling she had no idea that the dead chrysanthemum meant anything at all – and perhaps it doesn't. Oh, hang it all . . talking it through with you has left me more confused than before.'

'Thanks a lot!'

They were silent for a moment, meditating. At last Verity said, 'What *is* the significance of the chrysanthemum? I mean, are there myths and legends associated with it? I remember once, when I was a little girl, my father gave me a book called *The Meaning of Flowers* – or something like that. I'm afraid I never read it.'

'I looked it up,' Edward said smugly. 'Chrysanthemum, of course, comes from the Greek word meaning golden flower.'

'Of course!' Verity said ironically.

'In Japan, the imperial coat of arms contains a golden chrysanthemum. The Japanese legend – well, it's also a Chinese legend – tells of a terrible storm. A bamboo boat is blown on to an island. The boat's full of golden chrysanthemums tended by twelve maidens and twelve boys.'

'It's that sort of story, is it?' she interjected. Edward ignored her.

'They had been sent to trade the chrysanthemums for the secret of eternal youth but the island proved to be uninhabited so they settled down and built the Japanese empire.'

'But you said it was also a Chinese legend.'

'Patience! The aforementioned maidens and boys were Chinese. The chrysanthemum originated in China where it was so highly prized by the nobility that peasants were forbidden to grow them.'

'Is that it then?'

'No, actually. There's another Japanese myth about there being so many gods that some were sent down to earth. The god Izanagi strayed into Black Night. He managed to get back to earth and went for a bath to purify himself. The jewels he wore turned into flowers – specifically, his necklace was transformed into a golden chrysanthemum.'

'How confusing. Which legend do we go for?'

'I haven't a clue. None of them, probably.'

'What do we do then?'

With great difficulty, Edward refrained from smiling. It was just as he had hoped. Verity's naturally curious mind had taken charge. Instead of dwelling on the terrible events of the past weeks and the frustration of seeing her account of the massacre at Guernica ignored or dismissed as an exaggeration, she was concentrating on this new puzzle.

'We go to Brooklands on Saturday and keep our eyes open. My instinct – and it is rarely wrong,' he added to annoy her, 'is that Things are Coming to a Head.'

The gleam in his eye as he capitalized coming-to-a-head seemed to satisfy Verity and she smiled.

'Now, V, you must rest. I will telephone you tonight.' He kissed her on the forehead.

He felt at peace. Verity had been badly wounded but she was alive and she was safe. Europe might have begun its slide into the abyss but in England it was still safe.

14

It was, Edward thought as he parked the Lagonda and strolled into the crowded clubhouse, very much like Goodwood or the Epsom Derby. Although no one wore top hat and tails – suits were the order of the day – it was what *Tatler* referred to as a 'glittering occasion'. Society was well represented. Lord and Lady Mountbatten and their 'fast' set adored Brooklands though today, Edward noticed, Mountbatten was not with his wife but a startlingly pretty young actress whose name Edward could not remember. He raised his hat to the Kents – the Duchess elegant as ever in a silver fox tippet – and again to the Marlboroughs arriving in their Rolls with Margaret Whigham, top debutante of her year, shortly to marry the US golfer Charles Sweeney. As *Tatler* remarked after the last race meeting, 'Brooklands could hardly be called dowdy if Miss Whigham is there.'

As promised, Percy Bradley, the Clerk of the Course, had arranged for Verity to have a special seat on the roof of the pits where she could watch the parade and the races in comfort. These new ferro-concrete 'pits' had just been completed – the first of their kind in Britain – and provided drivers with the most modern facilities for repairing faults, changing tyres and generally getting their cars back on the track in the minimum of time. It was an added bonus that privileged spectators could watch the racing from the roof.

A steward went back to the Lagonda with Edward and escorted Verity – who had firmly refused a wheelchair – up the stairs while Edward and Fenton danced attendance. The Hassels were also coming but in their own car with Mrs Westmacott and Alice. As soon as Verity was seated, she was quickly surrounded

213

by friends and Edward was touched by the affection and respect with which she was greeted. Her reports from Spain had made her famous and her account of the razing of Guernica had drawn as much attention as George Steer's in *The Times*. The *New Gazette* was now acknowledged to have one of the finest foreign desks in Fleet Street.

Leaving Fenton to look after Verity and make sure she did not exhaust herself – this was her first social outing since returning from Spain – Edward went to stretch his legs and admire the real stars of the day – the cars, particularly those driven by the ladies. Many of the cars were having their final polish in preparation for the parade. Doreen Evans was surrounded by admirers in her special bodied single-seater MG. Jill Thomas in her Frazer Nash-BMW 328 and Margaret Allan in her husband's 4.5-litre Bentley which, she informed Edward, was much faster than his Lagonda, also drew crowds. It struck him again that so many of the ladies were tiny compared with the machines they drove and sometimes they had difficulty reaching the pedals or seeing over the steering wheel without artificial aids. Kay Petre, for one, looked quite unable to control her powerful car but Edward knew she was as effective and fast on the track as all but the very top male drivers. Georgina looked quite tall beside her. She was standing beside the Napier Railton she was to drive in the parade and talking to Barney. She seemed pleased to see him but was, understandably, preoccupied with the parade and her race which was to be the first of the day. He did not stay long but thanked her for introducing him to Percy Bradley who had made Verity's outing possible.

In the Paddock, Edward saw several people he knew, including Lord Weaver who introduced him to Sir Malcolm Campbell. Campbell was driving his V12 Sunbeam at the head of the parade and he urged Edward to join it in the Lagonda.

'It's a historic day. I am very proud of the new circuit, Lord Edward, and I want as much publicity for it as possible. Lord Weaver has promised us a "spread" in the *New Gazette* – I think that's what you called it, Joe, "a spread"?'

Weaver was an old friend of Edward's, and Verity's employer. He offered to go and sit with her so she would not feel out of things.

'You don't have to worry on that score, Joe. She seems to be the centre of attention, or at least she was a moment ago. I am suddenly aware she is famous.'

'She's a great girl and I'm proud of her. Backing her was one of the best things I ever did and, I have to confess to you, it was done in part to annoy my editor. He's a good man but he doesn't like Verity and I had to put my foot down. What's the point of owning a newspaper if you can't print what you want? I have to remind him of that now and again.'

'Actually, Joe, I'm surprised to see you here. Wasn't it only yesterday I read an article in your august organ accusing women racing drivers of "flirting with death" and "dicing with their lives"?'

Weaver had the grace to look shifty. 'I didn't write that article. I like Brooklands – always have.'

'Are you putting a bet on the first race?' Edward inquired.

As at any horse-racing course, betting was permitted and there was already a crowd in the Paddock examining the odds for the first race.

'No, I don't think so. Why, are you?'

'I think I will. A friend of mine, Miss Georgina Hay, is racing.'

'I know her name.'

'She's a well-known driver but I met her because she is the sister-in-law of the Foreign Office man, Charles Westmacott, who was murdered.'

'The Chelsea Bridge murder?' Weaver said, looking at him with interest. 'I might have known you would be involved. If you can give me a story . . .'

'Not yet, I'm afraid, Joe, but maybe soon. For the moment, take my advice and keep an eye on Miss Hay. She's a remarkable woman.'

'I'll do that. Thank you.'

Together, they left the throng and walked back to Verity who was still comfortably lodged in her armchair. Fenton stood at her elbow, prepared to take her down to the Ladies' Lounge when she was tired, but for the moment she was breathing in the tributes of friends and admirers like pure oxygen and there was a colour in her cheeks which had not been there before. She greeted Lord Weaver warmly and Edward left her in his charge as a steward informed him that, if he wished to take part in the parade, he must return to the Lagonda and be marshalled into

215

position. Verity and Weaver said they would wave at him. Verity had powerful Zeiss binoculars so she could see right across the circuit. Edward said he would return before the first race, in which Georgina was to take part. It would be a ladies' Short Handicap and the first of two short races before the main event – a long-distance race over a hundred laps for the new Campbell Trophy.

Dame Ethel Locke King, widow of Brooklands' founder, cut the tape and then drove forward in a 1903 Napier to begin the lap of honour. Behind her and Malcolm Campbell poured a host of cars, old and new – a veritable living history of the automobile. Edward modestly kept well back in the procession but he did feel proud to be there and proud of his Lagonda Rapier. Milk white and powered by a 4467 cc six cylinder Meadows engine, it was a magnificent machine. A similar model had won Le Mans in 1935. On this occasion, Edward was content to do a steady 5 mph but, even so, he was rather alarmed by the cloud of dust which enveloped him, thrown up by the cars in front. He slowed almost to a halt, not wishing to bump into the car in front – a black Armstrong Siddeley. Because of the dust he could not see the clubhouse and had no idea whether Verity could see him but, lifting the goggles he had put on for effect and which had no practical use, he thought he saw a face he knew. The young man was walking alongside the track with a crowd of enthusiasts.

It came to him that he knew exactly why the man was at Brooklands and he had to fight a desire to stop the Lagonda, vault over the barrier and collar him. A particularly heavy cloud of dust blinded him for a moment and, when he could see again, the man had disappeared. With a grim face, Edward completed the lap, fought his way off the course to park the Lagonda beside the clubhouse and leapt up the stairs to tell Verity what he had seen. He found her all alone except for Fenton, loyally standing at her elbow.

'Miss Hay . . . do you think she is in any danger?' Verity asked.

Edward rubbed his forehead vigorously. 'Of course, V, the chrysanthemum in her car. I must go and warn her.'

'I don't think she'll take any notice but go anyway. I wish I could come with you.'

'I wish you could too.' He leant over and kissed her on the lips.

'Stop that. You'll cause a scandal, Edward!' She clutched at him. 'Be careful. Now I've started having premonitions. I'll watch you through my binoculars.'

'Fenton, don't let her out of your sight.'

'I will not, my lord.'

He found Georgina – dressed entirely in black – talking to Kay Petre and Sir Malcolm Campbell. She always wore black, hating to appear after the race smeared in oil, but she must have been aware how good her yellow hair looked against it, at least until she put on her leather helmet. The car on the other hand – a supercharged Austin – was painted green, racing green, as it was called – to signify that it was English. Sir Vida Chandra was also there discussing technical details with Barney. He gave Edward a chilly nod and continued his conversation.

It suddenly seemed quite absurd to warn Georgina in front of Sir Malcolm that, because a dead chrysanthemum had been left in her car and he had glimpsed someone in the crowd whom he suspected of being a murderer, she ought to pull out of the race. If someone came to him with such a story, he would pooh-pooh it so why should he expect Georgina to do anything else? He compromised by breaking into Sir Vida's conversation to ask Barney if the car was ready for the race – a stupid question, he realized as soon as he had asked it. Sir Vida sniffed derisively but Barney, pipe between his teeth as usual, was polite.

'Tickety-boo, my lord. She's going like a dream.' He patted the gleaming metal as though it were a favourite dog.

A flurry of small boys whom the stewards had been unable to keep out of the pits clustered around Georgina and Sir Malcolm, seeking autographs.

'It doesn't look very substantial,' Edward said doubtfully, resting his hand on the car.

'It's strong enough,' Barney responded, 'but the main thing is that it's very light.'

Edward looked round and, to his amazement, found Verity standing beside him. She had got bored perched on the roof and had insisted on Fenton taking her downstairs. Fenton looked at Edward apologetically. 'Miss Browne insisted, my lord.'

'That's all right, Fenton, I know what it is when Miss Browne insists on something.' He introduced her to everyone.

217

'Miss Browne,' Georgina said, 'would you like to try it for size?' She indicated the car.

'Oh, may I?' Verity said, a huge smile lighting up her face.

'Of course – as long as you can climb in without opening up any of your stitches.'

'Here, let me help you,' said Kay Petre, who had walked over from her car.

Edward noticed that both women knew exactly who she was and how she had received her wounds and treated her with the same respect which she showed them. Sitting in the car, Verity looked very much at home though, to Edward's certain knowledge, she was an erratic, if dashing, driver. She had owned a Morgan when he met her first and, with her customary impatience, had not even discovered how to get into reverse gear before driving it for the first time. She had had no car for the last couple of years and, when she had insisted on riding a motorcycle the year before, Edward had found out she had no driving licence and had not passed a driving test.

He wished he had a Kodak with him to take her picture now. As if in answer to his wish, he turned to find André Kavan complete with camera.

'Good heavens! What are you doing here, Kavan? I thought you were in Spain.'

'No,' he said in his odd mongrel accent, 'I have had enough of Spain.'

Edward thought he understood why. Gerda's death at Guernica was reason enough not to want to return to that war-ravaged country.

'I saw your photographs – yours and Gerda's – in *Life* magazine,' he said awkwardly. 'They were extraordinary. Can anyone have ever recorded the horror and pity of war so vividly?'

'Thank you, Lord Edward,' Kavan responded gravely. 'Your praise means something to me as you were there. You have a right to judge my work. I have two or three of Gerda's photographs you might like to have. I know it was important to her that you liked her work.'

Edward remembered the way Kavan had taken her camera from him when she lay dead. There had been jealousy, even hatred, in his eyes then. He took these words – if not as an apology – at least as a gesture of reconciliation.

'I'd like that very much.' They shook hands solemnly and, in doing so, buried more than the antipathy they had felt for one another when they first met. They also put to rest their unspoken rivalry over Gerda. No doubt André still thought Edward had been to bed with her and it made little difference that he had not done so. He had wanted Gerda intensely and, talking to André, he felt the pain in his gut that he had never held her naked in bed and would never do so.

Verity, too, seemed delighted to see André again and let him take several photographs of her in the car, Georgina and Kay standing behind her.

'I am doing a spread for *Life*,' he explained, 'on the phenomenon of the lady racing driver. I am off to Italy and then Germany next week. Lord Edward, I believe you know Sir Vida Chandra. Would it be possible for me to meet him? I understand he plays a big part in the sport over here.'

'Of course, but here's the lady who should do that for you since he makes it possible for her to race. Georgina, may I introduce you to the celebrated photographer André Kavan? André, may I present Miss Georgina Hay who is shortly to race on this new track? By the way, where is Sir Vida? He was here a moment ago.'

'I have no idea,' Georgina said brusquely. 'I'm afraid we must go now. We are being ordered to prepare for the start.'

Edward was surprised at her sudden *froideur*. He wondered if he had made a faux pas. Perhaps she was embarrassed to have her sponsorship by the millionaire made public. Fortunately, at that moment Mrs Westmacott arrived with Alice, the Hassels and Miss Hawkins.

'Sorry we're so late,' Adrian said. 'We got caught up in the traffic and then the parade.'

'Well, you're here now,' Georgina said, kissing Alice. 'I'll see you all after the race.'

Verity was looking tired and Edward was glad when she was seated once again in her comfortable wicker armchair.

'Did you manage to warn Miss Hay?' she asked.

'I didn't have the chance, somehow. I don't know, when it came to say something, it all seemed so vague, I thought she

219

would laugh in my face if I told her to pull out of the race. I can't make up my mind whether I'm in the grip of some sort of fantasy or . . .'

'Oh well, it's too late now. Look, they are on the starting line.' She passed him her binoculars and he scanned the crowd, looking for the man he had seen earlier.

'That was Sir Vida Chandra, wasn't it? I wanted to meet him but he went away just as Fenton and I arrived. He is a friend of Mr Churchill's, you said?'

'Yes, he was there when I went to have dinner at Churchill's flat. He's got a finger in many pies. I don't know what to make of him. Sometimes I think of him as a patriot doing his best to help Churchill prepare for war and sometimes I wonder if there isn't something sinister about him.'

He continued to scan the circuit through the binoculars and his gaze came to rest on the Vickers Armstrong factory. It seemed so odd that the motor racing should take place in the same square mile as Vickers was developing its new aero-engines. He lowered the glasses and said to Verity, 'Am I imagining things or is this meeting a wonderful opportunity for a bit of industrial espionage?'

'What do you mean?'

'Crowds of people – anyone could walk into the Vickers factory and look about them. Then, what about the German connection? Didn't Mrs Petre tell me the drivers often went to Germany to race on the autobahns? Quite legitimate but what an opportunity for – what shall we say? – pursuing other interests.'

'Oh, that's nonsense, Edward. Are you thinking she or any of the other drivers could be spies?'

'No, of course not,' but he sounded doubtful. 'There was something Fred Cavens said to me . . . about fencing don't y'know. Now, what was it? I remember: "Himmler likes to penetrate British society through sport." Think of the propaganda triumph the Olympics turned out to be for Nazi Germany.'

'It's true . . .' Verity began, then she hesitated. 'Georgina was saying a moment ago that the bane of motor-racing was that it was becoming increasingly national – not one driver against another but one country against another country. If Kay wins a race, it becomes a Canadian victory. If Prince von Leiningen does, then it's a German victory.'

Edward lowered the glasses again and clicked his fingers. 'Hey, wait a minute: why racing cars? Why shouldn't one of the flyers carry secrets out of the country? They're popping over the Channel all the time.'

'I don't know, Edward. This is all wild guesswork. You've got no evidence of anything.'

'I know I haven't but I intend to get some,' he said grimly. 'I see there's a delay at the start. I'll do some scouting around while everyone is watching it being sorted out. Are you all right here for a few minutes, V?'

'Go,' Verity said dramatically, 'if it makes you happy. You won't find anything but go if you must. Still, why not wait until Georgina has raced?'

'I'll watch it as I stroll round the circuit. Sure you'll be all right?'

'I've got Fenton, haven't I? Go for God's sake.'

Reaching the Vickers Armstrong factory, Edward was frustrated but also rather relieved to find it closed – not only closed but locked and barred. Perhaps because it was a Saturday or, more likely, because this was a day of celebration for Brooklands, no one was at work. He peered through a dirty window but could see nothing. He tried a couple of doors and found them secure. He was about to turn back to the track when he was challenged by an elderly man in overalls.

'There ain't no one here. It's all shut up.'

'Are you the caretaker?'

'The janitor – caretaker – call me what you want. And I was told to keep an eye out for gentlemen as came snooping, d'y'see?'

'I do see and I heartily approve. In times like these you can't be too careful, eh?'

'I don't know about that,' the man said sententiously, 'but "no snooping, Bill" – that's what the governor told me.'

'Has there been "snooping", then?'

'I don't think as how I should be talking about it, begging your pardon, sir.'

'No, quite right. Well, Bill, I'll be off. Oh, by the way, was the chap they caught snooping a man about my age, short, with sandy hair and a crooked nose?'

'No. indeed, sir. He were a dark-haired young man . . . younger than you, sir. About your height, though.'

'Ah, well, not the man I was thinking of then. Good day to you.' He tipped his hat to Bill and went on with his walk.

He saw that Georgina's race still had not started. One of the cars seemed to have broken down and blocked the track. He thought he might still have time to get back to Verity before the flag went down.

Verity was in a fever of excitement when he returned. 'Guess who I saw?'

'I have no idea but you're going to tell me.'

'Guy Baron. He's here with André. I asked him why he was here, because he knows less about racing cars than I do, and he said it was "a good place to meet people". After all, he hadn't expected to meet me here and now he had. I really don't know what he was getting at. Oh, and the odd thing was, he was quite sober.'

Edward bit his lip. There were just too many people at Brooklands who had no business being there and, as Verity pointed out, most of them knew next to nothing about cars. Was it possible that, after all, he had got it wrong and the murderer was . . . but no, he was *not* wrong. It was two strands getting entangled. If only he could straighten out who did what to whom. He needed to know one thing more.

He saw the starter and Percy Bradley running around the broken-down car, gesturing and shouting. He could not make out what was being said but it was clear that the race was still some minutes away from starting. He told Verity he wanted to place a bet on Georgina but would be back in a moment.

'You're so restless, Edward. It's too late to make a bet. Sit down and relax.'

'I will in just a moment,' he said airily and slipped off to the Clerk of the Course's office. A young woman to whom he introduced himself obligingly allowed him to use the office telephone. He had Sir Robert Vansittart's telephone number – his direct line – but he was not there, it being a Saturday. With a finger in one ear to muffle the noise of roaring engines, he asked instead to speak to Mr Sanderson, the man who had dealt so efficiently with his diplomatic passport. This industrious minion was at his desk and Edward asked him to find out for him where and when a member of Desmond Lyall's staff had been born. When Sanderson understood why this information was important, he obligingly said he would ring Edward back in an hour when he had made his inquiries. Holding his hand over the mouthpiece, he asked the young woman whether he might give the Foreign Office Mr Bradley's telephone number to which she agreed, her eyes shining with excitement. This was clearly all much more thrilling than the racing.

He went back to Verity, having forgotten to put on his bet. She did not appear to have missed him and was once more surrounded by friends. Lord Weaver and his wife were sitting on either side of her. Guy Baron was lurking in the background talking to Adrian Hassel, and Alice and her mother were laughing with Charlotte. It was good to see Mrs Westmacott looking relaxed and happy.

Guy saw him and came up to him. 'Such a good crowd here, Corinth. And dearest Verity's being lionized, positively lionized. I so much envy you having been at Guernica. You saw history being made.'

Edward winced. 'It wasn't history I saw being made so much as the future. In the coming war I very much fear mass murder will become a commonplace. But don't let's talk about that now.' He had no wish to discuss Guernica with a man whom he distrusted and whose friendship with David Griffiths-Jones tarnished him.

'André's photographs made a great impact,' Baron continued to probe. 'Alas! Poor Gerda. Did you ever sleep with her? Kavan thinks you did.'

Edward looked at Guy with disgust. He felt the anger bubble to the surface but restrained it with a great effort. 'Where is Kavan?'

'He's taking photographs at the start. In fact, I think I'll go and join him.' He scurried off.

Adrian approached. 'I say, I thought you were going to hit the man. What did he do to annoy you?'

'He was attempting to make me lose my temper and, by jingo, he nearly succeeded. That's all.'

Suddenly there was a shout from Weaver. 'They're off! Look, at last they're off!' As the starter's flag fell, Adrian pulled Edward over to the rail and they watched the drivers rev their engines, desperate to be the first to get away. The growl of the motors was a sound he had never heard before and would never forget. He understood, really for the first time, what it was about the sport which hooked people. It was visceral and seemed to reverberate deep inside him, demanding a response over which he had no control. Momentarily, he forgot his anger and his concerns for Georgina's safety in the thrill of the chase.

The Austin took off like a swift among crows. Kay Petre, he noticed, was less fortunate and had to be push-started. There were twelve machines in all. The drivers were impossible to distinguish in their overalls and leather helmets – some had goggles, others visors – but each car was clearly numbered, in Georgina's case with a large white eight. By any reasonable reckoning, it had to be mad: these women driving at almost 100 mph in their fragile machines, with no straps to hold them in their seats, inadequate brakes, the cars always on the point of spinning out of control. But, as Edward watched, he saw that just because it *was* so unreasonable his heart beat faster and and his hands clutched the binoculars as though his life depended on them. The excitement of sheer, unadulterated speed gripped him so that it hurt.

The new Campbell Circuit was to be lapped anti-clockwise – each lap two and a quarter miles. The cars were to make twenty-five laps – a gruelling test for driver and car. They were to proceed down the Railway Straight, as they would have done before the Campbell Circuit was constructed, but make a sharpish left turn on to the new road. They then doubled back parallel to the Railway Straight, swung into the right-handed Aerodrome Curve and then into the Sahara Straight which ran parallel to the finishing straight. After a sharp left-hand bend at Vickers Bridge Corner, they crossed the Aerodrome road to the Fork turn and had to negotiate a climbing right-hand curve between embankments known as the Test Hill Hairpin before a left-handed swing round the Members' Banking.

It was a fast course and it was immediately apparent that several of the cars were simply not up to the job. One car had failed to start and the driver – Edward could not see who it was – suffered the indignity of having to be pushed back into the pits. Another car stopped dead on the eighth lap – knowledgeable folk saying that the gearbox must have seized up. Apparently it often happened.

It was frustrating for the watching crowds because the dust cloud was blinding and Edward wondered how the drivers dared to keep their speeds of over 70 mph when they must have very little idea of what was happening just a few yards ahead of them. He looked around him. Mrs Westmacott had her hands to her mouth and little Alice's excitement had turned to dismay. The noise of the engines, by now almost animal in ferocity, echoed up to the watchers on the roof. The dust began to make them cough and handkerchiefs and scarves were held to noses and mouths. It could not go on and nor indeed did it. In lap twenty, it seemed as though Georgina – the number eight momentarily visible as she took the lead – approached the Vickers Bridge Corner too fast, struggling in vain to combat the massive understeer. To the horror of the onlookers, her car struck the bridge parapet, tipped up on to its nose and rolled on to its side. Georgina was flung out and slid across the course but, by some miracle was not run over as the other cars, breaking to avoid the Austin, skidded across the track and concertinaed into one another.

Edward, aware that there was nothing he could do, nevertheless ran towards the carnage. A firetender was already there dealing with a burning car. Several drivers were walking around in a daze contemplating the disaster. He had no time to tend to anyone other than Georgina. She was being taken on a stretcher towards one of the three ambulances which had reached the accident within three or four minutes. Panting, Edward arrived just as the back doors were being slammed and the ambulance was preparing to depart.

'How is she?' he called to the driver.

'Badly hurt, I'm afraid, sir – broken bones but not dead, not by a long chalk.'

He sighed with relief and asked whether he could travel in the ambulance to the hospital. When he had to admit he was not a relative, he was refused permission.

'Where's she being taken?'

On being told it was Weybridge Cottage Hospital, he ran back to where Verity and the others were still sitting, hardly able to take in what had happened – it had been so sudden and so complete a disaster. Miss Hawkins was the first to grab him as he reappeared and ask after her friend. When she heard Georgina was badly hurt but not in danger of dying, she covered her face with her hands and collapsed into a chair.

Verity volunteered to look after Alice while Mrs Westmacott accompanied Edward to the hospital.

'Alice, do you know the way back to the house?' he asked.

'Of course I do. I've often come here with Aunt Georgina.'

'Good girl! Adrian, will you take charge of Alice and Verity?'

'Don't worry. You go off. We'll be all right,' Adrian reassured him. 'Just give me the key, will you, Mrs Westmacott?'

She handed over the key to the house, kissed Alice and told her not to worry. 'Lord Edward says Aunt Georgina is not going to die but we must go and find out how badly hurt she is.'

'Of course, mother,' the girl said, quite composed. 'I'll be all right. Give her . . . give her my love.'

Despite the drama of the crash, Georgina was the only driver who had been badly injured. They were not allowed into her room immediately because a doctor was still examining her. The cottage hospital, excellent in its way, was not equipped to deal with serious injuries and it was obvious that, as soon as she could be moved, Georgina would have to be taken to one of the big London hospitals. Among those receiving treatment for minor injuries was Kay Petre .

'Mrs Petre,' Edward said, 'Forgive me but may I ask if you are badly hurt?'

'Oh, it's you, Lord Edward. No, I'm not hurt – just my wrist . . . see? And a toe, but who needs toes?' She showed him her swollen wrist and hand. 'Not broken, I hope, but badly bruised. I won't be racing for a month or two, that's for sure. But poor Georgina . . . How is she?'

'Badly hurt but they say she'll live. We're just waiting for the doctor. He's in with her now.'

'Thank God! I think she was lucky to get out alive. I don't know what happened. One moment she was going like a bird and the next . . .' she raised her good hand to her head in a gesture of bewilderment, 'she didn't take the corner.'

Edward suddenly remembered his manners. 'Oh, Mrs Petre, this is Miss Hay's sister, Mrs Westmacott.'

'She wasn't . . . run over, was she, Mrs Petre?' Mrs Westmacott asked timidly.

'No, but as I say, I couldn't see exactly what happened. I was quite a long way behind after my rotten start but she was thrown a good way across the track. I've had several prangs in my time but nothing that bad.'

'From where we were, it looked as if the dust must have obscured her view at a crucial moment and she hit the embankment,' Edward said.

'The dust cloud was appalling. The track should have been swept more thoroughly. I'll tell Percy Bradley so. Of course, there'll have to be an inquiry.'

'You don't think there is anything fundamentally wrong with Sir Malcolm's new track?'

'No. It's fast, of course, but it's quite driveable. There are some nasty bumps in the concrete though. Perhaps Georgina hit one of them, or some debris left by the builders. We'll have to wait and see. I am sure the officials are examining the track at this moment. Oh dear, it will be headlines in the papers and they'll start saying that it's not a sport suitable for women and we can't drive safely and all that sort of rubbish.'

'Well,' Mrs Westmacott began, 'I was frightened before the start and I know Lord Edward was worried.'

'Not about women driving,' he said diplomatically. 'The best women drivers are no doubt the equal of the men but . . .' he saw Kay begin to frown and added hurriedly, 'but do women have the *strength* to drive such powerful cars?'

'Georgina has raced much more powerful cars than her Austin. She was perfectly capable of driving it much faster than she was when the crash happened. Perhaps she had a blow-out. It can happen. Who knows? Oh well, there's no point speculating.'

A nurse appeared and took Kay off to have her wrist and foot strapped up. At the same time, the doctor came out of Georgina's room and Edward introduced him to Mrs Westmacott.

'Is my sister going to be all right, doctor?' she asked nervously.

'She has a broken arm, a smashed shoulder and a broken rib but, as far as I can tell, she has not suffered any internal bleeding. We are waiting for an ambulance to take her to St Thomas's in London where she can be assessed properly. One thing is certain, she's had the devil's own luck not to be killed.'

Edward was relieved but wondered if the devil had not had something to do with the crash in the first place. It might have been an accident but he was prepared to bet that someone had made the accident happen. He blamed himself for not having insisted Georgina pull out of the race but he knew in his heart that she would never have agreed just to allay his premonition that her car had been tampered with. It remained to be seen exactly how it had been interfered with but he was convinced in his own mind that it must have been. Georgina was an experienced driver and a sensible woman. It was true the dust on the track had made it more than usually dangerous but he could not get the chrysanthemum out of his mind. The best he could do now was to put a stop, once and for all, to this series of deaths and near deaths.

In all the drama, Edward had quite forgotten that, as they left Brooklands to drive to the hospital, Mr Bradley's assistant had pressed into his hand a piece of paper on which she had written the answer to the query Edward had put to Mr Sanderson at the Foreign Office. He now took the crumpled note from his pocket and read what was on it: 'You were right. He was born in Munich on December 24th 1913. His mother is English and, when his father died in 1914, she came back to England. I won't do anything until you tell me. Sanderson.'

When Edward got back to Georgina's house, he saw at once that Verity was very tired and her wound was paining her. He kicked himself for taking her to Brooklands but he had hoped it would be a pleasant day out, not a day on which death would once again attempt to gather in its harvest. Oddly enough, Mrs Westmacott seemed to bear this new disaster with fortitude and was calm, even competent, when she might have been expected to have had a nervous collapse. She, too, had seen Verity turn very pale and insisted they take her home.

'You have been very kind – all of you – but there's nothing more you can do for the moment. As you know, Alice and I were planning to return home tomorrrow,' she said, 'and, since Georgina is being moved to St Thomas's, we may just as well go back. Alice has missed so much school already and I can get from The Larches to the hospital without too much difficulty.'

Edward said he would take Verity back to the Hassels' house despite Adrian and Charlotte assuring him they could cope with the invalid. However, when they were back in the King's Road, Charlotte was sufficiently alarmed by Verity's condition to call the doctor although it was already seven o'clock. Only when the doctor had convinced Edward that Verity was suffering from exhaustion and needed to be left alone to sleep, did he allow Fenton to drive him back to Albany in the Lagonda.

'Not all soda, old lad, if you don't mind,' he said an hour later, as he watched Fenton pour him a restorative. 'Have one yourself. We've earned it.'

He had already spoken to Pride and arranged to meet him at the Foreign Office at ten on Monday morning. Pride had told him that he had gathered in Miss Williams's boyfriend, Mervyn Last. 'I frightened the life out of him,' Pride confessed cheerfully. 'He turned out to be a postman – married of course – looking for a little bit on the side as you might say. I don't think he'll risk anything of the same again. I'm afraid the girl was rather cut up though. I tried to tell her gently but she went into hysterics. Told me I was a liar and I had scared off the love of her life.' He looked a little sheepish. 'I ought to have left it to you, I suppose, my lord. I think she would have taken it from you.'

'Don't blame yourself, Chief Inspector. The truth was always going to hurt. It almost always does. I'll talk to her – try and cheer her up a bit.'

Fenton brought over the two glasses of whisky and they both drank appreciatively.

'Thank you, my lord,' Fenton said, replacing his empty glass on the tray. 'Might I ask if you have established the course of events?'

'I believe so, Fenton. Chief Inspector Pride has agreed to go with me and re-interview the late Mr Westmacott's colleagues at the FO. I must say, he was most amenable about it. Do leopards change their spots, I wonder? I must also talk to James Lyall again.'

'May I inquire, my lord, if you have changed your opinion of the young man? You told me you did not believe he had been involved in his father's death.'

'I still think so but there are one or two points on which I think he was less than frank with me.'

The next day, Sunday, before he had eaten his breakfast, Edward telephoned the Hassels and was relieved to hear that Verity was very much better.

'She's asleep now but she says she has something to tell you – something she saw at Brooklands. She thinks it may be important,' Adrian said.

'Tell her I will come and see her about two o'clock tomorrow. I have a little sleuthing to do first. Tell her I think I know what she saw but I want to hear it from her own lips.'

15

'Miss Hawkins,' Edward said, addressing the white-faced but determined woman sitting straight-backed before him on the edge of her chair, 'Miss Williams said that she heard Mr Westmacott quarrelling with Mr Lyall shortly before Mr Westmacott disappeared.'

'Yes.'

'And you heard them too?'

'I heard raised voices. It wasn't my place to eavesdrop.'

'But you must have been curious as to why they were arguing? I gather it had not happened before.'

'It was not my business.'

'No one else heard the quarrel?'

'No, Lord Edward. They wouldn't have unless they had happened to be in my office.'

'I think you did hear what Mr Westmacott and Mr Lyall were quarrelling about,' Chief Inspector Pride interjected. 'It would have been unnatural not to have listened – particularly as you must have guessed it concerned you.'

'I don't know what you mean.'

'But you do,' Edward said, almost coaxingly. 'Lyall was trying to protect you, wasn't he? Westmacott was saying it was wrong of him to do so.'

'Protect me? Why would I need protecting?'

'Because you had been passing files to Mr Younger which he had no right to see, let alone take out of the office.'

'This is pure fantasy, Lord Edward. What possible reason could I have for letting Mr Younger look at files he had no right to see? In any case, he had every right to look at files in the department.'

'Not the file relating to the research being carried out at Bawdsey Manor.'

'I told you before, I don't know anything about such a file.'

'Miss Williams saw it on your desk and asked you about it.' This was Chief Inspector Pride at his most formidable.

'Mr Lyall may have had such a file. I did not. I don't even know what goes on at Bawdsey Manor.' Miss Hawkins was holding firm but Edward could hear the doubt and fear in her voice.

'Mr Lyall did indeed have a file on Bawdsey in his own cabinet where he kept the top secret files even you were not permitted to see,' Edward said. 'So, the question is: why did Miss Williams see it on your desk?'

'She can't have done.'

'But she did. She had no reason to lie and, of course, she had no way of knowing its significance. When it disappeared from the in-tray on your desk, you guessed who had taken it: Mr Westmacott. Foolishly, he took it home either because he picked it up with other files he was working on or because he was curious as to what it was. We shall never know. He came back to the office to ask Lyall to explain what the file was doing on your desk. Lyall said it was of no importance and that he would talk to you, Miss Hawkins, about it – something emollient like that. Westmacott got angry and threatened to tell Sir Robert about the lax way in which secrets were guarded in his department.'

'This is a tissue of lies. You've got no reason to attack me in this way. Why would I have one of Mr Lyall's secret files on my desk?'

'Because your son had just returned it to you.'

The blood left Miss Hawkins's face and she dropped her head, suddenly defeated.

'You know about Harry?' she asked in a low voice.

'We do,' the Chief Inspector said heavily. 'You were married in 1913 to a German by the name of Franz Junger. He died in 1914 and you made your way back to England with your baby. It did not do to have a German name in 1914 so you reverted to calling yourself Miss Hawkins. Is that correct?'

She shook her head. 'I called myself *Mrs* Hawkins. It did not do to have a baby but no husband. I explained I was a widow. There were many widows in those days. No one was particularly interested. I only became *Miss* Hawkins again when I joined the Foreign Office.'

'It must have been hard,' Edward said gently. 'With no pension and a baby to feed . . . How did you manage?'

'I had a little money from my husband. I found some rooms in the East End with a good woman who looked after Harry while I went out to work.'

'And you eventually took a secretarial course where you met Miss Hay?' Edward continued.

'Yes, the war was ending and I was still young. I took a Pitman's stenographer course and, as you say, it was there I met Georgina – Miss Hay.'

'Why did you never remarry?' Pride asked.

'Because Georgina and I fell in love.' She looked at the two men defiantly. 'I know what you think – that it was disgusting and that I am . . . perverted.'

'I don't think that,' Edward said mildly, aware that Pride would certainly be thinking exactly the opposite. 'Did you live together?'

'We thought it was better not to do so.'

'But Georgina – Miss Hay – knew about Harry?'

'Of course. We brought him up together.'

'Why did you revert to being *Miss* Hawkins when you joined the Foreign Office?'

'Don't you know, Lord Edward?'

'No.'

'They don't like you being married here. When Miss Williams gets married, she'll have to leave. They don't think it's suitable for married women to work. They'd rather you starve,' she added bitterly.

'When did you tell your son who his father was?' Pride asked.

'Not until two years ago. I had to. I was able to . . . to pull a few strings and get him a job in this department. It wasn't really his sort of thing but at least it was a job. I had to tell him then so he wouldn't say something and get me into trouble.'

'You mean you told your story to Desmond Lyall and asked for his help?'

'Yes. He was very kind,' she said miserably. 'I . . . I owe him a lot.'

'But your son wasn't satisfied?'

233

'No. He started to hate me. He brooded about his father. He kept on asking me questions . . . blaming me . . . I don't know what for. I tried to reason with him but he said I was betraying his father. He changed his name to an English version of his father's. He did not want anyone at the Foreign Office, other than Mr Lyall, to know he was my son. He started learning German so he could listen to . . . the wireless broadcasts . . . Hitler's, I mean. He learnt about the strength of the German air force as part of his work and he came to admire it and despise our government's weakness. He wanted to be an air ace . . . like Von Richthofen. He started going to Sir Oswald Mosley's rallies. Apparently, he was a flyer in the war.'

'So what happened? He began stealing secret papers and passing them on to . . .?'

'To a Major Stille. He's a German . . .'

'We know about Major Stille,' Edward said grimly. 'We know he is a Major in the SS, based at the German Embassy and that Ribbentrop uses him for all the dirty jobs he wants done.'

'How did they meet?' Pride asked.

'At Brooklands. I don't think it was an accident. He . . . Major Stille . . . kept an eye on who was flying there . . . oh, I don't know exactly . . .'

'But Stille wasn't satisfied with the low-level stuff Harry was giving him?'

'No. That was when he made me . . . borrow Mr Lyall's keys to his cabinet from his coat pocket.'

'And you got him the Bawdsey Manor file?'

'Yes.'

'It was remarkably casual of him to leave it on your desk when he had finished with it.'

'It was, but he was getting . . . reckless. He was thinking of taking a plane and flying it to Germany. That's what he used to say when . . . when he taunted me with what he called my betrayal.'

'But he was of more value to Stille here in London, surely?'

'Yes. Major Stille told him to stay.'

'So he said he couldn't because Mr Westmacott knew what he was up to?'

'Why had Westmacott come to suspect him?'

'Harry told me that Mr Westmacott had seen him with Stille in

St James's Park one lunch time and had seen him pass an envelope to him. He had followed Stille back to the German Embassy. When he got back to the office, Mr Westmacott asked Harry to explain himself. Harry said he had passed nothing to anyone and the man he had seen him with in the park was a German friend he had met at Brooklands who worked at the embassy. Westmacott pretended to be satisfied but Harry knew the game was up and it would not be long before the security services would be on to him.'

'*That* is what you heard Lyall and Westmacott quarrelling about?' Edward broke in.

'Yes, I overheard Mr Westmacott shouting at Mr Lyall. Desmond was trying to tell him he was mistaken. He simply would not believe Harry was . . . a spy.'

'And you warned Harry? You knew if Lyall refused to act, Westmacott would go over his head . . . to Vansittart?'

'I had to. What else could I have done? But I never thought . . . I never thought it would end with Mr Westmacott being killed. I swear it. It was a terrible shock.'

'But that wasn't the end of it, was it?'

'No,' she said in a small voice. 'When Mr Westmacott was found dead Desmond was distraught. He knew who was responsible and he blamed himself for letting his loyalty to me sway his judgement.'

'What happened? Did Mr Lyall threaten Harry with . . .?'

'I don't know . . . I don't know!'

'Well, I think he did say something to Harry,' Edward continued remorselssly. 'I think he told him to leave the country or he would be arrested.' Miss Hawkins said nothing but unconsciously twisted her hands in her lap, so Edward pressed on. 'And Harry couldn't leave. Stille wouldn't let him. So Mr Lyall, to whom you owed so much, had to die. Did you lure him out of the way so your son could put poisoned cigarettes in the box on his desk?'

'No! No, I swear . . . I would never . . . could never have . . . done that.'

'But he managed without you, somehow, didn't he?' Pride almost snarled. 'He even had time to leave his . . . his "calling card", his little joke, his dead flower. Did it give you a shock when Mr McCloud found it under the cigarette box?'

235

'I . . . I didn't believe it . . . not at first. Harry said he was going to get out. I didn't know that he was planning to kill Desmond . . . Mr Lyall. I would have stopped him. He knew I would have stopped him – that was why he didn't tell me. All he said was he thought, if he could take some plans of the new aeroplane Vickers are developing, he would be welcomed in Berlin.'

'He was going to take them from the Vickers factory at Brooklands?' Pride asked, looking up from the notebook in which he was writing.

'Yes. That's what he said.'

'But he didn't?' Edward chipped in.

'No. I . . . I told the whole story to Georgina. I was desperate. I didn't know what to do. She said to leave it to her. She met Harry and told him he had to give her his word that he wouldn't try and steal any plans or anything like that. She said she would warn Vickers to take extra precautions. She said he should just leave the country. She offered him some money. It was rash of her but she loved him, too, and she wanted to give him a last chance.'

'And, in return, he tried to murder her,' Edward finished up.

Pride looked at Edward. Then he said, 'I have to tell you, Miss Hawkins, that I have charged your son with murder and I shall now take you over to Scotland Yard where you will be formally charged with being an accessory to murder.'

He nodded to Edward. 'Good day, Lord Edward. Thank you for your assistance. I don't think your presence is required at the Yard, unless . . .'

'No. Thank you, Chief Inspector. My job is done, I believe.'

Miss Hawkins looked at him and a flare of unadulterated fury illumined her face.

'Yes, you're done! You, *Lord* Edward,' she imbued the word with sarcasm, 'have destroyed me and my son. It's so easy for you with all your privileges and your smug superiority. Who are you to judge me or my son? What have you ever known of hardship? Of surviving in a world where even your love is a crime? What do you know of love? And as for your patriotism . . . I spit on it.'

Verity heard what Edward had to say in silence. When she had considered the case against Miss Hawkins and her son, she said,

236

'So the man I saw in driver's overalls and helmet and goggles talking to Miss Hawkins was . . . ?'

'Her son.'

'They seemed to be quarrelling.'

'She was pleading with him not to do anything to hurt Georgina.'

'But he took no notice?'

'No, he thought Georgina had rumbled him – not just about his spying but about having murdered Desmond Lyall.'

'And Lyall – he blamed himself for Westmacott's death?'

'Yes. If he had done what Westmacott demanded, it would all have been out in the open and there would have been no point in Stille killing him. In fact, I believe he blamed himself for two deaths – his wife's as well as Westmacott's.'

'He went to see where Westmacott had been found hanging?'

'Yes, and perhaps tossed the thing he loved most, his wife's compact, into the river.'

'As a sort of offering?'

'Yes.'

'You said James had been less than frank about his last meeting with his father?'

'Yes. You see, his father made a sort of confession to him. He wanted to give James his blessing for having the courage he had lacked in going off to Spain to fight the Fascists. He broke down and told James that he felt responsible for Westmacott's murder. The boy was very upset and urged his father to go to the police or to me. He said he wanted to but he couldn't because he would never betray Miss Hawkins who was perhaps his only real friend. They certainly had some sort of bond. I think he felt he had betrayed one colleague and couldn't betray another. He probably knew he was signing his own death warrant. James said he was in a very confused state of mind and kept repeating that it was better to betray your country than your friends.'

'Was that why James rushed back to Spain?'

'Yes, V. He wanted to get out of the moral maze he found himself in. He thought that at least in Spain it was obvious who was right and who was wrong.'

Verity looked at Edward to see if he was being ironic but his face gave nothing away. 'I see,' she said slowly. 'Why did James not tell you about this earlier?'

'Because he would never betray his father and he had been sworn to secrecy. It was only when James saw that I had worked it out for myself that he thought it was all right to tell me what his father had confessed.'

'And did they part on good terms – the father and son?' Verity asked doubtfully.

'James said that, when he left, his father hugged him for the first time since he was a child and told him that he was right to stick to his principles and he wished he had had the courage. So, yes, I think they parted well.'

'I'm glad about that. I think his time in Spain has turned him from a boy into a man. We have had some long talks and I think he's going to do something . . . something good in the world.'

'Is he still a Communist?' Edward could not resist asking.

'He said he regretted nothing,' Verity replied with dignity, 'but that for the moment he has had enough of politics. He's thinking of becoming a Quaker and a pacifist.'

They both thought about this and then Verity asked, 'Do we know what Harry did . . . to the car, Georgina's, I mean?'

'Not yet. Something to the steering, I think, but the engineers are still working on it.'

'And the chrysanthemums? They had nothing to do with anything?'

'Not quite. They were a little joke. I discovered that – along with the Japanese and Chinese myths about chrysanthemums – there is also a German legend. On Christmas Eve a wood-cutter and his family who lived in the Black Forest were sitting down to their meagre supper when they heard a knocking at the door. They found a beggar on the step, blue with cold and starving. The wood-cutter fed and warmed the beggar who then revealed himself to be the Christ. The next day he was gone but he had left behind a white chrysanthemum.'

'And he . . . Harry was born on Christmas Eve in the Black Forest?'

'Yes, or at least near the Black Forest.'

'But the chrysanthemums were dead.'

'Yes, V. They were dead. That nice, callow boy who liked cricket was a bringer of death.'

'Oh, Edward, what a horrible mess. It was all so unnecessary. That hateful Major Stille. He seduced Harry – politically. He had

Westmacott killed in that revolting way to stop the boy leaving the Foreign Office.'

'Yes. He must have flattered him – told him he was too important where he was. It must have made Harry feel very proud.'

'At least we can get Vansittart to have Major Stille expelled, or whatever they call it.'

'I don't think so. It's much better Stille doesn't find out how much we know. That way we can keep an eye on him and perhaps feed him false information. Also, we don't want there to be a lot of questions in Parliament about why we are deporting a German Embassy official.'

'Oh God! How typical! I might have guessed you'd want to have it all covered up.'

'I'm afraid so, V.'

'Tell me, Edward, do I take it that you *are* a policeman now?'

'I think I'm a sort of policeman – a very irregular one and I don't seem to be paid anything. Do you mind awfully?'

'I thought so! I'm in love with a secret policeman! I can't believe it. Or rather I can.'

'Look, V, we had better have this out. In a year or two we will be at war, I'm sure of it. I know it sounds pompous but then, as you often say, I *am* pompous, but the country's security is worth defending. If Harry Younger, or people like him, are stealing secrets – details of our defences or the plans of aircraft engines Vickers Armstrong are developing – then we need to stop them. If I can do my little bit towards helping Britain prepare for that war, then I am proud to do it. It's not about stopping you and your Communist friends choosing to bark up a tree which you can't see – or won't see – is rotten at the top. If that's what you want to do, no one will stop you, as long as it doesn't involve helping David Griffiths-Jones and his kind undermine our capacity to defend ourselves. Right, lecture over. Now you can tell me I'm a Fascist and you don't want to have anything more to do with me.'

The expected outburst failed to materialize. At last she said, 'I'm not in any mood to throw bricks at you, Edward. I have had my eyes opened by what happened at Guernica. As I told you, I have had some long talks with James and I think you were right: David did send us to Guernica to witness the German attack knowing some or all of us might be killed. He did not try to warn the town about it because he wanted . . . he wanted the worst to happen so he could say to the world – look what these Nazis do. I don't altogether blame him. I can see the logic of what he was thinking and what did it matter if Gerda or I were killed?'

'Or me,' Edward added gently.

'Or you or André. David is utterly ruthless – I have always known that – but his object is still one I approve of. Even if Stalin is not . . .'

'The genial father of his people but a bloody murderer?' Edward said, suddenly angry.

'Even then, Communism is right, even if there are wrong things done in its name.'

'I get you,' Edward said bitterly. 'Just because the Borgias weren't very good popes, that doesn't make it wrong to be a Catholic?'

'Yes.'

'What else did James tell you?'

'He said it was quite true that the International Brigade was purged of its anarchists and Trotskyists. Everyone had to join the Party and take their orders from Moscow or be . . . liquidated.'

'Liquidated! Don't use euphemisms to me, Verity! You mean "killed".'

'Yes, I suppose I do,' she admitted sombrely. 'The logic of it is quite clear. We must be as ruthless as the enemy if we are to win.'

'But you admit the Republic is finished?'

'I do. I'm not a fool. Franco is too strong and the democracies have abandoned Spain, to their cost, but what you won't admit is that we were right to fight. To sit back in a defeatist way and say these bullies are too strong for us is not an option any of us should take. The longer we delay fighting the Fascists, the harder it will be to defeat them.'

'I do agree but I still think you cannot fight without the whole will of the people behind you. The failure of Baldwin and Chamberlain is that they have done nothing to harness that will. They have shown no leadership, preferring to do the "popular" thing and shrug their shoulders and say it will be all right. Which, of course, it won't.'

'The point I'm making,' Verity went on, as if Edward had not spoken, 'is that if the Republican government had not been the

Popular Front – a rag-bag collection of all sorts of anti-Fascists with nothing in common but their hatred of Fascists – if it had been a well-organized Communist government, then Franco might have been stopped.'

'But that's democracy, V. It may not be efficient but efficiency isn't everything. Why exchange one dictatorship for another? Don't you see,' he went on, suddenly in deadly earnest, 'that the individual human freedoms which you and I regard as the bedrock of everything we value in life are being reduced by force – I mean the tyrannical will of Hitler and Stalin – to nothing. We become corpses or slaves under their malign lust for power.'

'But the Communist ideal is worth striving for.' Verity refused to bow before his attack.

Edward looked at her, pale even against the white pillows behind her head, exhausted but determined not to abandon her faith. He had not the heart to argue further.

'Anyway,' she said, rallying, 'aren't you saying it's all right for you to be a policeman and defend the state, even if it involves sacrificing a few liberties along the way?'

'There are liberties which have to be sacrificed – temporarily – in the defence of democracy but that's a long way from saying the one-party state is a good thing. The means are *not* justified by the ends . . . but I don't suppose we'll ever agree about that,' he finished hurriedly, fearing that he was being too hard on her.

'But we're on the same side?' Verity looked at him pleadingly.

He touched her hand. 'One for all and all for one. Of course we are! I love you, V, whatever you call yourself. You can call yourself a dolphin for all I care.'

'Why did you say that . . . dolphin?'

'I was thinking of poor Lyall. When Westmacott's body was found he knew that in some way he was to blame. Maybe he hadn't worked out exactly how but he knew he ought to have listened to Westmacott and reported the security lapse to Vansittart. He went to pay his respects at the place where Westmacott had been murdered. He left in the water the most precious thing he owned – his dead wife's powder compact bearing the dolphin design. He always wore a ring with the same design. When she died, he kept the compact to remember her with.'

'Do you love me as much as that . . . as much as Lyall loved his wife?' Her eyes searched his face, as though she were trying to see into his soul.

'I do, V, I do.' He leant over her and kissed her on the lips.

'And I love you, Mr Secret Policeman,' she whispered. She smiled but her eyes were full of tears.

Fred Cavens was back from Germany and Edward was fencing fiercely with him as though he was trying to rid himself of a deep-seated anger. Fenton was watching anxiously. He still held to the view that, though Lord Byron might have fenced in his rooms in Albany with equanimity, it was now more seemly to take exercise in a gymnasium or some other place specially designed for the purpose.

'How was Herr Himmler?' Edward gasped as the bout ended. 'Did he ask your views on the will of the English to withstand a German offensive?'

Cavens blushed. 'No, my lord. We fenced. That is all.'

'I shall believe you, Fred, but you know, you must soon make up your mind on which side of the fence you stand, if you will forgive the pun. Sitting on the fence is a painful business.'

'I am not political, Lord Edward,' Cavens said with dignity. 'I fight as a profession, not for a cause.'

'I am afraid that will soon not be a good enough answer. All over the world there are people who say politics is a dirty business and they will have nothing to do with it but do you remember what the philosopher Edmund Burke said? "All that is necessary for the triumph of evil is that good men do nothing."'

'I know how to fight if I have to, Lord Edward. You seem to be angry about something, if I may say so. I hope it is nothing I have done?'

'No, I apologize, Fred. You are right. I am angry but not at you. Since you have been in Germany, I have suffered a loss. A girl called Gerda Meyer – a photographer – was killed by the Luftwaffe in an undefended Spanish town called Guernica.'

'Guernica! You were there?'

'I was and so was my friend, Verity Browne. We all nearly lost our lives. Miss Browne was badly wounded when the gallant Luftwaffe pilots machine-gunned the civilians escaping the fires

242

started by their bombs and incendiaries. Your friends in Germany are not playing games, Fred. They are leading us all toward Armageddon and, damn it, we are doing our best to make it easy for them. That is what makes me angry.'

'But what is this to do with me?' Cavens demanded, by now thoroughly perplexed and not a little insulted.

'I suppose I mean that I cannot any longer fence with a man who plays games with Himmler. You must choose, even if it is "not your business".'

'Then I choose not to stay and be insulted, Lord Edward,' Cavens said, beginning to gather up his weapons and leave.

Edward knew he ought to apologize. Why take out his anger on Fred Cavens? But then, he thought with a grin, why not?

Cavens left with the briefest of goodbyes. Edward knew he had seen the last of him and was sorry, but at least he had refused to compromise. He was no longer capable of shaking the hand of a man who had shaken the hand of Heinrich Himmler.

Fenton had watched this exchange with some amazement. He had not seen his master in this mood before. He seemed sterner and more hawk-like than just a few weeks ago. Fenton thought he had recovered from the experience of Guernica but now he recognized that he might never fully recover – might never want to.

There was a ring at the doorbell and he went to answer it. To Edward's surprise, it was Sir Vida Chandra.

'Sir Vida, forgive me for my *déshabillé*. I have, as you can see, been fencing. Mr Cavens has just left.'

'I met him on the steps. He looked . . . disgruntled.'

'Did he? I am afraid I have been guilty of bad manners. I told him I could no longer fence with a man who also fenced with Herr Himmler. You'll say I was unforgivably priggish but it's odd, it seems to me that, unlike a gun, a sword is never less than personal.'

'Not at all priggish. You are quite right, Lord Edward; the time is coming when we will all have to make it clear which side we are on. I have a feeling you may have thought I was on the wrong side.'

'I confess, I was alarmed when I heard you owned the house in which David Griffiths-Jones and Guy Baron were staying. I know something of both gentlemen and don't like what I know.'

'You'll have to believe me when I tell you I had no idea who Mr Griffiths-Jones was when I let him the house. Perhaps I ought to have known but I might still have let it to him. We do live in a democracy. What do you have against Communists? Surely your friend Miss Browne is also a Communist?'

'Leave her out of this, Chandra,' Edward said, angry again.

The Indian held up his hands. 'I had no wish to be offensive. I am just saying we are on the same side.'

'Was Westmacott coming to see you with secret papers when he was murdered?'

Chandra did not seem put out by this sudden change of tack. 'I was acting as an intermediary, certainly.'

'For Mr Churchill?'

Chandra bowed his head in tacit admission. 'It was not my fault Major Stille got to him first.'

'Oh, you know about that?' Edward said, momentarily discomforted.

'I do and I also know that you were instrumental in putting that silly young man – Younger, isn't that his name? – behind bars. You know, I think he is just a silly young man. He, too, made his choices but they were the wrong ones.'

'Maybe, but I beg to differ with you. He was not just a silly young man. He was a murderer . . . He even tried to murder Miss Hay who had cared for him as an honorary aunt all his childhood.'

'Why did he need to kill her?'

'Because she knew too much about his origins and he assumed that his mother had told her he was responsible for Westmacott's murder. As it happened, she knew nothing about that. She only knew that he had developed a fascination with Germany which had led him to hand over defence secrets to a certain Major Stille.'

'Ah well. You are probably right: the boy is rotten. But, Lord Edward, I have not come here to discuss ethics but to offer you a job. I happen to know that Sir Robert Vansittart is going to ask you to take over Desmond Lyall's department. The man he had in mind has had to go elsewhere, I understand, or maybe he's just not up to the job. I don't know. You have at least proved one thing – that the department requires completely reorganizing and re-staffing if it is to continue with its valuable work.'

'But you said you had a job to offer me?'

'I do. I have. An even more important job. I would prefer it if you would work with Mr Churchill. Notice I don't say *for* Mr Churchill. Marcus Fern warned me you were touchy about grammar. Mr Churchill needs someone like you to look after his security and help assess the value and reliability of the information he receives from his sources.' He held up his hand. 'Before you refuse and proclaim once again that you are not, and have no wish to be, Mr Churchill's private detective, let me make it clear that is not what is being offered to you. It is a much more important position than that though you would also be responsible for hiring and controlling his personal detective. I'm sure you would agree that Mr Churchill's life is too valuable to allow him to be assassinated by some madman or a foreign agent.'

'I am sorry, Chandra, but . . .'

'Come to Chartwell next week and we can talk some more. Mr Churchill wants to hear from you about the investigation.'

Without waiting for any further response, he left the room. He returned immediately to say, 'Oh, by the way, that amphora of yours – it's a fake, you know. Sonerscheins offered it to me but I turned it down.' And then he was gone.

'I am the more deceived,' Edward said to Fenton, as he went over to examine his treasure. 'Isn't it strange? When I did not know that this was a fake, I thought it was the most beautiful thing. Now I find it ugly.'

The telephone rang and he waved Fenton aside and went to pick up the receiver. It was Verity and she seemed to be crying.

'Edward, have you heard the news?'

'What news?'

'It was on the wireless a moment ago. The Hindenburg has crashed as it was coming in to land in New Jersey. It burst into flames and . . . and . . . It was supposed to be so safe.'

'Oh my God! Was Lord Benyon on it?'

'They haven't yet said who the passengers were but I am sure he was. He was in Frankfurt for a meeting and he said he was going on to the States in the Hindenburg. After what happened on the *Queen Mary*, he said he'd had enough of ships. He thought airships might be safer.'

'Oh, Verity, my darling. How awful. I'll telephone the Foreign Office and find out if . . if . . . You never know, perhaps he changed his mind at the last minute. Was everyone on board killed?'

'I think so... I don't know. Edward, tell me, will this never end? Will everything we love go up in flames?'

Edward shook his head but said only, 'I will come over as soon as I have rung Sir Robert. Be brave.'

He put the telephone receiver down and staggered a little. He put out a hand to steady himself on the table beside him. Benyon's death would be a blow not only to him personally but to the country. No man had done more to keep the national finances on a sound footing.

There was a cry of warning from Fenton. Edward had quite forgotten the amphora, sitting on the little table. He turned and made a grab for it but the vase slid out of his grasp. It hit the wooden floor, bounced and broke into a dozen pieces. Edward looked at the shards of ancient – or not so ancient – clay, hardly able to believe what had happened. Quite literally, he felt, the world was crashing down about his feet.